NIGHTMARE in TIMES SQUARE

James Bouvier

Bladensburg, MD

Nightmare in Times Square

Published by

Inscript Books

A division of Dove Christian Publishers

P.O. Box 611

Bladensburg, MD 20710-0611

www.dovechristianpublishers.com

Cover Design by Mark Yearnings

ISBN: 9781734303254

First Edition

Printed in the United States of America

Nightmare in Times Square is dedicated to my wife and best friend of fifty-two amazing years for her unwavering support and encouragement during the writing of this book; to our son Steven and daughter-in-law Amy for their love and continued support; and to their two children, our precious grandchildren, Riley Bouvier and Grace Bouvier, who are solid rock pillars of responsibility and integrity and role models for the youth of America (Riley is sixteen years old, and Grace is thirteen years old at this writing).

ACKNOWLEGMENTS

Sharon Bouvier—After spending hundreds, maybe thousands of hours and countless late nights helping me prepare my first book *Escaping Armageddon* for publishing, you would think my wife and best friend would tire of reading untold numbers of drafts of *Nightmare in Times Square* and providing me with constructive criticism. But that was not the case. I could not have completed this book without her unwavering labor of love and constant support and encouragement. I know she wanted to quit reading drafts as many times as I wanted to quit writing them, but she never hesitated to read a page, a chapter or two or three or the whole manuscript again and again and again when asked.

Thank you, Sharon, for giving your time helping me with this book when you had so many other things you would rather have been doing. I really appreciate your help and *Nightmare in Times square* is a better novel because of your fingerprints on every page.

Amy Bouvier—Encouragement from Amy, our daughter-in-law who is like a daughter to us, provided the fuel for the engine of creativity with her comments and tips regarding the writing of Nightmare in Times Square.

Sammie Maricelli— Having known Sammie most of our adult lives, she is one of our closest and best friends. She was the first person to agree to read the first few original chapters of the manuscript. The wisdom of her comments resulted in a complete rewrite of much of Nightmare in Times Square and has resulted in a stronger, more interesting, and easier to read storyline.

Roger Blake—Roger is one of our best friends and was the first to read a very early version of the complete manuscript. He returned the manuscript with numerous pages of helpful notes, criticisms, and suggestions that resulted in another major rewrite of the book. Nightmare in Times Square will surely be more successful because of the time Roger invested in it.

Emily Maricelli—Emily is the daughter of our best friends Sammie and Steve Maricelli. Among other things, she is a speaker and published author and offered to read selected sections of my book. Her comments from the perspective of one who has knowledge gained from a writer's conference and agent contacts contributed to a complete revision of the introduction of the book. Nightmare in Times Square has a much more powerful beginning as a result of Emily's comments.

Friends—Continued encouragement and a relentless interest in the timeline for the publishing of the book by many friends is very much appreciated and encouraging.

Contents

CHAPTER 1

THE NIGHT FROM HELL

Screams from the stands of the Times Square Ticket booth amphitheater pierced the frigid night air. "He's got a gun!"

A young man vaulted from the stands to the street below and broke into a run, yelling, "Yes, and I'll use it. Get out of my way!"

As the gunman vanished among the sea of fleeing bystanders, a father in the stands hugged his terrified wife and children and cried, "Let him go. It's too late for all of us, anyway!"

Gunshots, followed by muffled screams for help, were heard in the distance.

"As you can see Times Square, an enchanted wonderland of fun and entertainment that dazzles visitors from all over the world, has become a horrifying toxic war zone tonight, bringing the city to its knees. This is James Donaldson for CBN News bringing you live coverage of the night from hell. We're reporting from the corner of Broadway and West 47th Street near the Times Square Ticket booth amphitheater where thousands of spectators are rushing through the streets like stampeding cattle trampling anyone in their path."

Suddenly a man breaks from the crowd and attacks Donaldson knocking him to the ground while shouting, "This is all your fault, you should have given us more warning."

Leaping down the twenty-seven rows of the ruby red glass steps of the amphitheater, another crazed spectator heaved a young woman and her baby out of his way over the handrail. On her knees wiping blood from a gash on her head, the woman cried, "I can't move. Somebody, please help me find my baby!"

Fending off the attacker Donaldson continues, *"I can't believe my eyes... everyone is freaking out! Just moments ago, the crowd that packed Times Square was calm and passive. Now bodies are tumbling head-over-heels down the amphitheater steps as panic-stricken bystanders clamber over each other to reach the street level like a pack of hungry wolves in pursuit of wild game."*

A terrified newlywed separated from her husband by the mass of people cried, "I never dreamed it would end like this."

The roar of an approaching helicopter is heard over the clamor of the crowd. Illuminated by the brilliant lights of the animated billboards above 7th Avenue, the bright yellow CBN Air One News helicopter is spotted descending over the McDonald's restaurant and attempting to land in a roped off area in the plaza.

Approaching the landing area, Donaldson reports, *"I'll continue broadcasting live from Air One above Times Square."*

Suddenly, a frightened young man shouted to a group of angry followers, "Get that chopper. It's our only way out of here!"

"Stop, or I'll shoot," an NYPD officer guarding the landing area shouted to the crazed mob rushing the chopper, but he was trampled before he could fire his weapon.

Just as the helicopter touched down it was inundated by the throng of desperate people. Donaldson and his tech agreed the scene was too dangerous to go any closer.

While hurrying from the landing site and looking back over his shoulder, Donaldson continues, *"The rebels have opened the cockpit door and are forcing their way inside. Oh... the pilot is attempting to take off, but dozens of people are dangling from the open door and landing skids like clothes on a line. They won't let go! What a horrifying scene! The rotors of the chopper are whirring close to the ground like four giant razors threatening death to anyone in their path."*

"Oh my God, the extra weight is causing the helicopter to rotate

uncontrollably slinging screaming victims onto the street like rag dolls. Now the chopper is tipping dangerously close to the ground. I'm afraid it's going to...I can't look!"

"I'm begging you to let go! You're going to kill us all!" the pilot screamed over the PA system.

"It's true, if only they would have listened. Dr. Whitfield warned the White House and members of Congress of this harbinger of death and destruction months ago, but they ignored the warning. I guess I'm as guilty as the rest of them. It's too late now and..."

CHAPTER 2

THE PACKAGE

Six months earlier in a sleepy little suburban neighborhood near Princeton, New Jersey, home to Dr. Jonathan Whitfield.

Leaping onto the bed, the black miniature Schnauzer named Harlo rhythmically pawed Jonathan's pillow with the precision of a drumline. Awakened from a sound sleep, Jonathan turned over to find Harlo nose to nose with him.

Feeling the warm morning sun through his closed eyelids, Jonathan swung his legs off the bed, prompting his feet to blindly search the floor for his house shoes. Sitting motionless on the edge of the bed for a few minutes, he rubbed his eyes, attempting to shake off the lingering remnants of sleep.

Fumbling his way down the hall to the bathroom, he showered, shaved, and hastily ran a comb through his mop of brown hair that showcased a stylish touch of gray on his sideburns. Thick brown eyebrows complemented his dark brown eyes and neatly trimmed Johnny Depp mustache. Routine strenuous travels, long hours on archeological digs in the blazing sun, and exercising at the university gym gave Jonathan his youthful trim appearance and tanned complexion. A light brown safari shirt, khaki pants, and brown leather boots, sometimes accompanied by a dark brown leather jacket, completed Jonathan's usual dress attire. When his sable Fedora hat was adjusted at just the right angle on his head,

Dr. Whitfield boasted a distinguished appearance like the dashing Indiana Jones action movie character.

On the way to the front yard to pick up the morning paper, Jonathan stopped briefly in the kitchen to brew a pot of coffee. Believing coffee is the key to healthy living, he set no limit on the amount of this natural health drink he consumed.

After retrieving the paper, Jonathan returned to the dining room table and glanced at the date on the newspaper. Tears welled up in his eyes. It was Friday, May 14th, his 25th wedding anniversary. Staring at the carefully arranged place settings he kept on the table for his wife Deborah and son Ethan, Jonathan sat quietly with his head in his hands. He visualized Deborah with her short honey-blonde hair, girlish figure, and striking green eyes. He could even imagine the fragrance of her French perfume that lingered long after she left the table each day. However, Deborah and Ethan didn't come to the table this morning. In fact, they would never come to the table again. In the quietness of the moment, memories of the last thirty years washed over him like Niagara Falls.

After attending Collins High School together, Jonathan and Deborah enrolled in undergraduate studies at Columbia University where they remained best friends. After they graduated, they went their separate ways. Deborah accepted a second-grade teaching position at an elementary school in her hometown, and Jonathan joined the army where he rocketed to the rank of Lieutenant Colonel and met Steven Westin, who became his best friend. While serving in Turkey and Egypt, Jonathan was exposed to the mystery and aura of archeological digs and the ancient civilizations authenticated by the artifacts discovered. Before long, his acute interest in archeology was fueled and ignited by a summer university course entitled "Secrets of Lost Civilizations." After returning to the United States and rekindling his relationship with Deborah at their ten-year high school reunion, Jonathan and Deborah were happily married.

Soon after Jonathan's retirement from the Army, he and Deborah moved to a small suburb in Cambridge, Massachusetts near Harvard University, where he obtained his Doctorate degree in archeology. After graduation, they moved to a quaint little town in New Jersey near Princeton University, where Jonathan accepted an associate professor position. Ten years later, they had a beautiful baby boy named Ethan, and Jonathan was recognized as one of the youngest tenured professors at Princeton. The purchase of a cottage on the beach of the Atlantic Ocean in Chapel Hills provided a wonderful place for the family to get away for a weekend and completed their perfect world. Jonathan had it all, or at least it seemed that way!

Several months after celebrating their 20th wedding anniversary, Deborah planned a family outing for Jonathan's birthday at their beach cottage. With a backlog of work, Jonathan sent them on alone and promised to join them that evening. Immersed in his work, Jonathan was still working late when he heard a knock on his office door.

Opening the door, he was taken aback at the sight of a New Jersey Highway Patrol officer.

"Dr. Jonathan Whitfield?"

"Yes, officer, can I help you?"

"Do you live at 3418 Spyglass Hill?"

Silence.

"Dr. Whitfield? Did you hear what I said?"

With a painful stabbing sensation in his gut, Jonathan answered, "Yes! What happened?"

"Dr. Whitfield, please sit down."

Jonathan took a seat on the worn sofa, his eyes fixed on the officer, anticipating the worst.

"Is this about Deborah or Ethan?"

"Please Dr. Whitfield, I have some bad news. There was a catastrophic collision on Highway 525 just north of Chapel Hills and ..."

"What? Are Deborah and Ethan all right? Where are they?"

"Your wife was driving and apparently became distracted by something or someone. She didn't see an oncoming car suddenly swerve across the center stripe head on into her lane and ..."

"Please tell me, are Deborah and Ethan all right!"

"I'm very sorry, Dr. Whitfield, your wife and son were both killed instantly, but the driver of the other car has been arrested for drunk driving and is in jail awaiting trial."

Unable to believe what he just heard, Jonathan fell prostrate on the floor and sobbed hysterically. The lives of his wife and only son were snuffed out like a candle, leaving him in a world of darkness!

"Why, why? Why did this happen? Why did God let them die? I thought God was supposed to love people!"

With tears streaming down his face, he realized he had forgotten all about the outing that Deborah planned to celebrate his birthday.

Groping for words of comfort, the officer said, "Dr. Whitfield, I have learned that the driver of the other car has been arrested for drunk driving and is in jail awaiting trial."

"Do you know why they died?" Jonathan screamed! "They were going to give me a birthday party! If I had just gone with them and had been driving, the accident would never have happened. They died because of me, and God let it happen."

"I didn't even tell them I loved them the last time I saw them…"

Going without sleep or food for days after the accident, Jonathan was comatose during the funeral. Weeping openly, he interrupted the eulogy more than once blurting out loud, "I wish I had died with them. I can't live without them."

After the service, the pastor offered to help Jonathan with grief counseling.

"Do you really want to help me? Tell me why God allowed a drunken driver to murder the two people I love most in the world? I will never forgive that man for taking the lives of my wife and son, and I will never forgive God for letting it happen."

A few months later, the case of the drunken driver came to trial, and he was convicted of vehicular manslaughter. The judge sentenced him to fifteen years in prison, but Jonathan knew he could be out in five to seven years or less with good behavior.

Life went on for Jonathan after the trial, but he never stopped thinking about that tragic night when a drunken driver snatched the lives of his loved ones on a dark, rural highway. He often thought about what he would do if he ever saw that man again.

As the images of Deborah and Ethan's happy faces faded from the table, Jonathan snapped out of his walk down memory lane and focused on the morning TV news.

Sipping his coffee, Jonathan muttered. "Why do I even watch the news? The world is in such a mess, and the news is so depressing. Maybe Deborah had the right idea. I should just watch the cooking channel; it's definitely stress-free."

Grabbing the television remote, Jonathan punched the off button with a sigh of relief. Clutching his briefcase, he climbed into his 1967 classic Volkswagen to make the short drive to Princeton University.

Arriving early, the mild-mannered professor in his early fifties sauntered down the long hall of the Archeology Building to the office of his administrative assistant, Michelle Wilson. An attractive woman in her late fifties, Michelle was his administrative assistant for the entire time he had been at the university.

Completely devoted to the office of Professor Whitfield, Michelle arrived at the university early and is usually one of the last to leave. She knew almost as much about Jonathan as his wife Deborah, and she proved to be invaluable when preparing his notes and presentations for class, itineraries for travel, and just about everything else.

"And how are you this morning, Michelle?"

"I'm wonderful, Jonathan. It's Friday, May 14th, and I hope you have a great day. Here is your coffee just like you like it—strong and black."

"Thank you."

Taking his morning cup of joe which Michelle always had ready for him, Jonathan strolled unhurriedly to his office. Flanked on three sides by floor-to-ceiling bookshelves crammed with volumes of every possible genre, this cozy windowless office served as Jonathan's sanctuary from mankind. Flaunting the years of wear like a badge of academic honor, the large oak desk showcased towering stacks of papers and out-of-date academic journals with dog-eared pages. In one corner, sporting deep creases and cracks from years of wear, a small leather sofa extends an offer to anyone willing to escape the rat race for a few minutes.

Scattered about the floor from numerous digs are gratifying reminders of the joy of Jonathan's calling. Soft light from the desk lamp and the antique wood floors complemented by a hand-woven Turkish wool rug complete the warm environment of his refuge from the hectic grind of academic life. A two-hundred-year-old German Wag clock on the wall reminds the professor that even though he loves the freedom of exploration, he is still shackled to the clock.

With class notes in hand, Jonathan hurried down the long hall outside his office to his Introductory Class in Middle Eastern Culture. As a full professor, he only taught a few classes of his own choice each week, but with the ability to influence so many young minds in the direction of his own calling, this was his favorite class.

When Jonathan was not teaching, he was busy working on special projects for the university. Because of his worldwide notoriety, he routinely received grants from the United States Government as well as requests from the United Nations with projects proposed by the UNESCO (United Nations Educational, Scientific and Cultural Organization) World Heritage Center. Hand-picked graduate students eagerly provided low-cost labor for his projects, knowing they will gain valuable experience as well as an impressive resume that will certainly catapult them into a rewarding career after graduation.

While walking back to his office after class, Jonathan noticed a shadowy figure closing his office door and hurrying past Michelle's desk. Assuming it was the custodian, Jonathan dismissed any concern he had and slowly opened his office door. Staring him in the face was a large package nestled among the stack of papers on his desk.

As Michelle walked up, Jonathan asked, "What was that person doing in my office?"

Glancing up and down the hall, Michelle answered, "What person?"

"You must have seen the man that came out of my office a couple of minutes ago. He walked right past you."

"I haven't seen anyone near your office, and I've been at my desk all morning."

"Well, who put that package on my desk? It wasn't there when I left for class."

"Relax Jonathan. I haven't had an opportunity to tell you that the package was delivered by a UNESCO courier right after you left for class this morning. The courier said it was extremely important and that UNESCO would like for you to call them as soon as you have time to review their invitation. A decision is expected from you today by 5:00 P.M."

"Okay, I'll take a look at it right now. Wait a minute, Michelle, are you sure you didn't see anyone leave my office?"

"I'm positive, Jonathan. Seriously, I didn't see anyone."

Still baffled by the phantom visitor, Jonathan sat down and opened the plain brown paper wrapping on the package. Inside was a large manila envelope and a letter of invitation. Realizing UNESCO always brought interesting projects to the university, Jonathan excitedly read the letter:

"As you may know, in 1982, Saddam Hussein vowed to rebuild the great city of Babylon with its famous Hanging Gardens as a tribute to himself."

"After construction was underway, archeologists were shocked to find that he was building his new city on top of the ruins of the ancient city of Babylon, thereby potentially destroying valuable historical artifacts. Construction of Saddam's new city caused great concern since the ruins of ancient Babylon had been previously designated a UNESCO World Heritage site."

"On December 30, 2006, construction stopped on the new empire when Saddam Hussein was sentenced to death by hanging after being convicted of crimes against humanity by the Iraqi Special Tribunal."

"A joint venture to investigate the cost and schedule for repairing the ruins of the ancient city of Babylon by an elite group of invited archeologists has been funded by the United States government, the UNESCO World Heritage Center, and the Iraqi government. UNESCO has selected you to supervise the expedition. Enclosed is a letter of introduction to the Iraqi Government, airline tickets for you and your associate Grace Olivia, and directions to the site of the Babylonian ruins in Iraq. The names of the other members of the expedition and the location where you will rendezvous with them is also included."

In a separate envelope was a small piece of paper folded neatly with a handwritten note:

"Have a safe trip, Dr. Whitfield. Perhaps we will meet along the way."

The note was signed *Malachi*.

"What a nice touch to add a note for our safety and the safety of those traveling with us, but what does he mean 'perhaps we will meet along the way'? Oh well, maybe our paths will cross someday."

Elated about the assignment scheduled to begin in a week, Jonathan looked forward to the mystery and excitement that exploring the past always brought him. During the balance of the morning, Jonathan prepared notes for his graduate students who would teach his classes in his absence.

"It's only 12 o'clock, plenty of time to rest awhile and call UNESCO after class. I'll also call Grace and give her the news about the exciting assignment."

Before yielding to the call of the sofa, Jonathan phoned Michelle and asked that he not be disturbed until two o'clock, giving him time to prepare for his afternoon class.

CHAPTER 3

TAKEN

As the German Wag clock on the wall of his office struck 2 o'clock, Jonathan was jolted from a deep sleep by the incessant ringing of his office phone.

"Hello, who is it?"

"It's me, Jonathan. Michelle. Remember you asked me to wake you in time to prepare for your class? Well, it's 2 o'clock."

"Ok, I'm awake now, thanks."

Still drowsy with eyes threatening to close, Jonathan staggered back to the sofa, and within minutes he was sawing logs again.

No sooner was Jonathan settled into a peaceful slumber than he was awakened by the ring of his iPhone. Seeing the 20th wedding anniversary picture of Deborah on his phone brought back tearful memories even though he adamantly vowed never to remove the picture under any circumstances.

"Hello, Jonathan. Hello. Hello. Can you hear me?"

"Hi, Steven, I'm sorry, I was in the middle of something."

"If this isn't a good time, I can call back later."

"What time is it?"

"It's about 2:30 in the afternoon, why?"

"Nothing. It's okay. What's up?"

"Amy and I would like you and Grace to come to our home for dinner tomorrow night about 7:00 P.M."

"Of course, sounds good, and I'll check with Grace. I'm sure she would love to come if she doesn't have another commitment."

Steven and Jonathan became best friends after meeting in the military when Jonathan was in the Intelligence Department of the United States Army. He worked on some of the same projects as Steven, who was employed by the United States Central Intelligence Agency. Although retired from the CIA, Steven still worked as a consultant for the agency.

Jonathan loved the Westin family but hesitated to visit with them because it brought back painful memories of his wife and son. Ethan attended school with their children, Amy was Deborah's best friend, and Steven was Jonathan's best man at their wedding. Since Deborah's death, conversations with Steven invariably lead to advice about Jonathan's personal life, especially his relationship with Grace.

With each well-meaning discussion, Steven's counsel always sounded the same, just packaged a little differently. Of course, Jonathan was not interested in a relationship with Grace or anyone else.

Grace was a very attractive young lady in her mid-forties and doesn't look anything like Deborah. An eye-catching infectious smile highlighted the beauty of her natural curly auburn hair, alluring green eyes, long eyelashes that any girl would covet, and tiny freckles randomly sprinkled around her small, slightly turned-up nose. With the charisma of a politician, the charm and beauty of a fashion model, the courage of a pioneer, the intelligence of a scientist, and the grace of a princess, she was just as much at home in an evening gown and Prada shoes as she was in jeans and hiking boots. Grace had never been married, but it's only because she had lofty expectations for a husband, and she just hadn't met the right man. Her shapely five-foot-two frame and enchanting beauty attracted the eye of every man she met, but she showed no interest in any of them.

After graduating from Harvard University with a degree in Political Science and a major in Philology, the study of historical languages, Grace served as an interpreter for the United Nations. She is fluent in Farsi, Arabic, and Russian and studied archeology in the Middle East during the summers between semesters. Fascinated by the aura of the ancient past, Grace thrives on unraveling linguistic mysteries.

Jonathan met Grace at a formal dinner following a presentation he made at the United Nations about a year after the accident. Grace happened to be sitting next to him at the dinner table. Although he had no interest in a relationship, Jonathan was intrigued by Grace's charm, beauty, and credentials. Believing her abilities, natural curiosity, and acute knowledge of languages would be extremely beneficial in his work, Jonathan offered her a position as his assistant before dessert was served. Grace flashed him a smile and graciously accepted his offer on the spot. A few weeks later, Grace was settled in at Princeton and working at the university.

With her eyes on Jonathan for a relationship beyond that of an employee, she couldn't help but notice he had everything she had ever hoped to find in a husband except common religious convictions. In fact, the only religious convictions Jonathan had was that he had no religious convictions. With time, Grace believed God would change him, and she had the patience to wait.

While he liked to be with her, Jonathan considered Grace to be a good friend and a highly respected business associate. The one thing that irritated Jonathan about Grace was her love for her church and that she was a bold Christian. From time to time, she talked about God and frequently invited Jonathan to attend church with her.

Grace reminded Jonathan of his wife Deborah, who "religiously" attended church services with Ethan and was always volunteering to serve at the church. As much as Jonathan loved Deborah, he couldn't understand why she gave so much of herself to the relentless time-consuming religious services, committees, and programs. Jonathan occasionally attended church with Deborah at Easter and Christmas to make her happy but didn't really enjoy going. Besides, Jonathan traveled extensively, and when he was home, Sunday was his only day to rest, watch the football games, and catch up on his work.

Every time Grace brought up the subject of God or church Jonathan politely reminded her that the God she worshiped was the same God that allowed the love of his life and only child to be taken from him by a drunken driver. Despite their differences over religion, Jonathan always looked forward to a night out with Grace.

Without hesitating another minute, he called Grace and invited her to go to dinner with him at the Westin's on Saturday evening.

CHAPTER 4

A NIGHT OUT

Without a moment's hesitation, Grace promptly accepted Jonathan's invitation and expressed her eagerness to join him on the UNESCO expedition.

After spending much of the day Saturday at the university gathering materials for the UNESCO venture, Jonathan arrived at Grace's apartment precisely on time. Before he could get out of the car to meet her at the door, she sprang from the porch to the car like a schoolgirl on her first date.

On the way to the Westin's home, Grace talked excitedly about visiting with Amy, but Jonathan was unusually quiet. He was already pondering how he would deflect the unsolicited after-dinner counsel from Steven regarding his personal life. Wheeling into the driveway of the Westin's fashionable upscale Princeton home, Jonathan parked his vintage VW next to Steven's shiny new S Class Mercedes.

Opening the car door for Grace, Jonathan whispered, "Have you noticed that Steven always seems to have a new set of wheels every time we see him, an expensive set of wheels?"

"What about it?"

"How do you suppose Steven can afford such a pricy car and a luxurious home working for the government all his life? For years, he and Amy lived in a modest home in the suburbs, and then one day, they moved to this mini mansion with a pool in the posh part of town. He is probably just doing a little top-secret espionage work 'under the table.' I hear it really pays well."

"Jonathan, please stop it right now or I'm going back to the car!"

"All right, I'm sorry."

Seeing Jonathan and Grace walking up the long winding sidewalk flanked on both sides with gorgeous landscaping and a perfectly manicured lawn, Amy and Steven hurried to welcome them at the front door. As much as they loved Deborah, they believed Grace was the perfect woman to breathe new life into Jonathan if he would only give her a chance. She was beautiful, smart, caring, and has a passionate personality that reminded them of Deborah. Of course, Jonathan continued to recite his case that he is much too busy to get involved in a meaningful relationship with Grace or anyone else, for that matter.

After dinner, Amy motioned to Steven. "You guys go on to the study. Grace and I have a lot to catch up on. We'll call you when coffee and dessert is ready."

After Jonathan and Steven moved to the study, Steven asked, "Jonathan, what do you think about the situation in the world today, especially in the Middle East? Doesn't it seem like the world is just spinning out of control?"

With silence pervading the air, Steven eventually answered his own question and moved on.

"What do you think about the downward spiral of spirituality in America?"

Ignoring the question, Jonathan launched into a description of his latest exciting archeological adventure. Suddenly, the ringing of Steven's cell phone interrupted the narrative. Glancing at the number on the phone, Steven hesitated for a moment as though he were trying to decide whether he should take the call.

"Go ahead," said Jonathan. "I'll catch up on the latest sports in today's paper."

"This is an important call, Jonathan, but I promise I'll only be a few minutes."

Stepping into his private office adjoining the study, Steven carelessly left the door slightly ajar.

Overhearing the conversation, Jonathan crept quietly to the door. From what Steven was saying, it was obvious that he was talking to someone in the CIA, where he still receives routine contract assignments.

"You're saying you have evidence that some of our top-secret detonators for nuclear bombs are missing and the encrypted codes are compromised? We always knew it was possible for the detonators or their design to be stolen by spies working undercover in our government, but we know they're useless without the encrypted codes to the firing circuits. Those codes are routinely modified for specific detonators and maintained at the highest level of security. It's virtually impossible for anyone to obtain the codes that are worth billions on the black market without help from a mole.

"Do you have any idea who that person may be? Ok, I'll meet you in your office in Washington tomorrow. Don't discuss this subject with anyone until we talk, is that understood? No one! And don't mention to anyone that you called me! This is a matter of national security. Is that understood?"

Jonathan rushed back to his chair so as not to be discovered eavesdropping at the door, picked up the afternoon paper, and pretended to be engrossed in the sports page.

Jonathan's mind was racing. *Steven couldn't possibly be involved in any kind of national security espionage, although that would certainly explain his luxurious lifestyle. They say you're always shocked by the people that are involved in illegal operations, and they're always the people you least suspect.*

Walking slowly out of his office, Steven had a worried look on his face.

"Is everything all right, Steven? Is there something you need to take care of now?"

"No, it was just a routine call about a budget I was developing for an overseas assignment. I'm a little behind in my work, but I can take care of it later."

Jonathan thought *That didn't sound like a phone call about a budget.*

Noticing a definite tone of nervousness in Steven's voice, Jonathan tried not to reveal his skepticism. He couldn't help thinking about the mole that he mentioned on the phone.

There was no way to get the conversation he overheard out of his head, but Jonathan thought, *Steven couldn't possibly be involved in any kind of illegal covert espionage; he is too American, a real patriot.*

Noticing Jonathan was somewhat distracted, Steven asked, "Would you like something to drink, Jonathan? How about a cup of your favorite coffee?"

Jonathan quickly snapped out of his drifting thoughts of his best friend possibly being involved in selling secrets to the enemy and turned the conversation to baseball, one of Steven's passions.

"I was just looking at the Yankees' lineup for this year in the sports page. Boy, do you remember when the Houston Astros upset the baseball world with their win over the Los Angeles Dodgers in the 2017 World Series? That was some series, especially game five."

"Yes, I remember. Now, how about that coffee?"

"Sure, coffee would be great, and I'll just have mine black."

While they enjoyed the strong French coffee, Jonathan continued to describe the venture offered to him by UNESCO with the excitement of a child anticipating the first day of school. Although Steven shared his enthusiasm for the journey to Iraq, he expressed his cautious concern for the safety of his friends while on the assignment.

"Jonathan there is still great concern about the ability of the Iraqi government to retain control of their country. Although the strength of the ISIS military has been greatly diminished, they have not been destroyed, and don't forget the Al-Qaeda terrorists are still alive and well. In fact, the State Department recently issued a travel warning for U.S. citizens planning to travel to Iraq. Threats from insurgent groups and terrorists are almost routine vowing to target civilian aircraft landing and taking off at the Baghdad Airport. Small arms and stinger missiles left by the U.S. military and abandoned by the Iraqis in 2014 are now in the hands of the terrorists."

"I hear what you're saying Steven, but we're committed to this trip, and it's an awesome opportunity! We'll be traveling with heavily armed guards, and they will take all the necessary precautions to keep us safe."

After coffee and dessert, Jonathan and Grace thanked Steven and Amy for their hospitality and drove home.

All the way to Grace's apartment, the conversation centered on their exciting new adventure. There was so much to do and only a week to get ready. Jonathan didn't mention Steven's concerns for their safety or the mysterious phone call. It just didn't seem necessary to worry Grace.

The following week was spent researching documents related to previous archeological expeditions of the ruins of Babylon and obtaining the necessary paperwork, equipment, and tools they needed for the journey. To make room for their books, tools, and maps, they took the minimum change of clothes. By Friday, the day before they were to depart for Iraq, everything was ready. The team selected by UNESCO to accompany Jonathan and Grace to Iraq arrived in New York and assembled at the university Friday evening, where Jonathan briefed them on their mission.

Little did Jonathan know that he and Grace were about to embark on a mysterious journey to the unknown that promised to change their lives forever.

CHAPTER 5

MISTAKEN IDENTITY?

UNESCO arranged for Jonathan and Grace to travel to Iraq with a team of qualified, handpicked security personnel to ensure their safety. Their itinerary called for the team to take American Airlines flight 13 out of Newark Liberty Airport at 11:45 P.M. Saturday to Baghdad. After scheduled stops with layovers in London and Istanbul, they would arrive at the Baghdad International Airport. They would be met by Iraqi military personnel who would provide additional security while on their assignment in Babylon.

Saturday afternoon, Jonathan met Grace at her apartment. Since Jonathan's VW would hardly accommodate their luggage for the long trip, Grace agreed to drive her car to the airport. After dropping Harlo off at the Canine Hotel, they drove to a nearby restaurant for an early dinner. While ordering their meal, Jonathan received a text that their flight on American Airlines was changed to Swiss Air flight 26 departing at 9:00 P.M. The text directed Jonathan to go to the Swiss Air counter to pick up the new tickets and boarding passes for all their flights. With a quick phone call, he advised the rest of the team of the new arrangements, since he was not sure they received the update.

"Look, Grace, the message about the travel itinerary was sent from someone called Malachi—A Traveler's Friend."

"Malachi was the person who signed the note attached to the

airline tickets I received from UNESCO, so he must be associated with the travel agency they employ," Grace said. "I wonder why we haven't heard about the change from Michelle."

After meeting their team at the Swiss Air counter, Jonathan and Grace picked up their new tickets and boarding passes for all the connecting flights. Unexpectedly, Jonathan and Grace had both been upgraded to business class on the A340-500 Airbus. The upgrade was a shock because UNESCO never paid for anyone except executives to fly business class. With the difficulty of sleeping on long flights, this upgrade was a welcome change.

"Maybe we should check to see if there is an error in our seat assignments, Jonathan," Grace suggested.

"Are you kidding? No one questions an upgrade to business class, especially on a transatlantic flight."

"The overhead display indicates we have about an hour and a half before we board the aircraft. The Swiss Air attendant told me that the business class tickets permit us entry into the Lufthansa Business Lounge, so we may as well relax a little, grab a cup of coffee, and catch up on the latest news."

After finding a comfortable place in the lounge near a television, they settled down and waited for their flight to be called. They had only been seated a few minutes when Jonathan called Grace's attention to the breaking news announcement on the television.

A spokesman for the White House was speaking:

"Today, the United States Congress voted to join the proposed Eurozone that divides the world into ten regions and forms what will be called the New World Union. This new global organization has been in the planning stages for years spearheaded by the European Union. The New World Union is being established to execute a focused strategy to stabilize world markets, which are in a spiraling decline. Even the United States is on the slippery slope to bankruptcy with mounting unemployment, unbridled debt exceeding twenty-one trillion dollars, and financial markets that are dependent on the shaky global economy. This New World Union seems to be the only real solution."

"World leaders are also supporting a new global currency to

replace the American dollar. For some time, there has been talk of a new currency, but now the G7, the seven largest and most industrialized nations in the world, are seriously working to come up with a suitable cryptocurrency to improve the condition of global financial markets, restore confidence in the world banking system, and improve the efficiency of international trade. Many countries, including the United States, have already embraced bitcoin."

Hearing the announcement to board their flight, Jonathan and Grace departed the lounge, but as they walked onto the concourse, Jonathan stopped abruptly.

"That guy that just walked past us looked just like Steven Westin. Wait here. If that's Steven, I want to say hello to him."

Rushing through the crowded concourse, Jonathan tried in vain to catch up with the man he believed was Steven. As the man dashed down the jetway for his flight, Jonathan asked the attendant at the desk, "What is the destination of that flight?"

"After several stops, the final destination is Tehran, Iran."

Shocked, Jonathan thought, *why was Steven traveling to Iran? Perhaps it wasn't Steven, but he looked like Steven.*

Returning to the Lufthansa Lounge, Jonathan explained to Grace what he had seen.

"Are you positive it was Steven?"

"Well, he looked like Steven."

"But are you absolutely sure it was Steven?"

"I didn't talk to him, and I didn't see him up close, so I guess I don't really know for certain."

"Well then, that may have just been a case of mistaken identity. Besides, what business would Steven have in Iran?"

Puzzled by seeing a man who looked like Steven boarding a plane to Iran, Jonathan grabbed Grace and ran to board their flight. While waiting in line, Jonathan decided to call Steven. If he was at home, then it was clearly a case of mistaken identity. Amy answered the phone.

"Hi Amy, may I speak to Steven?"

"Well, he's not here. He's on a business trip."

"Oh? What exciting place did he go this time?"

With some hesitation in her voice, Amy answered, "Steven said he had a contract assignment for a business trip and the destination of the trip is classified. I can give him a message for you."

"No, I didn't want anything important. I'll just call back later."

Jonathan quickly put his phone away and didn't mention the call to Grace.

Could my best friend actually be conspiring with Iran? I just can't believe it, but why wouldn't Amy volunteer where he is going? Maybe it's reasonable that the destination was classified since it's a CIA assignment.

Eager to board their flight, Jonathan and Grace inched their way down the jetway packed with passengers. Arriving at a divide in the aisle, they were separated from those flying Economy and funneled through the forward door of the plane to the cabin reserved for business class passengers.

The bright young flight attendant directed them to their spacious accommodations to begin the twenty-four-hour journey to Baghdad. Both felt terrible that the support team traveling with them were not upgraded, but they were over their feelings of guilt before the appetizer was served.

One of the flight attendants was about to close the aircraft door when a profusely sweating passenger bolted through the door onto the plane. Jonathan and Grace were close enough to overhear the conversation between the flight attendant and the man, who was visibly shaken for some reason.

"Thank you," the man said. "I was scheduled to fly on American Airlines flight 13 through London and Istanbul, but I decided to take this earlier flight at the last minute."

"That's the flight we were scheduled to take, Jonathan." Grace focused on the man. "Wait a minute, I know that man. He's the American ambassador to Iraq. I met him in New York about a year ago where he was speaking at a Christian organization for World Missions. He is an amazing Christian, and I understand he is working with Iraqi officials to release a team of Christian missionaries who have been imprisoned for three years on 'trumped-up' charges."

No sooner did the aircraft door close than Grace pinched Jonathan.

"Ow, what?"

"Look at that man across the aisle from me dressed as an orthodox Jew. He keeps staring at me."

"Nonsense, Grace. You're just nervous. Try to relax before dinner."

Swiss Air 26 took off on time and after an eight-hour flight without incident landed in Zurich where the travelers had a six-hour layover. From Zurich, they flew to Vienna where they had another extended layover and a change of planes. Finally, they boarded Austrian Airlines for the last leg to the Baghdad International Airport operated by the Iraqi government.

More than a day after the archeological team left the United States, the group finally arrived in Baghdad at 10:30 P.M. Iraq time. However, even in business class, the frequent stops, layovers, and numerous servings of delicious meals made it difficult to sleep for more than a few hours at a time. Sleep-deprived and weary, Grace and Jonathan disembarked the aircraft and began their painstaking trek through customs and immigration. Sporting side arms and automatic rifles, the armed Iraqi guards insisted on redundant personal and baggage inspections and exhaustive questioning. As a linguist, Grace's perfection of the Arabic language was advantageous in the interrogations, but as she tried to gracefully challenge the increasing barrage of questions, the officer interrogating her just became more forceful. Finally, after more than a grueling hour, the officers were satisfied, and all the team was permitted to exit the customs/immigration area.

Checking in at the nearby Baghdad International Hotel, Jonathan, Grace, and the rest of the team found the rooms to be comfortable, but it was certainly not a four or five-star hotel, well maybe for Baghdad standards. All the rooms for the team were on the first floor, and Jonathan was concerned about noise disturbing their sleep at night. Exhausted from the flight, Jonathan collapsed in bed and was asleep before his head hit the pillow.

The next morning, Jonathan and Grace met the rest of their group at 7:00 A.M. for breakfast at the entrance to the restaurant and waited to be seated. An attractive young, dark-haired Arabic woman was seen conferring with two Iraqi military officers before seating the group in a rather conspicuous location at the center of the restaurant. Ignoring the table location, Grace ordered breakfast for everyone in perfect Arabic and then sat silently staring at the front page of the morning newspaper she picked up in the lobby.

The two soldiers cut their eyes toward the group but didn't say a word.

As Jonathan yawned from an apparent lack of sleep, he polled the group with curiosity.

"Did any of you hear a loud noise last night that sounded like an explosion? The sound woke me up from a deep sleep about 2:00 A.M."

Several of the team nodded sleepily in the affirmative.

One member of the team replied, "I think something serious happened near the airport because, after the loud noise, I heard sirens for what seemed like an eternity."

"Did you hear the noise, Grace?"

Ignoring Jonathan, Grace sat with her head buried in the Iraqi newspaper. She was the only one in the group who could read the paper because it was written in Arabic.

"What's wrong, Grace? You're white as a sheet!"

CHAPTER 6

A CLOSE ENCOUNTER

With her voice quivering, Grace choked out the words. "Jonathan, do you have any idea what happened here last night?"

"No, but I think you're going to tell me."

"What was the connecting flight we were originally scheduled on to Baghdad?"

"Why is that important now?"

"Please, just answer the question."

With a *I don't know why I'm doing this* look on his face, Jonathan pulled the original schedule out of his briefcase.

"Well, Grace, we would have been on Turkish Airlines flight 126 from Istanbul. Now, why did you want to know that?"

"That's what I thought! The paper says 'At approximately 2:00 A.M. this morning, Turkish Airlines flight 126 originating in Istanbul was the target of terrorists. Less than a half-mile from the Baghdad airport the aircraft was struck by a rocket and exploded in a fireball killing everyone on board in the fiery crash. It's believed that the American ambassador to Iraq was the target of the attack, but it has not been confirmed that he was on the aircraft."

Everyone at the table stopped eating. No one said a word while they digested the horrifying news.

Jumping up, Grace kicked her chair back and pounded the table so hard with both fists that it rattled the dishes. Raising her voice, she shouted, "What's the matter with all of you? Don't you get it? Everyone on Flight 126 is dead. We should have all been on Flight 126, and we should all be dead right now! What if the terrorists had learned he was on our flight?"

With the gentle persuasion of Jonathan's hands on her shoulders, Grace reluctantly settled back down in her chair with tears of gratitude gushing from her eyes while the others were locked in a complete stone face shock. The numbing fact that they had all escaped an apparent death sentence was slowly sinking in.

One of the team members finally spoke up. "I can't believe all the people on that flight died because the terrorist wanted to kill one man and he was actually on our plane."

At about that time, two of the armed Iraqi guards stationed in the restaurant, who were eyeing Grace intently, walked toward the table with a grimaced look and their hands on their automatic weapons.

Whispering, Jonathan said, "Now look what your outburst has caused, Grace. Try to pull yourself together and see if you can get us out of the trouble coming this way."

One of the soldiers barked in Arabic, "What's the problem here?"

In perfect Arabic, Grace politely replied, "No problem officer, everything is fine. We were just telling a joke. We apologize if we disturbed anyone, and we'll try not to be so loud."

Scowling at the group, the soldiers promptly asked to see each of their passports. After a careful examination of their papers and repeated questioning the soldiers seemed satisfied and walked away, but they stood noticeably nearby where they could watch and listen to every word of the group's conversation.

Grace leaned over and whispered to Jonathan.

"You have to call whoever it was at UNESCO that made that change in the itinerary and thank them. I don't care why they changed it, but they saved our lives."

"Grace, I talked to Michelle last night, and she said she didn't know anything about a revision to our arrangements. She spoke to my contact at UNESCO that booked the original flights just before we left and there was no mention whatsoever of any changes. They also said they have never used a travel agency called 'A Traveler's Friend,' and they don't know anyone named Malachi."

"I believe this whole near-death experience was a divine intervention by God with a guardian angel watching over us, Jonathan. How else can it be explained? Perhaps God has a special assignment for us. Isn't that exciting?"

Shaking his head in solemn disagreement, Jonathan could not believe God could possibly have a purpose for him, not after ignoring God his entire life and cursing God for killing his wife and son.

The conversation was interrupted by the young Arabic woman arriving with a wonderful assortment of Iraqi pastries, bigilla, kahi, and strong Iraqi coffee.

"I believe it was just a coincidence, Grace. Let's just finish our breakfast and load the bus to Babylon so we can get started on our project. I'm anxious to get out of here."

Grace sat quietly, toying with her fork in her food.

After breakfast, Jonathan waved to the young Arabic lady to bring the check for breakfast while Grace and the others returned to their rooms to gather their luggage.

Reflecting on their close encounter with death, Jonathan thought, *this had to have been a coincidence? How would anyone know about the planned terrorist attack, and how did the ambassador know to change his flight?*

Pulling out his iPhone, Jonathan looked at the message regarding the modified itinerary as if it would reveal a clue about the change.

What? The message is fading, and now it's gone completely.

With an unsettling feeling in his stomach, Jonathan decided not to mention this puzzling occurrence to the others. With the luggage and archeological gear loaded, the team boarded a dilapidated school bus for the trip from Baghdad to Al-Hillah, a small town just ten miles from the site of ancient Babylon. The bus looked like a 1950s prisoner transport vehicle, with torn seats and bars on the windows with cracked glass. The only air conditioning was by opening the windows, although there were only a few windows that went down.

Two military escort vehicles, each sporting a 50-caliber machine gun and a grenade launcher, were required by the government to travel with the team, one vehicle ahead of the bus and one at the rear. Several armed guards with automatic rifles were also riding on the bus with the team for security.

The vintage bus made the hot, dusty, sixty-mile drive over the sun-scorched terrain from Baghdad to Al-Hillah in record time, considering two brief stops were necessary to add water to the leaking radiator. As the bus passed close to Al-Hillah, the travelers got their first look at the massive palace constructed by Saddam Hussein with its awesome towering white columns silhouetted against the cloudless blue sky.

A group of French archeologists from UNESCO were already at the hotel in Al-Hillah to welcome Jonathan and Grace and the team from the United States, who were soaked in perspiration and exhausted from the blistering heat of the journey. The hotel accommodations were minimal, but the team was accustomed to staying in comparable hotels on archeological expeditions.

The group spent the first few days in the stifling heat familiarizing themselves with the layout of the ruins of the original city of Babylon as well as the new construction by Saddam Hussein. Much of the original Babylonian ruins had been desecrated by construction of the elaborate new structures.

After several days of carefully combing through the rubble on the foundation of the newly constructed Palace of Saddam Hussein which was built on top of the ruins of the ancient palace of Nebuchadnezzar, Grace noticed something that resembled the tip of an unexploded rocket protruding from debris.

It was common to find live bombs, land mines, and other munitions used during the war and the protocol was to notify the Iraqi military. Grace wasted no time finding Jonathan and reporting what she had found.

While they were talking, she heard a dozer start and proceed in the direction of what she believed was the unexploded rocket. With adrenalin surging throughout her body, Grace bolted toward the dozer rumbling rapidly away from her and screamed at the operator, "Stop, there is a bomb in front of you!"

Realizing what was about to happen, Jonathan sprinted toward Grace to save her from impending danger.

"Grace stop, he can't hear you!"

Unfortunately, no one could be heard over the roar of the huge D9 CAT diesel engine, and there was no way the dozer operator could see the deadly object hidden beneath the piles of crushed stones.

When the mammoth blade of the CAT struck the rocket, it detonated instantly in a firestorm destroying the equipment and killing the operator. The blast hurled rock and fragments of metal from the exploding rocket into the air like lethal missiles, creating a ballooning cloud of suffocating dust. Knocked to the ground by the blast, Grace and Jonathan suffered superficial wounds inflicted by airborne shards of steel and stone.

Trembling, Grace slowly picked herself up off the ground, holding her left arm that was bleeding profusely from a small but deep cut. Realizing her injuries were not life-threatening, she staggered to where Jonathan was lying unconscious.

"Jonathan, can you hear me? Are you okay?"

After a few minutes, Jonathan struggled to move, rubbing his head where the impact of an airborne object produced a large lump.

"Oh, man, my head is killing me!"

As soon as Grace realized he suffered only minor injuries, she screamed, "Do you realize we could have been killed by that blast? After two near-death experiences in two days, I think this mission may be too dangerous. Perhaps someone doesn't want us here."

Still in a daze, Jonathan sat up to find himself covered in blood with minimal cuts and bruises.

"Grace, I know the explosion scared the life out of you, but I'm sure we're just victims of two unfortunate random occurrences, and I'm positive this was just an accident. Besides, who would want to harm us, and why?"

"That's what you say, but how do you know for sure?"

Trying to calm Grace, Jonathan walked with her to the headquarters tent where they received medical attention for their superficial wounds. All work ceased immediately on the site until the military thoroughly examined the area for additional munitions and assured the team it was safe to resume work.

After receiving clearance from the military, work resumed the next day.

"Look, Jonathan, the explosion from the detonated rocket left an enormous crater in the foundation of Saddam's new palace and exposed about a twenty-square foot area of the original foundation below."

After carefully assessing the crater, Grace announced, "There is a hole about the size of a baseball all the way through the floor of the original foundation."

Out of curiosity, Grace peered into the hole, expecting to see the soil or stone directly beneath the foundation.

"Someone, please bring me a light, any kind of light, but hurry!"

Little did Grace know that her next move would open the door to the world of the unknown and begin a journey that would change her life forever.

CHAPTER 7

JONATHAN'S WORST NIGHTMARE

Pressing her face against the ancient stone foundation, Grace ignored the blistering surface scorched by the noonday sun. Squinting with one eye through the opening in the foundation illuminated by the beam of a small but powerful flashlight, Grace was overcome with euphoria at what she saw.

"Hallelujah! Jonathan, come here and look!"

A partial view of what looked like narrow stone steps emerged out of the darkness in the bright beam of her light. The breathtaking invitation from the abyss to come down and investigate was too much for Grace. Her imagination was running rampant.

Like a hungry dog with a bone just out of reach, Grace picked herself up, wiped the hot mixture of sand and sweat from her face, and shouted at the Iraqi workmen whom Jonathan had ushered to the site.

"Quick, clear this entire area of rocks and sand and enlarge this hole so I can get down the steps! Hurry!"

At Jonathan's direction, the workmen hastily cleared the area of rock and rubble several feet around the small opening. Soon, they had uncovered the edges of a three by five-foot stone door hidden in the floor of the ancient Babylonian foundation.

"This is my lucky day, a secret door! Hurry and move it out of the way! I have to get down there."

Struggling to remove the massive door, the workmen used a small crane to lift the huge slab of stone from its resting place and slid it aside using handholds carved in the surface by the Babylonians thousands of years ago. As the stone moved, exposing the opening, rays of light from the blistering afternoon sun shot into the depths of the dark chasm like blazing arrows exposing an underground passageway below.

"Grace, according to my research of this site, the explosion uncovered a secret entrance to an underground cavern or catacomb that before today has never been recorded. I must admit you're right! This is an astounding discovery, and it may even get your name in the record books."

Momentarily forgetting about the assignment from UNESCO, Jonathan called to several of the team members to quickly gather their equipment and meet him at the top of the steps to the underground cavern.

"We'll suspend our work temporarily and assist Grace in exploring the catacombs below."

Totally dismissing the recent close encounters with danger, Grace had only one thing in mind: finding hidden archeological treasure. Wasting no time, she donned her backpack with a few small tools and a flashlight and literally vaulted down the steps, throwing caution to the wind.

"Hold on, Grace, wait for us," shouted Jonathan from the top of the steps. "You can't go charging blindly into that cavern. Let's put our heads together with the other team members who will be here shortly and come up with a game plan to explore the catacombs."

By this time, Grace reached the bottom of the steps and disappeared down a narrow passageway into the darkness.

"Just follow me," Grace shouted. "I intend to search every inch of this place. I feel it in my bones; there is treasure hidden somewhere in this cavern, and I'm going to find it."

Worried about Grace's safety, Jonathan hurried down the steps and called for the others to follow. As they descended the last few steps, Jonathan noticed there was no sign of Grace's light in the dark tunnel ahead.

"Grace, please, will you just stop for a minute and let us catch up with you? You have no business exploring this passage alone; it's too dangerous. Remember, the Euphrates River runs through Babylon and parts of this ancient passage could be flooded. And don't forget we've seen ancient civilizations use booby-traps to protect hidden treasure, that is if there is any treasure down here."

No sooner had Jonathan said the words than the hushed darkness was shattered by an ear-piercing scream.

"Help!"

Scrambling to reach the sound of her voice, the group found Grace's flashlight lying on the ground but no sign of her. Beams of light from the team's flashlights danced wildly throughout the tunnel and suddenly revealed Jonathan's worst nightmare. Just ahead, obscured by the thick darkness of the passage, was a pit filled with water. Just as Jonathan's heart sunk imagining the worst, Grace's slim body rocketed up through the surface of the water like a porpoise, struggling and gasping for air.

After bobbing on the surface like a cork and nearly choking from inhalation of water, Grace struggled to hold on to the rocky edge of the top of the pit. With her elbows resting on the edge of the pit and gasping for air, she managed to scream, "Will somebody please help me get out of here before I drown?"

In one motion, Jonathan and several other men quickly pull Grace from what could have easily been a watery grave and set her on the floor against one wall of the passage. Opening the valve on a small canister he carried on all explorations, Jonathan administered oxygen until Grace began to breathe normally.

"Grace, for a minute, I thought you were…"

Struggling to stand up and get her balance, Grace ripped off the oxygen mask. "You thought what? I was dead? So, there are feelings for me in that stone heart of yours! Well, I'm fine now, but that pit must be twenty feet deep, and I went all the way to the bottom. With the weight of the equipment in my backpack, I thought I would never get it unbuckled and get back to the surface. Everything was lost except this small antiquity bag around my waist with a few tools."

"You do realize you're very fortunate, don't you, Grace? This pit was used as a deterrent to tomb raiders. Had it not been flooded naturally by water seeping from the river above, the fall would likely have claimed your life. Now please slow down and try to watch where you're stepping."

"I appreciate your concern for me, but I was never in any danger! I could have easily climbed out by myself."

Jonathan just looked at Grace and smiled without saying a word. This was a debate he knew from experience he couldn't win.

Once out of the pit, Grace outpaced the rest of the team again. Of course, no one could see the *Don't worry about me, I can take care of myself* look beaming from her face.

As the team followed Grace down the long musty winding passage, the darkness seemed to swallow the bright beams of their flashlights. They passed numerous narrow entrances, each leading to a small crypt or vault with plain-looking sarcophaguses stacked like cordwood.

Pointing to inscriptions above the entrances, Grace announced, "These rooms were used to bury the bodies of the King's personal staff and their families. Depending on their level of service in the King's court, the bodies were placed in different vaults along the passageway."

Opening one of the sarcophaguses, Grace explained. "Ugh, it looks like time has taken its toll. The Babylonians didn't mummify the dead like the Egyptians; they just painted their cheeks, darkened their eyelids, and wrapped them in linen." Grace marveled at the jewelry, coins, and even cookware and pottery placed in the sarcophagus by the Babylonians, believing they would be useful in the afterlife.

While Grace examined the sarcophaguses, Jonathan's light exposed hieroglyphs etched into a limestone coating plastered over the rock walls. Each vault exhibited similar walls with a representation of the roles of the servants buried in that vault etched in the limestone. There were impressions of cooks, chariot drivers, guards, animal keepers, scribes, and more, performing their daily tasks. Although there was a wealth of museum-quality artifacts found in the catacomb, there was nothing of earth-shattering significance, and there was no treasure!

"What a bummer, no treasure, Jonathan!"

With the hope of a world-class discovery completely dashed, Jonathan suggested he and Grace continue exploring the tunnel while the rest of the team begin documenting the contents of the burial vaults, which contained some archeological value. Everyone agreed to meet back at the entrance to the catacombs in two hours.

As the two explorers approached the end of the passage, their lights illuminated a narrow entrance to one last room.

"Look at this vault; there is a Z-shaped entrance preventing us from looking inside until we go around the corner," Jonathan observed. "Let me see if I can get through this narrow opening."

"Be careful, Jonathan."

Holding his breath to minimize his body size, Jonathan began to squeeze through the opening that is just large enough for a child to walk through comfortably when Grace screamed, "Wait, don't…!"

CHAPTER 8

ENTOMBED

"**D**on't go in there. The sign over the entrance says, 'ENTER AT YOUR OWN RISK, BEWARE OF THE CURSE OF LEB KA-MAI.'"

"Grace, Leb Kamai is an old Chaldean sorcerer, and I never put much stock in those ancient curses anyway," Jonathan explained. "Let me squeeze through this entrance, and then you can probably just walk through with your size two figure."

"Well, thank you for that compliment, but please be careful!"

After entering the vault, Grace was bubbling over with excitement. "Look, from the inscriptions on these walls, I would say this room may have actually been the real treasure room of King Nebuchadnezzar II. I knew it! I knew there was treasure down here. Perhaps his sarcophagus is even in here. You know his real tomb has never been discovered.

"Wait a minute, Jonathan. If this really is his treasure room, don't you think it's strange that we were able to just walk in?"

"Hold everything, look at this!"

"What?"

"This looks like a tripwire that I…"

"Wait, what's that sound?"

A low frequency grinding sound in the wall was followed by a deafening thud. Looking back, they saw the opening that teased them with the promise of ancient treasure was now sealed with a massive stone that threatened to entomb them forever.

"We triggered a booby trap. Well, now we know what the curse of Leb Kamai is! We should have been more alert!"

Realizing they may never escape the King's Chamber to tell the world of their discovery, Grace began to sweat profusely with her heart throbbing, and she collapsed into Jonathan's arms with fear-induced exhaustion. While embracing Grace, he sensed sensual feelings coursing through his body like an electric charge and found the lingering remnants of her French perfume a bit tantalizing.

Somewhat surprised, Jonathan silently reflected. *Emotions are bubbling up within me that I haven't experienced since my marriage to Deborah.*

Grace made no attempt to disengage herself from Jonathan's gentle grasp. With his mind wandering and his heart racing, the reality of the moment suddenly seized him. Shaking off the effects of his new-found feelings, Jonathan unwrapped Grace from his arms as though she was a delicate Christmas package and carefully slid her away. "If we're going to find a way out, we need to get started."

Pulling herself together and grabbing the light, Grace began to explore the chamber like a bloodhound hot on the scent of a fox. As Grace prowled the area with Jonathan trailing behind her in the darkness, the light exposed a short, narrow passage off the large room leading to a smaller vault.

"Look, Jonathan, shards of pottery that look like they're from jars used to store ancient scrolls, and there are fragments of scrolls scattered about the floor. This room must have served as an archive library, but it looks like someone took everything they could carry out and left in a big hurry."

While Jonathan looked for an escape route, Grace made her way through another narrow passage to a larger chamber, and there it was, big as life. A sarcophagus fit for a king.

Shouting in the darkness, Grace cried with exhilaration, "Here it is, here is the discovery of a lifetime. I knew it!"

For a moment both explorers forget about being entombed in the catacombs and huddle around the dim light pouring over the inscriptions on the sarcophagus. As Grace's fingers moved judiciously over each ancient letter, she announced with triumphant authority, "The writing on this sarcophagus authenticates the fact that this is the actual tomb of Nebuchadnezzar II, the King of Babylon, who began his rule in 605 BC. This is it, Jonathan, this is the real thing! Previous expeditions to the ruins of this city had located what they thought was his tomb on the opposite side of his palace, but the mummy proved to be the body of someone else. The large room we entered was most likely used to store the King's most precious treasures, and this smaller chamber the King's body. Just imagine, if we can retrieve this sarcophagus, we will finally be able to introduce the world to the real King Nebuchadnezzar II."

Suddenly reality set in and Jonathan decreed with obvious apprehension, "Great idea, Grace, but first, we have to find a way of escape."

Returning to the larger room, their attention was drawn to a strange hieroglyph etched in the limestone texture plastered on one face of the rock wall. The image of a large winged man was sitting suspended on a throne with a crown on his head surrounded by stars. He had what looked like the sun and moon in one hand and was reaching down with the other hand to a smaller figure of a man handing him a small box and a scroll. Emanating from the box were jagged lines resembling bolts of lightning.

"Jonathan, what do you think this pictograph means? These figures are not the king's servants like the ones we saw in the previous rooms."

"No, it looks like this hieroglyph is depicting someone or something with great power in the heavens or from another world giving a message and a box to a man portrayed as a servant on Earth. The box appears to have incredible energy, perhaps to fuel a machine or trigger destruction. This hieroglyph could be proof positive that someone or something from another world not only visited ancient Babylon but delivered a message and an object of enormous value and power to an earthling."

"What do you think the message means and what is inside the

box? I wonder where the box is now?"

"Great questions, Grace, but I don't have any answers. I do know the message must have been incredibly important for the king to have this event inscribed on the wall in his secret chambers. Why don't you search the rooms for any clues to the meaning of the hieroglyph, and I'll start looking for a way out of here."

"How can I search for anything? I can't even see my hand in front of my face without your light."

"Ok, let's look together."

Just when they were exhausted from searching every square inch of the chambers, the beam from the flashlight exposed the edge of a papyrus tucked into a crevice on a ledge in the smaller room believed to be used for archiving scrolls. With great anticipation, Grace delicately removed a set of scrolls in a corner away from the edge of the shelf. She also picked up as many fragments of scrolls that she can find scattered about the floor and carefully placed them in her antiquities bag.

"These scrolls may give us some clues to the meaning of the hieroglyphs and the identity of the strange visitor," Grace said.

"Great, but let's get back to searching for a way out, or we'll be living out the rest of our days down here with King Nebuchadnezzar II. These rooms appear to have no access to the outside world except back through the opening in the stone wall that is now impassable."

"What are you saying, Jonathan? We're not going to die, are we?"

"Of course not, but think about it. The sarcophagus couldn't have been brought here through that opening in the wall that we came through! There must have been another way in here at one time."

Just then, the light in Jonathan's flashlight went out, immersing the explorers in heart-pounding, deafening darkness.

Grace was hysterical until Jonathan pulled several candles from his backpack and lit them with a lighter he carried for just such an occasion.

"Here, hold these candles," Jonathan told Grace.

Eerie shadows created by the flickering flames of the candles made the pictograph figures on the limestone plastered wall seem to come to life and dance wildly.

Jonathan continued to examine the walls of the chamber by candlelight for any clue to a way of escape, and Grace remained glued to his side. As the candles burned out, returning the pair to total darkness, Jonathan walked slowly to one of the walls and laughed out loud.

Grabbing his shirt so as not to get separated in the darkness, Grace pleaded, "What has gotten into you? Are you delirious?"

"Turn around and look at the wall in front of you. What do you see?

"Nothing but darkness and an area that seems to be glowing green."

"Exactly, those rocks have an iridescent green color typical of radium."

"Okay, what's the point? And please light another candle. I can't stand this darkness."

"Listen, Grace, radium was applied to the dials on watches by female factory workers, called 'radium girls' in the early 1900s. The radium caused the dials of watches to glow in the dark. I would have never noticed the iridescent area of the wall had it not been for the darkness. I think that area must have originally been a shaft that was later sealed and plastered over to hide it, but the plaster has fallen away."

Jonathan continued. "Wait a minute, that's it! The sarcophagus was lowered into this room through a shaft from the outside. After it was secure in the large room, the shaft was permanently sealed by filling it with rock and sand. The slightly irradiated rock used to seal the cavity must be indigenous to this area. Sealing the shaft and plastering over the walls assured the King's body and his possessions were protected from tomb raiders. Even if someone stumbled upon the secret entrance to the treasure rooms like we did and avoided the trip mechanism, they still couldn't remove the sarcophagus."

"That's an incredible theory, Jonathan," Grace said, "but now you're telling me you're happy that we're trapped in this tomb with a glowing green spot on the wall."

"No, Grace, sometimes the darkness helps us to see the light. I think we may be able to dig our way out of here through what may be a secret shaft to the outside."

Leaning into his right ear, Grace whispered, "I hate to bring this up in the midst of your good news, but I'm standing in water!"

As Jonathan lowered the candle, the light revealed a shallow pool of water inching across the floor from the entrance of the room.

"It looks like water from the Euphrates River is seeping into the king's chambers and threatening to flood the entire area. The exploding munition must have weakened a substratum of this cavern beneath the river, causing the seepage of water to increase into the catacombs. Okay, help me, Grace. I don't know how long it will take for this chamber to fill with water, and I believe this shaft is our only way out. You hold the candle, so I can see to remove these stones."

After a few loose stones were removed from the wall, sand and rock spilled out onto the floor.

"It appears the shaft was originally five or six feet in diameter, although only a two or three-foot core is loosely packed and can be easily dug out."

With the removal of each stone, the opening grew larger, and rock and sand poured out, splashing into the pool of water that was growing deeper with every passing minute. When the sand and rock finally stopped flowing out of the shaft, a thin ray of bright afternoon sunlight emanating from the top of the duct chased the darkness from the cavernous room.

"Thank goodness! It looks like the shaft goes all the way to the surface. This is it! This is our way out, Grace!"

While Jonathan continued to remove rocks and sand from the shaft, Grace focused on a discovery of her own.

"Hey, take a look at this."

The bright beam of light from the shaft was focused like a laser on a small metal object in the shape of an octagon lying partially covered in the sand and water.

"Look at this medallion partially buried in the sand. The water must have uncovered it." After wiping the water and sand from the artifact with the care a mother gives a newborn baby, Grace studied the medallion with the curiosity of a cat. "You're not going to believe this. There is an inscription on the medallion."

"Well, what does it say"?

"The words 'Cyrus the Great, King of Persia' is scribed on the medallion. From these markings, the person who lost this medal was probably a member of King Cyrus' court, someone very close to the King who defeated Nebuchadnezzar II and took over his palace. Perhaps this treasure room was used to store his scrolls and artifacts while he controlled the palace. Jonathan, this medallion could be the key to another mystery."

With a wrinkled brow and ignoring her discovery, Jonathan climbed up into the shaft and began to remove more rocks. Pulling on his pants leg, Grace shouted, "Jonathan, are you listening to me?"

"Grace, I'm happy you found another stimulating artifact, but why don't we concentrate on getting out of here? With any luck, we can crawl up this shaft and dig our way to the surface before we drown."

"We can crawl up the shaft or do you mean *I* can crawl up the shaft?"

"Well, since you are obviously the smaller of the two of us, and the shaft is not that large at the top, you should be able to make your way up to the surface first and go for help."

"That's what I thought you meant, but I'm not getting into that small shaft; I'm too claustrophobic. Wait a minute, what's that weird sound? Something is crawling up my leg! I can't see!"

Shining his light on the floor, Jonathan chuckled.

"What's so funny? What is it?"

"That sound you hear is from hundreds of small hard-shell insects called Babylonian scarab beetles that burrow inside the flesh of dead bodies and eat everything but the bone. They emit a kind of chattering noise to signal other beetles that they have found food."

"Are you saying I'm food for beetles? But I'm not dead! Get down here and get these things off me. Hurry! I'm getting in that shaft!"

Jonathan brushed the insects off Grace's legs and helped her into the shaft.

Cleared of rock and sand, the shaft was about four feet in diameter at the bottom and rose about thirty feet to the surface at an angle of approximately forty-five degrees. As Grace inched up the shaft, she reported it was getting smaller in diameter with each move she made. About a foot from the surface, she shouted to Jonathan.

"I'm almost at the top, Jonathan, and I can see daylight, but I'm stuck. Sand is pouring in around my face and mouth, and I can't move up or down." Spitting sand from her mouth Grace cried, "Oh Jonathan, I think there's something else in this shaft besides me, and it's furry. Pull me out of here, quick! It's a big rat! Wait a minute, it just scurried up through the opening at the top of the shaft. Thank goodness it's gone!"

"Don't freak out on me, Grace. Try to stay calm. I'm coming up to help you."

Stepping out of knee-deep water, Jonathan climbed into the hole in the wall and tried desperately to crawl up the shaft but slid back down. After several attempts, he made his way up within three feet of Grace and realized he was wedged against the walls of the narrow shaft himself.

"I'm sorry, Grace, I can't reach you."

"Can't you do something? I know you don't pray, but please try to pray with me."

"Forget about praying, just keep digging your way to the surface. My feet are getting wet from water rising in the shaft, so we don't have much time."

As Grace tried desperately to move her arms, she prayed, "God, please don't let us drown in this shaft just inches from freedom. Please send an angel to find us! I know you must have something important for us to accomplish, and I promise we will be sensitive to your word!"

After Grace prayed, she said, "Wait a minute. Be quiet, Jonathan. I hear something!"

CHAPTER *9*

A ROCK STAR

Gasping for air, Grace heard a faint voice she recognized. "Listen! I hear a voice that sounds like Joshua."

Joshua was a burly, young, red-headed, bearded French archeologist who had worked with Jonathan and Grace many times before. Although he lived and worked in America for years, he still had an unmistakably strong French accent.

Spewing sand from her mouth like a geyser, Grace strained to yell as loud as she could. "Joshua, is that you? Can you hear me? It's Grace, please help us!"

"Yes, it's me, Joshua, but where are you?"

Feeling a sudden surge of relief at hearing a familiar voice, Grace cried out again as loud as she could. "I'm wedged in a shaft near the surface, and Jonathan is below me with water flooding the chamber. Please hurry and get us out. We don't have much time."

"Okay. Keep talking so I can pinpoint your location. I know I'm close to you, but I don't see anything that resembles an opening to a shaft."

After a frantic search for more than fifteen minutes and with time running out, Joshua noticed a desert rat about twenty feet in front of him. The rat was just standing there on his hind legs as if to say, "Look over here," and then scampered away. Out of curiosity, Joshua ran to the spot where he saw the rat and shined his flashlight down the small hole believed to be the rat's home. To his surprise, there was Grace's dust-covered but recognizable face inches below the surface.

"Grace, it's me, Joshua!"

Squinting from the light of Joshua's flashlight shining in her eyes, her fear of being trapped melted like ice on a sizzling summer pavement.

"It's Joshua, Jonathan, he found us; we're saved."

"Tell him to hurry; water is up to my ankles in this shaft."

After reassuring Grace that he would get them both out as quickly as possible, Joshua sent one of the other team members back to the headquarters tent for help. Meanwhile, he lowered a small hose from a portable oxygen canister he was carrying to provide fresh air for Grace and Jonathan. The other men soon returned with the necessary equipment to free the explorers from what would have certainly been a watery grave.

In less than an hour, both weary explorers were pulled from the shaft along with the scrolls, medallion and a few other treasures. Emerging into the daylight, Grace wiped the sand and sweat from her face and gave Joshua a hug of gratitude.

"Joshua, we can't thank you enough, but how in the world did you find us?"

Laughing, Joshua explained, "I didn't find you, Grace. When you and Jonathan didn't return to the entrance of the passage in two hours as agreed, we began looking for you in the catacombs. We couldn't find a trace of you, so we assumed you must have discovered an opening in the dead-end passage. We mapped the direction of the tunnel and believed it took you under the Euphrates River to the other side and began our search there. When we heard your muffled shouts for help, we followed the sound but couldn't find an opening in the ground that led to the underground cavern where we believed you were trapped."

"Okay, so how did you find the shaft?"

"Believe it or not, we saw a desert rat standing on his hind legs that seemed to be waiting for us. Out of curiosity, I examined the hole he came out of, and the rest is history. Without the help of that rat, we may have been too late."

"I guess that rat must have been what scampered past my head. I never thought I would thank God for a guardian angel disguised as a rat."

As Jonathan and Grace were walking away, they noticed water bubbling out of the shaft.

"We got out just in time, the chambers are flooded, and the shaft is collapsing, "Grace said. "I guess the world may never meet King Nebuchadnezzar II after all."

Jonathan and Grace returned to the headquarters tent with their treasure consisting of a few broken pieces of jewelry, several intact sets of ancient scrolls and fragments of other scrolls and of course, the curious medallion that Grace found.

"Well Jonathan, now do you believe God answered my prayer and sent an angel to signal our location to Joshua?"

"Maybe."

Grace just smiled.

After a short rest, Grace took some time to study her treasure. She explained to Jonathan that since the inscriptions on the intact scrolls were written in Chaldean, she believed they belonged to King Cyrus of Persia, not Nebuchadnezzar or Belshazzar.

"Grace, that means King Cyrus used the secret room to store his own archives of important documents after he conquered Babylon. This is a real treasure trove, even though we only have a few scrolls and fragments of other scrolls."

Work continued at the site of ancient Babylon with no further discoveries as great as that found in the secret chambers below. Each night after work, Grace poured over the scrolls she found. Soon it became clear that the manuscripts were part of a journal of King Cyrus' private daily life and must have been overlooked when the Persians hastily evacuated the palace.

Completing their documentation of the catacombs, Jonathan

and Grace received permission from the Iraqi Minister of Artifacts to take the scrolls they found back to America on loan for further examination. Anxious to begin work on the manuscripts, Jonathan called Michelle to make reservations for their flight home. The rest of the team remained in Babylon to complete the work assigned to them by UNESCO.

After a long, exhausting but uneventful flight, Jonathan and Grace arrived safely at Newark Liberty Airport.

The following morning, Jonathan arrived at the university early and began reliving the adventure in Iraq with Michelle. She was so thankful they were both home safe and sound after their harrowing experiences. Meanwhile, Grace arrived and took the scrolls into the laboratory to begin the tedious process of numbering and digitizing them so that the originals could be properly preserved.

When Michele brought in fresh coffee and an assortment of pastries, she found Jonathan and Grace glued to a televised newscast in progress.

"A bright new star on the political scene, Carpathia Romulus, has rocketed to stardom in the last few years. Considered by world leaders to head the recently formed New World Union Organization, this young man seemed to come into the political spotlight from nowhere. Reportedly born in a small town in Italy, the young statesman sports a colorful Roman ancestry with a law degree from Oxford University. However, no transcript of his education has ever been made public, and no alleged classmates or Oxford professors can be found that remember him. In any event, people don't seem to be troubled by the lack of background information for this new political champion."

"After graduation from Oxford, a powerful but stealthy political machine propelled him into British politics where he served two years in the London Assembly. Possessing the charisma of an evangelist and the popularity of a rock star, the handsome new statesman proposed solid ideas to jump-start the faltering global economy."

"Everywhere the young man goes, people are excited about his promise to change the world for the better. He proposes to stop the genocides that are killing people by the millions, make the world a safer place, and improve the standard of living for everyone."

"Although many long-time politicians believe he lacks the experience for the top job in the New World Union, this rising star seems to have garnered the support and confidence of world leaders everywhere. One of the first things the statesman pledged to do if elected head of the New World Union is inviting the Prime Minister of Israel to his headquarters to be established in Rome. To demonstrate his commitment for world peace, he plans to negotiate a seven-year peace treaty with their Prime Minister. Backed by the New World Union this treaty will certainly be welcomed by the Israelis since their only real ally is the United States. Most of the world's leaders seem confident that this new political figure could set the planet on a solid course of recovery for peace and prosperity."

"I don't know Grace," Jonathan said. "We have seen this kind of politician before. America elected as President of the United States a popular, charismatic guy who came from nowhere and look what happened to America. It's only because of the presidential election in 2016 that we're not in worse shape today."

Grace was distracted by something and didn't appear to be listening.

"What's on your mind, Grace? You look like you're in another world."

"Nothing. It just seems like all the events that are taking place in the world must have a more important meaning."

"What do you mean?"

"Never mind. Let's eat breakfast and get to work."

Grace worked long hours every day for more than a week with the scrolls and shreds of parchments while Jonathan fulfilled his teaching obligations at the university and coordinated the work with the team in Babylon. Each scroll was numbered and digitized so they could be studied at length even after the originals were encased with a preservative and shipped back to the Iraqi Antiquities Museum in Baghdad. Once the digitized copies were completed, Grace began the tedious task of interpreting the scrolls and methodically recording the notes in her journal. Late one afternoon, Grace called Jonathan into the laboratory to share take-out Chinese and to discuss her preliminary findings.

"Jonathan, I'm positive that the fragments of scrolls that were scattered about the room are related to the life of King Nebuchadnezzar II and King Belshazzar. Cyrus must have had the scrolls of Nebuchadnezzar and Belshazzar destroyed and used the room to archive his own documents during his stay in the palace. That would certainly explain all the fragments."

"The intact scrolls contain detailed notes describing the events that took place during the reign of King Cyrus, including his conquest of Babylon. Important conversations with others in his palace are also described in the scrolls. Unfortunately, my initial review of the scrolls indicates the journal of King Cyrus is incomplete."

Satisfied with the results to date and knowing Grace will not give up until she has bled every meaningful word from the parchments, Jonathan returned to his work at the university. Obsessed with finding the complete meaning of every symbol on the scrolls, Grace worked day and night piecing together the tattered pieces of papyrus and interpreting the intact scrolls. Working past the midnight hour at the university one night, she stopped what she was doing and made a crucial phone call.

CHAPTER 10

THE DOOMSDAY CLOCK

Awakened out of a sound slumber by the annoying ring of his iPhone, Jonathan fumbled in the darkness to confront the night-time intruder.

"Uh, hello, who is this? Grace? Is that you?"

"Yes, it's me, Jonathan. Are you awake?"

"Are you out of your mind? No, I'm not awake. It's 2 o'clock in the morning. What are you doing up at this…?"

"Just listen, Jonathan, I ..."

"Where are you? Are you in trouble?"

"No, I'm in the archive laboratory at the university, but please just listen to me for one minute..."

"What are you doing working this late by yourself? Don't you know you could be mugged or something worse, leaving the university alone in the middle of the night?"

"Gosh Jonathan, I love it that you're worried about me. But will you please listen to why I called?"

"Ok, so I'm concerned about your safety, but why can't we talk when I come to the office in the morning? You should call one of the security guards to escort you to your car and go home right now!"

"This can't wait until morning; you have to come to the university now! What I just discovered in the manuscripts I can't explain over the phone, but I promise you'll be elated you came."

"Oh, all right, let me get dressed, get a cup of coffee, and I should be there in about an hour, but this better be good!"

"Bring coffee for me, too, Jonathan; you'll not be disappointed."

Knowing Grace, she wouldn't call in the middle of the night unless she had truly discovered something of significant importance. Sitting up with a sigh, Jonathan turned on the nightstand light and cautiously opened one eye and then the other. After chasing away the cobwebs of a pleasant night's sleep, Jonathan showered, dressed and, on the way to the university, picked up coffee and pastries at an all-night coffee shop. Arriving at the university laboratory, Jonathan found Grace slumped over her desk, struggling to keep her eyes open.

"Okay, here I am, now, what's the big revelation?"

Aroused from her slumber by the fragrant aroma of steaming hot coffee, Grace helped herself to a large apple-fritter. Teetering on the edge of hyperventilation, Grace swallowed the last of the tasty pastry and, with rock-solid confidence, began to explain what she found.

"Okay, now listen to this! I was reading from this scroll that describes a conversation between a young Israelite man and King Cyrus."

"Whoa, stop right there. What you're saying makes absolutely no sense, Grace! Why would the Persian king be talking to an Israelite? The Israelites were slaves to the Babylonians, and later, they were slaves to the Persians."

"He was not just any ordinary Israelite. This very special young man gained a reputation for having unusual powers to interpret dreams for King Nebuchadnezzar II and King Belshazzar when no one else could. He was well respected by everyone and was even given a prominent position in the king's court by King Nebuchadnezzar II.

"Who was this unique young Israelite?"

Hesitating, Grace responded, "His name isn't recorded here."

"The story about an Israelite is interesting, but surely that's not why you called me at 2:00 A.M. this morning?"

"No, listen carefully to the rest of the conversation. The young man told King Cyrus he had been praying to God that all the Israelites who had been taken from Jerusalem by King Nebuchadnezzar II would be released. Jeremiah, an Israelite prophet predicted hundreds of years earlier that the captivity would last exactly seventy years and the Israelites had been captive in Babylon about that long."

"Seriously, Grace, I don't get it. Is this guy just asking the king to let him and the other Israelites captives go home?"

"Be patient. The next part of the conversation is the real reason I called you." Grace continued. "The young Israelite began to describe his recent encounter with a bizarre being he believed was from another world."

"What do you mean 'a being from another world'? What world? What kind of being?"

"Hold on a minute, please! He described a ghost-like figure of a man appearing out of thin air and flying. I'm sure the young man was frightened out of his wits, but he said when the being physically touched him and began to speak softly, he settled down and listened. When presented with an unusual timeline and description of future events, the Israelite was excited to recognize the only event on the timeline that made any sense to him was the imminent release of all the Israelite captives to return to Jerusalem.

"Of course, King Cyrus was extremely curious about this timeline, since any knowledge of the future would be extremely instrumental in expanding his empire. The young man explained to the king that there are three events on the timeline, and the last event will trigger the countdown to the beginning of the end of this world. Thrilled by the prospect of gaining greater power, King Cyrus asked the young man to describe each event in detail. Without question, he was particularly interested in the third event and the meaning of the countdown to the destruction of the world. No doubt he was contemplating using the information to become the ultimate conqueror of the world!"

"What does that mean the countdown to the end of the world, Grace?" asked Jonathan. "Is this Israelite saying the Earth will be destroyed by some powerful alien force, a 'Doomsday Clock' for planet Earth?"

Grace responded with, "Just stop talking, Jonathan, and listen to me.

"Unfortunately, the rest of this conversation between the young Israelite and the king is recorded on another scroll that King Cyrus must have taken with him. We'll never know the rest of the story without that scroll."

"Wait a minute, Grace; what are we saying? This idea of a Doomsday Clock for the destruction of planet Earth given to an Israelite by someone from outer space or another world sounds like something out of a blockbuster science fiction movie. This is a conversation between a king and some Israelite slave who would say anything to gain his freedom. I'm sorry, Grace. It's 3:30 in the morning and I should be home in bed."

Although thoroughly frustrated, Jonathan found himself torn between the mandate borne by his extensive experience to find a rational scientific meaning to everything he just heard and the desire to dismiss the conversation as another ancient mystery that would be proven to have no substantive basis. He had seen many of these so-called "too good to be true" findings in his career that turned out to be unsubstantiated accounts of an overzealous archeologist.

"Come on, Grace, let's go. I'll walk you to your car."

Jonathan got up from his chair and started toward the door but stopped abruptly and turned toward Grace with his face beaming.

"What?" Grace questions. "What are you thinking? I know that look, and you've got an idea."

"Don't you get it? Are we both asleep? Remember the mysterious hieroglyphs on the wall in the king's treasure room in Babylon?"

"Yes, but…"

"Remember there was a powerful man on a throne with the sun

and moon in one hand and stars all around him? He was handing an earthling a scroll and a small box with strange powers emanating from it."

With her green eyes widened in amazement, Grace shouted, "Are you thinking the man on the throne is the messenger from out of this world and the earthling is the young Israelite described in the scrolls?"

"Exactly, and the scroll he's handing the young Israelite is the timeline you're reading about, and the box is, well, the box may be the Doomsday Clock with the power to destroy the world. Grace, this may be the greatest archeological discovery since the unearthing of the Mummy of King Tut. I just need more proof that all of this is real."

Shocked wide awake now by the revelation, Jonathan's joyful shouts of victory echoed throughout the laboratory.

"But Jonathan, why would anyone want to destroy our planet?"

"I don't know, Grace; it all sounds so incredibly unbelievable! Maybe the hieroglyph is just a hoax. You know, maybe someone in the king's court drew the hieroglyph for entertainment or maybe it has a hidden meaning."

As the reality of the discovery set in, Grace and Jonathan settled down without saying a word. Both were thinking the same thing.

Finally, Jonathan broke the silence.

"Grace, just suppose the story is true. What if there is a Doomsday Clock? What if there is something that will trigger a third event on the timeline that initiates the destruction of the world?"

"Well if the timeline exists, why hasn't the earth already been destroyed? The message was delivered more than 3,000 years ago!"

"Maybe, just maybe, Grace, the clock has been hidden or lost for thousands of years waiting for the trigger that will activate it. Maybe the one who gave the Israelite the clock is waiting for something else to happen."

"Waiting for what to happen, Jonathan?"

"I don't know, Grace, but perhaps time is different for the one who visited our planet than it is for us, but we must do what we can to validate the timeline and locate the elusive clock of destruction to save the Earth."

Suddenly, Grace's face lit up like a light bulb, and with a twinkle in her eyes, she shouted, "Jonathan, I know exactly where to look."

"You know where the Doomsday Clock is?"

CHAPTER 11

MUSEUM CLUE

"Of course not," Grace replied. "I meant I know where the manuscript is that may give us the clue to where the Doomsday Clock is hidden. Think about it. King Nebuchadnezzar II placed his treasures and personal belongings in his secret treasure chamber, believing he would have access to them in the afterlife. Why wouldn't King Cyrus have done the same thing?"

Nodding in agreement, Jonathan swallowed the last bite of a chocolate donut and washed it down with coffee.

"So, you're thinking the missing scrolls are in the treasure room in King Cyrus's tomb?"

"Sure, why not?"

"Well that's a definite possibility, Grace, but it seems archeologists would have already found any manuscripts that were in the tomb during previous expeditions. Artifacts, manuscripts, and notes gathered from King Cyrus' tomb by archeologists in the early 1900s are preserved in the Freer Gallery of Art, in the Smithsonian Museum in Washington D.C. You know we have studied the artifacts and manuscripts in detail, and notes from the expeditions have even been used in my graduate classes.

"Grace, I think we should begin today to go over our notes from previous investigations of the tomb of King Cyrus to see if there is any clue that may point us to where the missing manuscripts of his journal are located. If we don't find anything, we should go to the museum in Washington and review the physical photographs, notes, and manuscripts from the tomb of King Cyrus again. If we don't find what we're looking for in the museum, we may have to consider traveling to the ruins of the ancient city of Pasargadae where the tomb of King Cyrus is located and look for the missing manuscripts ourselves. Of course, any artifacts still in the tomb are likely to be cleverly hidden, or they would have already been discovered."

Smiling like a Cheshire cat that just swallowed a canary, Grace was ecstatic at the prospect of personally exploring King Cyrus' tomb. She was even willing to first go over her notes at the university and then revisit the actual artifacts, manuscripts, and other material in the museum.

"Grace, there is just one problem! Gaining entry to Iran, where the tomb of King Cyrus is located, will likely be extremely difficult and dangerous in today's volatile world. We could be sentenced to prison or even shot as spies by the Iranian government just for being there."

Jonathan called the team in Iraq working on the UNESCO project and explained his dilemma. While wanting to return to Babylon to help them complete the assignment, Jonathan was now dedicated to solving the mystery of the Doomsday Clock for planet Earth. The group in Babylon was instructed to continue working with the plan they had and call if they needed assistance. He and Grace would return to Iraq as soon as they completed work on the scrolls of King Cyrus.

For several weeks, Grace labored over the notes of their past visits to the museum where they studied the Persian manuscripts, photographs, and artifacts. Concluding there was no additional information in her notes regarding the missing manuscripts, Grace called Jonathan at home one evening.

"Jonathan, I've been unsuccessful in finding any clues to the missing manuscripts in my notes. I'm leaving in the morning to go to the Freer Gallery of Art in the Smithsonian Museum. Hopefully, I'll find something that will help us unravel this bizarre mystery."

"Well, two heads are better than one. I'll pick you up in the morning, and we'll go together."

After a short flight to Ronald Reagan Washington National Airport, they arrived at the Smithsonian. They had no trouble locating the gallery in the basement of the Freer Gallery of Art where the Persian artifacts were on display. A special room was reserved for scientists and their assistants to study original manuscripts under strict security and carefully controlled laboratory conditions. After checking in with the curator, they were given access to the documents they wanted to research. The slim, all-business lady in her late 70s with her hair in a tight little bun and big horn-rimmed glasses resting low on her nose, sat up straight in her chair with a stone-faced look. Without cracking a smile, she meticulously recorded the presence of the researchers in her logbook and directed them to the appropriate areas.

In the event a trip to King Cyrus's tomb was necessary, Jonathan concentrated on drawings of the layout of the ruins, including photographs of walls, rooms, and passages prepared by other archeologists.

Meanwhile, Grace went straight to the area reserved for the examination of original manuscripts. Although indexed notes were provided to indicate missing sections, the precise interpretation of the documents was left to the individual linguist. As the hours dragged on, Grace found no reference to a timeline or manuscripts of a young Israelite speaking to King Cyrus. With the researchers being very thorough in their investigation, Grace and Jonathan were left with a disappointing and frustrating dead end.

By 4:45 P.M. both investigators were exhausted and ready to call it a day. Grace completed the documentation of the manuscripts and notes, and Jonathan finished his study of the photos, layout, and design of the tomb with absolutely no startling revelation.

As Jonathan approached the table where Grace was working, she whispered, "Look at that man across the room with the beard. He hasn't taken his eyes off me since we came in and doesn't seem to be studying anything, just watching me."

Looking around the room, Jonathan questioned, "What man? I don't see anyone. We're the only people in this room."

"Well, he was there just a minute ago. Maybe my imagination is getting the best of me; besides, I'm very tired, and I'm starving. You know we didn't even stop to eat lunch."

"Okay, come on. Gather your notes, and let's go."

"Wait a minute. Look, here is a photo that was inadvertently included with one of the lists of manuscripts I was studying."

Patting his foot impatiently, Jonathan pointed to his watch as Grace poured over her new treasure in the pile of notes. As some of the lights were being turned out nearby signaling the closing of the library, Grace broke the silence of the room with a shout, drawing the attention of the curator who stood to her feet and walked toward them.

"Jonathan, I don't believe it! How could I have missed this?"

CHAPTER 12

NEEDLE IN THE HAYSTACK

"Look at this photograph of one of the walls in King Cyrus' tomb."

"Grace, we have to go; they're going to turn the lights off."

"I know, I know, but sit down for just a minute and look closely at this picture."

"I've already examined all the photographs, and there is nothing there!"

"Well, you didn't look at this one! See that shady spot that resembles a depression in the wall?"

Squinting at the photo and trying to make out something meaningful, Jonathan replied, "Okay, Grace, so you found a hole in a wall. Let's go!"

As Jonathan turned to walk away, Grace grabbed his shirt sleeve and pulled him back. "Wait just one minute! Now look closely at this photo and watch when I zoom in on the depression. Don't you recognize the shape of the hole?"

"No, I don't. It just looks like a hole in the wall, and if we don't leave …"

Ignoring Jonathan's plea, but still holding on to his shirt sleeve, Grace held up another photo and reported with a smile of confidence on her face. "Now compare the shape of the depression in the wall with the picture of this medallion I found in King Nebuchadnezzar's treasure room in Babylon."

"What?"

"Don't you see, Jonathan? The shape of the impression in the wall looks exactly like the shape of the medallion."

"Well, I have to admit the shapes do look similar, but it could just be a coincidence. Let's go!"

"I'm betting the medallion will fit in the depression and perhaps unlock the secrets of a treasure room. If the guard who lost the medallion in Babylon was, in fact, a member of King Cyrus' inner court, he could have had the key to this secret room in his possession. This may even be the room where the missing scrolls are hidden."

Grace's mind was running like a buzz saw.

"Jonathan, we have to go to the tomb of King Cyrus."

About that time, the curator marched to their table and stood with arms crossed. With a scowl on her face, she pointed her long, crooked index finger toward the clock on the wall.

Smiling, Jonathan whispered, "I'm sorry, we're on our way out right now. I promise!"

Ignoring the drama of the curator, Grace declared to Jonathan, "Don't you get it? We may be holding the key to another undiscovered treasure room in our hands, possibly even the room where the missing manuscripts of King Cyrus are stored with clues to the location of the Doomsday Clock."

"You're not making sense Grace. Looking for that hole in the wall won't be like looking for a needle in a haystack; it will be like reconstructing the haystack straw by straw after a tornado struck and then looking for the needle. Even if we can obtain approval to explore the tomb, we have no idea where that photograph was taken. Then if we can find the depression and if the medallion unlocks a hidden room, we have no idea that the scrolls we're looking for will be there!"

"You may be right, but we have to try, please!" Grace pleaded. "Remember, to our knowledge, no one has discovered the manuscripts that chronicle the personal conversations between King Cyrus and the young Israelite in Babylon, and we already have part of that conversation in our possession. Aren't you at least curious that we could be on the precipice of a great discovery? Don't you want to know the rest of the story?"

"I guess you're right again, Grace! I'll see what's involved in planning for the trip as soon as we get back to the university. Right now, how about something to eat? It's been a long day."

"Sounds great to me; I'm starved!"

Energized with an exciting new sense of purpose, Grace returned the files, notes, and keys to the cases for the manuscripts they had been studying for almost eight hours non-stop, and they signed out with the museum curator.

In an accommodating tone of voice, the curator asked, "Well, did you find anything that was helpful in your research?"

"Yes," Grace responded. "As a matter of fact, the most helpful information we found was on a photograph that was inadvertently indexed with the notes for the manuscripts."

With her eyebrows arched and eyes glaring at Grace over the top of her horn-rimmed glasses resting near the tip of her pointed nose, the curator snapped, "Young lady, there are no photographs indexed with the notes. Look at this list of items you checked out. See, there are only manuscripts and notes, no photographs. Only the gentleman with you checked out photographs."

Not wanting to argue but determined to make her case, Grace smugly presents the curator with a copy she made of the photograph in question. Unwilling to get involved in the exchange, Jonathan gave Grace a gentle elbow in her ribs.

"Please, Grace, just drop the subject and let's get out of here."

After the curator suspiciously examined the front and back of the photograph for several minutes, she looked up at Grace and spoke with affirming authority.

"Here is the problem! I don't know how you obtained this photograph, but it doesn't have the museum identification serial number and indexing code that all materials in this room must have to validate their authenticity. We're very meticulous about our work here, and I can assure you this is not our photograph. I wouldn't base any of your research or findings on this unofficial photograph."

Grace and Jonathan politely thanked the curator for her help and left the museum somewhat confused.

"Grace, if the photograph doesn't belong to the museum and was not in the official list of documents, then where did it come from? How did it get in the document examining room and how do we know it's legitimate?

"I don't know, but it's another reason to go to the tomb of Cyrus and check it out. Maybe some other researcher left it here by mistake, but their error is our gain."

"Pasargadae is a long way to go to validate a photograph with an unknown origin even if we can gain entry to Iran."

"Yes, but all our other clues also point to the tomb of King Cyrus."

Two hamburgers and two chocolate shakes later, Grace and Jonathan took a taxi to Reagan National Airport and boarded the next available flight to Newark Liberty Airport. After the short flight, Jonathan dropped off Grace at her apartment and agreed to meet her at the university early the next morning.

As soon as Grace and Jonathan arrived at the university the next morning, Grace began working on preliminary plans for the trip to Iran assuming they would be able to obtain a visa through the State Department.

Jonathan made a call to his long-time friend Riley Morgan in Washington, D.C., who was the Director of Intelligence in the State Department. He had also worked closely with Riley when he was in the military. Jonathan explained, "I have something extremely important to talk to you about, but I don't want to discuss it on the phone."

"Well then, why don't you come to Washington and meet me in my office. We have a lot to catch up on since we haven't talked in a while."

Riley agreed to meet with Jonathan at 10:00 A.M. the day after the next. After a short flight to Reagan National Airport, Jonathan arrived at Riley's office a few minutes early.

After explaining what they found in the ruins of Babylon while conducting the expedition for UNESCO, Jonathan discussed how important it was to investigate the ruins of King Cyrus' tomb near the ancient city of Pasargadae, Iran. Riley had immense confidence in Jonathan's ability to use logic and good decision making in his exploits for archeological treasuries, even though he thought the idea of a Doomsday Clock was a little far-fetched. While discussing his plans to explore the tomb, Jonathan noticed Riley seemed a bit distracted, as though he had something more important on his mind.

Without saying a word to Jonathan, Riley asked his secretary to ensure they were not disturbed and closed his office door.

"Jonathan, it's very difficult for anyone to gain access to Iran right now except for the military and those involved in State Department business. However, your request today is very timely. I believe I can pull some strings and obtain a temporary visa for you to visit the tomb, but first I need to explain a few things."

"Sure! What kind of things?"

Riley stretched out a map marked Top Secret on the table. "You're probably aware that a nuclear arms agreement was negotiated between Iran and the United States a few years ago. With that agreement, Iran agreed to shut down and disable all the centrifuges in their nuclear facilities and dispose of the enriched nuclear fuel in their possession if the United States would immediately remove all sanctions imposed on their country. These centrifuges are necessary to convert the uranium isotope 238 used in nuclear-powered electric-generating plants to the highly enriched uranium 235 required to construct a nuclear bomb."

"And I guess we fell for that story and lifted the sanctions?"

"That's correct, the negotiation was consummated, and all the sanctions were lifted. IAEA[1] inspectors confirmed that Iran did shut down the centrifuges in all the known laboratories used to produce weapons-grade nuclear fuel. In addition, the small amount of enriched fuel that had been processed and documented by the Iranians was confiscated by IAEA inspectors. However, our intelligence satellite

---

1 International Atomic Energy Agency

photos have confirmed that there may be a secret Iranian nuclear laboratory hidden within the Zagros mountain range here," Riley pointed to an area circled in red, "less than a mile from the ruins of ancient Pasargadae and the location of King Cyrus' tomb."

Pointing to the tomb, Jonathan questioned, "Why would the Iranians build a secret laboratory that close to Cyrus's Tomb that would obviously be visited by archeologists and other scientists?"

Holding up a photo of a modern fighter jet, Riley continued. "The Iranian Republic News agency recently released a news bulletin describing the facility in question as a new high-tech plant constructed to manufacture jet engines for their new HESA Kowsar twin-engine light military fighter jet being developed by the Iran Aircraft Manufacturing Company. Besides, what better cover for a nuclear laboratory than to be located close to a UNESCO site?"

"That's fascinating Riley, but what does it have to do with me? I promise if you get me access to the tomb, I will neither venture anywhere near the alleged laboratory, nor will I discuss the location of the suspected facility with anyone!"

Ignoring Jonathan's comment, Riley continued. "The modern city of Pasargadae is approximately twenty miles from the alleged Iranian laboratory which was not on the list of facilities provided by Iran. However, the United States has had this location under satellite surveillance for some time. We suspect the Iranians removed fuel from the documented laboratories and secretly shipped enough enriched uranium for several bombs to this facility before the inspectors arrived. We also have intelligence that the Iranians may have installed new advanced technology centrifuges in this facility to produce additional high-grade nuclear fuel and may be working on a stealth program to advance the completion of their first nuclear warhead.

"Satellite photos reveal increased vehicle traffic to this facility, and seismic data recently recorded an underground detonation in a remote area about 50 miles from the facility that has all the earmarks of a nuclear bomb test. Our satellites have also detected what looks like the testing of a medium-range rocket, at the test facility near Shahrud, Iran, capable of carrying a nuclear warhead to Israel and American air bases in neighboring countries. If authenticated, this test is a direct violation of UN Security Council Resolution 2231. The successful development of a nuclear bomb capable of being deployed by a medium-range rocket will guarantee a nuclear arms race in the Middle East that could spark a world war of epic proportions."

By this time, Jonathan was unable to conceal a very troubled expression on his face as he digested the incredible secret intelligence he was being given so freely.

"Did something I said trouble you, Jonathan?"

"No, it's just difficult to believe the Iranians may be that close to having a bomb. I thought the United States pulled out of the nuclear arms agreement with Iran."

"That's true, Jonathan, but it's absolutely critical for the security of America and the world that we determine whether or not this facility is being used to enrich uranium and assemble a bomb."

"Wow, Riley. Well, you certainly have your work cut out for you."

The intelligence Jonathan received was fascinating and thought-provoking, but certainly not necessary to obtain a visa to explore the tomb of King Cyrus. It soon became shockingly clear why Riley shared this high-level security information with him.

CHAPTER 13

LIFE CHIP

"Since the aircraft engine plant is completely concealed within a mountain, the data from reconnaissance drone aircraft and satellite intelligence is inconclusive," Riley continued. "What better way for us to obtain more accurate information than by someone who has been trained in covert activities in the military but is actually engaged in a legitimate archeological expedition?"

Jonathan looked surprised. "Are you talking about me? You want me to be a spy? You must be out of your mind. I'm a lot of things, but I'm not a spy!"

"Jonathan, your archeological project is the perfect cover for this mission. And don't worry about the classified intelligence you've been given. I had your top secret clearance reinstated before you arrived.

"Make no mistake, Jonathan, this mission will be anything but easy since backing out of the Iran nuclear deal by our president has strained relationships between the United States and Iran. The bottom line is that this assignment could be extremely dangerous! I can get you and Grace into Iran for the sole purpose of exploring King Cyrus's tomb, but you will only be a short distance from what is believed to be the Iranian laboratory. Jonathan, you were trained for a mission like this, and it has your name stamped all over it. Of course, I'll certainly understand if you decline my offer."

"If you're sure they're building a nuclear warhead and a rocket to deliver it, why don't you just bomb the facility?" Jonathan asked.

"It's politics, Jonathan, complicated politics that could get a lot of people killed or even start a war. In addition, our intelligence cannot discern precisely whether this facility is being used to build a bomb as we suspect or is a manufacturing plant for jet engines as reported by the Iranians. Besides we're not sure our bunker bombs can penetrate the mountain where the facility is located. We also have intelligence that Russia may be providing Iran with SAM[2] missiles to protect the laboratory. Fortunately, the lynchpin to successfully constructing a nuclear warhead that can be carried aboard a rocket is a reliable miniature detonator, and we know the Iranians lack the technology to build the device. Without the proper detonator, a bomb designed to be delivered by a missile is useless."

"So, what are you saying?"

"I'm just saying I think we have some time before they complete a bomb, but we know sympathetic foreign powers like Russia and North Korea may make the detonators available to Iran at any time. The bottom line is we can't wait any longer. We must find out what's going on inside that facility."

Listening intently, Jonathan was not that interested in politics, but he did love adventure. For a moment, he thought about the conversation he overheard between his friend Steven and someone in the CIA about a mole and detonators for nuclear bombs.

This is the second time I've heard the subject of detonators for a nuclear bomb mentioned, he thought to himself.

Riley continued. "In addition to your official passports and visas, we will provide you with passports identifying you as a known international espionage agent accompanied by your personal assistant and linguist. We will also provide you with an electronic account number and password for a Swiss bank account with a verifiable balance of more than 500 million U.S. dollars. If you have the opportunity, let the Iranians know you are interested in negotiating for the purchase of a nuclear weapon for a billionaire terrorist you represent who will auction the device on the black market. If you can enter the facility, you may learn what is being produced there."

2 Surface-to-air

"I will make all the arrangements and cover all the costs for you to travel to Iran for an archeological exploration of the tomb of King Cyrus," Riley said. "Temporary visas for each of you will be obtained through the United States Embassy in Iran. In return, you must agree to do your best to provide us with any information that will help determine if the Iranians are, in fact, processing uranium and assembling a warhead."

"You will be provided with a small satellite radio designed to look like an ordinary cell phone that will serve as your umbilical to my department in the event there is any trouble. All outgoing conversations on the phone will be encrypted so your calls cannot be intercepted by the Iranians. The phone also has a built-in GPS so that we can always track your location. Unfortunately, the phone requires a satellite signal to operate, so if you are successful in getting into the underground Iranian facility, the device will not be functional. By the way, we will be unable to contact you directly, and you should only call us when necessary. Regrettably, we don't have any details of the design and layout of the Iranian facility to give you should you be successful in gaining entry to the laboratory."

"A SEAL Team Six military QRF[3] squadron will be standing by at the Saudi King Abdul Air Base just across the Gulf of Oman in Saudi Arabia. This squadron will monitor your satellite phone and can be activated in minutes with two MH-60 Black Hawk stealth helicopters to rescue you in the event it becomes necessary."

"Jonathan, please carefully contemplate the offer and let me know your answer in a day or two at the latest. I can't overly emphasize the danger of this mission, but I'll do everything I can to make it as safe for you as possible." Riley handed Jonathan a cell phone. "Just call the number 666 on this special untraceable iPhone and speak only the code word 'Geronimo' if you agree to accept the mission! We can meet again later to finalize the details of the plan. If I don't hear from you, I will understand you declined my offer."

Jonathan left Riley's office realizing the acceptance of this assignment was probably the only way he will ever gain access to the tomb of King Cyrus and possibly answer the questions plaguing him about the ancient secret of the Doomsday Clock.

---

3 Quick Reaction Force

After a short flight from Washington D.C., Jonathan arrived at the Newark Liberty Airport and called Grace. He arranged to meet her at their favorite coffee shop not far from the university.

As Jonathan was sipping his second cup of coffee and nibbling on a fresh-baked bagel, Grace walked in.

Waving his arms and pointing to the large flat screen television monitor on the wall, Jonathan shouted, "Hurry and sit down, Grace. There is going to be breaking news from CBN's Medical correspondent in Washington D.C. in about ten minutes announcing a medical breakthrough of some kind."

At the same time the latte Grace ordered arrived at the table, the CBN Medical correspondent appeared on the television screen.

"Today the Food and Drug Administration approved the immediate implementation of the new Life Chip manufactured by Modern Electronics Inc. Silently and invisibly, the microchip stores encoded information about the individual as well as his or her precise location at any time using the micro-GPS that is part of the implanted microchip."

"Using this device, the precise location of a kidnapped child or lost adult suffering from Alzheimer's disease can be determined in seconds and the person quickly rescued. The use of this new microchip will expedite police work for missing persons, give parents a new sense of security regarding their children, grandchildren, and aging parents, and revolutionize the maintenance of personal medical records for everyone. For those of you who may be concerned about the confidentiality of an individual's personal information, the FDA has assured the public that all information on the Life Chip is confidential and encrypted, so there is absolutely no possibility of anyone being able to hack into the device."

"The revolutionary new microchip can be harmlessly inserted under the skin of a person using a small syringe in a procedure that takes less than ten seconds. The forehead or right hand is the preferred location for the chip since those areas will be easy for special scanners to read the signals."

"The government will subsidize the cost of the implants and require that every baby born after the first of next month receive the chip at birth. Each adult currently diagnosed with Alzheimer's disease will receive the implant immediately. Older children and all adults will receive the chip on their next birthday or, in the case of Alzheimer's patients, as they are diagnosed. The United Nations has even agreed to promote the use of the implant globally."

Nodding his head, Jonathan confirmed the Life Chip sounded like a little good news for a change.

Whispering, Grace commented, "You have to wonder if there is any way that the chip could be used by sadistic people or terrorists or even the government for evil purposes. If everyone receives the implant on their next birthday beginning next month, everyone will possess the implant within a year. Hmmm! That means anyone with access to the GPS information in those implants would be able to determine the location of anyone anywhere, anytime and for any reason. With that information, a person could take over the world."

"Don't worry, Grace, most Americans have no idea that the government can already track almost everything they do by use of their social security number, credit card, and iPhone. Besides, no one can take over the world without having access to and control over all the world's computers, and there is no way that will ever happen."

"Why not?" Grace asked.

"Think about it, Grace. Every computer network in the world has robust security firewalls to prevent others from hacking or gaining access to the system without proper clearance, and new, more effective software is being developed every day to enforce that security. There would have to be a massive global crisis that required every nation to allow a single entity access to their business, government, military, and all privately owned computers. I'm talking about a global calamity that threatened the existence of planet Earth and the people who reside on it. Even then, specialized software would have to be developed and installed on every computer to override internal security measures. Can you imagine the United States government allowing the installation of software that gave anyone access to their military secrets for any reason? Nope! So, quit worrying about someone taking over the world, Grace. It's never going to happen, never!"

"Never say never, Jonathan!"

After the newscast, Jonathan shared with Grace the confidential conversation he had with Riley at the State Department. The longer Jonathan talked, the brighter Grace's face beamed with her insatiable appetite for curiosity and adventure.

"I've already decided to go to Iran, and I am going to call Riley in the morning, but because of the danger involved, I really think you should stay here."

Grace's body language tightened, and her forehead wrinkled as she stared at Jonathan for a few quiet moments. Then she shouted, "Jonathan, if you think you're going to leave me here while you go traipsing off to Iran on what may be the biggest archeological discovery ever, you're crazy!"

Every person in the coffee shop turned to look at Grace.

"Grace, please lower your voice; everyone is staring at us!" Jonathan urged. "Now, we're not talking about a little danger here. This may be a journey of life and death, and I don't want to endanger you. If something happened to you, I would never forgive myself. Besides, look at the harrowing experiences I've already exposed you to."

With her hands folded, Grace leaned across the small table, smiled sheepishly, and whispered, "It's amazing that you really care for me; I love it! Anyway, you're not going without me, and that's final! This will be the expedition of a lifetime, and I am not going to miss it. Call Riley and tell him to arrange for both of us to go. Tell him you need me as a translator for the Farsi Iranian language and that you absolutely can't go without me. Besides, this mission can't be any more dangerous than the expedition to Iraq."

Reluctantly, Jonathan turned aside so Grace couldn't see him blush a little from her affectionate reaction. "Okay, Grace. Against my better judgment, I'll tell Riley you're going to accompany me on the trip. Your linguistic ability will definitely come in handy."

The next morning, Jonathan used the phone that Riley gave him, dialed the number, and simply spoke the code word, "Geronimo." The next day, Michelle arranged for the round-trip flight from Newark Liberty Airport to Washington D.C. for Jonathan and Grace to rendezvous with Riley.

CHAPTER 14

DESTINATION

Jonathan and Grace flew to D.C. to meet with Riley in his office at the State Department to discuss their mission to Iran. After a briefing, Riley pushed a manila envelope across the table toward Jonathan with a list of contacts at the Embassy in Iran, instructions on how to use the compact satellite radio transmitter, and a package containing their arrangements for the trip. They would fly to the Mehrabad International Airport in Tehran, Iran. From Tehran, they would have to travel another 375 miles to the ruins of ancient Pasargadae where the tomb of King Cyrus and the suspected secret Iranian nuclear laboratory were located.

After the flight home from Washington, Jonathan dropped Grace off at her apartment to pack for the trip. Standing on the curb, she closed the car door, leaned in through the window, and whispered as though she thought someone may be listening. "There is definitely more drama and mystery associated with this trip than I even imagined. Are you sure we will be okay?"

Jonathan reassured her they would be fine and that Riley and his department will be watching over them every step of the way. Of course, he was thinking, *We will be all right if everything goes exactly as we plan.*

The real objective of the mission was to explore the tomb of King

Cyrus and look for the missing scrolls. Jonathan was only willing to attempt to obtain information about the work of the Iranians if the opportunity presented itself without potential harm to either of them. He would take no unnecessary chances!

When Jonathan arrived at Grace's apartment early the next morning, she hurried out the door right on time. Since they had already shipped their equipment and luggage to the Mehrabad Airport and had only their small personal bags to carry, Jonathan drove his VW to the airport.

After checking their bags, they proceeded through security and hiked to their gate where passengers were already boarding Lufthansa flight LH 401. Following an uneventful but practically sleepless seven-hour flight to Frankfurt, Germany with a twelve-hour layover, Jonathan and Grace boarded their flight to Tehran. Five hours later they arrived at Mehrabad Airport in Tehran. Military attendants in customs checked their passports and visas, inspected every square inch of their carry-on bags, and questioned them individually about their reasons for being in Iran.

Then, one of the officers rummaging through Grace's bag pulled out the medallion she found in Babylon. "What's this, and where did you get it?"

Grace swallowed hard and calmly responded, "That's a souvenir I purchased in Germany at the airport."

With a scowl on his face, the officer barked firmly, "Let me see the receipt for your purchase!"

Knowing she had no receipt, Grace reached into her purse. "I have it right here."

While pretending to search her handbag for the non-existent receipt, the men became distracted by a disturbance in another security line. "Never mind, but if you're on an archeological expedition, where is your equipment?"

Jonathan explained the equipment was shipped ahead and they were to pick it up on arrival at the airport. The weary travelers were detained by one of the officers while the other officer recovered their luggage in baggage claim. When a thorough inspection of their tools and other equipment failed to produce anything suspicious, Jonathan and Grace were permitted to leave the Customs area.

Before leaving the airport, Jonathan called a special phone number Riley gave him and checked in with the State Department at the U.S. Embassy in Tehran. After giving the officer their schedule for the exploration of King Cyrus' tomb, they were instructed to check in with the Embassy Duty Officer each day before midnight to verify their safety.

Three hours later, with more than 100 miles of rugged, mountainous terrain in the rearview mirror, Jonathan and Grace arrived in Pasargadae. Utterly exhausted from their twenty-seven-hour journey, they happily checked into their rooms at the Homa Hotel and proceeded to the hotel restaurant for a quiet dinner. They were within twenty miles of their destination, the coveted tomb of King Cyrus.

Following a welcomed night's sleep and an early breakfast, Jonathan and Grace packed the car and drove to the ruins of the ancient city of Pasargadae and the tomb of King Cyrus. About a thousand yards from the entrance of the tomb, they arrived at a barricade across the road. Two smartly dressed, heavily bearded Iranian soldiers armed with automatic weapons emerged from a small concrete bunker and motioned for the travelers to pull over and get out of the car.

One of the guards instructed Jonathan and Grace in broken English to leave everything in the car and stand by the bunker while they inspected the vehicle and examined their bags.

Holding up an object, one of the guards snapped, "What's this?"

Jonathan whispered to Grace, "Look, he has the special satellite radio Riley gave us."

Jonathan replied calmly, "That's my cell phone."

The guard examined the phone carefully and put it back, muttering, "Okay, it doesn't matter. There is no signal out here anyway."

After their passports and visas were determined to be in order, the guards pointed the way to the entrance of the tomb on a makeshift road that led in the opposite direction from the alleged nuclear facility. After logging in the time, one guard warned the explorers, "You must be out of the tomb and checked out with us here at the guard gate no later than sundown."

While the stone-faced guards completed their paperwork, Jonathan and Grace stared at the double row of razor wire fencing that protected the perimeter of the laboratory. There was a similar fence around a nearby electrical substation.

Jonathan whispered to Grace, "If this is the nuclear laboratory, that substation must provide the power for the vast number of centrifuges required to produce weapons-grade nuclear fuel. The stealth location of this facility makes it impossible for the United States surveillance satellites to observe what's taking place inside the facility under tons of solid rock. However, it's equally difficult for the Iranians to conceal the increase in truck and personnel traffic entering and leaving the facility due to the lack of cover in the desert."

"Don't go near that fence," one of the guards barked. "It is electrified and dangerous. There are also guards with automatic weapons every fifty yards. Anyone approaching that fence will be shot without warning. This plant is designed to manufacture classified military jet engines and there is absolutely no access to the public."

Smiling, Jonathan thought, *Well, at least his story is consistent with the information the State Department was given.*

Acknowledging the warning, Jonathan and Grace collected their papers from the guards and jumped in the car. As they drove toward the tomb with the sight of the secret laboratory fading in the rearview mirror, Jonathan remembered what the hotel clerk said last night when he was asked about the Iranian facility.

"That building is strictly off-limits to everyone except those who work there and live in the dormitory on the premises. All food and supplies are brought in, so there is no contact with the outside world. We're told that the proprietary nature of the casting process used to produce aircraft engine components there for the military makes it necessary to maintain an elevated level of security. Everyone believes the story is just a cover-up for something far more sinister, but no one is interested in trying to discover the truth. Also, many of the townspeople that work in the fields several miles outside of town have broken out in a puzzling rash lately and become deathly ill. The local doctor suspects it may be radiation poisoning, but he has been threatened with his life by the military not to make that diagnosis public."

As Jonathan and Grace approached the tomb, they were awestruck at the sight of the entrance located at the top of six massive stone steps that majestically rise out of the ground to meet them. The incredible sepulcher that appeared to be literally carved into the face of a mountain exhibited an enormous set of thick ancient wooden doors flanked on each side by colossal stone pedestals.

Standing at the top of the steps leading to the doors of the tomb, Jonathan saw the entrance to the secret Iranian laboratory built into the side of the mountain about 1000 yards in the distance. Checking his compass, Jonathan noted the facility to be due east of the entrance to the tomb.

"Grace," said Jonathan, "the 'manufacture of aircraft engine components' is the perfect cover for a secret laboratory where a nuclear warhead is being assembled. But there is no way I'm going to get into that facility on the pretense of negotiating a deal. Let's get on with our work."

Before entering the tomb, Jonathan switched on the power to the lights that had been installed inside by previous expeditions. However, the curator of the tomb they met in town told Jonathan he was not sure the lights were working since they had not been used in years.

With all the gear unloaded, Jonathan unlocked the chain on the heavy wooden doors with the key he was given by the curator, and they proceeded cautiously inside down steep stone steps. After descending several levels of stone steps and sidestepping deep pits intended to slow down any intruders, they start down a damp, musty passageway with electric lights hastily strung along the ceiling. As Grace walked, she scanned the walls of the tunnel looking for the depression she saw in the museum photograph.

After walking no more than one hundred yards from the entrance, the explorers were struck with a deafening, ear-splitting sound that reverberated throughout the tunnel, violently shaking the ground and walls of the ancient tomb. With the passageway threatening to collapse, the electric lights flickered and then went out, plunging the pioneers into total darkness. Without warning a blast of choking dust and debris blew past them like a violent windstorm followed by a dreadful crushing roar like massive boulders shifting. Losing her balance and falling to the ground, Grace struggled to find Jonathan in the darkness and the suffocating cloud of fine dust. Grace screamed at the top of her lungs, "Where are you, Jonathan?"

"I'm right here, Grace. That sounded like a horrific underground explosion."

"Jonathan, I can't see a thing. Where are you?"

Fumbling in the darkness, Jonathan found Grace and helped her to her feet. Taking her by the hand, he said calmly, "Let's find our way back to the entrance. I want to go outside and look around."

Struggling to breathe the air that was heavily laden with debris and fine powder-like dust, they covered their faces with handkerchiefs and proceeded carefully back to the entrance. What they observed left them in utter shock!

CHAPTER 15

MISSING SCROLL

Jonathan froze when the beam from his flashlight exposed what had been the entrance and their only way out of the tomb just minutes earlier. Stumbling backward in the darkness, Jonathan inadvertently bumped Grace, who was walking so close behind she was practically joined at his hip.

"Get back, Grace. The entrance is completely blocked by tons of rock and debris that look extremely unstable."

"What do you think caused the rockslide?"

"Based on the intelligence Riley gave me, that blast must have been the detonation of a nuclear bomb deep underground. The violent earthquake generated by the explosion caused the rockslide and knocked out the generator that powers the electric lights in the tunnel."

"Well, how do we get out of here?"

"I just tried the radio, but there is no satellite signal inside this mountain. Remember, the good news is that we're supposed to check in with the State Department every twenty-four hours. If we don't check in tonight, they'll call the Iranian guards at the gate and verify we didn't leave the area today. Realizing we're still in the tomb they'll send someone to investigate, but it will take time to arrange for heavy equipment to arrive and free us. We have extra flashlights and food and water, so we're good for a couple of days, maybe more."

"Since we have some time before we're rescued, I suggest we proceed very carefully back down the passage where the air may be better. We can at least spend the time we have in here looking for the treasure room of King Cyrus as we planned."

"Jonathan, if there was a nuclear explosion, won't we be exposed to radiation?" Grace asked.

"No, there is no danger of radiation poisoning. That blast was deep underground probably twenty or thirty miles from here, and we're shielded from any trace amounts of radiation in the air by tons of rock."

Convinced they were safe and help was on the way soon, Grace relaxed and set out determined to obsessively scour the walls of the passageway looking for any sign of the depression in the wall. About twenty-five yards from the entrance, Grace pointed out the burial vault of King Cyrus a few feet off the main tunnel as documented in Jonathan's map.

"According to the inscription on the wall, this large vault is where the sarcophagus of King Cyrus was originally located. We know from notes of previous archeologists that a golden coffin, where the body of King Cyrus the Great was interred, was in this chamber resting on a table with golden supports. Of course, tomb raiders desecrated the sarcophagus when they confiscated as much gold as possible and removed the king's body, which was never found."

Several other chambers off the main passage were explored, but all were found to be void of any valuable artifacts. Soon the explorers came to a fork in the tunnel where the passage branched to a deep cavern to the right and a narrow passage to the left. The deadening silence of the tunnel was abruptly broken by a strange noise emanating in the cavern.

"Jonathan, do you hear that? It sounds like leaves rustling in the wind. I can't see anything even with my light, but the noise sounds like it's getting closer."

"Yes, I hear it, but I don't know what…"

Instantly, the sound became thunderous, and both explorers

staggered backward falling to the ground, flailing their arms wildly to fend off thousands of vampire bats that were flooding the passageway. As the deafening storm of tiny winged creatures continued to rocket past them for what seemed like an eternity, Jonathan and Grace felt the flying creatures thrashing along their bodies ripping their clothes. At last, the horde of vampire beasts disappeared down the tunnel, and Jonathan and Grace managed to get up off the ground, shaken but unharmed.

"Are you all right, Grace?"

"I guess so. It's not every day that I'm attacked by a swarm of bats."

"According to the map, the cavern to the right is a dead-end about twenty yards from here so let's take the tunnel to the left."

Walking unhurriedly, Grace methodically combed the walls for clues for more than an hour. Except for being frightened out of their wits by the colony of bats, the exploration of Cyrus' tomb was completely and disappointedly uneventful so far.

Looking at his compass, Jonathan commented, "We have been walking east in the direction of the Iranian laboratory since we left the entrance. I estimate we're about a thousand yards from where we entered the tomb and thirty or forty feet below the surface. The map indicates we're not far from the end of this passage."

As they turned another sharp corner, the passage narrowed. Judiciously flashing the beam of her light up and down the faces of the rock walls, Grace suddenly shouted, "Look, Jonathan, there in the distance. I think that shadowy depression in the wall is what we're looking for. I knew we would find it."

While Grace stopped to search for the medallion in her bag, Jonathan sensed she was about to sprint to the wall as soon as she retrieved the artifact. Without hesitation, he grabbed her shoulders from behind, whirled her around, and shoved her firmly against the wall behind them.

"Hey, what are you doing? You hurt my back."

"Look, Grace, right in front of you is a clear sign we may be on the brink of discovering something of great importance."

Illuminated by the beam from Jonathan's flashlight was a deep open pit more than ten feet across that spanned the width of the passageway.

"Take a look into that pit, Grace."

Inching forward cautiously, Grace leaned over the edge of the dark chasm and shined her light to the depths below. Adrenaline shot into her bloodstream from the sight of deadly slithering Caspian Cobras, causing her to drop her flashlight and lose her balance, tipping toward the edge of the abyss. Grace's fall was arrested as Jonathan grabbed her belt and pulled her to safety.

Jonathan knew that once a person was bitten by one of the vipers they would die in a matter of minutes. "I told you not to get too close!"

Frozen in her tracks with her heart pumping and hands trembling, she choked out, "That pit is crawling with hundreds of creepy snakes, Jonathan, and you know how I hate snakes. How are we going to reach the other side?"

"The pit is too wide to jump, so the Persians must have had a way to cross it hidden somewhere close by."

As the light from Jonathan's flashlight danced around the walls, he shouted, "There it is, a plank hidden in that crevice in the ceiling."

After removing the cobwebs and brushing away several creepy, black spiders, Jonathan carefully removed the foot-wide plank from the wall and placed it across the pit.

"How do we know the board isn't rotten Jonathan?"

"It looks okay; it's actually petrified from age. I'll go first. If the plank holds me, it will surely hold you."

"What if it doesn't hold you?"

With the beam of his flashlight illuminating the way, Jonathan stepped off onto the board and called out, "Well, let's find out!"

As Jonathan quickly traversed the pit, the board creaked and groaned but remained intact.

Stepping safely onto the other side, Jonathan yelled, "Okay, the board is perfectly safe. Come on, and I will light the way for you."

Nervously, Grace began to slowly navigate the plank across the snake-laden pit, placing one-foot heel to toe in front of the other.

"Grace, whatever you do, don't look down!"

About halfway across the abyss, Grace froze as she heard a loud cracking sound. While glancing down into the pit thick with snakes writhing in the beam of her light, she hyperventilated and momentarily lost her balance. For a minute or two, she just rocked back and forth on the board like a seesaw with her arms outstretched to steady her like a tight rope walker. With each movement of Grace's body, the board groaned and threatened to topple her into the chasm. Grace teetered side to side as she tried desperately to regain her composure. Watching with fear in his heart, Jonathan realized there was absolutely nothing he can do to help her.

Using his flashlight to illuminate the path, Jonathan called out calmly, "Stop looking down, Grace! The board will hold you. Just relax and keep looking at me."

"Easy for you to say! I'm the one standing on this creaking board over all those slimy snakes!"

Standing motionless for a full minute, Grace took a deep breath and started to move.

"Good, now walk slowly putting one foot in front of the other foot while I illuminate the board with my flashlight."

Leaning slightly forward with arms reaching out to Jonathan, she strained to reach his outstretched hands, but his grasp was inches away. With one more step, Grace lunged at Jonathan as he grabbed her wrists and jerked her to safety in one motion of animated flight. As Grace sprung to safety, she inadvertently kicked the board away from the edge and watched it disappear into the darkness.

"Now look what you did, that board was our only way back across that pit and out of this tomb."

"Well, it was your idea to use that old board. Besides, I could have fallen into that pit with the snakes, and I'm lucky to be alive."

"Don't worry, I have a rope in my backpack. If I can tie it off somewhere one of us can go down and retrieve the board."

"One of us? If you think I'm going down into that pit with all those snakes, you're out of your mind."

"Well, you're the lightest, and it will be easier for me to stay up here and let you down on the rope."

With her curious spirit of investigation trumping her fear of retrieving the board from a pit full of snakes, Grace announced, "Maybe, but right now I want to see if this medallion fits into the depression."

Her exuberance was quickly doused with a heavy dose of disappointment when the medallion didn't fit regardless of what position she tried.

"Oh man, I was sure this was the right place! Now, what do we do?"

Sitting on the floor with her back against the wall, Grace abruptly jumped up with a renewed spirit of enthusiasm and shouts to Jonathan. "I know why the medallion didn't fit. This is not the right place. Think about it. If tomb raiders were able to traverse the pit with one of the guard's medallions, they would be frustrated by the fact that it didn't fit the obvious keyway and leave. Don't you see? The real keyway must be somewhere nearby, but out of sight."

Encouraged by Grace's assumption, both explorers began to scour every inch of the walls.

Near the end of the passage, the beam from her flashlight exposed what resembled the elusive depression in the wall, blanketed in thick cobwebs and home to a family of very large hairy brown spiders. With hands trembling, Grace gingerly brushed the spiders aside and cleared the cobwebs from the slot in the wall to make room for the medallion.

"Ughhh, I hate spiders almost as much as I hate snakes." Carefully placing the medallion into the depression, Grace shouted, "Perfect!"

Hyperventilating, Grace tried to turn the key, first to the right, but it didn't move. With great relief, the medallion turned easily to the left. After making nearly a full revolution, the medallion turned no further and abruptly disappeared into the wall with a click as if sucked in by a supernatural force. Awestruck at the mysterious phenomenon, Grace and Jonathan were momentarily speechless.

After a few seconds, there was another loud click, followed by a protracted low-frequency grinding sound. A doorway in what was a solid wall began to open slowly. The light from Jonathan's flashlight was swallowed by the foreboding darkness inside. Grace's pulse was racing as she threw caution to the wind, grabbed Jonathan's light, and bounded inside like a hound hot on the trail of a fox. Her efforts were rewarded with the sight of a King's treasure trove. Bursting with gold and silver artifacts of all shapes and sizes, the room also contained several earthen jars like those used to store ancient manuscripts.

Overwhelmed with euphoria, Grace grabbed one of the jars. "Jonathan, do you realize we've found the king's treasure room, and we may even find the missing scrolls inside one of these earthen jars."

Holding her breath, she carefully broke the clay top of one of the jars stamped with the seal of the king while Jonathan retrieved another flashlight from his bag and cautiously entered the room.

"Extracting the ancient documents from one of the jars, Grace announced, "This is an incredible find, these manuscripts are intact and perfectly preserved."

While Grace meticulously pored over the manuscripts, Jonathan documented the physical dimensions of the room as well as a general description of the priceless artifacts it contained.

Noticing the Hebrew word for Israelite was used several times in one of the Persian manuscripts, Grace concluded, "I think this is it—the missing scroll. Finally, our persistence paid off."

After carefully securing what was believed to be the object of their quest in her antiquities bag, Grace was anxious to get out of the tomb and take the manuscripts home where she could study them in detail.

"That's good news, Grace, but stop what you're doing for a minute and come over here. It appears this wall of the chamber is bulging inward as if it was subjected to enormous pressure from the other side."

"So, what?"

"I don't know, but help me remove some of these stones that are loose and perhaps we can see what is on the other side. This may be our way out."

Fortunately, Jonathan had packed a small folding pick in his backpack for just this kind of situation. Working feverishly, he removed enough rocks from the wall to partially expose the secret hiding just on the other side of the king's treasure chamber. Bending down on one knee with his light shining through the opening, Jonathan called Grace.

"You're not going to believe this!"

CHAPTER 16

THE LOCKER ROOM

Edging Jonathan aside, Grace crouched down on the pile of rocks next to the wall. "Move over and let me see!"

"What's all the excitement? I don't see anything but another solid surface."

Jonathan gently moved Grace out of the way and, using the pick, enlarged the opening and exposed a wall made of gypsum wallboard with vertical aluminum supports. "See, Grace, this is the same material used in the construction of modern office buildings."

After punching a hole in the wallboard with the sharp point of the pick, a thin shaft of bright light chased the darkness from the tomb.

"Can you believe this, Grace? I think the secret Iranian laboratory is just on the other side of this wall. The construction of the underground nuclear facility must have caused this area of the tomb to be shoved inward and compromised the strength of the wall! In the rush to complete the facility, no one noticed they almost breached one wall of the tomb."

They froze upon hearing muffled voices coming from the other side of the wall. Glued to the opening, they saw Iranians dressed in what appeared to be white cleanroom suits.

"Shh, Grace, listen. Can you understand what they're saying?"

"Yes, they're grumbling that their break is over, and they have to report back to work."

"Well, it looks like we may have possibly found the missing scroll we were searching for and be able to do our country a service by obtaining intelligence on the operation inside that facility."

"We have what we came for Jonathan. Why not just wait to be rescued and get back to the good old U.S.A.?"

"Grace, we may be able to obtain intelligence on the construction of the nuclear bomb, intelligence that will be critical to the safety of America and Israel! We can't stop now; we have to do what we can."

"What happens if we get caught?"

"They'll probably shoot us!"

"That's not funny, Jonathan."

When the voices of the Iranians faded, and Jonathan was sure the room was void of workers, he quietly began to chip away at the weakened stone wall. Jonathan and Grace quietly squeezed through the opening made between the aluminum supports into the adjoining room.

"It looks like we're in a locker room where the workers' uniforms, respirators, radiation monitors, and cleanroom suits are stored. Fortunately, I can move that storage cabinet in front of the hole we made to conceal our entry."

Jonathan opened one of the dozens of lockers and took out two jumpsuits and two sets of cleanroom coveralls with caps, radiation monitors, and handkerchiefs.

"Hurry, Grace. Put on this jumpsuit and pull the cleanroom coveralls on over it. Wear this cap with your hair tucked under it and use this handkerchief to fashion a makeshift Islamic Niqab headscarf to cover your face. Hopefully, these clothes will disguise our appearance."

With no one in sight, Jonathan and Grace left the locker room, ventured out into the hall, and located a stairwell. All the signs were in Farsi, the primary language of Iran. The numeral -۴ scribed on a placard on the wall indicated they were on the fourth level below the surface.

"Grace, we know the only way out of here is up, so let's take the stairwell."

Walking up to level -٣, the third level below the surface, they cautiously slipped out into the hall to look around. A room next to the stairwell boasted a sign in Farsi that read "DANGER. DO NOT ENTER." With no one else in the hall, curiosity transcended Jonathan's cautious nature as he tried unsuccessfully to open the door.

"Here, Jonathan, let me try. I'm guessing this magnetic card attached to my suit will work."

Grace swiped the card on the door's magnetic scanner. After a few seconds, a small green light flashed three times followed by an audible click, and the door popped open.

"We're in."

"Clever work, Grace. Let's just take a quick look around in here."

The well-lit room beckoned Jonathan and Grace to examine boxes of expensive-looking state-of-the-art tools and electronic hardware as well as a mountain of electrical devices and countless spools of wire of assorted colors and sizes. As Jonathan hurriedly took stock of the contents of the room, Grace drew his attention to a large locked case with a clear front panel marked "WARNING! DO NOT TOUCH." On closer inspection, Jonathan was blown away by what he saw.

CHAPTER 17

WEAPONS GRADE U-235

Being familiar with miniature detonators used in nuclear warheads carried by missiles, Jonathan was positive there were several of them right before his eyes.

"These detonators are precisely what Riley said the Iranians need to complete a bomb carried by a rocket," Jonathan told Grace. "There is no doubt now that the Iranians plan to assemble a bomb in this facility right under the noses of the IAEA inspectors and the United States."

Inching closer to the clear front panel of the case that separated him from the detonators, Jonathan strained to read the fine print stamped on the devices. "Wait a minute! The inscriptions on these devices indicate they were made in America. Riley said the Iranians would do anything to acquire American-made detonators, and it looks like they did, but how did they get them? More importantly, how did they obtain the encrypted codes embedded in the hardware that are necessary to enable the functionality of the firing circuits? Without the codes, the detonators are useless. There is no way Iran could get their hands on the codes unless they had someone on the inside."

"Are you talking about a mole, a spy?" Grace asked.

For a minute, Jonathan thought about the phone call he overheard at Steven's home and the discussion about detonators and a possible mole. "Yes, but surely Steven didn't…. no, no way! He couldn't possibly be involved in selling hardware to the Iranians, but I did see him at the airport on his way to Tehran! Well, I think I saw him!"

"That's right Jonathan. You have no proof, and Steven is your best friend."

"My first impulse is to break open the case and take the detonators. The missing devices will certainly slow the progress of the Iranians, but if we're caught with the hardware, we will be shot on the spot."

Using the camera in the special satellite phone, Jonathan took photographs of the detonators as well as the identifying inscriptions.

"Jonathan, why is a detonator made in America so important to the Iranians?"

"A reliable miniature detonator is one of the most critical pieces of hardware for the successful initiation of a fission reaction in a nuclear bomb carried by a missile. The Iranians have only land-based detonators used for underground nuclear tests like the one we experienced today that are too large to be carried aboard a rocket. The United States was the first nation to design and test the technology during the development of the atomic bombs dropped on Nagasaki and Hiroshima, and they build the most reliable, miniature detonators in the world. Therefore, the Iranians would do anything to obtain that sophisticated hardware."

With every frayed nerve in their bodies on alert that they may be discovered at any moment, they stealthily slipped out of the room and started toward the stairwell.

"Listen, Grace! Do you hear that? That's the muffled hum of large motors running."

Leaving Grace and walking cautiously across the hall, Jonathan peered through a window in a set of double doors leading to a cavernous room. He couldn't believe his eyes.

"Take a look; there must be hundreds of new high-technology centrifuges housed in this room."

"What's the purpose of those machines?"

"They convert Uranium 238 into weapons-grade Uranium 235

which is the radioactive material used in making a nuclear bomb," Jonathan explained. "I've seen enough; we need to get out of here before we're discovered!"

Faced with the shocking reality that they confirmed exactly what Riley suspected, Jonathan and Grace quickly re-entered the stairwell and continued up to Level -2 to search for a way out of the facility. Suddenly, a muscular Iranian guard, armed with a Russian PPSh-41 submachine gun slung over his shoulder, threw open the stairwell door above them and vaulted down the stairs as if the building were on fire. Stopping abruptly in front of them, the guard glared at them with a feral look without uttering a word. The cleanroom suits they were wearing, the makeshift Islamic Niqab headscarf covering Grace's face, and Jonathan's dark skin and mustache made it difficult for the guard to recognize them as Americans.

The stone-faced guard barked, "Where are you two going?"

Grace answered in perfect Farsi dialect. "We just received word to report to the cleanroom immediately."

Without speaking, the guard eyed them skeptically with his finger tapping nervously on the trigger of his machine gun. Wrinkling his brow, he gave a cursory nod in the affirmative and continued bounding down the stairs.

"That was too close for comfort, Jonathan. Thankfully, there are so many workers in this building, no one knows them all."

"Grace, did you notice he was carrying a Russian-made machine gun? Riley said, 'There is speculation that the Russians are providing the Iranians with SAM rockets and we know they are providing them with the expertise to enrich U-238 to weapons-grade U-235 nuclear fuel.'"

At the top of the stairs on level -2, Jonathan carefully cracked open the stairwell door not knowing whom or what they may encounter. The view through the opening exposed a long white sterile hall with oversized double doors at one end. With the curiosity of a cat, Jonathan crept toward the doors like a lion on a hunt and peered through one corner of the glass windows in the doors so as not to be detected. A group of technicians in cleanroom suits was laboring over a device that was partially hidden from view. While hurrying back to the stairwell, Jonathan stopped and observe a large duct suspended from the ceiling.

Opening the stairwell door, Jonathan whispered to Grace, "There is a large cleanroom at the end of the hall where they may be assembling a nuclear warhead, but I can't be positive. We must find a way to observe exactly what they're doing and hear what they're saying. Wait here in the stairwell and don't make a sound. I have an idea. I'll be back before you know it."

"Okay, but hurry! Please don't be gone long."

Knowing all cleanrooms operate under a slight positive pressure to prevent airborne contamination, Jonathan studied a large aluminum duct hanging from the ceiling that carried fresh air into the cleanroom.

"Assuming clean air is distributed throughout the area by vents in the ductwork over the ceiling, I know exactly how the workers can be observed," Jonathan said to himself.

A small ladder in a nearby storage closet provided Jonathan access to the duct. With the ladder in place, he hurriedly removed a large inspection cover and returned to get Grace. Opening the stairwell door, he called softly, but there was no answer. Looking up and down the stairwell, Jonathan saw no sign of Grace. Forgetting about everything except finding Grace, instant panic set in that she had been discovered.

CHAPTER *18*

THE REPORT

A soft whisper from behind the door broke the silence. "Here I am. I was hiding to avoid being seen."

"Grace, you scared the life out of me. I thought you had been arrested."

"Really, you were frightened I may have been taken? I love it!"

"Seriously, Grace, come on, and I'll explain what you need to do."

"What I need to do? Why do I always have to be the one to do everything?"

Walking to the duct, Jonathan pointed to the inspection plate opening and explained his plan. "Now listen carefully. We must find out what those technicians are saying, and you know I don't understand a word of Farsi. Since you love adventure and understand the language, here is a golden opportunity with your name written all over it. This inspection plate opening is just large enough for you to squeeze through. After I boost you up into the duct, just crawl quietly along until you come to the vent closest to the area in the cleanroom where the technicians are working. From that vantage point, you should be able to hear and see everything."

"Wait a minute! You're going to put me inside that duct and close it up? I could hyperventilate just thinking about it! You know I'm claustrophobic. Where are you going to be?"

"Relax, Grace, I'll be nearby. Now, hurry and take off your shoes because they'll make too much noise as you crawl along the duct. We can't take a chance on you being discovered."

"When I'm on my way back, how will I know when I've reached the inspection opening?"

"I'll leave a few screws out of this inspection plate when I replace it. When you see the light shining through the holes, you will know you've reached this spot. Tap lightly on the sides of the duct, and I'll remove the inspection plate and help you out."

"What if someone hears me tapping on the duct?"

"Let's just hope they don't. Are you ready?"

"If I have to! First I have to get these coveralls off so I can move about easily."

With some hesitation, Grace climbed up the ladder and wriggled into the duct to begin her reconnaissance mission. Stepping to the back of the storage closet behind some boxes, Jonathan left the door slightly ajar. Meanwhile, Grace inched her small frame silently along the duct and soon made the short trip to a vent a few feet from one of the groups of workers. Even though the air in the duct was cool, she was breathing heavily and sweating profusely due to the confined quarters.

Through the vent opening, Grace could see a frightening-looking shiny metal object bulging with a massive bundle of tiny multi-colored wires, yet to be connected. *That may be the nuclear warhead, but I need to be sure of what I'm seeing,* Grace thought.

Several Iranians were hovering over the device methodically connecting the bundles of wires according to a towering stack of drawings nearby.

Overhearing the technicians talk about their plans to complete the device is easy, but they never refer to it as the warhead or bomb. What is it?

Joking loudly as they worked, the technicians had no idea that a novice spy was listening to every word they uttered and watching every move they made. Suddenly, the work was interrupted by a claxon bell ringing and a flashing red light on a nearby phone.

One of the technicians dropped what he was doing and sprinted across the room to answer the phone as if he knew there was a high-ranking official on the other end. The only words Grace can hear were the staccato responses of the technician to the voice on the phone as he clicked his heels together. "Yes, yes, yes, sir, right away, sir. We will be ready, sir."

Hanging up the phone, he shouted with a recognizable sense of urgency in his voice to the others in the room. "Listen up, everyone, and stop what you're doing. That was headquarters on the phone, ordering a surprise meeting to review our progress on the projects."

Review their progress on what projects? Why don't they say what they're working on?

"General Ataollah Akbar will be here in an hour with Nuclear Chief Mohsen Ashtiani, Mohammad Farhadi, and Russian Defense Minister Vladimir Shoigu. Gather all the necessary reports and prepare the classified briefing room immediately for their arrival and order refreshments for everyone. Hurry, we don't have much time!"

The technicians halted all work and scrambled to carry stacks of top-secret drawings, schedules, and charts to the briefing room that adjoined the cleanroom.

Grace knew from news reports that General Ataollah Akbar was the commander of the Iranian army in charge of their nuclear program, and Mohsen Ashtiani was known as the 'father' of the Iranian nuclear bomb. Mohammad Farhadi was the primary negotiator for the Iranian nuclear deal.

This must be an incredibly important high-level meeting, but why is the Russian representative attending?

It was common knowledge that Iranian officials often scheduled secret meetings like this with little or no notice to minimize any possible leaks to the International Atomic Energy Agency.

All Grace could think about was finding a way to hear what was going to be discussed in that briefing room. Surely the ductwork that delivered fresh air must run over the briefing room, but could she possibly crawl close enough to hear the conversation without being discovered? She shuddered as she remembered Jonathan's words:

"We'll be shot as spies if we're caught."

Nervously but quietly, Grace continued her way along the duct with her destination still more than twenty feet away. Stopping at each vent, Grace looked down through the opening and assessed her position. Arriving at a vent near one corner of the briefing room, she was elated she had a bird's eye view of the briefing table and seating for all the attendees. While waiting for the meeting to begin, she became heavy-eyed watching the time on her watch drag by in what seemed like slow motion.

With the dignitaries laughing, the Officer-in-Charge directed them to the briefing room. "Right this way, gentlemen."

Finally, the loud laughter of the arriving Iranian and Russian leaders aroused her. The attendees took their places at the table with the Iranian Officer-in-Charge for the nuclear laboratory seated at one end of the table. When Mohsen Ashtiani, the Iranian "Father of the bomb" arrived, he was seated at the head of the table. Introductions were made and refreshments served.

Ataollah Akbar, the commander of the Iranian army, called on Behram Jafari, the Officer-in-Charge, to give a report on whether the nuclear arms agreement had impacted the schedule for the assembly of the nuclear warhead.

Oh, my gosh! They said the magic words! They are assembling a nuclear warhead right here in this cleanroom.

After some preliminary discussion, the Iranian Officer-in-Charge stood up, clicked his heels together at attention and proudly stated with authority, "Sir, we are on schedule to have the warhead ready to load the nuclear core in six months or less. Our underground nuclear tests have been completed, and I am also proud to announce that an Intercontinental Ballistic Missile designed to deliver the warhead has been successfully test-fired. With a range of more than 6,000 kilometers, the rocket will be able to deliver our warhead to Israel, the eastern shores of America, and anywhere in between."

The room rocked with an outbreak of heavy laughter and deafening applause in response to the announcement.

"Although U.S. officials have accused us of violating the Iranian nuclear agreement[4] as well as the U.N. Security Council resolution by testing the launch vehicle, we maintained the rocket was designed and tested for the launch of an innovative technology weather satellite. I promise, sir, the Americans don't suspect a thing even though they have withdrawn from the Nuclear Arms agreement!"

Swallowing hard, Grace was horrified to learn they were so close to having perfected the bomb and that they had a rocket capable of delivering it to America.

Grace flinched as General Ataollah Akbar, commander of the Iranian army, pounded his fists on the table hard enough to rattle the dishes and barked gruffly. "What are we doing to convince the IAEA that we're abiding by all the terms of the nuclear arms agreement? The infidels must not suspect our work on the bomb."

Mohammad Farhadi, the primary negotiator for Iran, responded, "Don't worry, my friend."

Standing and pounding the table with his fist, General Akbar shouted, "Don't tell me not to worry. My job is to worry when there is nothing to worry about, and I'm not your friend!"

Mohammad Farhadi continued. "The agreement gives us twenty-four-hour notice before the IAEA inspectors arrive to perform inspections in any facility. Furthermore, we're permitted to execute and report on some of the inspections ourselves. Of course, we are always reporting glowing progress on the dismantlement of our nuclear arms program in all the facilities we identified to the IAEA!"

"Sure, we are disassembling the centrifuges used to enrich the percentage of U-235 in U-238 as promised in the agreement, but we never agreed to give up 100% of the U-235 material we already processed. Besides, we had already relocated most of the enriched uranium and installed thousands of new Zippe centrifuges we purchased from our friends in Russia to this secret location before the IAEA inspectors were scheduled to arrive in Iran."

"Our schedule will actually be enhanced using the new Zippe centrifuges since they represent an improvement on the standard gas centrifuges we gave up as part of the agreement."

Slapping Vladimir Shoigu on the back with laughter, Farhadi

---

4 Joint Comprehensive Plan of Action

continued. "With the billions of dollars in unfrozen cash assets the United States was obligated to give to the Islamic Republic under the terms of the original agreement, we have additional finances to buy even more of the hardware we need to destroy America and Israel. The nuclear deal was further sweetened by lifting the arms embargo and allowing us to purchase S-300 surface-to-air missiles from our good friends in Russia."

What? Russia is providing Iran with SAM missiles? We allowed that in the agreement?

"Finally, even if the Americans plan an attack and locate this laboratory, which is highly unlikely, their bunker bombs are unable to penetrate the solid rock of this mountain to reach us deep underground. General Akbar, I promise you, we have absolutely nothing to worry about!"

The solemn air of the room was broken by thunderous applause by all on cue by General Akbar.

Reassured with what he heard about the nuclear warhead program, General Akbar requested Russian Defense Minister Vladimir Shoigu give a progress report on the delivery of the S-300 SAM missiles to Iran.

Vladimir Shoigu stood up and proudly announced, "The first shipment of the S-300 surface-to-air missiles to Iran to protect the laboratory and rocket test facilities was delivered on schedule in 2016 and are in operation hidden from the view of American drones and satellites. The next shipment will be delivered in three months. Mounted on mobile trucks, these rocket launchers can be moved around and prepared to fire in less than five minutes."

Convinced that the secrecy of the facility was secure and the nuclear project was on schedule, the conversation turned to the newest project being developed jointly by the Russians and Iranians.

The Iranian OIC announced, "We have a separate team of technicians and engineers working on the EPGS666 project, and we are on schedule to launch the first trial satellite in six months."

"The launch of the first trial satellite is on schedule?" Grace muttered. "*Now* what are they talking about?"

General Ataollah Akbar interrupted abruptly. "It's imperative that the EPGS666 project, as well as the completion of the nuclear warhead, stay on schedule for us to defeat the United States and destroy Israel in a surprise attack."

What? They're planning a surprise attack?

"As soon as we complete the warheads and finalize the EPGS666 project, we will launch the last jihad and Allah will be overjoyed with our extermination of the foolish Americans. We warned them of a harsh retaliation after their terrorist airstrike that killed our beloved General Farshid, head of the Islamic Revolutionary Guard. Of course, our work could never have been possible without the help of our friends in Russia who helped us with the technology for the bomb and our friends in North Korea that supplied the technology for the missile to carry the warhead. And remember, we are most grateful to the supporters of Allah in the United States who generously provided the miniature detonators that are critical for the bomb until the detonators arrive from Russia."

"We gave them the detonators?" Grace gasped in disbelief. *"They didn't steal them? I don't believe it."*

General Ataollah Akbar took several copies of a report stamped *Top Secret* out of his briefcase and distributed them to the attendees.

"This is the estimated damage assessment report for the combination of the EPGS666 project, which is launched first followed by the launch of the nuclear warhead. Study this report carefully, and I will answer any questions at our next progress meeting."

Oh no, they're not going to discuss the other project. I must know what's in that report that describes the EPGS666.

The attendees took all the copies except one and handed the last copy to the Iranian OIC to place in the briefing room safe. The document would be removed later and placed in the master vault downstairs in a secure area for safe keeping.

The Iranian OIC pulled back a large painting of Mohsen Ashtani on the wall that revealed a small wall safe next to a compartment containing a remote keypad.

Grace's heart skipped a beat as she shifted a little to relax cramped leg muscles. "I have to get into that safe."

Recalling a scene from a James Bond movie, Grace was ecstatic with the idea that popped into her head to obtain the code.

Boy, this spy stuff is a piece of cake. I'll just use the zoom on the video camera in the special cell phone to record the keys on the keypad as he inputs them. After the last shift change, hopefully, Jonathan and I can slip back in here and enter the passcode and retrieve the report.

Studying every move, Grace watched as the OIC depressed each key on the keypad.

Noticing there was a different tone emitted as the keys were depressed Grace thought, *Wow, that safe must open when the correct sequence of tones is entered on the remote keypad.*

However, Grace's heart sunk when one of the men stepped in front of the safe and partially obscured her view before the complete code was entered. Only the first four of the five keys entered on the keypad by the OIC were visible.

Oh man! I can't see the last keys the OIC entered. I don't believe it! Now we'll never see what's in that report and learn what the EPGS666 project is all about.

As the meeting adjourned, Grace waited for everyone to leave the room and then began her quiet retreat down the air duct. Sweating profusely, she stopped momentarily over a vent opening to check her location. Unexpectedly, one of her earrings fell off and rolled right over the cover of the vent opening and lay delicately balanced between two louvers. With trembling hands, Grace attempted to grasp the earring with her sweating fingers knowing the slightest mistake would send her jewelry through the opening and alert the workers to her position.

Holding her breath and realizing her life may be hanging in the balance, Grace nervously reached for the earring with her thumb and index finger, but…

CHAPTER 19

THE ESCAPE

Daring Grace to come any closer, the earring rocked lazily back and forth, threatening to slip between the vent louvers. Just as Grace touched the small but heavy gold loop with fingers dripping with perspiration, the slippery loop seemed to smile 'goodbye' as it dropped through the opening. The sound of the metal loop hitting the floor shattered the silence.

Oh man! I'm dead now!

One of the workers turned abruptly and barked, "What was that noise?"

Walking to his workstation, the OIC replied, "I didn't hear anything."

Pointing in the direction of the vent where Grace was situated, the worker insisted, "I know I heard something right over there."

Walking toward the vent, he surveyed the floor and stared up at the ceiling for what seemed to Grace like an eternity. Looking into his dark eyes with a stare as cold as ice water, her heart was pounding so hard she was afraid he would hear it.

Fortunately, the earring rolled under a counter where it was completely out of sight.

Impatient with the distracted worker, the Officer in Charge

snapped, "You're just hearing things, and stop staring at that vent! There is nothing up there but air. Besides, no one could breach the security of this facility even if they could find it. Now get back to work; we have a tight schedule to keep."

"Yes, sir!"

Overjoyed at not being discovered, Grace wriggled her slim perspiration-soaked body backward down the duct at a snail's pace. Her mind was running rampant with what she had seen and heard. Arriving at the inspection plate and seeing the light shining through the holes, she tapped quietly on the duct hoping only Jonathan will hear her. Responding to the signal, Jonathan immediately retrieved the ladder from the closet, and in a matter of minutes, Grace was safely out of the duct and in the storage closet for a debriefing.

"What have you been doing? I was worried sick that you had been discovered."

Practically hyperventilating, Grace told Jonathan about the schedule for the bomb and the new secret device described in a Russian report that was locked in the briefing room safe. There was so much to tell, and Grace was talking so fast she could hardly make a sentence.

Holding up the special phone, Grace announced with a triumphant smile. "Look, I recorded video of the passcode characters required to get into the safe to retrieve the report, but I couldn't see the last three characters. I'm afraid there is no practical way to guess the combination of characters to complete the code."

"That's all right, Grace. Based on what you've told me, it's imperative that we get our hands on that report."

"I know, but it's impossible to open the safe without the last three characters."

"Don't worry! You recorded sound as well as video of the Iranian official entering the passcode, so you recorded the distinctive sound each character made when it was depressed on the keypad."

"Okay, but how does that help?"

"All we have to do is depress each key on the keypad until we match the sound of the fifth tone as it was recorded on the video.

Then we simply enter all the tones in the correct order by depressing the correct keys. Let's wait in the storage closet until the last shift leaves and then slip into the clean room."

After waiting patiently for more than an hour, they heard three blasts from a claxon horn, immediately followed by the orderly shuffling of feet and loud voices of people in the halls.

"That horn must have signaled the end of the last shift," Jonathan whispered.

After donning their coveralls and caps, Jonathan and Grace opened the closet door and joined the ranks of workers anxious to get to their living quarters. No one seemed to notice the two intruders as they joined the crowd and later entered the cleanroom. The briefing room was unlocked, so they went in and left the door slightly ajar. The safe that held the Iranian secrets was in plain sight and beckoned Grace and Jonathan to try their luck extracting the report.

As Jonathan suggested, Grace used the video she made to re-play the sound of the fifth tone as it was entered in the keypad by the Iranian Officer. Meanwhile, Jonathan methodically depressed each key, listening for a match to the sound. Bubbling with excitement, Grace now had the entire five-tone passcode and was about to enter the code in the keypad when they heard footsteps in the clean room.

"Shh, quiet, Grace. Someone is coming."

Peering through the opening where the briefing room door was left ajar, Jonathan saw two Iranian workers enter the cleanroom. Looking around the room, the workers glanced at the briefing room door, picked up some papers on a desk, and left.

"Okay, quick, Grace, enter the complete passcode and let's hope there is not an alarm of some kind on the safe."

After carefully entering the code, a light on the keypad blinked green three times and the thick safe door silently sprung open.

"Wow! We did it, just like in the movies."

"Grace, will you please just look for the report?"

"Here it is, Jonathan; Estimated Damage Assessment Report for Project EPGS666."

Grabbing the report out of her hands, he began scanning the pages as quickly as possible.

"Look at this summary of the demonic device, Grace."

The Americans will be looking for a nuclear bomb, and instead, we will give them something they never dreamed of. On our command, this conventional-looking 'weather satellite' will launch many smaller satellites all over the northern hemisphere from a stationary earth orbit. When activated, each satellite will direct pulses of electromagnetic energy at predetermined targets in America. These pulses will completely disable all electrical communications within a radius of more than one thousand miles. All domestic and military operations in the area as well as anything else that is dependent on electronic communication, like military and commercial airlines, will be paralyzed. In addition, all electrical grids in range will be totally disabled.

All guidance systems, radar, and satellite GPS will be inoperative. Mass chaos will blanket the nation. Then while the United States is in a state of turmoil, we will launch the rockets with nuclear warheads and destroy Washington D.C. and other major targets in the United States as well as Israel. Without radar, anti-ballistic missiles will be unable to locate, lock on, and destroy our incoming nuclear missiles. The most powerful nation in the world will fall to Iran. Allah will finally be glorified. Even the best American intelligence sources have no idea that we have already successfully developed the Electromagnetic Pulse Generator (EPG).

"Grace, with a weapon like the EPG, the United States doesn't stand a chance against a nuclear attack. The result will be the destruction of the world, beginning with the United States and Israel. This may even cause a chain reaction in the bowels of the Earth. What an incredible apocalyptic device.

"I am afraid this may be the beginning of what will be World War III and perhaps the last war on this planet. Quickly, photograph the report and put it back in the safe. With the safe locked, it may take a while for the Iranians to discover we were here. We must find a way out, so we can contact the QRF to pick us up."

With everything secure, Jonathan and Grace crept quietly out of the cleanroom, entered the stairwell, and proceeded cautiously up the stairs, occasionally passing other workers and guards armed with automatic weapons. However, with each encounter, a reassuring word from Grace sent the guards on their way. Reaching ground level, the two novice spies found themselves in a large room with several lines for security checks each having an electronic card reader. Most of the workers had already vacated the building after the last shift change, leaving only a few workers still being processed.

"Grace, it appears all the workers go through a full-body scanner and ID card reader when entering and leaving the facility. Hopefully, we'll be able to use our magnetic cards to safely pass through the scanners. If our identity is questioned, you should explain we were radicalized in the United States and defected to join the work on the bomb. If all else fails, make a run for it and hope the guards are poor shots."

"Yeah, right!"

About that time, Grace nervously pulled on Jonathan's sleeve and whispered, "Look, they're searching the workers."

"What are you worried about? We don't have anything except this satellite phone and a few old manuscripts."

Grace pulled on Jonathan again.

"Well, I have to confess I took this very small gold Persian statue from the treasure room."

Before Jonathan could answer her, the guard barked in Farsi, "Step over here. I've never seen you two before. What are your names and how long have you worked here? Give me your papers!"

Grace answered. "He is Abdullah Namdaranand. I'm Partow Sossonabadi. We have only been working in this facility about three weeks."

The guard pulled up a list on the computer and asked, "What group are you in and who do you report to?"

"We're both working on project EPGS666."

Pointing to Jonathan, the guard snapped, "What's wrong with him, can't he talk?"

"He just got out of the infirmary with a severe sore throat."

Stepping away from Jonathan, the guard growled, "Okay, but what's the name of the person you report to?"

Grace knew they were about to be discovered. With authority, she proclaimed, "We have been assigned to the Iranian Officer in Charge Behram Jafari."

"Okay, but I'll have to call him and verify your identity and work area. Now give me your papers."

About that time, several guards congregated at the other end of the room to arrest someone trying to smuggle a laptop computer out of the facility. As the guard walked toward the disturbance, he shouted, "Wait right here, both of you. I'll be back in a minute."

In the confusion, Jonathan and Grace quickly scanned the cards attached to their suits in the card reader and proceeded out the door with several other workers. Once outside the facility, they shoved their way hurriedly through the open gate of the electrified fence and ran for open ground, disappearing into the thick darkness of the desert night.

The stillness of the evening was suddenly broken by a screaming siren, and a voice over a loudspeaker shouting in Farsi, "Shoot them, they're spies!"

About that time, Jonathan and Grace reached a clearing a few hundred yards from the entrance to the compound and were caught in what appeared to be a violent sandstorm. Fierce winds knocked them to the ground, and they struggled to get back on their feet. The roar of the wind in the darkness was terrifying, and neither Jonathan nor Grace could see which direction to run because of the blinding sand. Wind and airborne dust became even more brutal in the glaring beams of brilliant spotlights that penetrated the darkness and danced along the landscape illuminating their presence.

Realizing the Iranian guards had spotted them, Grace fell to the ground freaking out and screaming her head off. Jonathan put his arms around her, anticipating what was going to happen next. The deafening sound of gunfire was coming dangerously close, and a rain of bullets could be heard whizzing over their heads as they lay prostrate with their faces buried in the sand. Both explorers braced for the inevitable.

CHAPTER 20

THE INTERROGATORS

Expecting to feel the sharp pain of a searing bullet penetrate his body at any moment, Jonathan glanced skyward, squinting in the bright lights. Wiping perspiration-drenched sand from his face, he realized the violent dust storm was caused by the powerful rotors of two MH-60 radar-evading, stealth Black Hawk helicopter gunships appearing out of the darkness. With the capability to move about undetected by conventional radar, these were the same type of aircraft used in the raid on Bin Laden years before. The Iranian military never saw or heard them coming. When Jonathan spotted the two rescue choppers proudly sporting American flags on their fuselage, he shouted for joy. With a sigh of relief, he knew they were a part of the Quick Reaction Force (QRF) from the American airbase in Saudi Arabia, but believed they arrived too late. The Iranian guards were rapidly closing in on them.

Descending rapidly into crisscrossing beams of powerful Iranian floodlights, one of the helicopters descended to a few feet from the ground. Two 7.62mm machine guns emerged from the open cargo door and returned fire to the Iranians.

With their ears ringing from the sound of the thunderous gunfire, Jonathan and Grace heard voices inside the helicopters screaming, "Give me your hands and climb in, hurry!"

In the wake of the intensified gunfire from the Iranian guards,

Jonathan and Grace felt surges of adrenalin course through their bodies, giving them an overwhelming dose of superhuman strength. Lifting their bodies from the ground, they propelled themselves skyward toward the chopper's open door. With arms outstretched, they struggled desperately to grab the soldier's hands reaching down to them from the helicopter, but the crewman's hands were just out of their grasp.

With the Iranians moving close enough to have Jonathan and Grace clearly in their gunsights, the helicopter descended another few feet. Thrashing in the air with outstretched arms, the two Americans were snatched by the crewmen. Clumsily yanked safely aboard the helicopter, Jonathan and Grace's legs were left dangling outside the doorway. The pilot was given the signal to "go" by the crewman in charge of the rescue, and the chopper sprung vertically into the night sky like a rebounding bungee cord jumper. At that instant, the Missile Warning System light on the helicopter's Caution and Warning Panel lit up like a Christmas tree, and a loud pulsating clanging sound signaled an approaching rocket. Only the pilot and crew knew what would happen next.

Without warning, the aircraft pitched upward violently and simultaneously banked away from the Iranian compound at a dangerously steep angle. Flung completely into the cabin by the ninety-degree snap roll of the helicopter, Jonathan and Grace were slammed against the opposite side of the gunship like two rag dolls.

The cabin lit up like the fourth of July as the fiery trail of an accelerating missile rocketed alarmingly close to the open doorway, narrowly missing the aircraft.

Following a rapid climb to two thousand feet, the helicopter abruptly rolled back, and the pilot pitched the nose down and accelerated while Jonathan and Grace rolled uncontrollably back across the cabin. Grabbing their arms as they slid helplessly toward the open door, the crewmen arrested their fall from the helicopter just in time and pulled them both safely inside.

"Man, that was close, but that wild, skillful maneuver saved all our lives." Jonathan's appreciation for the crew's flying skills drew a grin and a nod of acceptance from the pilot who had momentarily turned around to see if his passengers were okay.

As Jonathan and Grace watched, the silhouette of the second gunship in the Iranian spotlights hovered high over the nuclear facility and returned fire from the Iranian guards. Soon the Iranian compound, illuminated by searchlights dancing about in the night sky, vanished in the darkness behind them. Jonathan and Grace were out of harm's way, and both Black Hawk helicopters were safely on route to an American airbase in Saudi Arabia.

Staring out the window into the darkness, one question was still nagging Jonathan. *Who called the QRF to pick us up and who knew we would be at the agreed-upon pick-up zone at the precise time they arrived? I was never able to use the satellite phone, and no one could have possibly known about our escape.*

After a hot meal and a few hours rest at the American airbase in Saudi Arabia, Grace and Jonathan were flown to a United States military base at an undisclosed location in Germany. Their plane was met by United States intelligence personnel who debriefed them for hours on their findings at the Iranian nuclear laboratory. The expert interrogators were extremely interested in information about the detonators, the schedule for completion of the nuclear warheads, and the Electromagnetic Pulse Generator project.

Anxious to share his findings with Riley, Jonathan asked to speak with him by phone. However, the person in charge of the debriefing responded with authority, "That's not possible. Riley is tied up with an investigation of a retired Central Intelligence agent named Westin who died in a recent car crash."

"Steven, Steven Westin, are you positive about that name? He was my best friend."

"Yes, and the details about the accident are sketchy, although foul play is suspected."

"What kind of foul play? Who would want to kill Steven?"

"I'm sorry. The accident is under investigation, and we're not at liberty to discuss the matter any further."

With sharp pangs of sadness in his heart, Jonathan choked out, "When is the funeral?"

"A private service is scheduled for tomorrow, but unfortunately, you will not be home in time to attend."

Suffocating in a heavy blanket of grief by the news of his best friend's death, Jonathan called Amy to express his sorrow and to obtain more information. There was no answer.

After several more days of intense interrogation, Grace and Jonathan were released to return to the United States by way of commercial aircraft. Arriving at the Charles De Gaulle Airport in Paris confused and heart-broken, Jonathan sat down with Grace at a restaurant in the airport food court for dinner.

"Jonathan, you've been very quiet since we arrived in Paris."

"I know, I was just thinking, is it remotely possible that Steven was involved in espionage and was caught in the crossfire?"

"You know Steven better than that. Do I have to keep reminding you that he was your closest and best friend? I believe you're just in shock over his death."

"I know, Grace, but lately there have just been too many unexplained coincidences."

When the waiter brought the check, Jonathan asked Grace if she had money to pay the bill.

"Why? I never knew you to be without cash or at least a credit card."

"During our flight to Germany, I realized I lost my wallet somewhere in the Iranian laboratory, but I didn't tell anyone during the debriefing. I've already canceled all my credit cards, but of course, I don't have any cash. Thank goodness the American State Department paid for our flight home, and if my passport had not been in my backpack, I couldn't even have made my way through security at the airport."

"Sure, I'll pay for the meal, but what will happen when the Iranians find your wallet? It has your address and university information. Your wallet even has your car license on the insurance form and the parking ticket that tells where the car is parked at the airport. Finding us will be like taking candy from a baby."

"Honestly, Grace, I don't believe the Iranians will want to spend the time and expense to hunt down a couple of university employees like us."

"Are you kidding? You think they don't want to find two Americans that breached the security of their top-secret nuclear laboratory and had two helicopter gunships rescue them and shoot up their facility?"

"Well, when you put it like that ..."

Jonathan was trying to hide that he *was* extremely worried about the Iranians hunting them down, believing they must be secret agents posing as university employees. After dinner, Jonathan and Grace proceeded to the security area and then made their way to the gate just in time to board their flight.

After another exhausting but uneventful flight in coach, Jonathan and Grace finally arrived at the Newark Liberty Airport physically and mentally drained. Since they left Iran in a hurry, they had only the clothes on their back, the manuscripts and the one small gold Persian artifact tucked safely inside a small backpack Grace purchased in the Paris airport. Thankfully, the journey through the security and immigration areas in the Newark Liberty Airport was without incident.

As they walked through the airport parking lot, they spotted a man in a long black trench coat bending over the windshield of Jonathan's car.

"Look, Grace, I think that guy is trying to break into my car. And why is he wearing an overcoat in this warm weather?"

Running toward his car, Jonathan shouted at the suspicious-looking guy, "Hey, you, in the black coat, what are you doing?"

At the sound of Jonathan's voice, the stranger bolted and quickly vanished in the parking lot.

"Where did he go?"

"I don't know, Grace; he just disappeared into thin air!"

Jonathan looked over his car and said thankfully, "Oh well, it looks like we came along just in time. No windows are broken, and I don't see any damage."

"Look at this, Jonathan. There is a note on the windshield that says, 'Don't touch the car! Take a taxi home. The answers you're looking for are at the wall'. Now, what is that supposed to mean and who do you think put this note on the windshield? The note is signed, 'your friend, Malachi.' There is that name again! Do you think the man running away from the car left this note? Was that Malachi?"

"I don't know, but if he did, why didn't he just hang around and tell me what he wanted to say? Grace, this is either a practical joke or the real Malachi, whoever he is, is trying to tell us something. But why would he say take a taxi home? What's wrong with driving my car? I'm not going to pay a hundred bucks for a taxi to take us home when I have a perfectly good car to drive."

Jonathan put his hand on the door handle and was just about to open the car door when Grace screamed…

CHAPTER 21

THE RIDDLE

"**S**top, Jonathan!"

Jerking his hand off the car door as if it were a hot rock, he irritably shouted, "What are you yelling about?"

"What if the Iranians discovered that we stole secret information from their safe? They could have sent that guy in the black coat to cut the brake lines and cause an accident or, worse yet, plant a bomb in the car to stop us from talking, permanently!"

"You've been watching too many James Bond movies, Grace. Besides, we left the report locked in the safe! Even if that fellow did tamper with the car or plant a bomb, why did he write a note warning us not to touch the car?"

"I don't know, Jonathan, but I have a strong feeling that we should do as he says; call it woman's intuition. Remember, the Iranians know exactly where your car is parked here at the airport. It would be child's play for them to track us down if they wanted to kill us. Come on, let's get out of here and take a taxi home."

"I guess you're right, Grace. With our track record, why take a chance? Let's go back to the terminal and grab a taxi. Tomorrow, I'll have the car towed to a repair shop and call Riley to send someone who specializes in this kind of thing to check it out."

"Great, my stomach already feels better!"

As Jonathan and Grace were walking away, a large white van raced past them and wheeled into the parking space next to their car.

"Man, that guy must think this parking lot's a racetrack, and look how close he is parking to my car. Why do people do that? There are plenty of empty parking spaces! He can't even get out of that van without..."

At that instant, the driver of the van threw his door open in the tight parking space and bounced it off the side of Jonathan's car.

Waving his arms in the air, Jonathan shouted, "Hey man, you in the white van, what's the matter with you? You're going to pay for the damage to my..."

Before he could finish the sentence, Jonathan's car exploded in a flaming inferno. The fiery blast belched flames and a cloud of thick black smoke into the air that could be seen for blocks, triggering a violent shock wave that set off every car alarm in the parking lot and showered the area with burning debris. Slammed to the ground on their backs by the blast, Jonathan and Grace had the wind knocked out of them. Revived by the intense heat and pungent odor of burning rubber from an airborne car wheel landing close enough to set their clothes on fire, Jonathan and Grace sat up in a daze. The car and the van were destroyed in the explosion, and the driver of the van was killed instantly. Several vehicles parked nearby were also engulfed in flames.

With their heads spinning, ears ringing, and pulses racing, Jonathan and Grace slapped embers from their clothing and crawled away from the burning tire dripping with molten rubber.

"Are you all right, Grace?"

"Yes, but good grief, Jonathan, we would have both been killed if you had opened the door of your car. Shouldn't we call the police?"

"No, there is nothing we can do for the driver of the van, and my car is a total loss. Besides, the police will be here shortly. Everyone in the terminal area probably heard the blast, and I'm sure the black smoke from the burning cars is visible for several blocks." Jonathan looked at Grace with gratitude. "Your intuition was correct and thank goodness I listened to you."

"But shouldn't the police be looking for the man who planted the bomb? He was probably the man running from your car."

"No, even if the guy we saw was involved, he was too far away for us to identify him and he is long gone by now. Anyway, I'm guessing the Iranians must have discovered that we obtained intelligence on their secret, monstrous projects and instructed one of their operatives in America to eliminate us before we passed on any more information to our government."

"That's what I said earlier, Jonathan!"

"Ok, so far you're always right, but at least I think the Iranians believe we were killed in the explosion. Now let's get out of here and get back to the terminal building where we can get a taxi to take us home."

After hurriedly making their way through the smoke-filled parking lot to the terminal, Jonathan and Grace found a waiting taxi.

"Isn't it unusual to find a taxi just waiting for a fare at this busy time of day?" Grace remarked.

"Yes," Jonathan nodded his head in agreement, "but I think we should take it."

The parking lot was already becoming congested with police, fire, and other emergency vehicles as well as a crowd of curious spectators. Pulling away from the airport parking area, the taxi driver remarked, "I just arrived at the airport a few minutes ago and saw all the smoke in the parking lot. Do you folks have any idea what happened?"

"Someone said a car exploded causing a second vehicle to be destroyed!"

"Do you know whether anyone was in the vehicles? Were they able to get out before the explosion?"

Jonathan looked at Grace with suspicion and cautiously replied, "Some guy that arrived on the scene right after the blast said it looked like the passengers in both vehicles were killed instantly."

"Oh, that's too bad. Where did you folks fly in from?"

Jonathan looked at Grace, pleaded silence with his index finger to his lips, and replied, "Oh, we just arrived from Florida. We've been visiting with relatives in Tampa and had a wonderful time just relaxing on the beach."

Grace leaned over and whispered to Jonathan. "This taxi driver is asking a lot of very specific questions, and he looks Middle Eastern. He could be an Iranian operative."

"You're right, Grace," Jonathan whispered. "It's best we don't say anything else."

To avoid going to the address in his wallet that was in the possession of the Iranians or to Grace's apartment, Jonathan had the driver drop them off at a department store near Grace's apartment. Later, Jonathan called a taxi to take them home and had a rental car delivered to his home.

Jonathan agreed to meet Grace at the university early the next morning so they could begin deciphering the manuscripts they found in King Cyrus's tomb. Believing they were getting close to having the answers to all their questions, he suspected the demonic Iranian weapons may be connected to the Doomsday Clock puzzle. However, he needed a well-deserved night's rest, and he recommended Grace do the same.

Early the next morning, Jonathan dragged his sleep-deprived body out of bed, had his usual breakfast, and proceeded to the university in the rental car. The jet lag from the exhausting flight would be with him for several days to come and he was still shaken from yesterday's harrowing near-death experience at the airport. Grace arrived at the university a few minutes later with the manuscripts.

"Well, did you get a good night's sleep, Jonathan?"

"Are you kidding? Pondering Steven's tragic death and trying to understand why he would help Iran with the development of the nuclear bomb kept me up most of the night. He was my best friend, and I just don't get it. I also tried to call Amy last night, but no one answered the phone."

"Recalling all the strange circumstances and near-death experiences we have encountered that began with the UNESCO expedition to Babylon didn't help me sleep better either. It's almost as though something or someone is leading us through a maze of mysterious clues to take us deeper and deeper into the unknown while protecting us from certain danger. I'm actually a little nervous about where we're being taken, by whom and why!"

"Okay Jonathan, so do you really think someone is orchestrating our every move?"

"I don't know, Grace, but with the close calls we've had, it sure seems to be the case."

Jonathan asked Michelle to bring in coffee and pastries, but Grace was too excited to eat as she hurriedly prepared the scrolls to be digitized. Jonathan went to his office to prepare for the next day's class and left Grace in solitude to begin her work in the archive's laboratory.

Having completed the tedious process of digitizing the manuscripts and ensuring the long-term integrity of the original documents, Grace began to prepare detailed notes as well as a voice recording of her interpretation of the ancient conversation recorded on papyrus. She was absolutely mesmerized as she laboriously poured over each line of the manuscripts. It was as though she were eavesdropping on the private conversation between King Cyrus and his trusted young Israelite slave that took place more than 3,000 years ago. With her eyes closed, she could almost see and hear them talking.

A few days later, Jonathan walked into the laboratory where Grace was still laboring over the manuscripts.

"How is it going, Grace?"

"Jonathan, the document is extremely enlightening, but it seems like the timeline of events that the Israelite is talking about was written in a secret code."

"Good, I love codes; tell me more. I brought sandwiches for lunch, and we'll order dinner in should we decide to work late."

Accepting a sandwich, Grace began to methodically explain to Jonathan her translation of the manuscript. "When the king was told about the Doomsday Clock, he anxiously asked the Israelite to tell him more about the timing of the events on the clock. The servant explained the timeline for the clock not only revealed how long the world would exist once destruction began, but there were a description and timing of three extraordinary events that would take place before the world ended. When the king asked how long before the world will be destroyed, the Israelite replied, seventy weeks.

Now, what do you think that means, Jonathan, seventy weeks?"

"I don't have any idea. What else does the Israelite say about the events that make up the seventy weeks?"

"The servant indicated that the first event in the timeline, which would last seven weeks, was the rebuilding of the walls of Jerusalem and the Temple of Solomon that King Nebuchadnezzar destroyed in 586 B.C. The second event on the timeline that would last sixty-two weeks, he explained, is the time until the introduction of the Messiah promised by the Old Testament prophets."

With a twinkle in her eyes, Grace sighed. "The Israelite is talking about Jesus, the Son of God—the Messiah. Jonathan, the coming of Jesus had been prophesied for more than 700 years."

"Grace, do we have to bring religion into this discussion? Just keep your mind on translating the manuscript."

"The third event is actually the duration of the destruction of the world and is documented as being only one week."

"The entire world destroyed in one week? That's impossible!"

"Listen, Jonathan, and let me finish. If you total the time for the three events, you have exactly seventy weeks, just like the young Israelite said. The young man told the king that the beginning of the last week of the world's existence will be initiated by a very significant event. He even gave the king a riddle that contained a clue to the identity of the man who will initiate that event and rule the world during the last week."

"You're telling me there is a riddle about the future recorded in this ancient manuscript written more than 3,000 years ago? And you believe that riddle explains how to recognize some guy who is destined to arrive on the scene, perhaps in our future, and rule the world during the last days? Seriously, Grace?"

"Yes!"

"Well, this is all a little too far-fetched for me. This whole story is too bizarre! What one individual could possibly rule the entire world while some other out-of-this-world force orchestrates the destruction of the entire planet?" Jonathan stared at Grace with a wrinkled forehead and raised eyebrows that visibly validated his disbelief.

Believing Jonathan doubted her ability to accurately interpret the conversation in the manuscript, Grace explained further. "In fact, the riddle contains two clues. First, the manuscript says, 'The people of the prince that shall come shall destroy Jerusalem and the temple and he shall confirm the covenant with Israel for one week.' In other words, the prince who will rule the world will be a descendant of the people who destroyed the Temple in Jerusalem after it was rebuilt by the Israelites."

"All right, Grace. Even *I* know the Romans destroyed Jerusalem and the Temple in 70 A.D. Therefore, I guess the ancestry of the prince or man who is to come must be from the Roman Empire."

"Correct, but a one-week treaty with any country doesn't hold any water."

"No, somehow we still must find the key to decode the timeline and unravel the real meaning of a week as it was used by the Israelite."

It was early afternoon, and the sandwiches were gone, and Jonathan was more confused than ever about what appeared to be a coded timeline for the Doomsday Clock.

"So, what do you think, Jonathan?"

"I think we should go home and get some rest, but I feel like you're on the edge of a major discovery, and I don't want to quit now."

Jonathan picked up a history book he borrowed and opened it to a bookmarked page. Suddenly, with enthusiasm, he stood up and shouted with victory in his voice.

"I have it, Grace! I believe the pieces of the puzzle are falling into place."

CHAPTER 22

DECODED

"**L**isten to what this book of Babylonian history says." Jonathan began reading.

"'After the fall of Babylon to the Persians in 539 B.C., the prophet Ezra was given permission by King Cyrus to return the Israelite captives to Jerusalem.' History proves this act ended the captivity of the Israelites in Babylon exactly seventy years after it began, just as stated in the manuscript."

"After some delays due to political problems, the rebuilding of the wall and temple in Jerusalem was initiated during the reign of King Artaxerxes of Persia. A decree was given to the prophet Ezra to begin the reconstruction, and the project was completed in exactly forty-nine years, a fact authenticated by historical documents."

"Did you get that, Grace? It took exactly forty-nine years to rebuild the Jerusalem walls and temple. If the timeline in the manuscript indicates seven weeks for this event, then one week would be equal to seven calendar years. Applying that theory to the sixty-two weeks for the second event on the Doomsday Clock timeline would yield 434 years until the appearance of the prophet the Israelites called Jesus. Using that interpretation of the timeline would put the birth and ministry of Jesus at about the turn of the century from B.C. to A.D. or a little more than 2,000 years ago, which is also corroborated by historical documents. Now we have some cold hard facts to work with."

"Great, Jonathan. By the way, did you notice that two of the three prophecies given to the Israelite came to pass precisely as stated in the manuscript?"

"Correct, but what are you saying?"

"If the Doomsday Clock contains a total of seventy weeks or 490 years, there is only one week or seven years left to the end of the world from the last recorded event on the clock. If the first two events took place exactly as written, then it's safe to assume the third event will also happen exactly as documented. However, for some unknown reason, the clock stopped after the second event, and there have been no signs that it has started again."

Scratching his head, Jonathan listened intently as Grace grappled for an explanation.

"Remember the second part of the clue? The prince that will be a descendant of the Roman Empire will negotiate a treaty with Israel for one week? Now we know that the treaty will be signed for seven years. It's possible that the seven-year duration of the destruction of the world corresponds to the same seven-year period as the treaty with Israel."

With raised eyebrows, Jonathan leaned back in his big leather chair and struggled to absorb the entirety of Grace's hypothesis.

"Don't you see Jonathan? When the prince of the Roman Empire inks the treaty with Israel, the countdown to the end of the world and the beginning of the last seven years on the Doomsday Clock will commence. It appears the signing of the treaty is actually the trigger that initiates the destruction of our world."

"Grace, you hit one out of the ballpark this time, but we still don't know when it will happen or who this prince character is. Right now, this whole Doomsday Clock affair isn't making any sense to me, but it's frightening, to say the least. There must be a higher force from another world involved with the Doomsday Clock that has supernatural powers completely unknown to us."

"Are you talking about God?"

"Of course not. I meant there must be some extraterrestrial being with advanced intelligence from another world in deep space behind this whole Doomsday Clock idea, but why? What's the purpose of the obliteration of Earth? Whoever or whatever is behind this Doomsday Clock is probably watching us right now as we struggle with the answers to this riddle. Do you think it's possible that whoever is behind the destruction of the earth is the same powerful stranger from another world that gave the information to the Israelite?"

"All I know, Jonathan, is that only God controls the destiny of the world."

"So, are you saying the same God that you believe created the world is planning to destroy it? Why would God want to destroy what He created?"

"I really don't know, Jonathan, but shouldn't we tell someone in Homeland Security or the FBI or someone about what we've found?"

"Are you kidding, Grace? People will think we're crazy with no more to go on than what we have. We have to find the Doomsday Clock, and then we can report our findings to the authorities."

With Jonathan's fingers moving quickly down the lines of a dog-eared page in the history book, he called Grace to look over his shoulder.

"Look at this, here is why the clock stopped after the second event. Israel was scattered to the four corners of the Earth when the Romans destroyed Jerusalem in 70 A.D. The last group of Israelites hiding out in Israel died on a mountain top called Masada near the Dead Sea and the nation of Israel and their Hebrew language no longer existed. To complete the riddle, Israel had to become a nation again, and that didn't happen until 1948. Therefore, the clock could not possibly have been reactivated until sometime after 1948."

"Great, Jonathan, but Israel became a sovereign nation again more than seventy years ago, and there hasn't been a recorded seven-year peace treaty signed between any nation and Israel since then."

"I know, but think about it. The person who will negotiate the treaty with Israel must be a recognizable ally to Israel and hold a position of international power. There is no international figure that fits that description, and Israel has no true allies.

"What about the United States?"

"Seriously, Grace? The United States hasn't been a real ally to Israel in many years. In fact, our previous Washington administration snubbed the Prime Minister of Israel many times and ignored his concerns regarding the Iranian involvement in building a nuclear weapon to use against them. We even abstained on a UN vote that allowed passage of a resolution condemning Israeli settlement expansion in the occupied West Bank. The failure of the United States to veto the measure was viewed as a double-cross of Israel by the U.S. Only since the election of President Trump has the White House attempted to improve relations with Israel and promised to stand beside them. In fact, in 2018, the United States not only recognized Jerusalem as the capital of Israel but moved the U.S. Embassy from Tel Aviv to Jerusalem."

"Then perhaps the prince in the riddle who will negotiate the treaty with Israel hasn't arrived on the political scene yet," said Grace.

"Wait just a minute, Grace. Remember the television newscast we saw that announced the candidacy of a bright young politician for president of the newly formed New World Union? His last name was Romulus, I think. Didn't he hail from a Roman ancestry and say that he planned to negotiate a treaty with Israel as one of his first actions if elected President of the New World Union?"

"Oh my gosh, you're right!"

"Well, then this young man could be our prince in the riddle. If that's the case, we may not have much time to locate the Doomsday Clock before he takes office and the treaty is signed."

"But we don't know where to start looking, and we have no clues!"

"Let's go back over the manuscripts, maybe we missed something."

After working all night and coming up empty-handed, Jonathan could hardly keep his eyes open. As the antique German Wag clock in his office struck 6:00 A.M., Jonathan suggested they go home and get some rest and come back later in the afternoon. The golden rays of the morning sun were just washing over the tops of the trees when

Jonathan walked Grace to her car.

"Grace, do you remember the note we took off the windshield of my car at the airport?"

"Of course! I have it right here in my purse. 'Take a taxi home. You will find all your answers at the wall,' and the note was signed Malachi. There is no doubt about the meaning of the first line, but what do you think the part about finding all your answers 'at the wall' means?"

"This Malachi person, whoever he is, seems to know exactly what we're looking for and is providing clues to help us," Jonathan noted. "Let's just assume the last part of the note is a simple instruction like the first part. 'Find all your answers at the wall.' What wall? We know there are or were at least three famous walls in the world; The Wall of China; the Berlin Wall which has been taken down and the Western Wall in Jerusalem. Of course, the Wall of China has no relation to any of the events we have been studying in the Middle East. So, the wall in the note must refer to the Western Wall in Jerusalem."

"Does that mean the Doomsday Clock is hidden somewhere around the Western Wall?"

"That's what I would assume right now!"

With a twinkle in her eye, Grace smiled.

"I know that look, Grace, and I know what you're thinking. Okay, I admit you're right on target, and we should book a flight to Israel right away and check out every inch of the Western Wall. For some reason, this Malachi person seems to be leading us to the Doomsday Clock, but there is something I need to do before we leave."

"I called Amy again last night to express my sorrow at Steven's death and asked if she had any information about what caused the accident. All she knew was he died instantly in a one-car crash in Washington D.C. while driving to a hotel after work one night. During the conversation, I noticed a bit of guarded apprehension in her voice that didn't seem quite natural for her. I believe there is something else going on, and I want to talk to Riley in Washington. If there is more to be learned about Steven's death, Riley will know the complete story. I'll call him in the morning and arrange a meeting as soon as possible somewhere private away from his office. Michelle can make all the arrangements for us to travel to Washington D.C. and then on to Tel Aviv, Israel from the Dulles International Airport."

Later that afternoon, Jonathan called Grace.

"Grace, we have a meeting with Riley at 2:00 P.M tomorrow. I'll pick you up in the morning at 10:00 A.M. in the rental car for the flight to Washington D.C. We can have a quick lunch downtown, visit with Riley, and easily make our 6:00 P.M. departure for Tel Aviv."

After their flight the next morning from Newark to Ronald Reagan National Airport in Arlington, Virginia, just outside of Washington D.C., Jonathan and Grace hailed a taxi and arrived at a Starbucks Coffee Shop, where they had lunch and agreed to meet Riley. Arriving fifteen minutes late, Riley apologized and sat down with Jonathan and Grace on a large sofa in a quiet corner of the shop.

Riley spoke first. "Jonathan, I know you're anxious to learn more about Steven's tragic accident."

"Yes, you know he was my best friend, but there were some red flags popping up in Steven's behavior lately. When I heard about the fatal accident, the first thought I had was that he was caught up in espionage."

"Don't worry, I'll explain everything, but first, I want to thank you and Grace for your help. The information you obtained from the secret nuclear laboratory in Iran has already proven to be invaluable for validating our own intelligence as well as developing a strategy to prevent the Iranians from completing the assembly of a nuclear bomb. I'm also very happy you were successful in obtaining what you were looking for in the tomb of King Cyrus."

"While we're talking about the Iranian laboratory, there is a question that's been nagging me," said Jonathan. "Although we greatly appreciate being rescued safely, how did the QRF know to pick us up at the precise time we arrived outside the facility compound when we didn't even know exactly when we would make our escape or where we would be?"

"That's easy, Jonathan. The Commander of the base in Saudi Arabia called me and said they received a transmission from the encrypted frequency of your satellite phone with the code alerting them that you were in imminent danger. With your precise location and time transmitted from the phone, the QRF immediately launched the helicopter team, and the flawless rescue was executed exactly as planned."

"Yes, Riley, but there is just one catch. We never transmitted a signal to rescue us. As you warned, the phone would not function inside the mountain. So how could the QRF have possibly known when to pick us up?"

"Unfortunately, I don't have the answer to that question. Perhaps the QRF monitored the GPS in your phone and by watching your movements realized that you were in trouble. Anticipating your escape, they launched the rescue team in time to arrive at the clearing outside the fence when you exited the laboratory."

"Maybe that's the way it happened, Riley, but that sounds like a real stretch to me. Okay, never mind. What I really want to hear about is what happened to Steven."

Leaning closer to Jonathan, Riley began in a whispered voice so as not to be overheard. "Several years ago, Steven was involved in the development of updating top-secret encrypted nuclear codes. These codes protect the security of the firing circuits for miniature detonators used in nuclear warheads designed to be deployed by our missiles. Recently, Steven was working undercover with Iranian agents to learn more about their progress on the development of the nuclear bomb."

"Having learned that Steven had access to American detonators for nuclear bombs as well as the associated encrypted codes, the Iranians approached him with the prospect of becoming a multi-millionaire overnight. Evidently, the deal was tempting and seemed worth the risk of the penalty for espionage. Unfortunately, when Steven made the deal to deliver the detonators and codes to the Iranians, he unknowingly sealed his fate."

"I don't understand how top-secret material like detonators for nuclear bombs could be removed from a classified storage area without someone's knowledge," Jonathan stated.

"That's simple, Jonathan. Steven's top-secret clearance gave him complete access to the computer inventory for the codes and detonators. Adjusting the inventory in the computer to account for the detonators he removed was easy. We didn't discover the discrepancy until the routine physical count of detonators was made sometime later."

"We presume that after the hardware was delivered, the Iranians decided to eliminate the only conceivable way the breach of American intelligence could be exposed by eliminating Steven. In that way, no one would ever know they had obtained the detonators and codes necessary to complete the bomb. An Iranian agent in the United States compromised the brake system on Steven's car, causing him to careen off the road on the way home from the office and plunge into the Potomac River. He died in what was reported to be an unfortunate car accident. The cover-up by the Iranians was complete! I'm sorry, Jonathan. I know how much you thought of Steven."

Jonathan struggled to hold back the tears but to no avail.

"Do you have any idea what it's like to lose your best friend only to find out that he was selling secrets to the Iranians?"

"I'm really sorry, Jonathan."

Grace was shocked speechless.

Jonathan regained his composure and shook Riley's hand. "Well, we should be leaving now to catch our flight. Thanks for taking the time to give us the explanation, but I still can't believe it!"

On the way to the airport, Jonathan asked the taxi driver to stop by Riley's office near the coffee shop where they met. He explained to Grace. "The cell phone Riley gave us is still in my briefcase, and I want to return it. Don't worry, we have just enough time to return it, have dinner at the Dulles Airport, and make our flight to Tel Aviv. Please wait in the car, Grace. I will only be a few minutes."

Jonathan made his way to Riley's office and opened the outer office door expecting to be greeted by his cheerful assistant, but there was no one there. Noticing his office door was slightly ajar, he overheard a conversation that almost caused his heart to leap out of his chest!

CHAPTER 23

LEGOS

"**W**ell, Riley, do you think he bought your story?"

"Of course, he bought it, hook, line, and sinker. Jonathan trusts me. I didn't want to lie to him, but with our national security at stake, I had no choice."

Jonathan's heart sunk. *That's Steven's voice, I would know it anywhere. But it can't be. He is…well, he's dead.*

Jonathan quietly and instinctively peered through the opening left by the door slightly ajar and to his amazement there was Steven, very much alive and well, sitting on the sofa having a conversation with Riley.

There is not even a scratch on him.

Unable to contain himself, Jonathan angrily threw open the office door and stood there glaring at both men, struggling with words to speak. For a moment, there was an awkward, hushed silence in the room.

With their discussion abruptly interrupted by the sound of the door slamming against the wall, Riley and Steven were stunned to see Jonathan standing in the doorway. Vacillating between happiness that Steven was alive and anger that he had been deceived, Jonathan burst out shouting in a rage that could be heard down the hall.

"You both have a lot of explaining to do!"

Steven leaped from the sofa and bolted across the room to give Jonathan a manly hug, but Jonathan hastily retreated with his hands outstretched to resist Steven's advance.

"Whoa, Steven, wait just a minute! You have some serious explaining to do."

"Please, Jonathan, close the door and come in and sit down. I promise I can explain everything."

With his hands on Jonathan's shoulders, Riley gently slid him into a chair near the sofa. "Let me begin by saying that what I'm going to tell you is highly classified, and I don't want one word of what I say to leave this room! If the press gets hold of this story, I'll lose my job, and our national intelligence will be compromised. Do we understand each other, Jonathan? Are we perfectly clear?"

Nodding in the affirmative, Jonathan replied, "Of course, I understand Riley, but ..."

"We planned to explain everything to you in due time, but we had to wait until the time was right. Amy was even advised not to give anyone any information regarding Steven's travel plans to Iran."

"Jonathan, we can't thank you and Grace enough for providing the vital intelligence that confirmed the Iranians are in fact assembling a warhead in the underground facility in Pasargadae. We also suspected they were making progress on a missile capable of delivering a warhead to Israel, but we had been unable to confirm they had tested a long-range rocket capable of deploying a warhead to the shores of the United States. Nor were we aware of the development of the EPG, which is definitely a game-changer in our international relations with Iran."

"Now, here is the truth, the whole truth about Steven. We were afraid the Iranians were getting too close, too fast, to completing the development of a nuclear warhead. The one thing the Iranian scientists desperately needed to complete the assembly of a bomb to be deployed by a missile was a reliable miniature detonator. Believing they may be negotiating with the Russians for the hardware, we simply accommodated them by leaking information that one of our undercover agents in Iran had access to American detonators. Iranian scientists knew the firing circuits of the coveted American devices were superior to and more reliable than those developed by Russia and North Korea."

"Steven's position and top-secret security clearance permitted him access to the detonators and the confidential, encrypted codes for the firing circuits. Also, his financial records were modified to indicate he was bankrupt due to large gambling losses and was desperately in need of cash to pay off a mountain of debt. While in Iran working on a covert project, Steven signaled he was willing to sell the critical hardware to the Iranians for the right price. A meeting was arranged with an Iranian agent in Tehran, and the delivery was made for an agreed-upon price payable after testing the functionality of the detonators. With the successful testing of one detonator, the jubilant Iranians arranged a cash payment to Steven a few weeks later. Of course, the cash went to the U.S. Government."

"To ensure there were no further contacts with Steven by the Iranians, we fabricated the car accident and the story of espionage. As far as Iran and the rest of the world know, Steven died in a tragic car crash. A press release was prepared, and we enacted a mock burial for Steven. The entire espionage transaction, as well as Steven's death, had to look authentic to anyone watching, especially the Iranians, who were monitoring our every move. Steven and his family are now enrolled in a government Witness Protection Program for their safety and security."

"Do you mean Steven and Amy and the children will have to move away from all their friends?"

"I'm afraid so, Jonathan, but Steven understood the conditions before agreeing to participate in this critical mission."

"I still don't understand how you could justify giving the enemy the vital components necessary to successfully build a nuclear bomb to be deployed by a missile."

"We didn't, Jonathan. That's the beauty of the strategy behind this mission."

"But you just said..."

"I know what I said, but what the Iranians didn't know was only one of the five devices we gave them was functional. It's common knowledge that before closing the deal, the Iranian scientists would demand that one of the detonators be tested in their laboratory to ensure functionality. However, when one of our detonators is electrically tested live, the device is rendered useless. Anticipating they would only test one device, we just gave them one live detonator. It will be impossible for the scientists to discover the other four devices are non-functional until they are actually deployed by a missile and there is an attempt to detonate the warheads."

"But how…?"

"Listen, each detonator was packed for delivery to the Iranians in a different colored box with a picture of a Lego toy on the box. You see, Steven was posing as an American toy manufacturer on his way to an international Toy Trade Expo in Paris, France as cover for the exchange. Steven met the courier in Tehran and provided him with the devices that he packed with several boxes of the newest children's Lego toys intended for distribution at the convention. After the exchange, Steven continued on to Paris and attended the Expo as part of his cover."

Reaching into his coat pocket, Steven pulled out a couple of small Lego toys. "See, Jonathan, I even took a few Lego toys like these characters to hand out at the Expo. You know Lego toys are very popular among kids all over the world these days. Here, keep one as a reminder of this conversation."

With a perplexed look on his face, Jonathan questioned, "I still don't understand how you could possibly have known with certainty that the Iranian scientist would choose the only authentic detonator for the test? Had they chosen one of the others, your entire plan would have been exposed."

Chuckling quietly, Riley replied, "That's easy, Jonathan."

"We just played on the ego of the Iranians. One of the boxes of detonators had a picture of a Lego model of a rocket, and the other four boxes were pictures of Lego models of American cars, ships, and trucks. The Iranian scientist was so excited that they would now have everything necessary for a reliable rocket mounted nuclear warhead, that he chose the box with the rocket on the cover, the box with the live detonator."

"Well, if you knew the fake detonators would slow the Iranian progress on the bomb, why did we risk our lives to obtain intelligence on their schedule for assembly of the first bomb?"

"Jonathan, Iran may eventually purchase additional detonators from Russia or North Korea. We had to know where their secret laboratory is located and where the warhead is being assembled. Besides, the information you gave us on the EPG project will prove to be invaluable. Remember, this facility has been kept secret from the United Nations and the IAEA inspectors. Undoubtedly, the fake detonators will just set their timeline back until we can find a way to stop them permanently."

"I'll have to say that story sounds like it was taken right off the pages of a James Bond novel."

As if on cue, Jonathan got up and gave Steven a manly hug boasting, "I just couldn't believe you were actually involved in illegal trafficking of top-secret military hardware. I am ecstatic that you were not selling secrets, and I am overjoyed that you are alive and well."

"I appreciate your confidence in me, Jonathan, but this may be the last time we will be able to talk due to changes in my lifestyle required by the Witness Protection Program. However, you will always be my best friend, and we will find a way for you and Grace to catch up with us."

As Jonathan walked toward the door, Riley added, "By the way Jonathan, we had you and Grace under surveillance since you returned from Iran and we know about the attempt on your lives at the airport. For your protection, the story has been leaked to the press that 'Two American university employees returning from an archeological expedition in Iran died in an unfortunate freak explosion in an airport parking lot. The cause of the explosion was later determined to be due to a leaking fuel tank on the car and has been ruled accidental.' We also intercepted a message to Iran from your taxi driver at the airport in which he assured them you were both killed in the explosion. The Iranians will assume you're dead and will not be looking for either of you."

Jonathan was grateful to Riley for his help and his explanation of the cover story for Steven, but his heart was breaking that he may never see his best friend again. With tears in his eyes, Jonathan gave Steven a hug without words and hurried to meet the waiting taxi.

As Jonathan opened the car door and excitedly hopped into the taxi, he leaned over and whispered to Grace, "My conversation with Riley is top-secret, but everything is all right."

Grace gave Jonathan one of those looks that said, "I don't understand what you're saying, but I'm happy if you're happy."

After checking in at the Washington Dulles International Airport and making their way to the security line, Jonathan stopped to read a sign posted at the entrance.

"Look, Grace. The new Life Chip we heard about on television already has a new application. 'Beginning January 1, next year, we are introducing a new program called Easy Fly. The Transportation Security Administration has approved the use of the Life Chip to store your encrypted boarding pass and all flight information including travel preferences. You will no longer need a paper boarding pass or luggage receipts, and you will be able to bypass long security lines as well as customs and immigration lines.' Well, I don't know about having all my confidential information stored on an electronic chip in my hand!"

"I don't know, Jonathan. It will not be long until our entire life history will be stored on the Life Chip, and we will buy and sell everything with a wave of our hand. Doesn't that sound scary?"

"Yes. Anyone in government intelligence will have access to all our personal information and our whereabouts. If desired, they could even dictate what we do and where we go by remotely reprogramming the chip without our knowledge or approval. I don't even want to think about it!"

Following a tiring journey through the long lines for security screening, Jonathan and Grace proceeded to the food court for hamburgers and shakes. After dinner, they walked to their gate and arrived just as passengers were beginning to board the aircraft.

"Grace, you know, after navigating the crowded security lines, I think I may consider being a proponent of the new 'Easy Fly' program."

After almost twelve hours flying non-stop, the Lufthansa flight landed on time at 10:30 A.M. at the Ben Gurion Airport a few miles from Tel Aviv, Israel. After claiming their luggage, Jonathan and Grace proceeded to Passport Control where they were confronted by a young Israeli officer who politely, but firmly, asked to examine their passports. While comparing their photos to their faces, he methodically studied each page of their passports. When he came to the pages with the Iranian stamps, he closed the passports and shouldered his Israeli Tavor automatic weapon.

"Come with me!"

Additional officers were summoned, and Grace and Jonathan were ushered to a private sterile-looking room off to the side of the main lobby. Once the two travelers were seated at a small metal table, the door slammed shut with two armed officers standing nearby. The Officer in Charge sat down across from them with each of their passports open to the page with the Iranian stamp. For what seemed like an eternity, no one spoke a word while the officer thumbed back and forth, scrutinizing the pages of their passports. An almost frightening silence blanketed the room as the Officer in Charge laid the passports down on the table and stared straight into the eyes of Jonathan and then Grace.

CHAPTER 24

THE WESTERN WALL

The Officer in Charge, who took a seat at the table opposite Jonathan and Grace, must have been all of twenty-five years of age but was exceptionally professional. Jonathan was not at all surprised by the interrogation process since Ben Gurion Airport had a reputation for having the strictest and most comprehensive security of any airport in the world. As a result, it was also the safest airport and was a model for other cities throughout the world seeking to improve airport safety and security.

Looking directly into their eyes and watching for any involuntary movement that may signal an untruth, the officer finally broke the deadening silence. He questioned Jonathan first and then Grace.

"Explain to me why you traveled to Iran and describe the specific purpose of your visit to Israel."

While Jonathan articulated the purpose of their expedition to the tomb of Cyrus in Iran, one of the other officers ransacked their luggage and meticulously removed and examined every single item. Repeatedly emphasizing they were American archeologists, Jonathan stated they were visiting Israel to observe the ongoing excavation near the Western Wall. Jonathan showed the officers papers certifying their registration with the Hecht Museum at the University of Haifa, Israel through the International Archeological Association (IAA). After exhaustive questioning, the officers finally seemed satisfied with their story. The Officer in Charge hesitated as if having second thoughts and then pounded a page in each of their passports with his Israeli stamp. The weary travelers were permitted to stuff their disheveled clothing back into their luggage and exit the interrogation room.

Greatly relieved, Jonathan and Grace continued through the Customs portal. Entering the arrival lobby of the airport, they observed a large group of men and women smartly dressed in business attire being escorted by armed military personnel. There was a sense of urgency to their mission as they quickly disappeared behind a set of double closed doors, leaving a trail of anxious reporters frustrated and disappointed.

Puzzled by the unexplained drama in the lobby and still recovering from the mental drain of the exhaustive interrogation, Grace decided they should get coffee from the nearby food court to take on their drive to Jerusalem. After ordering, she asked the attendant, "What's all the excitement about? And who are those people the reporters were following?"

"You haven't heard? It's all right here in the newspapers."

Picking up a copy of the New York Times, Jonathan sat down with Grace at one of the tables for two and spread out the front page.

"Grace, look at these headlines. Here is the reason for all the commotion here at the airport."

"A new encrypted computer software virus has been detected in airport Air Route Traffic Control Centers (ARTCC) and computer-controlled radar systems in London, Paris, Washington D.C., and Tel Aviv airports and is spreading to computers worldwide like wildfire. There seems to be no way to eradicate the virus or safeguard a computer from being infected by it. The deadly new virus, called 'Trojan-Ware,' is designed to mimic components of any computer security system and penetrate the computer's operating programs without detection. Once the virus is released, the owner of the computer system has seven days to meet the monetary demands of 500 million dollars of the monster that created the virus."

"If the demands are not met, the lethal bug will spread throughout all interconnected computer systems in the network and trigger a self-destruct function rendering the entire system inoperable. At the speed the virus is spreading, computers throughout the world could be infected in seventy-two to ninety-six hours. It appears no computer system is immune, and the world will soon be held for ransom by an unknown demented fiend. It's not known if the virus is a result of terrorists or simply a rogue madman."

"Grace, imagine what would happen if the virus was introduced into our military weapons computers. Our country would be helpless against any enemy."

"Could this virus be the global crisis you were talking about that would lead to one man being able to gain control of the world's computers?" Grace asked.

"I don't know, Grace. I guess it's possible. At least we will be able to fly out of Israel before the deadline on the demand is up, if that's any consolation. Who knows what will happen after that? Look, our coffee is ready, let's go!"

After picking up a rental car, they made the hour-long drive to Jerusalem. Exhausted after the long flight, they checked into the Prima Royale Hotel located just a short distance from the Jaffa Gate, one of several original entrances to Old Jerusalem. Although Jonathan was ready to unpack, Grace was much too excited to even think about resting. Desiring to take a walk around Old Jerusalem, Grace convinced Jonathan to go along with her.

"I know you're determined to walk your feet off, and I can't have you wandering around Jerusalem alone, so let's have lunch and find the Jaffa Gate together."

"I love it when you're so concerned about my safety."

After sharing a pizza at a small deli near the hotel, the travelers continued their walk and soon arrived at the majestic Jaffa Gate entrance to Old Jerusalem. Inside the walls of the ancient city, the narrow passages and stone walkways were teeming with the sights and smells of vendors and throngs of people of every nationality.

"You know Jonathan, I feel like we were transported back in time more than 2,000 years when we walked through that gate."

"You're right, and I hope we find what we're looking for here. Let's ask someone for directions to the Western Wall. We'll never find it on our own in this maze of passages."

Grace was impressed by the presence of so many young men and women smartly dressed in Israeli Defense Force military uniforms and carrying automatic weapons. It seemed that all of Israel was on constant high alert as a matter of routine. The visibility of so many military personnel made Grace feel safer, but she was still concerned about missile attacks by terrorists. Multiple rockets had been launched by Hamas into Israel from the Gaza strip just a few days before they arrived.

The travelers threaded their way through the narrow streets and crowded shops alive with the babbling of diverse languages of the throng of people, doing their best to follow the directions they received from a friendly shopkeeper. Eventually, they arrived at a security checkpoint overlooking the plaza where the Western Wall, or Wailing Wall as it's sometimes called, was in sight.

"Look, Jonathan, the Western Wall. I can't wait!"

With his arms out an armed guard barked, "Wait, you must go through the scanner! Take everything out of your pockets."

Everyone entering the area was subject to being searched and was required to pass through an airport-type security scanner portal.

The Western Wall served as the retaining wall for the Temple Mount complex, the site of the ancient Jewish Temple. The temple was destroyed during the Roman Siege of Jerusalem in 70 A.D. when the Jews were scattered across the planet. In 691 A.D., the widely recognized Islamic Shrine called the Dome of the Rock was constructed on the Temple Mount at the site of the ruins of the Jewish Temple.

After passing through security, Jonathan and Grace walked down several flights of steep stone steps leading to the plaza across from the Western Wall.

"You go ahead, Grace. I'm going to wait right here!"

Excited by the stark presence of the great wall cloaked in colorful history, Grace quickly made her way through the crowded plaza and down a ramp to the area of the wall reserved for women to pray. Bowing her head, Grace approached the wall reverently and wrote a prayer on a small scrap of paper as is customary for residents as well as visitors. After delicately folding the paper and wedging it in a crack between stones in the wall, Grace walked back up to the plaza to meet Jonathan.

With a tantalizing twinkle in her eye, Grace said, "Okay, now I'm ready to do a little shopping."

"All right, but only for a little while. You know I'm not much of a shopper, and I'm very tired."

After a strenuous afternoon dragging Jonathan into one small crowded shop after another, Grace said she was ready to head back to the hotel where they could both get some much-needed rest.

"It's about time! We must have gone in every shop in Old Jerusalem."

As they were walking back toward the Jaffa Gate, Grace stopped and pulled on Jonathan's arm. "Look, there is a food court where we can get a falafel. Please, Jonathan, falafels are a favorite Jewish food, and I've always wanted to try one."

"Grace, you know I'm not Jewish, and neither are you. Why do we have to try a falafel?"

"Please, Jonathan, do it for me!"

"Ok, at least we can sit down while we eat."

After finishing off his plate of falafels with an unexpected smile of enjoyment, Jonathan suggested they start back to the hotel, unpack their luggage and rest a while. After a wonderful dinner at the hotel, they walked to a nearby shopping center for ice-cream. Staying up as late as possible would help adjust to the eight-hour time change and the jetlag.

The next morning, Jonathan was up early studying maps and details of the excavation of the Western Wall obtained from the Hecht Museum through the International Archeological Association (IAA). After breakfast, they returned to the Western Wall where they had arranged for a private tour of the excavations. Since they were members of the IAA and were registered with the Hecht Museum, they were given exclusive privileges to examine areas of the excavation that were off-limits to the public. Before entering the tunnel, Jonathan was given a kippah, since it was customary for men to wear a skull cap in the tunnel to show respect for God. They would be walking near the Holy of Holies, where the ancient Jewish Temple was once located.

Entering the tunnel from the plaza, Jonathan and Grace walked along the narrow passage adjacent to the wall. Inching along slowly, they scoured the ancient wall for any clues that might lead them to the location of the Doomsday Clock as the stranger Malachi had suggested. Although there were no clues to be found, they were awestruck by the precision with which the massive stones were placed in the wall.

Jonathan commented, "Look at these huge blocks of stones that were laid without the use of any mortar. The sides are cut so perfectly you can't even put a knife blade in the cracks between the stones."

As they passed the Western Stone, the largest stone in the wall, weighing 570 tons and stretching almost 45 feet long and 10 feet high, they marveled at its enormous size. After meticulously combing the entire Western Wall and inspecting the most recent excavations they found nothing that helped them in their quest for the Doomsday Clock. Greatly disappointed, Jonathan and Grace exited the tunnel on the north side of the Temple mount onto the Via Dolorosa.

As she stepped onto the cobblestone street, Grace smiled. "Jonathan, can you believe this is the very same street that Jesus walked on his way to the cross at Golgotha?"

As he kept walking, Jonathan just shook his head from side to side and mumbled something unintelligible.

Tired and frustrated that they were completely unsuccessful in discovering a single clue at the wall, they decided to eat lunch at the Basti Restaurant in the Jewish Quarter, recommended by the hotel clerk.

Following a wonderful lunch and an amazing lemon drink with mint made famous by the restaurant, Grace and Jonathan returned to the hotel to review their notes and photographs taken during the examination of the wall. After hours reviewing all the results of their investigation and believing they may have missed something, they decided to return to the wall again the next day more determined than ever.

As the morning sun washed over Old Jerusalem and morning prayers from a nearby Muslim minaret broke the silence, Jonathan and Grace finished breakfast and began their trek to the Western Wall with a renewed spirit of excitement and determination. However, after studying every square inch of the subterranean face of the Western Wall for a second time as well as an in-depth study of the unofficial results of the on-going excavations, they emerged from the tunnel completely exhausted and disheartened.

Stepping out into the daylight, Jonathan declared his irritation. "Grace there just doesn't seem to be a single clue here! I can't believe we made this long, expensive trip based on a note from some guy we don't even know named Malachi. We must have been out of our minds to take that note seriously."

"Yes, Jonathan, but remember the first part of the note saved our lives from the explosion at the airport."

"You're right, Grace, but maybe this Malachi character is not even a real person. We've never met him, have we?"

"No, but…"

"Well, maybe he is just a fictitious character conjured up in the mind of the person or thing that is really behind the Doomsday Clock. I can't believe I've been so naïve."

Frustrated and confused, they walked to the plaza and sat down on the stone bench at the bottom of the steps to reflect on the disappointing results of the day.

Grace looked at Jonathan with a puzzling gaze and asked softly, "Well, what do you think we should do?"

"I don't know about you, Grace, but we may as well head home because I think we're at a dead-end with no hope of finding the Doomsday Clock. It looks like it will always remain a mystery."

Looking toward the Western Wall, Grace replied in a soft voice. "I'm going down to the wall to pray again, and I will be back in a few minutes. Please don't move from this spot!"

"Don't worry, Grace, I'll be right here!"

As she walked toward the area of the wall reserved for women, she noticed a man standing in the plaza who appeared to be watching her every move.

That man is dressed in the same traditional black robe and hat, characteristic of Orthodox Jews, as the man in the airport parking lot. I wonder if that's him.

Grace approached the wall thinking, *Maybe he's not even Jewish. Maybe he's a terrorist disguised as a Jewish man, but I know he's watching me!*

After praying, Grace turned around slowly, expecting to see the stranger waiting at the top of the ramp, but he was nowhere in sight. Somewhat relieved, she walked briskly up the ramp to the crowded plaza hoping to spot Jonathan.

She spotted the stranger instead. *Oh no, there he is!*

What does he want with me anyway? I know there have been attacks by Palestinians reported in this area and he has probably singled me out for a tourist robbery or stabbing.

At that moment, the stranger began walking straight toward her.

With Grace's imagination intensified, she broke into a run for her life through the crowded plaza toward the steps where Jonathan was waiting for her. Her only hope was to reach him and safety before the stranger caught up with her. Successfully fighting her way halfway across the plaza through the host of people, Grace stopped for just a moment to catch her breath and look around.

Oh, man, there he is behind me, and he's still coming.

Her legs ached, her mouth was dry as desert sand, and her pulse was racing, but she forced herself to run. As tears flowed from her eyes, she cried out loudly for help, but people just stared at her. Shoving her way through the sea of people, she finally saw Jonathan standing on top of the bench straining to see her. With her heart beating like a bass drum and powerless to run another step, Grace stopped and looked back over her shoulder.

Where is he? Where did he go? Thank goodness, I think he's gone, and I thought he had me for sure.

The stranger could not be seen anywhere, and Grace assumed she had escaped her would-be assailant.

Feeling a rush of relief, she turned around hoping to signal

Jonathan, only to realize she was standing face-to-face with the man she was running from. Paralyzed with fear, she stood frozen as the stranger reached inside his coat pocket. All Grace could think about was how did the man get in front of her? She was so far ahead of him.

She was panic-stricken and wanted desperately to run, but her legs seemed to weigh a thousand pounds. Unable to cry for help, her throat and mouth felt like they were packed with sawdust.

With her mind working overtime, Grace thought, *I knew he was really a Palestinian. What if I'm abducted, carried off to a remote location, and murdered? Jonathan would never know what happened to me. And how could he possibly get along without me?*

Mentally assessing a list of offensive measures that she learned in self-defense classes, Grace evaluated her first move. Unfortunately, while her mind was delivering lifesaving commands, her paralyzed body was unable to carry out any instructions.

Where are all those young military men and women with the big guns when you need them?

As the stranger stepped closer to Grace, he reached out for her hand and pulled something out of his coat pocket. Everything seemed to be moving in slow motion as she broke out in a cold sweat and felt faint.

They say that's what happens right before you die. Oh, where is Jonathan when I need him?

Anticipating the worst, Grace closed her eyes tightly and fell to the ground in the shadow of the stranger. Every muscle in her body tensed anticipating the sharp pangs of a Palestinian blade.

And then, out of one eye, she saw his hand coming at her…

CHAPTER 25

THE GUARDIAN

"Shalom Grace," the stranger spoke in a soft, compassionate voice as he gently took her hand and helped her limp, perspiration-soaked body up from the ground.

"Please take this tissue and wipe your eyes. I've been waiting for you and Jonathan. In fact, I've been waiting a very long time for this moment."

Her eyes popped open. She was not dead or being abducted, and the stranger was not going to stab her with the package of tissue he was offering her. Feeling a strange calming sensation, she was comfortably drawn toward the man in black as if he were an old friend. Wiping tears from her eyes, she asked politely, "Who are you? How do you know our names, and why have you been following us?"

"One question at a time, Grace. Let's just say, I have been keeping an eye on you and Jonathan until the time was right."

At that moment, Jonathan spotted Grace talking to the stranger and rushed to see what was going on.

Noticing Grace's red eyes and clothes soaked with perspiration, Jonathan shouted, "Grace, is this man bothering you? Do you want me to call the police?"

"No, Jonathan, everything is all right; he's a friend."

The stranger's eyes met Jonathan's eyes with a captivating gaze that took his breath away.

"Shalom, Jonathan, my name is Malachi, and I have an appointment with you and Grace."

"You're Malachi? You're the mysterious Malachi?" Jonathan questioned with a lump in his throat. "How do you know my name? I'm sure we've never met, and we don't have an appointment with you."

"Yes, I'm Malachi. I've known you both for a long time although we've never been formally introduced. Jonathan, you may remember the note from me attached to the letter from UNESCO regarding your expedition to Iraq."

"Yes, I remember the note."

"Do you remember the change in your flight plans to Iraq that saved your lives as well as the lives of your team? The American Ambassador to Iraq was also supposed to be on the doomed flight you were scheduled to be flying. In fact, he was the target of the terrorist rocket that brought the plane down. Remember, he boarded your flight at the last second to avoid alerting the terrorist network of his change in plans.

"How did he know about the planned rocket attack on his flight?"

"Let's just say he had a very strong feeling about it. You see, he is also one of my clients."

"Wait a minute, are you calling us your clients?"

"Did you wonder how Grace discovered the clue in the Smithsonian Museum that led you both to the tomb of King Cyrus? Did you think it unusual that no one could determine who activated the QRF that rescued you from the nuclear laboratory in Iran? Do you remember the note on your car in the parking lot at the airport that warned you before the explosion?"

Jonathan and Grace were speechless. Finally, Jonathan choked out the words. "You were responsible for all those things, but how…?"

Without hesitation, Grace snapped out of her trance and, with tears streaming down her face, hugged the man. She thanked him for watching over them and saving their lives on several occasions.

"You've been like a guardian angel to us on this entire mysterious journey, and we didn't even know it, but why are you protecting us. What do you want?"

Interrupting, Jonathan argued, "Don't get me wrong, Malachi. I'm ecstatic that you claim to have kept us safe, but how and why were you providing clues that led us on a wild goose chase all over the Middle East with a dead-end here in Israel? Do you know something about the Doomsday Clock or the power that's behind this apocalyptic device?"

Smiling, the stranger replied softly, "You may think of me as your guardian, and I will explain everything in due time, but for now, your journey is just beginning. I promise your trip to Israel is not a dead end. Now, please come with me."

Standing with his feet firmly planted and with suspicion in his voice, Jonathan declared, "Wait a minute, Malachi! You never said who you are or where you're from or who you work for."

Walking away, Malachi agreed, "You're correct, I didn't."

"Are you with the State Department, the military or CIA? Because I don't want to be involved in any more foreign espionage."

Continuing to walk, Malachi replied, "Let's just say I come from a place far from here and I've come to give you something that money can't buy and death can't take away that will change your future and the future of others forever."

"Can or will change our future?"

"That depends entirely on you, Jonathan."

"What is this going to cost me? I'm sure there is a catch."

"It will not cost you anything, and there is no catch; just come with me, and everything will be much clearer in a little while."

Reluctantly, Jonathan and Grace left the plaza and walked with the stranger for several minutes winding through the crowded streets. Stopping in front of a small shop on the congested Via Dolorosa, Malachi opened the door. With one arm extended toward the open doorway, he motioned for Jonathan and Grace to step inside.

"Please, come in."

Standing outside the door, Jonathan hesitated and whispered to Grace. "We have been at this exact same spot each time we came out of the Western Wall tunnel, and I never saw this shop."

"I didn't see it either. How could we have missed it? Oh well, we went in so many shops maybe we just didn't notice it."

As Grace pulled him in by his shirtsleeve, Jonathan looked at his watch and noticed the time was 11:20 A.M.

"Come on, isn't this what you wanted, answers to all your questions?" said Grace.

"Yes, but what if this is a hoax or a scam? How do we know if he was really watching over us and how could he possibly have changed the course of events anyway?"

"Come on! Let's just see what he wants. He seems sincere, and I believe he is harmless. Besides, if we're not comfortable, we can always leave."

Hesitantly with a quick backward glance, Jonathan entered the shop and noticed there was nothing in the room except two old comfortable-looking reclining chairs.

In a reassuring voice, the stranger spoke softly. "Please, both of you sit down and relax."

Muttering under his breath, Jonathan sat and replied, "I hope this is not one of those scams where they make you watch a presentation to get a gift, and then try to pressure you into buying something expensive you don't need and don't want."

Suddenly, the door closed with a solid thud. Glancing toward the door, Jonathan tried to stand but couldn't move. It was as if some mysterious force was restraining him in the chair.

"This was your idea, Grace. Now I can't move, and we may be trapped in here with a madman. Who knows what he intends to do to us and we're totally helpless. No one even knows we're here."

Looking around the small shop, Grace asked, "Why are there no customers in this shop? The streets are jam-packed with people, and the other shops we passed are crowded, but there is no one in here but us."

"I'm the keeper of this shop, and I only have business with the two of you," Malachi replied. "Grace, I know you and Jonathan made a great discovery in Iraq regarding the Doomsday Clock, and you're still searching for clues that will enable you to locate what you believe is the clock. I'm here to help you in your quest for truth."

Abruptly, Jonathan questioned, "What do you know about the Doomsday Clock?"

"I know you and Grace have many questions about the clock and the imminent end of the world that it promises to initiate. Now please just sit back and try to relax, and I promise all your questions will be answered in due time."

The light in the room began to dim, and suddenly Jonathan and Grace were immersed in complete darkness and a hushed silence.

CHAPTER 26

DNA

"Please, just try to relax, I promise no harm will come to you. You are about to observe actual scenes of the sights and sounds of the Israeli civilization during events that took place more than 2,000 years ago. Now please just watch and listen."

Before Jonathan could ask a question, he and Grace felt a calming effect come over them as if they were being submerged in warm water. As the room slowly brightened, a life-like three-dimensional vision of robust Israeli craftsmen meticulously cutting massive stones for a huge structure appeared in front of them.

"That looks like a high-tech hologram. I can't believe my eyes," Jonathan said.

"Please, Jonathan, be still, watch and listen," said Grace.

Incredible life-like images bounded to life and filled the room with all the sights, sounds, and smells of ancient Jerusalem. Watching in awe, Jonathan and Grace witnessed twenty years fast-forward like the wind as the backbreaking construction of the magnificent temple of King Solomon was completed in all its beauty on the temple mount of Jerusalem in 960 B.C.

Malachi narrated the vision. "It wasn't long after the new temple of God became the centerpiece of worship that the people of Israel drifted from God and embraced the idol worship of their pagan neighbors. Because of their disobedience, God used the powerful Assyrians to attack Israel as a warning of future judgment if they did not repent and worship only Him.

"Following a brief period of repentance, the fire of revival in Israel cooled. Once again, the people retreated from God. By the way, Jonathan, the heinous terrorist attack on the United States on 9/11 was a similar warning for America to repent."

"What do you mean, 9/11 was a warning?" Jonathan asked.

"Do you remember the days that followed 9/11? Churches were packed on Sundays and sometimes during the week, at least for a few months. Even politicians prayed openly and sang praises to God on the steps of the Capitol Building in Washington. It seemed that the surprise attack and the destruction of property and death of almost 3,000 innocent people by terrorists sounded the alarm for Americans to stop the spiritual downward spiral and return the nation to God.

"Unfortunately, the flames of repentance ignited by destruction and death quickly grew cold and faded from memory. The concrete and steel rubble where the twin towers of the World Trade Center once stood in New York City was cleared away, and a new, taller, stronger Freedom Tower was constructed in their place. Americans have continued to blatantly reject God since 9/11 and are following in the footsteps of the disobedient Israelites. You might say both nations have the same DNA.

"God was very patient with the Israelites because he loved His chosen people, but they continued to mock His prophets, ignore their message, and worship pagan gods. As a result, the enemies of Israel were used by God to inflict more forceful warnings."

"In 606 B.C., King Nebuchadnezzar II of Babylon laid siege to Jerusalem and carried many of the bright young boys into captivity in Babylon. In fact, one of the young boys taken captive from Jerusalem during this siege grew up to be the young Israelite slave you read about in the manuscripts of King Cyrus. His name was Daniel, and I will have much more to say about him and his conversation with a strange visitor to Earth later."

"You know about that conversation between the Israelite and the strange visitor from another world?"

Malachi ignored the question. "In 605 B.C., the siege of Jerusalem by King Nebuchadnezzar II continued. More than 10,000 people were carried to Babylon in captivity for seventy years."

The images raced forward in time.

"Israel continued a path of flagrant disobedience to God for many years following intermittent, short periods of repentance, but after countless warnings and years of rebellion, Israel arrived at a tipping point. Locked in the crosshairs of God's judgment with no hope of escape, the prophet Jeremiah articulated the main points of Israel's guilt."

"The Israelites mocked the prophets of God and their message as they pleaded with them repeatedly to repent and return the nation to God."

"Ignoring the principles God had put in place for them to live by, the Israelites chose to adhere to the evil code of their heathen neighbors. Even the priests polluted the altars with their defiance of God's laws and became an abomination to Him."

"The Israelites abused God's prophets and the laws they represented. The final straw was King Jehoiakim burning the scrolls with the written warning of the prophet Jeremiah as he begged the people of Israel to repent."

"As a result, God used Nebuchadnezzar II as His servant to accomplish the destruction of Jerusalem, the murder of thousands of people, and the burning of the temple in 586 B.C."

Shrinking down in their chairs, Jonathan and Grace were riveted to the deadly scenes of destruction unfolding before their eyes. Entire families were murdered right in front of their eyes. Sobbing uncontrollably, Grace watched the walls of Jerusalem crumble, the temple and its contents plundered and burned, and thousands of men, women, and even children slaughtered by the razor-sharp swords of the Babylonian soldiers. Searing heat and thick, pungent smoke of fires burning caused the time travelers to sweat profusely and gasp for air.

At that moment, a soldier raised his blood-drenched sword above the head of an innocent child while her hysterical parents were forced to watch. They pleaded for mercy, but to no avail.

"Please, Malachi can't you do something to save that child, that innocent little girl?" Grace begged.

"Remember, you're watching those things that have already taken place. There is nothing you can do to save these people."

Unable to watch any longer, Grace and Jonathan turned away as the callous soldier's blade found its mark, but they couldn't block out the screams of the terrified parents witnessing the heartless, cold-blooded execution of their innocent daughter. In less than a heartbeat, the screaming stopped, and the sword-slashed bodies of the mother and father lay beside the lifeless corpse of their little girl in a pool of blood.

With the merciless scenes of murder burned in his brain, Jonathan shouted angrily. "Why didn't the Israelites just do what they were told? They were warned so many times."

Malachi walked slowly to Jonathan, put his hands on the arms of his chair, and looked straight into his eyes.

"I hope you will remember what you just said, Jonathan!"

CHAPTER 27

THE TIME MACHINE

A few heart-breaking minutes later, the images of smoke and fire faded, and the stench of death subsided. The cries for help from the suffering Israelites grew faint and became deathly silent as the images blurred and evaporated. As they struggled to recover from their mind-bending journey over hundreds of years of incredible, gut-wrenching Israeli history, Grace and Jonathan were bathed in an atmosphere of soothing, cool, blue vapor that chased the darkness from the room and quelled their trembling bodies.

"Malachi, did you hypnotize us?" Jonathan asked. "I feel like we've been traveling in a time machine."

"It's not important, Jonathan, how you visualized the past; just pay close attention as we prepare to embark on a journey through the portals of time to the future."

Leaning close to Jonathan, Malachi whispered, "Only you will remember everything you see and hear today, although later it will seem like a dream, a very real dream.

"As you begin the voyage to the future, keep in mind that America, the lighthouse of Christianity for the world, has passed the same tipping point that Israel did just prior to the destruction of Jerusalem in 586 B.C."

"What are you saying? Is God going to destroy America for

rejecting God? People in the world have done much worse things. What about Hitler and his attempted genocide to exterminate the Jews?"

"Let's focus on America, which has been blessed by God beyond belief but has refused to return to the fundamentals of God's laws on which the nation was founded. Foreign religions that worship false gods have been invited to corrupt your beliefs, your education, your politics, and even your judicial system, in the name of religious tolerance and freedom of speech. As a result, your nation has shunned the Bible and mocked God's Word. Rather than defending the one true God on which your nation was founded, you apologize for offending those of other religions and cults, even those who seek to kill you. Marriage and the family are no longer sacred, with same-sex marriages embraced by many people, ignored by the majority, and legalized by the Supreme Court in 2015."

"Millions, even billions of dollars are spent each year to protect certain species of turtles, birds, and even insects in the environment. Sadly, there is no remorse for the more than fifty million innocent unborn babies murdered since the passage of the landmark Roe vs. Wade Supreme Court decision in 1973. Even late-term abortions are performed with the blessing, encouragement, and even the liberal funding of the federal government. In 2015, after learning the federal government-funded Planned Parenthood organization was allegedly selling body parts of aborted babies, a bill was proposed in the Senate to defund the organization." "Regrettably, the Senate with a Republican majority could not even garner the votes to bring the bill up for a vote. In 2019, New York Governor Andrew Cuomo was successful in passing a late-term abortion law making abortion legal up to and even after birth in some cases."

"The hallowed beliefs of religious organizations and churches are routinely pushed aside for the sake of political legislation and a platform to acquire votes in the next election. The thunderous cries of a few have resulted in banning students from wearing crosses, prohibiting prayers at school athletic events, and even removing crosses along public highways that memorialize the deaths of those who died in our nation, as well as those who died for our nation."

"Therefore, it's with a heavy heart that I inform you that if the deterioration of America's spiritual condition continues, God's judgment will be imminent. Jonathan, when you and Grace found the scrolls with the conversation between King Cyrus and the young Israelite, you were reading about the timing of God's ultimate judgment, the supernatural apocalypse that will destroy the world as we know it. The timing for the apocalypse that you call a Doomsday Clock has been idle for more than 2,000 years while God waits patiently for mankind to repent and return to Him."

"Okay, but is there anything that can be done to disable the Doomsday Clock?" Jonathan asked.

Ignoring Jonathan, Malachi continued. "I know you're both very curious about the clock and what the end of the world will be like, so I'm going to let you experience God's judgment, known as the Tribulation, in its full life-like seven-year-long entirety during the next few minutes.

"Once the clock starts ticking again, the countdown for the last seven years of the world's existence will be set in motion, and the clock cannot be disabled or slowed down. Now brace yourselves! You're about to observe supernatural events that will surpass anything you've ever imagined or experienced even in the most bizarre, shocking blockbuster science fiction movies. Remember, everything you will see is real, and will take place someday!"

CHAPTER 28

THE LAST LETTER

"The supernatural invasion of planet Earth you're about to experience will not be an assault by aliens from Mars or visitors from another planet in deep space, but by the awesome power of Holy God, the only true God."

"So, you're telling me that God is going to destroy the world and everyone in it, the world that Christians believe He created?" Jonathan asked. "Are you kidding me? Are you saying God is in control of the Doomsday Clock? Then why did God give the clock to that young Israelite and what did he do with it?"

"Please, Jonathan, no more questions right now. By the way, you were exceptionally perceptive to observe that the Doomsday Clock couldn't possibly be activated before Israel became a nation again in 1948. Of course, even then, many of the other elements of Biblical prophecy necessary to start the clock ticking again were not in place. Today, everything is ready for the end of the world to begin. We are just waiting on the signal from God. In fact, that's why it was critical to help you find your way here today."

"Everything you're saying is so far-fetched. How can I be sure any of this story about the future has a shred of truth to it?"

"Biblical prophecy, Jonathan, is the truth!"

"Okay, but it's difficult, without seeing some concrete evidence, for me to believe that the entire world could be destroyed by anyone."

"Jonathan, I know you're a very intelligent man, but think about this question for a moment! How much of all the information on every subject in all the books in all the libraries in the world do you think you know?"

"Well, uh…maybe two percent, no, maybe one percent at the most."

"Good. Then, do you think it's possible that the prophecy you're about to witness could be in the ninety-nine percent of the world's information that you don't know?"

"Well, when you put it like that, I guess anything is possible!"

Smiling, Malachi continued. "During the last few minutes, you witnessed some of the significant life-changing events of Israel's past. Now you will experience what it will be like on Earth during the seven terrorizing, excruciatingly painful years of the apocalypse called the Tribulation. Although you can't prevent the events that you will experience from taking place, you can avoid destruction for yourself as well as others, and you may even be able to delay the ultimate judgment of God for a season. We will have time to talk about this in more detail later."

Before Jonathan could ask another question, darkness chased the light from the room, and an image of a television newscast already in progress leaped to life in front of them. The journalist at the CBN news desk announced that the United States Congress was debating the President's recommendation for America to become a member of the newly created New World Union. As the vision seemed to fast-forward in time, the images blurred for a few moments and then sharpened again as time advanced to a bright sunny day in Rome several months in the future.

"Jonathan, remember we saw the news bulletin announcing the United States joined the New World Union," Grace said.

"Shh, please be quiet," scolded Malachi.

All cameras were focused on the most extravagant processional the world has ever witnessed as the news commentator described the event:

"Arriving on the scene riding a magnificent high-stepping white Lipizzaner Austrian stallion is the man who will soon be inaugurated as the first President of the New World Union, Carpathia Romulus. Flanked on each side of the president-elect is a brigade of highly decorated, colorfully dressed military dignitaries on horseback with sabers gleaming in the sunlight. Following the military unit is a motorcade of black limousines carrying celebrities and heads of state from the four corners of the world. Police and military personnel providing security for the new monarch are visible along the entire route of the procession as it makes its way down the streets of Rome to St. Peter's Square and the Vatican. Crowds of cheering spectators line the streets of the procession and strain to get a glimpse of their new messiah as his splendid steed gracefully prances by."

Listening and watching the pomp and circumstance, it was soon clear to Grace and Jonathan that the entire world embraced this new politician, who seemed to appear from out of nowhere.

Crowds in St. Peter's Square chanted, "Long live Carpathia Romulus," as the procession entered the square.

Pointing at the young politician, Grace cried out, "Is that man the anti-Christ?"

"Yes, Grace," Malachi answered. "He is the demonic politician better known as the anti-Christ who will soon take control of the world."

"Jonathan, did you hear that? Carpathia Romulus is the man we saw on the evening news last week who is being considered for the Presidency of the newly formed New World Union."

"You're right, Grace. It looks like the future is closer than we thought, although the inauguration hasn't taken place in our time."

"Malachi, what do you mean he will control the world?" Grace asked.

"Grace, the anti-Christ has a clever plan to take control of the world and those who reside in it. One of his demonic accomplices will introduce a rogue computer virus that will quickly spread to every computer system in the world. If exorbitant demands for money and power are not met in a timely manner, the computer system will self-destruct. With the world in turmoil, the same demonic accomplice will secretly develop and market a security software system almost overnight that will instantly disable and destroy the deadly virus in any infected computer system. The world will appear to be safe from the lethal menace. Unknown to owners of the computer systems, the new software, once installed, will contain an undetectable encrypted algorithm that will render complete control of the entire computer system to the anti-Christ. On his command, he will gain control of all financial transactions and the movement of all goods and services worldwide. Eventually, people everywhere will willingly hand over the ownership of America and the world and even their souls to him."

"Wow, what a scheme!" Grace responded.

"Yes, but hold on, there is more to come."

As the festivities in the St. Peter's Square following the inauguration of the president concluded, the images blurred again and time accelerated to a crowded conference room in Independence Hall in Tel Aviv, Israel. Cameras flashed, and television reporters scrambled to secure the coveted positions near the table where the dignitaries were seated.

The journalist covering the story for CBN News in Israel announced, "The newly installed President of the New World Union just completed negotiation of a seven-year peace treaty with the Prime Minister of Israel and is seated with him here in Independence Hall."

"Look, Jonathan, that's the anti-Christ seated next to the Prime Minister of Israel."

Excited, Jonathan whispered to Grace, "If I can make out the date on the Israeli newspaper on the table, we'll know exactly when this treaty is going to be signed in our own time."

Jonathan struggled to move closer to the table. "I can almost make it out…the year is two thousand…I just need to get a little closer."

Just as Jonathan was close enough to clearly read the entire date, a strange force pulled him back into his chair as though he was attached to a powerful bungee cord.

Malachi interrupted, "Jonathan, remember you can't do anything but watch, and you will not be permitted to see the date on the newspaper. We'll talk later about what you can do."

At that very moment, the anti-Christ inked the last letter of his signature on the treaty with Israel, and the meeting was abruptly interrupted by a high-pitched siren-like noise. The sound shook the historical structure and sent the journalists and crowd of spectators stampeding madly for cover as the dignitaries were whisked out of the building by security.

Everyone in the crowd was screaming, "We're under attack."

The next moment, the vision shifted to the streets of Manhattan in New York City. It looked like 9/11 all over again, but the devastation and chaos were much worse.

"Another terrorist attack on America," Jonathan shouted, "I knew this was going to happen!"

The scene in the vision rapidly shifted again to a newscast in progress where multiple plane crashes were reported at La Guardia and Newark Liberty Airport. There was an accident of some kind on almost every street corner in New York City, and clothing was scattered everywhere, sailing wildly through the air like kites pulled loose from children's hands by the gusting wind. Subways and trains were speeding out of control. Everyone was freaking out and screaming hysterically about missing men, women, and children.

"I can't believe it, Grace! This looks like the beginning of World War III."

It was soon apparent from the newscasts that other large cities around the world were experiencing similar chaos. There was world-wide pandemonium with reports of millions of men, women, and children of all ages, races, and occupations who suddenly went missing with no apparent connection between them.

A television newscast flashed pictures of an empty elementary school classroom with children's clothes laying in the seats of the desks as if they just stepped out of them and walked away. In fact, there was not a young child to be found anywhere in the world. Husbands were hysterically searching for their wives, wives were looking for their husbands, and parents were hunting for their children. Some commentators attributed the chaos to an invasion of aliens from outer space harvesting humans for food with plans to take over our world.

Jonathan blurted out loud. "Wait a minute, this is not a terrorist attack, is it, Malachi?"

"No, Jonathan. It's the beginning of the end of your world."

"You said my world, Malachi?" Why did you say my world?"

"Never mind. We will talk about that later."

"Now I think I know what's happening," Grace sobbed. "This time of world chaos is what my pastor called the Rapture of Christians prior to the beginning of the Tribulation. He talked about it one time in church but never took the time to really explain it because most of the congregation didn't want to hear it. It all sounded so scary and unbelievable, like something out of a sci-fi movie. People were more interested in sermons that were positive and made them feel good."

"You're so right, Grace. God will not allow his own children to be harmed by the incredible destruction and suffering of the Tribulation that is coming. Therefore, God will take all the children and the Christians to heaven in a supernatural act called the Rapture before the apocalyptic destruction begins. The departure to heaven will be announced by a piercing sound like you heard after the signing of the seven-year peace treaty in Israel."

"Malachi, are you saying the only way to escape the Tribulation is to be a Christian?" Jonathan asked.

"Exactly, Jonathan."

"What does it mean to be a Christian? Oh, I know, you'll tell me later."

"Just pay attention to the vision, and we'll talk later about what you must do to save yourself as well as others."

Grace noticed Jonathan had his head buried in his lap with his hands clasped over the back of his neck. "Are you all right, Jonathan?"

"I think so." Jonathan looked up. "I'm just trying to digest everything." He turned to Malachi. "Since this hasn't really happened in our time yet, why can't you tell us where the Doomsday Clock is located and give us the key to disarm it?"

"Sit tight, Jonathan, for just a little longer and I will answer all your questions…"

"I know, I know, you will answer all my questions later."

"That's correct, Jonathan, now please try to pay attention. The Tribulation has just begun. There is so much more to come!"

Restlessly, Jonathan settled back into his chair just as the scene shifted to Washington, D.C. The President of the United States was conferring with his military advisors and cabinet members in the Situation Room in the bowels of the White House. The vision zoomed in on the faces of men and women staring glassy-eyed at a bank of television monitors.

Wrinkled brows projecting spasms of grief and frozen terror on each face in the room telegraphed the horror of the imminent chain of events without anyone uttering a word.

CHAPTER 29

SILHOUETTES OF DEATH

Captivated by the events that sent shock waves throughout the White House, Jonathan and Grace listened intently to the nation's leaders deliberate strategies. Multiple terrorist attacks were erupting in cities across the nation. With America's relaxed immigration policy, Islamic extremists had begun streaming across the Mexico/United States border while Congress pointlessly debated the rights of illegal immigrants. Crossing the border under cover of migrants fleeing Syria, South and Central America and other countries, the terrorists easily entered the United States under the radar of Immigration and Customs Enforcement (ICE). Marching stealthily across the country undetected by authorities, they activated countless organized sleeper terrorist cells and struck carefully pre-selected targets. With all resources focused on defending the nation, the search for the millions of people who mysteriously vanished earlier was quickly abandoned.

Struggling to get up, Jonathan shouted, "How could this happen? Isn't there something that can be done to stop this madness?"

"Jonathan, please sit down. I told you we'll discuss what can be done later!"

"Why is everything *later*?"

The vision flashed to the newsroom of CBN Nightly News more

than a year later where the spokesman for the White House was reporting on the world chaos:

"Military advisors have informed the President of the United States that there have been unrelenting attacks on America's allies around the world as well as major cities here at home. It seems the entire world is at war with terrorists as well as third world nations armed with nuclear and chemical weapons. The Department of Homeland Security has elevated the security level in the United States to 'SEVERE,' indicating an increased risk of attack from nations armed with nuclear weapons. Almost one-fourth of the population of the Earth has been destroyed by the storms of war."

"There have also been reports that some cities in the United States have suddenly lost radio and television signals for some unexplained reason. Other areas of the nation are in a total blackout having lost their complete electrical grid and communications network. Nonfunctioning radar is causing chaos with both commercial and military aircraft. Scientists have postulated the phenomena may be due to unusually high sunspot activity creating an electromagnetic mist or haze over parts of the Earth. Fortunately, we've had no interruption in communications here in Washington D.C., and NASA scientists anticipate the problem is only temporary."

"Wait a minute! Our broadcast has just been interrupted by an alert from the Pentagon that the military is tracking an intercontinental ballistic missile from the Middle East, possibly Iran, targeting Washington D.C. The air raid siren just sounded, and we've been told the Pentagon has six minutes to launch an interceptor missile to destroy an inbound rocket. We'll continue to keep you updated by broadcasting from our emergency headquarters underground ..."

"What happened?" Grace wondered.

"It looks like they lost all communications, Grace," Jonathan answered. "Remember the Electromagnetic Pulse Generator we discovered in the secret Iranian report?"

"Yes."

"Well, they planned to release the satellite carrying the EPG just prior to launching a rocket with a nuclear warhead. Since Washington lost all communications, it looks like the Iranians were successful, and the attack on America is about to take place exactly as they planned."

"Does that mean the tracking radar used to guide our rockets to destroy the inbound missile will not function?"

"Probably not, Grace. I'm afraid the people in Washington D.C. are doomed in less than six minutes!"

With his face in his hands, Jonathan couldn't hold back the tears. "What am I going to do? I have so many good friends in Washington, and they are all going to die."

"Remember, Jonathan, this is the future, and none of what you're seeing has actually happened or has to happen."

Relieved, Jonathan looked up. "Are you saying that you're going to show us where the Doomsday Clock is and how to disarm it so those people don't have to die?"

There was no answer.

As the chaos in the world progressed, the young President of the New World Union made one television announcement after another from his headquarters in Rome. He continued to assure the world's population he would put an end to this madness and seek out and punish the perpetrators. Meanwhile, as the days and months raced by in the vision, headlines painted a devastatingly graphic picture of nations on the edge of bankruptcy due to soaring prices of goods and services and sagging economies.

A CBN News commentator reported, "Famine and disease are rampant worldwide, and hospitals are unable to care for the multitude of the sick, injured and dying. Even water and food are scarce due to some unexplained extreme increase in air temperatures around the world. Water reservoirs everywhere have dried up, and entire fields of crops have been destroyed by the scorching heat. Every patch of shade is a battleground for armies of sun-blistered people searching for temporary relief from the intense sun."

As the world reeled from the pandemonium that seemed to worsen by the hour, Jonathan and Grace wondered if it could possibly get any worse. And then it happened—an unimaginable weapon of mass destruction took center stage during the onslaught of Earth. As the vision flashed from Los Angeles to New York and from Paris to

London, they watched in horror as one massive flaming asteroid after another streaked across the sky from deep space striking and completely disintegrating entire cities, unmercifully destroying thousands of people.

A newscast from California, where communication had not yet been lost, featured pictures of a horrific radioactive mushroom cloud rising menacingly above Washington D.C., where the military was unable to stop the Iranian nuclear rocket attack.

Fighting to hold back the tears, the journalist reported, "No one was able to escape the deadly Iranian missile strike on the Capitol Building and White House, leaving the entire nation in utter chaos. The Federal Government has been virtually destroyed, and America is now under military rule until further notice."

After a few moments of deadening silence in respect of the loss of so many people in Washington, the journalist announced, "We now bring you a special bulletin from the NASA JPL Laboratories in Pasadena, California, where a NASA scientist will update us on the latest attack on our planet from deep space."

The scientist began his report. "Thank you. As you know, the Earth has been bombarded by deadly flaming asteroids from outer space. NASA has been tracking these space bodies for decades traveling harmlessly in predictable paths. Without warning, many of the asteroids we routinely track abruptly altered their trajectory as if on a signal from a powerful force beyond this planet and barreled toward a precision collision course on Earth with specific targets on every continent. We have no explanation for this astronomical phenomenon, and it seems there is nothing we can do to stop the barrage of projectiles."

As the newscast concluded, the room darkened, and the scene in the vision shifted to a vast field illuminated by the light of a full moon, with only stubble remaining from the recent harvesting of corn. Overcome with grief from witnessing the nuclear attack, Jonathan and Grace watched in awe as a mound of dirt slowly erupted out of the flat, barren field and rose toward the sky growing in height and size every second. It was as if something or someone buried beneath the surface were struggling to get out. Glued to the vision, they witnessed a multitude of hideous-looking beings bursting through the crust of the towering earthen cone as other mounds emerged across the fields.

As the creatures clawed and shoved their way to freedom, clouds of thick black smoke belched into the moonlit sky. It seemed the hideous, demonic-looking creatures would never stop boiling out of the mounds as they spread their bat-like wings and bolted to freedom.

Raising her hand and pointing to the alien beings, Grace trembled. "What are those repulsive-looking creatures, and where did they come from? They look like giant mutated insects, the kind of creatures you only see in science fiction movies."

There was no response.

The air was heavy with screams from the creatures' prey as the repulsive beasts seized their unsuspecting victims without warning and repeatedly stung them with poisonous venom from their scorpion-like tails. Victims begged in vain to die because of the intense, torturous pain. Overcome with the terror of the demonic beings, Jonathan and Grace watched as the scene shifted to the countryside just outside their hometown in New Jersey.

Light from the full moon cast silhouettes of death creeping across the grassy fields while another horde of ghastly creatures more terrifying than the first alien-like beings prowled the open countryside.

With their bulging fly-like eyes scanning the horizon and their erect antennas listening intently for any signs of life, the gruesome creatures spread out and silently stalked their unsuspecting prey in nearby towns. As the light of the morning sun washed over the countryside sparkling with dew, the ghastly creatures, numbering in the millions, moved like a well-organized army leaving a bloody trail of dead and mutilated bodies. Slipping quietly into the quaint town of Princeton, the creatures arrived just as classes began at the university.

"Oh no, there's our hometown and our university," Grace noted. "Look, Jonathan. Students are being yanked out of the classrooms kicking and screaming through the shattered windows and dragged away by those hellish creatures. What are they going to do with them? Malachi, can't you stop them? I can't watch this!"

Glancing in her direction, Malachi said, "Please, Grace, try to remain quiet."

A local news station was on the site covering the horrendous story:

"An enormous group of repugnant beings are roaming the university campus and randomly grabbing humans with razor-sharp claws and murdering them in a manner that no one should have to witness, much less endure. Their agility and speed make it almost impossible for any earthlings to escape their assailants, and the police are helpless. Wait… they have seen me, and they're coming toward…"

With scores of innocent people screaming for their lives in streets where blood was flowing like a river, the scene in the vision shifted again to a newscast in progress from Los Angeles:

"There are reports that strange-looking mounds vomiting thick black smoke with the stench of sulfur are erupting out of the ground all over the world allowing millions of winged alien-like creatures to escape from the bowels of the earth. The beings are ruthlessly murdering people on the spot wherever they find them, and it seems there is no way to kill the beasts or even slow them down. Some scientists believe the creatures arrived in alien spaceships disguised as asteroids that recently crashed on Earth."

"It has been more than three years since the global chaos began with the mysterious vanishing of millions of men, women, and children into thin air. In fact, we still have no answers for their sudden disappearance, and not a single missing person has been found. Scientists speculate that aliens may have left a dying planet in another solar system and arrived here to harvest a food supply and eventually inhabit the Earth."

"We've also been advised that one-third of the world's population that was spared in the recent widespread wars has been murderously exterminated by the terrifying alien creatures. In other words, almost one-half of the entire population of the world has now been eliminated in less than three and one-half years. Dead bodies litter the landscape of the world and are stacked like cordwood everywhere.

Hospitals are helpless to take care of the wounded and the dying, and there is no escape from the overpowering smell of death that permeates the atmosphere."

Suddenly, the air in the room was filled with the rancid smell of sulfur and the pungent stench of death. Without warning, one of the satanic creatures pounced right in front of Grace as if it had singled her out as the next victim. While edging closer, the creature stretched out his wings from one side of the room to the other and with a cold, piercing stare gazed into Grace's eyes. She could almost touch the slimy skin of its body and recoiled from the putrid smell of death on the creature's hot breath. The ghastly being tilted his head slowly from one side and then to the other as he studied her. Pressing hard against the back of the chair, Grace, trying to make herself invisible, pulled her legs up against her stomach as far away as possible from the creature, but with each move she made, the being inched closer.

Fearing for her life, Grace screamed, and Jonathan cried out, "Please Malachi. Do something, I'm begging you to help her!"

With each yell for help, the repulsive creature moved closer to Grace, staring at her with bulging eyes that seemed to burn like hot coals. Then without warning, it lurched toward her, snarling with its mouth open-wide and its deadly razor-sharp claws extended toward her face. Grace closed her eyes and turned her head sharply, avoiding looking straight into the being's fangs dripping with saliva and exposing the bloody remnants of its latest victim oozing from its mouth. Frantically pushing harder against the back of the chair, Grace hoped to escape the inevitable, but it was too late…

CHAPTER 30

RESURRECTION

Feeling the creature's hot breath on her face, Grace grimaced, squeezed her eyes closed, and screamed for help. Suddenly, the creature halted within a whisker of Grace's quivering face muscles as though it jerked against an invisible leash restraining its movement. Frustrated and unable to grasp its prey, the beast pawed angrily at Grace's chair with razor-sharp talons and turned away to join the others on their march for new victims. Stomping away angrily, the monster abruptly hesitated, pulled in its wings and widened its stance as if to plant itself on the spot. Looking back over its shoulder at Grace with a stare cold as ice water there was no mistake that the look on its face was meant to say, "Okay, so I can't have you, but there are so many others out there!"

As the drama of the demons subsided, Jonathan turned to Grace. "Are you all right?"

With fear and trembling, Grace whispered, "Yes, I think I'm okay."

"Look at your chair, the arms are torn to shreds from the creature's claws. Thank God he couldn't reach you!"

"You said 'thank God,' Jonathan!"

Shrugging his shoulders, Jonathan replied, "Grace, that's just an expression."

She smiled and then caught a twinkle in Malachi's eyes.

"I thought this was supposed to be a harmless vision for information purposes, Malachi," said Grace. "You know we could have been killed."

Stepping closer to Grace, who was still shaking in shock from the horrifying encounter, Malachi reassuringly took her hands.

"Don't worry, Grace. The creatures can't harm you, but I wanted to show you and Jonathan in the most realistic way that this is your world during the Tribulation. The vision is real, the creatures are real, and death is real, but you haven't seen anything yet."

"What about these claw marks on my chair? They certainly look real!"

Ignoring the question, Malachi began to narrate the next scene as the vision shifted to a crowded room in the Vatican. "At this point, the Tribulation has been in progress for about three and one-half years. The anti-Christ has played out the role of messiah to reassure and encourage a frightened world with rapidly disintegrating political, economic, and financial factions. Wars, deadly climate changes, supernatural asteroid strikes, and the unexplained invasion of alien-like creatures from Hell have claimed the lives of more than one-half the population of the planet."

"Much of the United States has been destroyed in nuclear attacks along with many of their allies while Israel has been protected by God as prophesied in the Bible. Rome has been established as the capital of the New World Union by the anti-Christ where he is making his third State of the World address today. Let's join the press conference in Rome that's just about to get underway."

The Press Secretary of the New World Union stepped to the microphone. "Good morning, ladies and gentlemen. During today's press conference, the President of the New World Union will discuss the State of the World and his plans to continue restoring order and improve worldwide economic conditions. This historical room, located in the Palace of Justice in Vatican City, was chosen to showcase his promise of a world where peace triumphs over evil. The center stage where the president will speak is flanked by ten life-size sculptured statues of valiant peacemakers of the past including a bronze statue of David with the head of Goliath at his feet and Goliath's sword in his hand."

With arms outstretched towards the president the press secretary announces, "Ladies and gentlemen, please welcome President Carpathia Romulus, President of the New World Union, the messiah and savior of planet Earth!"

Pompously sauntering toward the podium, the anti-Christ grinned impertinently as if he owned the world while the audience saturated the room with more than three solid minutes of a boisterous standing ovation. The young statesman approached the microphone with an assertive look of arrogance and supremacy. What happened next would stun the world and shake the foundations of political circles and financial markets everywhere.

Unexpectedly, a reporter sitting in the front row leaped from his chair as if on cue and pulled the sword of David loose from the statue. Operatives within the Vatican had previously modified the bronze sword on the statue of David so that it could be easily removed by the assassin and used in the attack on the president's life.

In one swift motion, he vaulted onto the stage and lunged at the president, slashing his head before the security personnel could draw their weapons. Slumping helplessly to the floor, the young world leader began bleeding profusely from a deep gash in his head without ever uttering a sound. Chaos erupted, and the president, surrounded by armed guards, was rushed backstage where doctors and other emergency personnel sprang into action.

Believing their own lives may be threatened by the attacker, the attendees in the audience bolted from the room. Only the journalists remained behind with the television techs continuing to broadcast the commotion.

Sprinting down an aisle and stumbling while attempting to leap over a row of chairs in his escape, the assailant fell to the floor from several gunshots fired by nearby guards.

After more than twenty minutes, the attending physician approached the microphone as if it were a cobra poised to strike. Hesitating, with tears in his eyes, he began to speak as his voice cracked with grief. "With much sadness, I must announce to you and to the world that our president has been pronounced dead from a massive head wound."

You could literally hear the oxygen being sucked out of the room as those remaining gasped in one accord.

Behind the stage with the deceased president, the press secretary thought, *It's not possible! Our messiah can't be dead. He was our only answer to the chaos in the world.*

After a barrage of questions from reporters and journalists, the physician urged all those remaining to leave at once. Muttering beneath their breath, the crowd shuffled out slowly in a state of shock and disbelief.

As the reality of the president's death soaked in, world leaders of the newly created New World Union met in an emergency session to discuss what action should be taken and who should fill the vacancy as acting president. Almost immediately, elaborate funeral plans were formulated to properly mourn and honor the death of the great statesman. To give the world time to grieve the loss of their messiah, they decided that the chief executive of the world should lie in state in St. Peter's Basilica. Three days after the historic murder, reporters and camera crews from around the world, as well as thousands of dignitaries and millions of spectators, poured into Rome to pay their respects to the fallen world leader.

Malachi continued. "Let's listen in to a television journalist who is reporting live in St. Peter's Basilica."

"It's a beautiful sunny Sunday morning here in Vatican City and St. Peter's Square is overflowing with onlookers who have been waiting all night to get inside the Basilica and catch a glimpse of the closed casket containing the fallen young president. Bright sunlight shining through the transparent panels in the dome of this magnificent church is illuminating the solid pearl white casket resting on a golden stand on the stone floor near the four columns of St. Peter's Baldachin. Silence pervades the Basilica except for the soft rhythmic tap, tap, tap of a solitary drummer concealed in the shadows of the ancient church's massive arches. Shuffling slowly around the casket to the steady cadence of the lonely drumbeat, the long lines of mourners and dignitaries from all over the world stretch beyond the towering Egyptian obelisk in St. Peter's Square."

Observing a strange phenomenon developing before his eyes, the journalist moved cautiously closer to the casket and motioned for his camera technician to follow. In a whisper, the journalist reported on what he was witnessing.

"I've just noticed a strange pulsating glow and the sound of a low-frequency drone emanating eerily from the casket where our fallen president lies in state."

"Listen! The drumbeat abruptly stopped as if on cue."

As the light pulsations increased with each throb of his heart, the journalist began nervously backing away.

"Now the light pulsations are closer together in rhythm with the drone, that has become painfully earsplitting, echoing throughout the halls of the church. The casket of our fallen president is radiating like the sun and threatens to explode at any moment. Many people in the crowd are hastily retreating outside to St. Peter's Square in fear. I have no idea what's going on, but I'm moving back with my camera technician as well. Wait a minute…!"

While backing away from the casket, the journalist stopped in his tracks and put one hand out to his side, motioning for the camera technician to stop alongside him.

"The pulsating drone and light show from the casket has suddenly stopped, and there is a frightening silence here in the church. I've never witnessed anything like this in all my years as a journalist."

"What the… a strange, black, vaporous-looking form that resembles the shape of a man just appeared out of thin air in the middle of the Basilica. What is that ghostly thing?"

Motioning vigorously to the camera technician with one hand and pointing toward the middle of the Basilica with the other, the journalist raised his voice. "Quickly, over there, get your camera on whatever that thing is."

As the dark, but transparent vapor began to move toward him, the journalist lowered his voice to a whisper as if he didn't want to be overheard by whatever it was.

"Gliding silently and effortlessly through the church, the

apparition-like form is now hovering directly over the casket! Shifting from one side and then to the other, the thing seems to be studying those in the crowd who are noticeably petrified with fear and unable to move."

At that moment, the vaporous form whirled around and moved within inches of Jonathan and Grace, who were mesmerized watching the lifelike vision. The demonic spirit floated right up to them and stared as if to state their unwelcome presence in the vision of the future. Without hesitation, the form quickly spun back around and abruptly returned to the casket as though it was responding to an urgent call from the corpse inside.

"I can't believe my eyes," cried the journalist, "I just heard a loud whooshing sound, and the apparition, or whatever it is, was just sucked through the solid metal top of the casket."

"Wait! I heard a loud click coming from inside the casket. Now, folks, I know this is impossible, but you're watching it live on television! Somehow the lid of the casket has been unlocked and is opening by itself. Now I can see the body of the dead president inside moving as if he is alive, but he can't be alive! He's dead! He was murdered three days ago, and I was there and witnessed it."

Watching the body writhe and struggle in his prison for the dead for almost a full minute, the reporter almost passed out as did others in the crowd. Pulling himself together, he yanked the camera technician over by the shirt sleeve and urged him to get a closer picture of the dramatic battle for life over death.

"You can see the president's body thrashing around, and it seems to be gaining strength. Believe it or not, I think our fallen messiah is about to get out of this coffin. Yes, now he is climbing over the side onto the floor right before my eyes and is bending over struggling to stand to his feet. This is impossible! Do you believe this, a dead man is being resurrected on live, worldwide television?"

"The fallen world leader shuddered as though electrical energy was coursing throughout his body. While glancing around the chamber with only a sparse crowd of fearless spectators remaining, he is attempting to stand upright."

Taking a few moments to regain his composure, the resurrected leader walked slowly over to Grace and Jonathan and with a triumphant menacing smile stared directly into their eyes. Showcasing the absence of the deadly wound on his head, the president offered proof to the world that he had been miraculously healed.

"Everyone inside the Basilica is rushing out the doors through St. Peter's Square shouting to the heavens."

"He's a god! He was dead and now he's alive. Only a god could do that. Our messiah is alive!"

In the vision that followed the "resurrection" of the anti-Christ, Jonathan and Grace witnessed the most ruthless dictator in the history of the world as he was reinstated in leadership and took the reins of planet Earth. Quickly, the vision shifted from the Vatican to a large auditorium where a man impersonating the anti-Christ was speaking to a huge crowd of people.

As the vision flashed pictures of crowds listening to young political figures in cities around the world, Grace exclaimed, "Look, Jonathan, there are hundreds of young men all over the world that look and sound exactly like the anti-Christ."

"Those men are not human, Grace," Malachi interrupted. "They're robotic reproductions of the anti-Christ powered by the spirit of Satan. They look, speak and act like the anti-Christ, but they're not human."

"Well, what do they do and why are there so many of them?"

"The mission of the anti-Christ during the Tribulation is to steal the souls of humans for all eternity. Going throughout the world, he must explain the 'benefits' of the New World Union, which can only be accessed by accepting a special code or mark that the anti-Christ offers. To obtain his code or mark, people must openly reject the one true God and swear allegiance to the anti-Christ as the only god they will worship. By accepting the mark, people forfeit their soul to Satan for all eternity. With only a few years left before the end of the world, one man cannot possibly reach everyone with that diabolical message. By reproducing the appearance of the anti-Christ in thousands of locations at the same time with lifelike robotic replicas, everyone can be reached with his demonic message in the fleeting few months that remain. No one will even realize they're not talking to the real anti-Christ."

"Is the code you're talking about the number '666' we have all heard so much about in books and movies?"

"Yes Grace, but the mark of the anti-Christ may not actually look like the numbers '666'. Your world will soon require every man, woman, and child to accept an implanted RFID or radio frequency identification device that contains that individual's personal information including a micro-GPS which can be used to determine their exact location at any time of the day or night. Easily programmed, this device can be read by scanners like those used in the grocery store or 'Easy Tag' lanes on your highways. This 'electronic micro-chip 'will be the perfect tool for the anti-Christ to use to ultimately steal the souls of mankind. Although relatively new, this technology has been commercial for some time and is even used in implants in hospitals to store, retrieve, and transmit patient information."

"I believe this RFID implant is the Life Chip we saw introduced by the FDA on television just a few weeks ago," Jonathan explained. "This is incredible and extremely scary, Grace! The future we're witnessing in this vision is already coming to pass in our lifetime."

The scene shifted to a large room of a building in a suburban area where a crowd was watching a video explaining the benefits of the New World Union and narrated by one of the robotic impersonators.

"Every person on Earth will have ninety days to attend a seminar explaining the New Society at one of the New World Union Education Centers like this one. After introducing people to the New Society, each person will be given an opportunity to acknowledge Carpathia Romulus as their one and only god. If they're willing to worship him and accept his 'mark,' their micro-chip will be programmed with his code. With this code, you will be able to buy or sell food, clothes, shelter, schedule transportation, cash checks, etc. Life will be amazing!"

Malachi explained, "With a totally cashless economic society and complete control of the world's computers, it will be possible for the anti-Christ to electronically control the movement of all goods and services and all financial transactions. He will literally control the world and everyone in it. By the way, Jonathan, your world is very close to a cashless, electronic economic society today. In fact, there are some plans to replace the United States dollar with an electronic cryptocurrency like the Bitcoin."

Watching a group of people being taken away who refused to accept the mark, Jonathan asked, "Malachi, where are those people being taken?"

"All who refuse to accept the mark are being led to another location where they will be given a final opportunity to worship the anti-Christ while standing in the shadow of macabre guillotine death machines. In fact, they will be forced to watch as each one who refuses the 'mark' for the last time has their head restrained under the massive razor-sharp blade of one of the machines. On cue from the executioner, the blade will rattle down the tower and decapitate the screaming victim in less than a heartbeat. The body will be quickly removed in preparation for the next subject. No doubt the gruesome execution will send a powerful message to those next in line contemplating their decision to worship the anti-Christ."

"You're saying all those people will be executed just because they won't acknowledge the anti-Christ as god?"

"Yes, and since everyone has a microchip, it will be easy for the satanic army of the anti-Christ to use the GPS in the chip implant to track down, locate, and execute anyone who refuses to attend one of the New Society seminars. Scanners strategically located in all places of business throughout the world will be used to check each person's implanted chip for the programmed Satanic code before any transaction takes place. Anyone found without the code will be arrested and executed."

"For the last three and one-half years, the world will experience massive destruction, and billions of people will suffer and die. Toward the end of the Tribulation, God will give the people remaining in the world one last opportunity for survival. However, even with all the death, disaster, and chaos that the world will experience, many people will still reject God's gift of eternal life."

"Finally, the Tribulation will end in a massive fiery battle we call Armageddon, beginning in the valley of Jezreel in Israel and ending near Jerusalem. In fact, Jesus will return to the exact spot on the Mount of Olives, where He ascended to heaven more than 2,000 years ago, to destroy the remaining armies of the world. Jonathan, the place where Jesus will return is less than a mile from where you're sitting. Just think about it; the one who came to save the world will destroy it because most of the world relentlessly rejected His offer of grace, the gift of eternal life in heaven."

While the mind-blowing images were still spinning in his brain, Jonathan asked, "Is everything I've seen today things that *will* be or things that *may* be?"

"Unfortunately, Jonathan, for most of the population of the world these are the things that *will* be. However, all those who have accepted God's gift of eternal life will be supernaturally removed from the Earth in the Rapture you saw earlier before the apocalypse even begins. Of course, all those who accept Christ during the Tribulation will spend eternity with God in heaven, but they will not be immune from suffering a painful death on earth."

Without thinking, Jonathan blurted out, "That vision of the future scares the pants off me."

"It should!" Malachi responded sternly. "It should, indeed."

As the images of the future faded, Malachi vanished into thin air. Jonathan glanced around and noticed the small empty shop they entered earlier was now crowded with tourists. An elderly gray-bearded man with a weathered, kind face was stooping over his chair looking straight into his eyes. Dressed as an orthodox Jew, he appeared to be the shopkeeper.

"Can I help you?"

"Where am I?"

"You and your friend came into my shop and sat down in these chairs to rest. Perhaps you were just tired from walking so much and fell asleep."

The shopkeeper offered Jonathan and Grace a glass of water and helped them on their way.

As they left the shop, Jonathan asked Grace, "What happened in here? Were we hallucinating or what, and how did that guy called Malachi just vanish?"

Totally confused, they decided to go somewhere for lunch and discuss their harrowing experience. A small food court was just around the corner and seemed like a good place to talk.

"Grace, do you know what time it is?"

"It's about 11:50 A.M. by my watch."

"That's what I thought. I looked at my watch just before we went into that small shop with Malachi and it was 11:20 A.M."

"That means the entire vision of hundreds of years of the past and the seven years of the future was only thirty minutes. That's impossible!"

"Jonathan, I was just thinking. Remember the article in the newspaper at the Tel Aviv Airport describing the strange computer virus infecting computers all over the world? Do you think that virus could be related to the scheme the anti-Christ has to take control of all financial transactions in the world? Could that vision we just saw be coming to life today?"

"I don't know, Grace, but I have to admit those were the most bizarre events I ever saw and heard in my life!"

Emotionally drained, Grace and Jonathan finished their lunch and were getting up when the waiter handed Jonathan a note.

In perfect English, the young Israeli waiter said, "A Jewish man appeared out of nowhere and asked me to give you this note with a map."

"What man? Where is he?"

"I don't know, I don't see him! He just gave me the note, pointed to you, and put five American dollars in the palm of my hand. When I turned to thank him for the tip, he was gone."

The note was written in English, and Jonathan read it to himself, laughing out loud.

"I don't believe this. It must be a joke."

THE EBENEZER STONE

"The note says we're to drive to the ruins of the ancient city of Mizpah in the morning, where Malachi will meet us."

"Mizpah? Where is Mizpah, Jonathan?

"From the map attached to the note, it looks like the ruins of Mizpah are located just outside the city of Tel en-Nasbeh, about eight miles northwest of Jerusalem in the West Bank. The note says there will be a road sign indicating where we're to turn off the main highway, and it will be obvious when we've arrived at our destination. Malachi will explain the significance of a large rock in Mizpah called the Ebenezer Stone and how it relates to our quest for the Doomsday Clock."

"A meeting with Malachi to explain a rock located in the ruins of an ancient city sounds really weird to me, but then what do we have to lose? Maybe the Doomsday Clock is buried near the Ebenezer Stone," Grace said with excitement in her voice.

"You had better get a good night's sleep," Jonathan chuckled. "The last line in the note says, 'You must arrive at the ruins of Mizpah no later than 5:00 A.M.'"

"Arrive at 5 A.M.? It's still dark, and we won't be able to see anything."

"I know, Grace. This Malachi character is certainly a strange bird, but we've come this far, I guess we should humor him and arrive at the site as he requested."

Returning to the hotel, Jonathan checked with the concierge, hoping to obtain additional information regarding directions to Mizpah while Grace continued to her room. Without hesitation, the aging Jewish resident of Jerusalem replied in perfect English while stroking his long, bushy grey beard.

"Archeologists have been excavating for the exact location of that ancient city for years but have had no success. You're wasting your time looking for something that hasn't been found! Besides, I've traveled that road out of Jerusalem many times, and I'm certain there are no road signs that indicate the location of excavations for Mizpah."

After relating his conversation with the concierge to Grace, they reluctantly decided to trust Malachi and look for the ruins of Mizpah in the morning anyway. After a meager breakfast of coffee, rolls, and dates, they left Old Jerusalem and began their journey with guarded excitement. Leaving the soft glow of the city lights in the rearview mirror, they drove for twenty minutes through the stark Israeli landscape cloaked in total darkness. Having no idea where to turn off the main highway to the alleged ruins of Mizpah, Jonathan drove slowly, straining in the darkness to see a road sign as the note indicated. Suddenly the headlights flashed on a large marker that read 'ruins of Mizpah' and sported a large arrow pointing to the turnoff.

"Look, Jonathan, there it is, the marker telling us where to turn just like the note said."

"Yes, but don't you think it's strange that the concierge, who lives here, said there were no markers and no ruins out here?"

"I don't know, Jonathan, maybe it's a new sign. Besides, I'm getting excited about the possibility of finally finding the Doomsday Clock!"

Leaving the highway, they were forced to drive at a snail's pace as the car rattled every bone in their body bouncing into and out of every hole in their pock-marked path. Hanging by a thread of patience, Jonathan said, "This… is not …even… a road, when are we going to get to this …special rock?"

Grace shouted with enthusiasm. "Look, there is a light at the top of that hill. Yes, I see someone waving. Well, it looks as if we've finally arrived at our destination.

Opening the door before the car came to a complete stop, Grace shouted, "Come on, Jonathan! That man by the light must be Malachi motioning for us to come closer."

Walking toward Grace and whispering so as not to be heard, Jonathan said, "Grace, have you noticed that we haven't seen any ruins? I'm tempted to leave right now while we're still able. Who knows what this guy is going to do with us out here in the middle of nowhere in the dark?"

Ignoring Jonathan's plea, Grace hurried ahead and greeted Malachi with a cheery "Good morning," but there was no response.

As if on cue, Malachi said, "Stop where you are, don't come any closer," and began to slowly wave his hands over the small nondescript stone next to him. Sand and dust began to spiral up mysteriously from the ground over the lackluster rock like a west Texas dust devil.

Malachi's movements in the light that seemed to have no visible source created shadows that danced wildly as he appeared to be conducting an invisible orchestra. Without warning, the ground began to shake and groan with a thunderous sound deep under the surface as if something buried alive were struggling to escape.

Backing up a few steps, Jonathan and Grace had no idea what was about to be unleashed from the bowels of the earth.

Shaking violently, the small stone groaned as it began to ascend deliberately out of the ground, shedding thousands of years of soil and remnants of ancient civilizations. Through the thick curtain of dust created by the eruption, Jonathan and Grace watched as the ground belched dirt and rocks into the air. Growing larger with each passing second, the stone seemed to exhibit a life of its own. When the movement ceased, and the bright light from the rock faded to a soft glow, Jonathan and Grace were staring at a massive stone standing ten to twelve feet above the ground and more than twenty feet in diameter.

"Whoa, what an incredible sight! How did you do that?" Jonathan asked.

Ignoring Jonathan, Malachi continued.

"This is the ancient Ebenezer Stone of Israel. Come closer and sit down, and I will explain why you're here today."

After that astounding exhibition, Jonathan and Grace were all ears and quickly took their seats on nearby rocks.

Malachi began a brief dissertation of the history of the stone.

"More than 3,000 years ago in the valley of Ebenezer not far from here, the Israelites, who had been rejecting God and worshiping the idols of their pagan neighbors for some time, were attacked by the Philistines and lost 4,000 men in a devastating defeat. The discouraged Israelite leaders pondered why God allowed such a demoralizing conquest and the loss of so many men in a single battle."

Jonathan interrupted with impatience in his voice, "With all due respect Malachi, what does this old Israelite war story have to do with us and the Doomsday Clock?"

"Shh, please be patient, Jonathan!" Malachi continued. "The Israelite elders rationalized the battle was lost because they didn't have the Ark of the Covenant with them. You see, when Moses led the Israelites out of Egypt, God instructed the Israelites to construct a special box called the Ark of the Covenant. The Ark was to be a Holy sanctuary and the place to offer sacrificial offerings to God. Unfortunately, the Israelites believed God resided in the Ark, and they could carry Him around and call Him out whenever they chose."

"Now the Ark of the Covenant was in the small town of Shiloh about ten miles north of here, which was the ancient capital of Israel for 369 years. Believing the Ark would have guaranteed victory had it been in their possession during the battle, the Israelites immediately retrieved the Holy Ark from Shiloh."

"Similarly, in the United States immediately after 9/11, many people believed if they went to a church or synagogue, and millions did, they could petition God to protect them from their enemies and future attacks. After all, wasn't God supposed to live in the church, waiting for them to come to Him? Many people still don't understand today that it's their personal relationship with God through His Son Jesus Christ that's important, not church membership or even church attendance. God doesn't live in the church or any building any more than He lived in the Ark of the Covenant."

"After retrieving the Ark from Shiloh, the Israelites engaged the Philistines in a second battle, believing that God would surely bless them with a great victory."

Jonathan interrupted, "Well, I guess the Israelites won that battle since they had the Ark, right?"

"Wrong Jonathan! There was absolutely no change in the hearts of the people toward God. They selfishly wanted the Ark in their possession so they would be victorious. Having willingly rejected God and worshiped stone and wooden images of heathen gods for years, the Israelites didn't understand their lives were to reflect the presence of God in their hearts. They had no intention of changing their lifestyle or worship, so it shouldn't be a surprise that they were defeated again, and this time they lost 30,000 men. Worse than the enormous loss of men, the Philistines stole the Ark of the Covenant. After seven months of painful judgment by God for taking the Ark, the Philistines gladly returned the Ark to the Israelites."

Standing up to stretch, Jonathan took Grace by the hand and tried to politely help her up, but she pulled him back down.

"Let's go, Grace. That is an interesting story, but I don't see how it has anything to do with our quest for the Doomsday Clock."

Malachi walked slowly over to Jonathan and spoke softly. "Jonathan, I am just asking you to let me finish. I promise I will tell you about the Doomsday Clock."

Shaking his head in disbelief, Jonathan sat back down.

Malachi continued. "After the second defeat, Samuel told the Israelites, 'If you want God to bless you and protect you and your nation from your enemies. You must;

1. Return to the Lord with all your heart,

2. Put away all the strange gods and

3. Worship only the Lord.'

"With their hearts broken by the words of the prophet, the Israelites admitted they had willfully disobeyed God, and they repented of their disobedience. Symbolically expressing their genuine commitment to God, they poured pitchers of water out on the sun-parched ground. Since water was and still is a precious commodity in Israel, this physical act was a meaningful demonstration of their sacrificial commitment to God. During this very moving experience, Samuel sacrificed a burnt offering to God where the people worshiped God from the heart for the very first time in a long time. While the worship experience was in progress, a bizarre phenomenon took place."

"The ground shook as thousands of mighty Philistine warriors marched up the hillside with swords flashing in the sunlight. The sight of the heavily-armed wave of Philistines covering the hill struck fear in the hearts of the Israelites. Defeated twice and knowing they were no match for the Philistines, Samuel raised his arms to the heavens and cried out for God to protect the repentant nation of Israel."

"In the twinkling of an eye, the once clear-blue skies became black as coal and were ripped apart by herculean winds, creating a blinding dust storm that lobbed deadly rock projectiles throughout the ranks of the approaching enemy. Thunder that sounded like the hoofbeats of a million horse-drawn chariots and meandering fingers of lightning flashing from the heavens sent the frightened Philistines running haphazardly in every direction. In the confusion, most of the terrified Philistines killed each other. Those who were left were confounded and easily slain by the Israelites, who were emboldened by the display of the power of God. For the first time in many years, the Philistines had been overwhelmingly defeated by the Israelites, although everyone knew the victory was due only to the awesome power of God."

"Malachi, did the fact that the people repented of their heathen lifestyle make the difference in the outcome of the battle?" Jonathan asked. "I mean, did God actually destroy the enemy and protect the Israelites from harm because of the change in their hearts and lives?"

"Yes, Jonathan, you're exactly right. I'll talk more about God's amazing grace..."

"I know, later!"

Grace just smiled, thinking that everything she had been telling Jonathan over the years was finally starting to soak in.

Malachi continued. "As a permanent physical reminder of Israel's commitment to repent and serve God, Samuel set a stone memorial in the ground, this stone, that became known as the Ebenezer Stone. Unfortunately, as you witnessed in the vision yesterday, the Israelites' commitment didn't last, and ultimately, Jerusalem was destroyed in 70 A.D. The people were scattered to the uttermost parts of the world, and the nation of Israel ceased to exist."

"Don't you see, Jonathan? Your nation is in the same spiritual spiral to destruction as was Israel, rejecting God and His commandments and worshiping anyone, anything and everything except the one true God. If America doesn't repent of her stubborn disobedience and return to God, history will surely repeat itself."

"History will repeat itself? Are you saying America will be destroyed by her enemies?" Jonathan asked.

There was no answer. As the golden rays of morning sun peaked over a distant hill in the East and daylight diluted the darkness, Jonathan noticed faint, unintelligible letters in Hebrew appearing on the smooth face of the Ebenezer Stone.

Jonathan leaned over and whispered to Grace. "Look, letters are appearing on the stone, but I can't make them out."

With a cracking sound like a whip, a laser-like beam of light penetrated the heavens and began to burn the first letter deep in the stone, removing thousands of years of deposits until the letter was clearly visible. Rock particles and flaming embers shot out of the rock and ascended high into the still, crisp morning air as the beam was skillfully guided from one letter to the next by an unseen power.

When the last letter was visible, Jonathan got up slowly and moved closer to the stone still smoking from the heat. Intrigued by the clear, but unintelligible words branded into the face of the rock, he asked, "What do those words mean, Malachi?"

CHAPTER 32

THE MESSAGE

"The word is Ebenezer, and in Hebrew, Ebenezer means 'God saved us from destruction,'" Grace said softly.

"That's correct, Grace," responded Malachi. "God did save the Israelites because they repented of their worship of idols and solemnly committed their nation to serving God again. America is a land that was chosen by God just like Israel, and I was sent here to offer the United States, the spiritual flagship of the world, one last opportunity to defer the ultimate judgment of God. Your nation, Jonathan, holds the keys to the destiny of the world, but with God's patience running out, Americans must repent of their worship of the idols of the world and commit their lives to serving God without delay."

"You were sent here to save America? Who sent you and where did you come from? Why do you say, 'your nation'?" Jonathan asked.

There was no answer.

Once again, Jonathan questioned Malachi, "What do you mean Americans must repent, repent of what? We don't worship idols."

"Jonathan, all men were born with the desire to live their life as they pleased, giving their time, resources and energy to the worship of the idols of wealth, power, fame, entertainment, possessions, abilities, etc., without consideration for the God who created and loves them. That lifestyle of selfish living is called 'sin,' and the penalty for sin is eternity without God. Thankfully, more than 2,000 years ago, God sent His Only Son, Jesus Christ, to die on a Roman cross and pay the penalty for the sin of all mankind that came after Him. Now, all a person must do is repent and turn away from the sin in their life and accept Jesus Christ in their heart, and the debt for their sin—past, present, and future—is paid in full, forgiven and forgotten forever."

Noticing Jonathan was visibly shaken by what he had to say, Malachi continued. "The message that you must take to America's leaders and to the world is the very simple gospel message of the amazing grace of Jesus. You must warn them of God's judgment if they refuse to repent and return the nation to God."

"You want me to take that message and a warning of judgment to America's leaders? Me? I don't know, Malachi. I'll admit I felt something come over me that I didn't understand when you were talking about what Jesus did for me, but I don't know if I can accept this Jesus. Having worked with numbers and cold hard facts all my life, it's difficult for me to accept such an intangible God. How can I present a message to others that I'm not even sure I believe?"

"That's okay, Jonathan. Take your time. God is patient, although His patience will eventually run out. God has tried to reach people with the gospel of Jesus Christ for centuries, and while many people have accepted Jesus, many more have rejected Him. America is the lighthouse for evangelism, supporting most of the Christian missionaries in the world. If America returns to God, the gospel will spread to the outermost parts of the world like a firestorm. We're talking about a worldwide revival, Jonathan, that will start with you. I know Grace is a Christian and that she has been praying for you for years."

"How do you know that?"

"I don't know how he knows, but it's true, Jonathan," Grace admitted. "I want you to believe in Jesus more than anything in the world."

Moved by what was being said, Jonathon felt an awesome burden in his heart. "Why do you think America's leaders will pay any attention to me and what will convince them that I'm telling the truth? They'll think I'm a religious fanatic."

Smiling, Malachi replied, "I'll talk to you about that later, Jonathan."

"Of course, later, everything is later. But when is later? We're leaving for home tomorrow."

"Go back to your hotel room and get a good night's sleep. I promise I'll see you before you leave Jerusalem."

Walking back to their car, Jonathan stopped and surveyed the landscape. "Well, now that it's daylight, it's obvious."

"What's obvious, Jonathan?" Grace asked.

"There are no ruins of any kind here, and there is no excavation. We're out in the middle of nowhere."

Glancing around, Grace announced, "Did you notice Malachi is gone and we have not seen or heard a car leave? You know, Jonathan, come to think about it, I didn't see another car parked anywhere when we arrived. How did Malachi get here? Everything about him is so mysterious."

As they left the area and turned on to the main highway, Jonathan stopped the car and looked up and down the road.

"Now, what are you doing?"

"I'm going to take a picture of the sign pointing to the non-existent Mizpah that we saw this morning and show it to the concierge. I know he'll be surprised."

"Jonathan, I don't see the sign."

"It was right over there, I think. Maybe it was to the left. Oh well, it was dark then, and now I'm not sure where the sign was. Never mind, let's go, I'm ready for a real breakfast!"

Jonathan and Grace dropped off their bags in their hotel rooms and made some notes about the perplexing early morning meeting with Malachi. After breakfast in the hotel dining room, they went for one last walk in Old Jerusalem. Later that afternoon, they returned to the hotel for an early dinner before packing for the trip home.

Arriving in the dining room a few minutes late, Jonathan sat down at the table, and Grace announced, "Jonathan, I have prayed for years that God would use me in some way to reach many people for Jesus Christ, and I believe this is it."

"Yes, Grace, but remember, I'm supposed to go to the leaders of our nation when we get back to the United States and proclaim this prophecy of warning; not you."

Reaching across the table with tears in her eyes, Grace gently squeezed Jonathan's hands and smiled. "Yes, I know, Jonathan, but I believe I'm the one God sent to share the gospel of Jesus with you, so you could take the message to others. I've just been waiting for the right time."

Jonathan finished his second cup of coffee without looking up. "Well, I don't know Grace. I haven't made any decisions yet."

"I know, but listen to God's still small voice and don't wait too long. Please don't wait until it's too late."

After dinner, Jonathan said goodnight to Grace and returned to his room to finish packing for the early flight to Newark Liberty Airport in the morning. He had so much to think about. His head was spinning, and his heart was moved by the words of Malachi, the vision he experienced, and the concern Grace expressed for his spiritual condition.

As Jonathan was about to get into bed, he had the strangest feeling something or someone was in the room with him. He turned around and…

CHAPTER 33

CHOSEN

There was Malachi standing in his room nose-to-nose with him. "You almost gave me a heart attack! How did you get in here? I know I locked the door."

"It's not important how I entered your room, but I do require a few more minutes of your time before I leave you to complete the mission for which you've been chosen."

"Did you come to tell me about the Doomsday Clock? You never told me where the clock is or who has it."

"Please!" With his right hand extended to Jonathan's shoulder, Malachi gestured for him to take a seat in the chair at the small desk. "I must be honest with you. There is no Doomsday Clock, and there never was a Doomsday Clock."

"What? There is no clock? What about the timing of the events documented in the ancient scrolls that the young Israelite man said was given to him by the stranger from another world? What about the riddle describing the prince of the people who destroyed Jerusalem? He's supposed to negotiate the peace treaty with Israel and start the clock ticking again in the future. We've seen that man, and we know he is real. Who or what is controlling the timeline if there is no timing device?"

"Jonathan, the documentation you and Grace discovered that

describes the things that must come to pass before the end of the world begins is ancient prophecy recorded in the Bible. We're talking about the prophecy of the Tribulation that was revealed to you in the vision you witnessed here in Jerusalem. I guess you could say the prophecy of the timeline is like a clock, and it does certainly describe what will be the doomsday for the world. However, the timing of the events leading to the end of the world is controlled solely by God, not by a clock or any other device or individual."

"Are you saying everything we discovered in the ancient manuscripts is recorded in the Bible that I could have just ordered online?"

"Yes! In fact, everything I showed you in the visions of the past and the future is documented in the Bible."

"Okay, what about the etchings on the wall we found in the tomb of King Nebuchadnezzar II? Those sketches depicted a god from another world handing a scroll and a box emitting lightning bolts to a young man on Earth. How do you explain that?"

"I have to confess I left that clue for you on the wall. I knew your curiosity about the meaning of the pictures would compel you to continue following the trail that eventually led you here!"

"You left that clue? Why did you have us run all over the world following your clues and risk being killed several times? If you had something to say, why didn't you just come out and say it?"

"Jonathan, some people like you have to discover the grace of God for themselves in the only way they can understand and accept it. I knew you would never read the Bible or listen to the gospel of Jesus from a preacher or even from a person you love like your wife or your assistant Grace."

"I never said I loved Grace!"

"And because you blamed God for the death of your family, I knew it would take a journey in the supernatural fueled by your obsession for archeology and your passion for discovering secrets of the past to get your attention. Besides, I was watching over you and Grace every minute of every day. I would never have let anything happen to either of you."

"Well, thank you for that bit of good news, although I'm still not convinced you had anything to do with our safety."

"Jonathan, I know you're not a religious man, and I'm not here to talk you into anything, because someone else could just talk you out of it. I do pray that you will accept the gift of life everlasting offered to you by the amazing grace of Jesus Christ that you have been introduced to during the last two days. Once you accept this gift, no one can take it from you, and you can never lose it. Your life will be changed forever, and you will be assured of spending eternity in heaven with the God who created you and loves you."

"The truth is, Jonathan, I brought you here not only to see your life changed but, hopefully, to change the lives of Americans and people all over the world. You've been chosen to be the messenger to deliver God's last warning and to share the vision you witnessed of God's judgment in the future with the leaders of your great country."

"I understand what you're saying, and I wouldn't want anyone to experience what I saw in the vision of the Tribulation, but why did you choose me to deliver the message? Why not ask one of the many important religious leaders in the world?"

"With your impeccable reputation in many professional fields and the utmost respect that many world leaders have for you, I believe Americans will listen to you and believe you. Besides what's paramount in the messenger is the dramatic transformation of the heart and soul of that person that will make him authentic and believable."

"But I haven't experienced that transformation."

Smiling, Malachi replied, "I know, but you will.

"You must tell your leaders that the only way to escape the cataclysmic events of the Tribulation and the end of the world is to repent of their evil ways and begin the arduous process of returning America to God. Their commitment must be physically demonstrated by erecting their own Ebenezer Stone in a permanent location where millions of people will see it. I believe the best place for the stone is on the National Mall near the White House, the epicenter of legislation. The modern-day Ebenezer Stone will be a symbolic reminder to the current generation and generations to come of America's promise to return the nation to God. Jonathan, your message will be the final warning to America before the judgment of God, but remember you are only accountable for sharing what you have been told, not for the results. You are just the messenger."

Burying his head in his hands, Jonathan pondered the magnitude of his mission. "Are you saying the future of America depends on me?"

"Absolutely not, Jonathan. The future of each individual depends entirely on their own decision to personally accept the gospel of Jesus Christ in their heart. The future of America depends on the nation's decision to repent and return to God."

"Malachi, the warning of the Tribulation sounds so bizarre. If I could only see a sign that proved there was some truth to everything you said that will happen, perhaps I could believe the message and carry it to others."

"I will give you and your leaders a rather spectacular sign from God, but I warn you even a supernatural phenomenon may be rationalized away and only result in dangerous worldly skepticism."

"What kind of sign?"

"You will inform your White House Administration that several months from now, NASA scientists will announce that a massive asteroid the size of a small luxury yacht has departed from the predictable orbit it's been traveling in for centuries and is now on a collision course with Earth. Unable to explain the abrupt change in trajectory, NASA will attribute the altered course to an unknown but powerful magnetic force field due to mammoth solar activity on the sun. Hurtling toward Earth at more than 25,000 miles per hour, the asteroid will strike a moderately populated area on the west coast of America exactly forty-five days after NASA scientists make the public announcement about the impending collision. You will also warn America's leaders that they must not attempt to stop the speeding missile or alter its course, but rather use the time before impact to carry out an orderly evacuation of the target zone so there will be no casualties. This will be the ultimate test of their faith in your message from God."

"But Malachi, why not send the asteroid to a completely unpopulated area if it's just a warning?"

"Jonathan, forty-five days is more than enough time to evacuate the population of the target area even if the nation waits until NASA announces their discovery of the asteroid. I will give you the exact coordinates of the target zone later, which you will deliver in your address to the nation. Once the asteroid is observed to change course toward Earth, NASA will calculate the time and location of the target zone on Earth, which will be precisely what you gave the nation in your message. NASA's announcement will authenticate your warning and validate your message from God."

"Remember, Jonathan, you must give God's message and His warning of judgment to the nation, with your account of the future of planet Earth during the Tribulation, precisely as you witnessed it in your vision."

"Okay, I'll do it, but I don't know if anyone will believe me." Grabbing a pencil and paper off the desk and poised to write, Jonathan asked, "By the way Malachi, where will the asteroid strike?"

Jonathan turned around to see that Malachi had vanished as suddenly as he had appeared.

CHAPTER 34

TROJAN-WARE

"Why didn't he tell me where the asteroid will impact?"

Without hesitation and almost hyperventilating, Jonathan fumbled with the phone and called Grace.

"I know it's late, Grace, but I have to talk to you right now! Meet me in the lobby."

In a few minutes, Jonathan and Grace were comfortably seated on a small sofa in the dimly lit lobby. At one in the morning, the lobby was deserted, so it was private and quiet. Jonathan was sweating profusely and somewhat emotional as he explained to Grace the conversation that he had with Malachi in his hotel room a few moments before. Grace was not surprised at what Jonathan was sharing with her.

"Well," she said. "What are you going to do?"

With heart-pounding, hands trembling and head spinning, Jonathan said, "I told him I would do it, but now I don't know."

Grace smiled with her eyes meeting his. She took both of his hands in hers, leaned close, and whispered. "God wants to save you, Jonathan. Everything you're feeling is God's Holy Spirit calling you. Just pray this simple prayer: *Lord, I believe you sent your only Son Jesus to die for my sins, and I am sorry for rejecting you all these years. Please save me and guide every step I take from this moment on. I invite Jesus into my heart, and I only want to serve, honor, and please you for the rest of my life.* That's all there is to it, Jonathan. Please pray now; don't wait any longer."

Jonathan was silent, but after a few moments, he leaned over close to Grace and, in a fashion totally uncharacteristic of him, affectionately kissed Grace on the cheek. "I'm very close to praying that prayer. I just need a little more time."

With her face blushing and heart beating like a bass drum, Grace instinctively kissed Jonathan. Both sat quietly in a romantic embrace for a few more minutes without speaking a word.

Then Jonathan wiped the tears trickling down her cheeks and released her as if his time in the passionate setting had expired. "It's late, we had better return to our rooms and get ready for our flight home in the morning."

Grace smiled as they walked in silence to the elevator for the next few minutes with hands intertwined. On the way to the room, Grace prayed silently that God would touch Jonathan's heart and save him before it was too late. Unsure of exactly what had happened tonight, she believed Jonathan had seen her for the woman she was for the first time and hoped he would pursue this new relationship with her. Jonathan walked Grace to her room and then returned to his room.

"What is wrong with me? There were so many things I wanted to tell Grace. Why didn't I tell her how I feel about her? We were all alone, and she gave me every opportunity. Why didn't I pray with her and ask Jesus to save me? I was so close, but I just want to be sure of what I'm doing."

After tossing and turning all night, Jonathan met Grace in the lobby early the next morning, and they drove to the Tel Aviv Airport.

While checking their bags, Jonathan questioned the airline agent. "Is the schedule for the flight out of Tel Aviv to Washington Dulles International Airport this morning affected by the Trojan-Ware virus we read about when we arrived?"

"No. Haven't you heard? The story is all over the news this morning. New security software has been developed and installed in ARTCC and computer-controlled radar systems in Tel Aviv and many airports around the world. I understand the new software immediately disables and destroys the Trojan-Ware virus. It's amazing; as soon as the software is installed in all computer systems, the world will be safe, thanks to some incredible, innovative new computer geek in California that no one has ever heard of. It's amazing how he developed the software so quickly."

"Well, thank you, sir. That's one less thing we have to worry about!"

As Jonathan and Grace passed through security and walked toward their gate, Jonathan commented to Grace. "Don't you think it's strange that the software could be developed almost overnight and function perfectly the first time? Are you thinking what I'm thinking?"

"Yes. Could this virus be the same bug that the anti-Christ will use to gain control of the computer systems in the world just like in the vision of the future we saw? Could we be witnessing the future unfolding right before our eyes with the anti-Christ implementing the first phase of his plan to control all financial transactions and the lives of everyone on the planet?"

"I don't know Grace, I really don't know what to think, but all this does seem to be very coincidental and frightening."

"Jonathan, I would like to hear the whole story about that software and its developer. Look, there are several vacant chairs near our gate where we can sit down and watch TV. Maybe we can catch the story on the news."

After several minutes of advertisements, there was a breaking news story on CBN News.

"Look, there it is!"

"Good morning from the CBN News Desk in Washington D.C. The breaking story of the day is the development of the revolutionary computer software called SCIV (Stop Computer Infectious Viruses). The developer of SCIV, Dr. Anthony Romulus, created the amazing encrypted security software almost overnight. Trials have already proven it will disable and destroy the recently discovered Trojan-Ware computer virus within seconds after being downloaded to the infected operating system. We know little about this developer except that he has a brother in British politics and the headquarters for the company is in Rome. Recognized experts in the computer industry in Silicon Valley said they know nothing about the man. In fact, the website for SCIV just appeared the day after the Trojan-Ware was detected."

Whispering, Grace said, "And the man's name is Romulus? He has the same last name as the President of the New World Union? Oh, my gosh, this man is related to the anti-Christ. This virus is all part of his demonic scheme to take over the world's computer systems, and no one suspects anything. We have to tell someone."

"Are you kidding, Grace? People will think we're crazy. We have no proof, just our story of a vision and a strange man we know nothing about."

"Shh, listen," Grace whispered as the journalist continued.

"With no other alternatives available and the clock ticking, the United States Government purchased and installed the software on all infected ARTCC and computer-controlled radar systems at the Ronald Reagan Washington National Airport in Washington D.C. area this morning as well as several military installations. To the government computer geek's amazement, within seconds after the new software was downloaded, the Trojan-Ware virus was totally encapsulated, disabled, and destroyed. With the computer systems returned to normal operation, there appear to be no residual effects of the Trojan-Ware or the SCIV software."

"The new software is already being downloaded on all infected computers around the world, and within another forty-eight to seventy-two hours, every major operating computer system will be armed with SCIV software. The President of the United States is already planning a ceremony at the White House later this week to present Mr. Romulus with the Presidential Medal of Freedom award for his development of the now-famous SCIV."

"Jonathan," said Grace, "if what we saw in the vision is true, no one knows about the undetectable, dormant algorithm that has been implanted in every computer system loaded with the SCIV software. Once the anti-Christ becomes President of the New World Union, he will simply trigger the algorithms and take control of the world's computers and every human implanted with the Life Chip. The anti-Christ will have the power to rule the world."

"I know. The Tribulation is imminent, and the United States is in the crosshairs of destruction if I don't carry out the request of Malachi and warn the White House."

"Exactly, Jonathan!"

"But you know I haven't …"

"I know Jonathan, but don't worry."

After the newscast concluded, Jonathan and Grace boarded their plane without uttering a word. Following a tiring non-stop flight to Newark Liberty Airport in New Jersey, they picked up their luggage and made their way to their rental car in the parking lot.

Chapter 35

May 14th Again

After picking up Harlo at the Canine Hotel, Jonathan dropped Grace off at her apartment. As she was getting out of the car, Jonathan asked sheepishly, "I would like to take you out to dinner after work tomorrow night, Grace. What do you think?"

"Sure, where are we going?"

"What do you think about your favorite Italian restaurant, the Teresa Café near the university?"

Grace and Jonathan had often been to dinner together with business associates, but this was the first time he had asked her to have dinner with him alone. Grace sat back down and moved over close to Jonathan and whispered, "Is this a date? Is this a real date?"

"Let's just call it dinner."

"It's okay if you can't bring yourself to say it's a date, but I know it's really a date."

Excitedly, Grace leaned over and kissed him rather gingerly on the cheek and with a warm tantalizing smile that could charm a snake answered, "Of course I'll go, and I can't wait!"

"Great! I'll see you in the morning at the university, and we'll go to dinner right after work. I'll make the reservation."

Overcome with euphoria by the impromptu invitation to dinner,

Grace closed the car door and skipped up the sidewalk to the front door of her apartment like a schoolgirl.

Arriving home, Jonathan went straight to the bedroom and settled Harlo in her basket. Opting to skip dinner and unpack tomorrow, Jonathan collapsed in bed from exhaustion. Tossing and turning for more than an hour, he couldn't get his mind off the appeal he was compelled to make to the President of the United States regarding the unbelievable story of a rogue asteroid, the message to return the nation to God, and the imminent judgment of God called the Tribulation.

Even the dinner plans with Grace were somewhat disquieting because Jonathan didn't completely understand his feelings for her that had been aroused during the quest for the Doomsday Clock.

As the stately Howard Miller grandfather clock in the living room chimed 3:00 A.M., Jonathan finally drifted off to sleep. It seemed like only a few minutes had passed when he awoke to the morning sunlight washing over the room. Startled that it was already 7:00 A.M., he sat up on the side of the bed and strained to open his eyes as he squinted to adjust to the light. With his head spinning, there was one throbbing question on his mind.

What are they going to do to me when I tell them that a mammoth runaway asteroid is on a collision course with Earth? When asked, NASA will report that all space bodies are in stable trajectories where they have been for thousands of years. People will think I'm out of my mind! What was I thinking when I agreed to deliver this message?

After dressing for work, Jonathan opened the front door to observe a beautiful, cool spring morning and was shocked to see his VW parked right where it was supposed to be.

"Hey, what the…? What's going on? What's my car doing in the driveway? It was destroyed by terrorists in the Newark Airport parking lot when we returned from Iran."

After pinching himself to see if he was dreaming, Jonathan retrieved the morning paper from a nearby bush and glanced at the date.

"What? Now, wait a minute! How can today be… Friday, May

14th. I know for a fact I was in my office on Friday, May 14th when Michelle gave me the package delivered by UNESCO for the trip to Iraq, and that was months ago."

Contemplating the sobering dilemma of the appearance of his car and today's date in the newspaper, Jonathan settled down at the dining room table for breakfast. "Was everything just a dream, a very real dream?"

As he unfolded the paper, the sight of the headlines plastered across the front page caused him to drop his coffee cup, which exploded in a million pieces on the tile floor.

"A bright new young diplomat, named Carpathia Romulus has been appointed to head the New World Union Organization."

"What! Carpathia Romulus? That was the name of the unknown, but bright new star that rocketed to stardom on the political scene in the last few years and was identified as the anti-Christ in the vision of the future we experienced in Jerusalem."

The column under the headline continued: "If confirmed, the new president will be inaugurated in Rome following the most extravagant processional any monarch has ever enjoyed. In a press conference yesterday, the president-elect thanked world leaders for their support and promised to embrace their ideals while improving the quality of life in the world for everyone. He also praised Dr. Anthony Romulus for his research and development that resulted in the SCIV software that destroyed the lethal computer virus, Trojan-Ware. Later this week, the President of the United States will present Dr. Romulus with the Presidential Medal of Freedom Award."

Sinking back in his chair and perspiring profusely with a sick feeling in his gut, Jonathan pushed the breakfast bowl of bran flakes aside.

"I have to get the university!"

CHAPTER 36

DÉJÀ VU

"Good morning, Jonathan, you look like you're going to a fire."

Rushing past Michelle and ignoring her friendly offer of morning joe, Jonathan sprinted down the hall, stopping abruptly in front of his office.

Pushing the door open slowly, he stood in shock. Taking a blind half-step backward, he didn't see Michelle as she rounded the corner.

"Watch where you're going! You almost spilled coffee everywhere! By the way, you walked right past me without saying a word this morning, and now you look like you've seen a ghost. Are you all right?"

"I don't think so!"

"I thought you would be excited about the package from UNESCO I put on your desk this morning. Awarding you such an important assignment, they knew you would want to look it over before you went to your first class. By the way, here is your coffee, thank you very much."

Recoiling from the sight of the package as if it were a snake poised to strike, Jonathan muttered, "This is déjà vu; I don't get it!"

"What do you mean 'déjà vu'? And what don't you get?"

"Did you put this package from UNESCO on my desk?"

"Yes, I just told you I did! FedEx just delivered it this morning. Why?"

"Have ever seen this package before today?"

"No, I just said it was delivered this morning. Are you sure you are all right?"

"This isn't the same package from UNESCO that you put on my desk the last time?"

"There was no last time, Jonathan. I told you I've never seen this package before today. FedEx delivered it this morning."

Sitting down and leaning back in his chair, Jonathan rubbed his head. "How can it be Friday, May 14th again? I must be losing my mind."

"Your mind is fine; just look over the package. UNESCO is expecting your call today. I have work to do, and I'll come back when you're in a better mood."

Removing the plain brown paper wrapping exposed a large manila envelope marked, "Dr. Jonathan Whitfield, for your eyes only." There were maps, instructions, and a letter of invitation with two airline tickets inside, one for him and one for his assistant, Grace.

"I have already seen everything in this package. Wait a minute, I remember the last time there was a small envelope with a folded note from someone named Malachi." Shuffling randomly through the papers, Jonathan confirmed his suspicion. "Of course, there it is!"

Carelessly ripping open the envelope he found a small note folded neatly inside the letter. "Yes! 'Have a safe trip, I'll see you later,' signed Malachi. This is the exact same note I read when I opened the package the first time."

"I can't believe it. It's like I've been in this same time and place before, unwrapping the same package, seeing the same material, and reading the same small note on Friday, May 14th. What does this all mean? Maybe I'm in a time warp or having a nervous breakdown. I have been under a lot of stress lately."

"Wait a minute. What is this?"

While stuffing the contents back into the package, a small piece of paper fell from an envelope addressed to Dr. Jonathan Whitfield. "Don't put it off. Read I Thessalonians 4:16-17"

Stomping down the hall to Michelle's desk with the paper, Jonathan barked, "Who left this note on my desk about one Thessalonians?"

"You don't have to shout, Jonathan. I'm right here, and I have no idea who left the note. No one has been in your office since you left yesterday. And for your information, First Thessalonians is a book in the Bible, although I can't imagine why anyone would leave you a Bible verse."

"This is a Bible verse? I don't even own a Bible."

"Yes, I know, and to my knowledge, you've never read a Bible verse in your entire life, although it would certainly do you some good to read one now and then."

Puzzled, Jonathan made his way to his class and then had an early lunch. Mentally exhausted from the morning's strange events, Jonathan yielded to his sofa's invitation for a nap after calling Michelle to wake him at 2 o'clock in time for his afternoon class.

As requested, Michelle called at precisely 2 o'clock. Stumbling to his desk while shaking off lingering fragments of a deep sleep, Jonathan fumbled to find the phone among the mountain of papers.

"It's 2 o'clock, Jonathan. Time to prepare for your class."

"Ok, Michelle. Thank you. I'm awake, I promise!"

With his eyes threatening to close again, Jonathan staggered back to the sofa, and within minutes he was sawing logs.

Suddenly the annoying sound of his iPhone that he forgot to silence jolted him from a sound sleep. Straining to open his eyes and focusing on the German Wag clock on the wall, Jonathan took a deep breath. "It's exactly 2:30 in the afternoon, and I remember Steven called me in my office at 2:30 P.M. on Friday, May 14th, so that must be Steven."

"Steven, is that you?"

"Why, yes. How did you know?"

"Just curious, Steven, are you calling to invite me and Grace to dinner tomorrow night?"

"Yes, as a matter of fact, I am. What are you, a mind reader?"

"No, it was just a hunch. I haven't seen you and Amy in a while, and I thought it was about time you called, but we will be glad to come."

"Great, see you tomorrow night."

This is weird, I knew Steven was going to call, and I feel like I already know everything that is going to happen tomorrow night, if there is a tomorrow night.

CHAPTER 37

Don't Put It Off

After his last class, Jonathan grabbed his briefcase and walked past Michelle softly stating, "See you Monday, unless it's Friday the 14th again!"

As he started down the steps of the university to the parking lot, Jonathan stopped abruptly, holding his ears.

"Good grief, that must have been a sonic boom from a jet aircraft, but I don't see anything."

Driving out of the university parking lot, Jonathan noticed large crowds gathering everywhere. Abandoned cars in the streets made navigating through the snarled traffic almost impossible. Small groups of people standing on the sidewalks looked like zombies staring mesmerized at the clear blue cloudless sky. A mother was screaming, "My baby is gone," while another woman shouted from her car window, "John was driving a few minutes ago, and he just disappeared from the car. Where is my husband?"

Someone nearby screamed, "Run for your lives! That small plane just cleared the top of the university and is going to crash."

Rushing to the aid of those in the burning single-engine plane, one man freaked out, screaming, "There is no one in this plane."

Jonathan could only conclude that something horrifying had happened. *Perhaps this was a terrorist attack, but how do you explain the missing people and the plane crash with no pilot?*

Several pieces of clothing blew onto the windshield of the car, totally obstructing his view. Stopping to remove the clothes, Jonathan noticed the streets were littered with clothing. Seeing a department store delivery truck overturned in the street, Jonathan concluded the driver had an accident and lost a load of clothes.

With the wind blowing as hard as it is that truck driver will never find all the clothes. Oh well, they'll be a gold mine for the homeless people.

Approaching the Princeton Junction Railway station a few miles from Grace's apartment, Jonathan watched as the 10:33 A.M. New York to Penn Station train flew past the railroad station where it was scheduled to stop. Terrified passengers were hanging out the windows waving their arms, screaming, "Somebody help us, we're all going to die."

That train must have been going over one hundred miles per hour. Something is terribly wrong.

The music on the car radio was interrupted by a news bulletin:

"There have been strange reports of accidents and people mysteriously disappearing all over the country. Some reporters are speculating that planet Earth is experiencing an invasion of aliens from deep space who came to harvest humans because of a dwindling food supply on their own planet."

Jonathan thought *I'd better check on Grace. Michelle said she left early today, so she must be home by now.*

Arriving at Grace's apartment, Jonathan noticed her car was in the driveway, and the front door was unlocked.

Walking through the house, Jonathan called out to Grace in every room, but there was no answer. All the lights were on, the television was on, and there was a tea kettle with water boiling on the range top. Clothes lying on the floor in the kitchen were a clue that something serious had happened, but Grace would never leave clothes on the floor or go off and leave the range top on. Jonathan sat down at the kitchen table with his head in his hands.

"Could that loud noise I heard have been the Rapture Malachi talked about? It would certainly explain the chaos and disappearance of so many people. I can't even believe I'm saying this!"

Jonathan pulled out the note that was left in his office. "Don't put it off! I Thessalonians 4:16-17!"

"Don't put off *what*?"

Grabbing Grace's Bible from the table where she kept it, Jonathan realized this was the first time he had ever opened a Bible and had no idea how to find the verse in question. After searching the table of contents for the page number of the book of First Thessalonians and probing the pages, he found the verse. Clearly, the scripture indicated a *sound like a trumpet* will announce the coming of Jesus Christ to take away all the Christians and children from the Earth before the Tribulation begins.

Now it all makes sense, the clothes everywhere, the accidents, the train out of control and the missing people. This is what Malachi was talking about in the vision in Israel. It has happened just like he said. He told me I would remember everything I saw and heard. The Christians and children have all been taken to heaven and will escape the death and destruction that has begun. All the things I saw in the dream were convincing, but I wanted more time. I needed more proof. Numerous times, Grace tried to warn me when I felt God tugging at my heart. I knew He was calling me, but I put it off. Grace is in heaven now, and I've been left behind.

"What a fool I've been not to accept Jesus Christ when I had time!"

Looking up, Jonathan met the eyes of a familiar person sitting across the table with a reassuring smile. He seemed to have materialized out of thin air.

"Relax, Jonathan. The fact that you're concerned about your spirituality is a sign that it's not too late for you!"

"But the Rapture…Grace is gone…and I've been left behind. I waited too long to accept Jesus."

"I promise you, Jonathan, it's not too late, and you still have time. Why don't you lie down and rest a while? I promise everything will be crystal clear to you when you wake up. You must believe me!"

"What I wouldn't give for just one more opportunity to accept Christ before the Rapture!"

"What would you give, Jonathan?"

"I would give my life to Christ and do anything I could to share the gospel!"

Collapsing on the sofa in Grace's living room, Jonathan was sound asleep in less than a minute.

Suddenly he was awakened by a blinding white light and a booming voice that pierced the silence calling his name.

"Jonathan!"

CHAPTER 38

WARNING

"Wake up, Jonathan. It's after 2 o'clock in the afternoon. You've been sound asleep for almost two hours, and you have a class in an hour."

Desperately trying to identify the source of the voice, Jonathan sat up, squinting at the bright light.

"Michelle, is that you? What are you doing here?"

"I'm sorry about the light, but when I called to wake you up, you sounded drowsy, so I came down to be sure you were awake, and I found you sound asleep."

"Searching for words, Jonathan muttered, "The last thing I remember was resting on the sofa at Grace's apartment."

"You have not been at Grace's apartment; you must have been dreaming. After you reviewed the UNESCO package and had lunch, you fell asleep on the sofa. You've been sawing logs right here in your office for the last two hours."

"You mean I've been dreaming for two hours? I can't believe it! Everything was so real."

"What was real?"

"The trip to Iraq, the secret laboratory in Iran, the Ebenezer Stone in Israel, the computer virus in Tel Aviv, everything!"

"Jonathan, whatever you think you did and wherever you think you went was definitely a dream. I promise you have not left this sofa for the last two hours. But don't worry. Everybody dreams. It's perfectly normal!"

"No, you're wrong, Michelle. This was not a normal dream! I have been given the single biggest opportunity of my life, and I'm not going to blow it! What is the date today?"

"Jonathan, really? It's the same day it was when you came to work this morning. Friday, May 14th, all day long."

"What time is it?"

"It's 2:15 in the afternoon. Why?"

"When Steven Westin calls me at 2:30, tell him I can't talk to him. I have to go."

"How do you know Steven is going to call at exactly 2:30 today, and why don't you want to talk to him? What about your class this afternoon?"

Shuffling through a pile of disheveled papers on his desk, Jonathan handed Grace a folder. "Just give one of the graduate students these notes and have him or her teach the class."

"But, Jonathan, are you going to accept the assignment from UNESCO? Remember, they were hoping to hear from you today, and I know you haven't called them."

"Michelle, I've already accepted the assignment of a lifetime, and I know now that I've wasted too much time in my life. I have some important things to do, and time is running out."

Leaving his briefcase, Jonathan bolted past Michelle, leaving her standing in the doorway.

"Sometimes I really don't know what to think about that man!" Michelle said, returning to her desk.

Rushing down the hall to the outside, Jonathan ran through the parking lot to the spot where his VW was usually parked and to his surprise, there it was. With a sigh of relief, he began his drive home and noticed everything looked normal. There was no chaos, no clothes sailing in the air, no people shouting hysterically, and no plane crashing.

Walking in the front door, Jonathan stood staring toward the kitchen table. "Oh no, it's not you again, the man in the dream. I thought I was finally awake."

"Relax, Jonathan, you're quite awake," said Malachi. "Please have a seat. It's true that everything you experienced in Iraq, Iran, and Israel was a supernatural dream you had during the two hours you were asleep on the sofa in your office today, Friday, May 14th. The truth is everything you witnessed in the dream is true and will come to pass exactly as you experienced it, but I promise you're not dreaming now."

"What about my new-found feelings for Grace in the dream?"

"That relationship is real, Jonathan, if you want it to be real. You will have to express your feelings to her yourself. Remember, you're the only person who actually lived the dream.

"As I told you, I was sent here specifically to get your attention, so I could share the gospel of Jesus Christ with you in the only way you could understand and to give you a critical message from God to deliver to America. The dream and the vision of the past and future you experienced was my way to communicate both the gospel and God's message to you. However, I allowed you to exercise some of your own deep-seated desires and feelings during the dream. One of those feelings was your longing to begin a real relationship with Grace, but down deep in your heart, you were afraid Deborah would not approve. Well, you are now free to express your feelings to Grace, and Deborah will confirm that approval later with a sign you will recognize."

"How do you know about Deborah and what sign are you talking about?"

"Never mind how I know about everything in your life, but you will understand the sign later."

"Well, if I'm not dreaming, are you real?"

"Yes, I'm very real, and you might say I am here to follow up on our conversation in your dream about your need to accept Jesus Christ and your mission to deliver God's warning to America. You have no idea how long Grace has prayed for your salvation. By the way, your wife and son are not lost forever. Once you become a believer, you will be able to spend eternity with them in heaven after you breathe your last breath on earth. I know you miss them, but I promise you will see them again."

Jonathan's heart was pounding. He knew God was speaking to him. "Thank God this is no dream, and it's not too late for me!"

Bowing his head, Jonathan prayed aloud with help from Malachi. He never actually remembered praying to God, although he often cursed Him after his wife and son were killed in that horrible car crash.

"Jesus, I beg you to forgive me for living a selfish life without regard for the sacrifice you made for me. Please come into my heart now, and I promise I will live the rest of my life serving and honoring you in everything I do."

Instantly, Jonathan felt an awesome surge of power within his body. Knowing this was the real thing, he wanted to share what he experienced with Grace first and then with America! Malachi was right! Everything he experienced in the dream and the visions were preparation for his salvation at that very moment. Now he was ready to share the gospel and deliver the warning from God with the leaders of America.

"I feel like a tremendous burden has been lifted from my shoulders. I don't know how I could have been so blind to the truth for all those years."

"Before I go, there is one more thing I must give you," Malachi told him.

"Written on this piece of paper is the exact location of the target zone of the approaching asteroid I described to you in the vision. You're to give the location of the impact zone to your leaders when you deliver the message and insist evacuation of people from the target zone begin immediately to avoid catastrophic destruction. By the way, your government will name the asteroid Genesis, since it's the first cosmic body of this size to threaten the modern civilization of Earth."

"Genesis will impact planet Earth at exactly 34 degrees 8 minutes 33 seconds North and 120 degrees 15 minutes 15 seconds West."

Quickly googling the latitude and longitude, Jonathan determined the impact zone was the precise location of the town of Glenway, California. With a population of about 30,000 people, the city was located 100 miles north of Los Angeles in the foothills.

With guarded apprehension, Jonathan carefully folded the paper and put it in his shirt pocket.

"Okay, Jonathan, you're ready for your mission. You know what to do, and I will pray the best for you."

"Malachi, will you be there with me when I deliver the message to the President of the United States?"

"Let's just say I will not be far away, but you will not see or hear me. You'll be fine. Remember you're only the messenger."

There was a knock at the door.

"Wait here, Malachi."

Cautiously opening the door, there was Grace, beautiful as ever.

Hugging Grace like he thought he would never see her again, Jonathan said, "Wow, thank God! It's you!"

Somewhat surprised at the overwhelming embrace that was uncharacteristic of Jonathan, Grace was speechless, but certainly didn't resist.

"Are you all right, Grace?"

"Of course, I'm fine. Why do you ask?"

With excitement that the Rapture had not occurred and that Grace was still there, Jonathan could hardly speak.

"Grace, this is the happiest day of my life. Come in, I want you to meet Malachi, the man I was telling you about in my dream. He's here in real life."

"All right, but I don't see anyone."

"Well, he was sitting right here at the table."

"Jonathan, are you sure you're all right? I didn't see anyone leave your house and there was no car parked outside. I went by your office, and Michelle said you woke up from a nap and left in a hurry to go home without any explanation. She said you were shouting at her and acting irrationally. You do sound kind of different."

"I'm fine, Grace, but I am different. I've been given another opportunity for life and another chance to deliver a crucial life-changing message to our nation, but I need to talk to you right away. Do you have time to talk now?"

"Well I was just getting ready to go back to the university, but you're the boss."

"Forget about going to the university. We have the most important assignment of our life ahead of us."

"We have an assignment?"

"Yes, come on in and sit down."

The dream of the journey to Iraq and Iran for the elusive ancient treasure and the mystery surrounding Malachi in Israel sprang to life for the first time outside of the dream as Jonathan relived every electrifying moment in meticulous detail. Hanging on every word, Grace couldn't take her eyes off Jonathan as his description of the journey progressed and excitement mounted. Like the crescendo in the last movement of Beethoven's Fifth Symphony, Jonathan stood with outstretched arms and raised his voice from a make-believe pulpit as he verbalized the mission Malachi gave to him.

"We must warn America to repent and establish an Ebenezer Stone on the National Mall as a constant reminder of the nation's commitment to return to God or face the judgment of God called the Tribulation. Finally, we must warn America of the approaching monster asteroid from deep space that will authenticate my message from God. This is our opportunity to turn this nation around for God!"

"Jonathan, I have been praying for God to touch your heart in some way for several years. For the last three days, I've been praying every minute that God would do something special, something supernatural in your life to convince you of your need to accept Jesus Christ. Believe it or not, I woke up this morning and had the weirdest feeling that God was going to do something wonderful, something life-changing in your life today. In fact, I prayed specifically for you this afternoon."

"Exactly what time did you pray?"

"It was right at 12:00 noon."

"That is exactly the time I went to sleep on the sofa in my office."

"Wow, I know now the dream Michelle said you had in your office today was the answer to my prayer."

"One more thing, Grace, I know it's going to happen in our lifetime."

"What?"

"The Tribulation. I don't know exactly when, but I know it will be soon. The good news is I did pray for Jesus to come into my life and to give me the boldness to carry out the mission I've been given. In fact, I must begin working on the presentation that I'll make to the President of the United States, and I need your help. We can talk about it over dinner. And there is something else, Grace."

Looking straight into Grace's sparkling green eyes, Jonathan confessed. "Although most of the vision I had is a little unnerving, the one part I like is that it made me realize I have feelings for you that I've not known in a long time. And Grace, I know those feelings are real, and I have just been afraid to admit it to myself."

Grace was a little too choked up to talk, so she just smiled and squeezed his hands a little tighter. *Jonathan, you don't know how long I have patiently waited for you to say those words.*

Grace gave Jonathan a hug and a kiss as light as a summer breeze. "Hey what's that in your shirt pocket?"

Jonathan carefully unfolded the paper as if it were a delicate ancient papyrus. "Look at this. I have physical evidence that Malachi was here. He gave me this note with the precise location where the asteroid named Genesis will impact our planet. I couldn't have been given a physical note in a dream, and I couldn't possibly make up these coordinates. Of course, how do I know this location is accurate?"

"You don't have to know, Jonathan. Just do what God directs you to do and use what you've been given. I believe you've been visited by a guardian angel named Malachi, a supernatural being from heaven sent by God, and I do believe you actually talked with him."

The next morning while having breakfast, Jonathan called his friend Riley Morgan in the State Department and asked him to arrange a meeting with the President of the United States in the White House. While explaining his mission to Riley, Jonathan glanced at the television. The coronation of the man elected to be the President of the New World Union was being broadcast live from Rome, Italy.

"That's the most elaborate coronation ceremony I have ever witnessed, and that's the most magnificent white horse that he is riding. All this pomp and circumstance seems vaguely familiar to me as though I have seen it before. Of course, it is the coronation of the man called the anti-Christ in the dream."

"Riley, I don't think we have much time."

Riley was skeptical of Jonathan's story and his request, but he was a committed Christian and took Jonathan at his word. He even noticed an obvious change in his voice, his demeanor, and his passion for doing something for others. This was not the old selfishly motivated Jonathan he had known for years. Since Jonathan's message included allegations of what could be construed as terrorist activity, Riley was successful in arranging a brief meeting between Jonathan and his close friend, the President of the United States.

With every nerve in his body on edge, Jonathan accompanied Riley into the Oval Office for the very first time. Sitting behind his vintage desk was the President of the United States with the head of the Department of Homeland Security, the Chief of Staff and the White House Press Secretary standing close by. After brief introductions by Riley stating the purpose of the meeting, Jonathan articulated details of his discovery of the secret Iranian nuclear laboratory, the covert work of the Iranians to destroy America, the presence of Russian supplied SAM missiles, and the message for America to repent and return to God or face imminent judgment. Of course, he failed to mention that a dream was the source of his entire account.

The president seemed a bit aloof as Jonathan verbalized the details of an asteroid that was already on a collision course with Earth that would not be identified by NASA for several months. When the meeting concluded, the president asked Jonathan and Riley to wait outside his office while he conferred privately with others in the room. Jonathan's heart was pounding, wondering if his message was heard and understood. As the door to the Oval office closed with a solid thud, Riley and Jonathan were left standing in the hall with only a security guard for company. After ten or fifteen tense minutes that seemed like an eternity, the door to the Oval Office opened.

CHAPTER 39

HOMELAND SECURITY

Emerging from the Oval Office, the Press Secretary announced he had been instructed by the president to arrange a meeting between Dr. Whitfield and members of the Congressional Committee on Homeland Security as soon as possible. Jonathan breathed a noticeable sigh of relief, believing the audience granted with members of Congress signaled his message had been heard and accepted.

With the wheels of bureaucracy grinding slowly, it took several months to set a date for the congressional meeting. Finally, on the afternoon of August 1, a courier arrived at Jonathan's home with a letter from the House Committee on Homeland Security. With an air of excitement anticipating a cordial invitation to share his message with Congress, Jonathan ripped open the envelope. He was shocked to find a subpoena.

"Dr. Jonathan Whitfield: You are summoned to appear before members of the Full House Committee on Homeland Security in an emergency session scheduled for August 7. You are required to appear in room 2154 of the Rayburn House Office Building in Washington D.C. at 9:00 A.M. It will be necessary for you to provide detailed testimony under oath of your knowledge of an imminent attack on the United States. Please bring all supporting documentation for your testimony."

The increasing number of terrorist attacks throughout America and the world by Islamic extremists resulted in America being on the highest security alert. Unfortunately, Jonathan's warning of Iran's development of weapons of mass destruction and the alleged imminent attack by a rogue asteroid had all the earmarks of a terrorist conspiracy.

Monday morning, August 7, with Grace at his side, Jonathan arrived thirty minutes early at the Rayburn House Office Building located at 45 Independence Ave SW, across the street from the Capitol Building. A White House military police escort met them in the lobby and ushered then to a large room where the lengthy Benghazi hearings had been conducted. Representatives of the thirty-one-member House Committee on Homeland Security were already seated around the expansive semi-circular theater-like forum. Congresswoman Sharon Bovia, Chairperson of the House Committee, introduced herself to Jonathan and Grace and explained the procedures that would be followed throughout the hearing.

This was not a closed hearing, so there were several journalists and television media represented who were salivating to hear Dr. Whitfield's story and the committee's reaction to his allegations. Jonathan took his seat at the small rectangular table in front of the committee opposite Mrs. Bovia. Grace was seated at his side. Ms. Bovia explained to Jonathan that he would be answering all questions under oath. She explained to him this was a hearing, not a trial, and after administering the oath, she invited him to give his opening statement to the committee.

Resting his elbows on the table with his fingers intertwined under his chin, Jonathan leaned in toward the microphone and before speaking, silently surveyed the representatives, with impertinent grins, seated in front of him. Then, as if on cue, he sat back and began to articulate his message for the nation to repent and return to God before His dreadful judgment is unleashed on America. With boldness in his voice, Jonathan could feel the apprehension in the air intensifying the longer he spoke.

"We have embraced the lifestyles of those of alternative sexual orientation in our courts, schools, books, and movies while abandoning the age-old Biblical sanctity of marriage between a man and a woman and the importance of family values. Unborn but living children have been refused the God-given as well as constitutional rights to 'life, liberty, and the pursuit of happiness' for decades under the pretense of safeguarding the rights of women. We have accepted the murder of more than 60 million unborn babies since Roe vs. Wade while legislation to protect certain species of birds, animals and even insects has flourished."

"As a nation, we accommodate all religious beliefs in our social, educational, political, and even judicial systems except Christianity, including those who want to kill us. Embracing freedom of religion, the Bible, the cross, and the worship of the one true God, as well as adherence to the Godly principles that this nation was founded on, have been swept under the rug of political correctness. America is now squarely in the crosshairs of God's ultimate judgment, as His patience with America is running out."

Jonathan concluded his opening statement by hammering home the fact that the accelerating downward spiral of moral and spiritual values and decaying family principles in America over the past decades with no signs of reversal will accelerate God's imminent judgment if there is no repentance. Finally, Jonathan stated that a commitment to lead America in repentance must be symbolized by erecting a twenty-first-century Ebenezer stone in a public setting near the United States Capitol building. This monolith would be a constant reminder to Americans of the commitment they made.

Settling back in his chair, Jonathan relaxed.

Chairperson Bovia leaned into her microphone. "Thank you, Dr. Whitfield, for that explicit thesis on spiritual and moral values and Israeli history, but what is this judgment of God that you speak of and what does it have to do with the Iranian arms build-up that you claim to have knowledge of?"

Jonathan pulled the microphone a little closer and articulated the best he could the seven horrifying years of holocaust called the Tribulation.

With many of the members looking a little glassy-eyed, one U.S. Congressman stood to his feet and interrupted, "That's great material for the next blockbuster science fiction movie, but it has no place in the agenda of this Committee."

"Thank you, Dr. Whitfield," replied Chairperson Bovia. "Now will you please tell us what you know about Iran's plans to develop nuclear weapons for an attack on America and how you acquired that information?"

Without mentioning the vision, Jonathan began by explaining his journey to Iraq and Iran and describing in detail how he and Grace stumbled into the alleged secret nuclear facility while exploring the tomb of King Cyrus of Persia. Painting a graphic picture of Iran's intent to destroy America and Israel, Jonathan articulated the plans and schedules for the weapons of mass destruction under development by the Iranians. "In addition to the assembly of a nuclear warhead, Iran has already developed and tested what they call an Electromagnetic Pulse Generator or EPG, carried by a ballistic missile under the guise of expanding weather satellite technology. Launch of the EPG will complete the first of two phases in Iran's plan to destroy America. When introduced into the northern hemisphere by satellites in earth orbit and activated, the EPGs are designed to completely disable the nation's electrical grid and all communications, rendering the United States vulnerable to enemy attacks. America will be virtually blind to incoming enemy aircraft and missiles. Following the communications blackout, Iran will launch intercontinental ballistic rockets carrying nuclear warheads that are being assembled in the secret Iranian laboratory as we speak. Global World War III is imminent if we don't begin now to return this nation to God."

The U.S. Congresswoman from Virginia interrupted. "Dr. Whitfield, you're telling this committee under oath you actually witnessed the Iranians working on these projects in a secret laboratory near Pasargadae, Iran?"

"Uh…yes, I did, Congresswoman!" Believing it was time to confess to the rest of the story, Jonathan leaned into his microphone with his head down and nervously spoke in a whispered voice. "I did witness everything exactly as I described it to you, but I experienced everything in an extremely realistic…uh… a very real… vision or dream of…"

Chairperson Bovia interrupted. "What? Will you please speak up Dr. Whitfield? We can't hear you! Did you say you had a vision or a dream?"

"I said…"

"Please speak up, Dr. Whitfield!"

"I did witness everything exactly as I described it to you, but I experienced everything in a very realistic supernatural vision given to me by God."

With that statement, you could hear the oxygen being sucked out of the room as the members of Congress leaned back in their plush leather chairs and gasped in shock. Chairperson Bovia took off her glasses in disgust and threw them on the desk in front of her, knocking over her glass of water.

Flashing a furrowed brow, she spoke, raising her voice. "A vision! You're telling this committee that everything you have testified to us today was given to you in a dream?"

"But this was not just an ordinary dream; it was a vision given to me by God. You must believe me! The work of the Iranians, the warning of an attack, and the plea to return America to God or face judgment are all as real as today's sunrise."

With some members chuckling in the background, Chairperson Bovia raised her gavel to adjourn the hearing for lunch recess when Jonathan stood and announced in a loud, bold voice.

"Wait, Madam Chairperson! Please, I have one more critical message for the committee."

With hand motions impatiently prompting Jonathan to sit down, Mrs. Bovia reluctantly agreed to humor him while other members shook their heads in disagreement. "Dr. Whitfield, we're very disappointed that a man with your credentials and reputation would bring such allegations without any corroborating evidence before this committee. We will indulge you for five more minutes, hopefully, to tell us what you really know."

"Thank you. Anticipating your reluctance to believe me, God has already put a supernatural event in motion that defies the laws of physics to convince you everything I said is authentic. A massive asteroid in deep space has made a sudden departure from the orbit it has been in for centuries and is now on an irreversible collision course with planet Earth. The potentially deadly impact of this colossal space projectile on American soil will authenticate the truth of this prediction as well as validate the message you heard from me today. It will be futile to contact NASA regarding this phenomenon as God has blinded scientists from detecting the asteroid's change in trajectory for several months."

A U.S. Congresswoman from Arizona stood and spoke up. "Dr. Whitfield, this is preposterous. You're an archeologist with no formal training in astronomy! How can you expect us to believe you have any knowledge of an astronomical body that violated the laws of the universe?"

Others in the committee applauded loudly while closing their notebooks, indicating they had heard enough.

With his throat parched dry as desert sand, Jonathan reached for the glass of water nearby. After a few sips of water, he responded in a firm but quiet voice. "I'm pleading with you to believe this message from God, but I realize I'm only the messenger. You must make your own decision."

Looking at her watch, Chairperson Bovia interrupted, "Dr. Whitfield, thank you for your most interesting testimony. We will take a recess for lunch and resume the hearing at 2 o'clock this afternoon."

Following lunch, the hearing reconvened on schedule although Jonathan and Grace were much too anxious to eat and didn't leave the room.

"Dr. Whitfield, during the recess for lunch, several members of Congress made calls to associates with NASA and the Jet Propulsion Laboratory in California to see what they knew about the subject of rogue asteroids like the one you described. NASA scientists reported that they have no data on any asteroids that are on a trajectory anywhere near a collision course with Earth neither now nor in the next twenty or thirty years."

Jonathan stood.

"I told you, NASA will not discover the asteroid for several months, so I'm not surprised by the information you were given. The advance information I gave you is intended to provide more than sufficient time to evacuate the area of impact to minimize the loss of life while validating the fact that my message to you is truly from God."

Another member spoke up. "Dr. Whitfield, I suppose you're going to give us the location of the target zone for this fantasy asteroid?"

"Yes. I'll provide you with the exact information I was given." Reaching into his coat pocket, Jonathan retrieved the note given to him by Malachi. "The asteroid will impact at exactly 34 degrees 8 minutes 33 seconds N. and 120 degrees 15 minutes 15 seconds W., or the location of the city of Glenway, California."

A young tanned freshman Congresswoman from California with sun-bleached hair stood. "Not that I'm worried about this imaginary asteroid, but why did you choose that city? Glenway is my hometown, with almost 30,000 residents.

"I didn't choose the city, Congresswoman. The location was given to me, and I advise you to begin evacuating the city immediately if you have any concern for the safety and welfare of your constituents."

An aging, white-haired U.S. Congressman from South Carolina with a strong southern drawl spoke up. "With all due respect, Dr. Whitfield, do you expect us to incite panic across this nation based on the knowledge of an approaching asteroid that you obtained from some imaginary stranger in a dream?"

Chuckles from members of Congress permeated the room.

Chairperson Bovia's gavel pounded the desk. "Order, please!"

A short recess was declared to prepare an official response for the record. After about thirty minutes, Ms. Sharon Bovia returned to the room with the other members.

"Dr. Whitfield, we appreciate you coming today, giving your testimony, and answering our questions. You are certainly entitled to your religious beliefs, including your conviction that the world may end soon. Unfortunately, we cannot issue any statements to the nation regarding your prediction of an approaching asteroid that would inflame those of other religions without any real facts to verify your statements. We have also listened carefully to your testimony, weighed all the facts, and dismissed any possible charges regarding your involvement in a covert conspiracy of terrorism. We thank you for your time today, Dr. Whitfield, and you're excused."

As they left the building, Grace smiled at Jonathan. "Well, you did your best, Jonathan. Remember, you're only the messenger. They will believe you soon enough."

As they walked down the steps, Jonathan stopped and looked back over his shoulder. "It was not that long ago that I would have agreed with those politicians if I had heard a ridiculous-sounding story like I told them. Now, I understand why God destroyed Jerusalem. The Israelites wouldn't believe the prophets of God any more than these leaders of our nation believe my message from God."

A few weeks went by after the hearing without news of an asteroid approaching Earth, and liberal journalists were having a field day with Jonathan's testimony at the recent Congressional hearing. Labeling the archeologists an "extremist Christian alarmist," newspapers gave a skeptical slant to his message and the warning of an approaching asteroid. Mocking his message from God as a doomsday prophecy based on a fantasy dream, newspaper cartoonists had a mother lode of new material to work with.

Then, one evening, while Jonathan was having dinner out with Grace, there was late-breaking news on television. The President of the New World Union announced he was planning to meet with the Prime Minister of Israel to discuss potential peace talks because of increasing attacks on Israel by Islamic extremists in Syria.

Jonathan looked at Grace. "It's almost the beginning of the end, Grace, and people still refuse to believe the warning from God. Americans are going down the exact same path as the Israelites thousands of years ago. I guess people really haven't changed that much"

Knowing the clock was ticking, Jonathan thought, *There is something very important I have to do in the morning.*

CHAPTER 40

CONFIRMATION

Following a restless night, Jonathan was awake early the next morning, dressed, and out the door as the darkness evaporated in the first light of the morning sunrise. Picking up two small bundles of fresh flowers he purchased from a nearby florist the day before, he drove to a small cemetery a few miles outside of town. Turning off the main highway, he drove slowly through the open gates of the massive ornamental arched iron entrance and passed a sea of polished granite headstones standing tall like soldiers at attention out of respect for the fallen residents. Neatly manicured lawns with droplets of morning dew sparkling like diamonds in the sunlight flanked the winding road Jonathan had driven so many times.

As the limestone crunched under the pressure of the slowly turning wheels of his VW, Jonathan reminisced about the experience he endured here five years ago that crushed his heart. Arriving at the rear of the cemetery, he parked the car near a massive oak tree overlooking a small tranquil lake that was home to a family of ducks.

"Deborah loved trees and water, and it was only proper that she should be buried alongside Ethan in this picturesque location."

Nostalgic memories of his wife and son washed over him like Niagara Falls, but then Jonathan felt a peace come over him that he had never experienced before. Without a doubt, he knew now that his loss of Deborah and Ethan was only temporary. Since he accepted Jesus and was assured eternity in heaven, he knew he would see them again. A few sobering moments later, Jonathan walked unhurriedly to their gravesites.

Kneeling at Deborah's cross-shaped tombstone, Jonathan placed the fresh flowers in a small iron container. Years of wonderful memories symbolized by the dash between the dates of her birth and her death on the tombstone flooded his mind and brought tears of joy to his eyes.

"I miss you so much, and yet I yearn to be with Grace. I know you are dancing in heaven about my new relationship with Jesus, but Deborah, I need confirmation from you that it's all right to marry Grace, a sign of some kind, any kind of sign."

After a heart wrenching, emotional few minutes, he finally stood to his feet.

"Maybe it was silly to think Deborah's spirit could communicate with me from heaven and give me an answer about Grace. Or maybe she doesn't approve of Grace. Maybe no sign is a sign."

As Jonathan walked to his car, he decided to call Grace, although he didn't really have any idea what he would say to her. Turning on his cell phone, Jonathan glanced at the anniversary picture that Ethan put on the "lock screen" of the phone. Suddenly Deborah's picture began to slowly fade from the screen right before his eyes until it completely vanished, leaving Jonathan in the photograph all alone. In place of Deborah was a picture of a single red rose petal. Jonathan turned the phone off and on several times, but the picture was always the same. Deborah was gone, and the rose petal was there in its place.

Jonathan shouted to the heavens right there in the cemetery, startling a flock of birds feeding in the grass nearby and causing them to take flight into the crisp morning air.

"Of course! The single rose petal is the sign from Deborah that Malachi was talking about. She approves of me marrying Grace."

Jonathan quickly turned and ran back to Deborah's grave. Kneeling at the headstone, he whispered, "Thank you, Deborah, thank you, and by the way, I will see you and Ethan in heaven, and it may be sooner than we think. I know you know what I'm talking about since you have the inside line now."

With a great burden lifted, Jonathan called Grace on the way home to arrange dinner at her favorite restaurant. He proposed to her that evening, and she said yes before the appetizer arrived. They went shopping together the next day, and Grace found the perfect engagement ring.

On September 1, Grace and Jonathan were married by the pastor of Grace's church in a small private ceremony. Steven and Amy Westin and their children, as well as Michelle and a few close friends from the university, attended the wedding.

During the reception, Jonathan saw what looked like a Lego character on the floor near Steven and picked it up. Placing the toy in Steven's hand, Jonathan asked with his mouth twisted in a one-sided smile, "Is this yours? It must have fallen out of your coat pocket when you were taking out your car keys. It looks like a toy Lego character."

While waiting for Steven's answer, Jonathan reflected on the dream when Steven was involved in a covert plan to sell nuclear detonators to Iran packed in boxes disguised as Lego toys. He remembered Steven always carried one of the Lego toys in his coat pocket. Suddenly, reality smacked Jonathan in the face as Grace walked up in her beautiful white wedding dress.

Pulling on his coat sleeve, Grace chuckled, "Aren't you guys too old to play with toys? Come on, sweetie. Everyone is waiting for us to cut the cake."

"Why yes, Jonathan," Steven finally replied. "This toy probably belongs to one of my kids. You know Lego toys are…"

"Really popular among kids all over the world these days."

"What are you? A mind reader? That's exactly what I was going to say."

After the reception, Jonathan and Grace left for a two-week honeymoon in the beautiful Cayman Islands. The Discovery Point Condominiums on Seven Mile Beach provided pristine white sand beaches where they could relax away from the crowds. Shopping in George Town, tacos at the Sunshine Grill, and swimming with the stingrays in Sting Ray City in the North Sound rounded out a fantastic honeymoon.

After returning home, Jonathan sold his home and most of his furniture and moved into a new home with Grace.

One night after dinner, Grace called Jonathan to the television. "Come look, there is breaking news on CBN."

"We are interrupting our regularly scheduled programming tonight to bring you a special news bulletin."

"Good evening, I'm James Donaldson reporting for CBN's Nightly News, and we have an unbelievable breaking news story coming to us tonight from deep in outer space. We're delighted to have Dr. James Morrison, of the NASA Jet Propulsion Laboratory in California, as our guest tonight to describe this mysterious cosmic phenomenon. All I can say is fasten your seat belts folks!"

CHAPTER 41

GENESIS

"Thank you, James, for having me on the show. For the benefit of your viewers, let me begin by giving a little tutorial on asteroids, meteors, and meteorites. Millions of massive rocky space objects called asteroids have been harmlessly orbiting the sun in our solar system for thousands of years. In fact, every day, Earth is pelted with more than 100 tons of small fragments that are constantly spalling off the asteroids. Most of the fragments, called meteors, create an impressive light show as they streak through the Earth's atmosphere, but burn up completely before reaching the ground. Larger fragments that strike Earth's surface have been given the name meteorites, but usually result in little or no damage to people or structures. Only once every few thousand years has an intact fragment of an asteroid large enough to threaten Earth's civilization entered our atmosphere as a colossal meteor. This was the case with the 14,000-ton Chelyabinsk meteor that exploded in the heavens over Russia in 2013, injuring more than 1,500 people with thirty times more energy than was released from the bomb detonated at Hiroshima.

"Now, for the news you have been waiting to hear. On October 19th of this year, we received data from JPL's Deep Space Network in Goldstone, California that, while monitoring a spacecraft probing the outer reaches of space, an asteroid, about the size of a small luxury cruise ship, was discovered to have mysteriously departed *from the path it had been on for centuries and has taken direct aim at planet Earth. This asteroid had been tracked by the Asteroid Terrestrial-Impact Last Alert System (ATLAS) for decades, and the abrupt change in trajectory defies all laws of astrophysics. On your screen is a spectacular photograph of the asteroid we have named Genesis, weighing in at approximately 16,000 tons, which is slightly larger than the Chelyabinsk meteor. When this photo was taken by the new James Webb Space Telescope launched into Earth orbit in 2021, Genesis was more than twenty-five million miles from Earth."*

"Dr. Morrison, that's an impressive picture of the asteroid, but what do we have to worry about if Genesis is more than twenty-five million miles away?" James Donaldson asked.

"James, notice I said Genesis was more than twenty-five million miles away. The rogue asteroid is now on a precise collision course with Earth and is traveling at a speed of more than 25,000 miles per hour. Assuming the asteroid remains on the present course and speed, we estimate Genesis to impact our planet in about 41 days or sometime on November 30th of this year."

"Now, that news is somewhat frightening, Dr. Morrison. Do you have any idea where it will impact?"

"If Genesis remains on the same trajectory and speed, it is predicted to strike our planet at exactly 34 degrees 8 minutes 33 seconds North and 120 degrees 15 minutes 15 seconds west. These are the coordinates of the city of Glenway, California, north of Los Angeles."

"Jonathan, did you hear that?" asked Grace. "NASA just announced that the asteroid will impact at the exact location you gave the members of Congress several months ago. I'll bet they believe you now."

With a wrinkled brow, Jonathan responded, "Perhaps, Grace."

"Dr. Morrison, you said if Genesis remains on the present course, it will impact Glenway, California. Do you believe there is a chance it will deviate from its present course and avoid Earth entirely or fall harmlessly into the ocean?"

"First of all, there is no reason for people in Glenway to panic because NASA has already developed a joint plan with the military to

deflect the asteroid safely away from Earth. As you may know, NASA has not developed a new launch vehicle since the space shuttle fleet was retired and the program terminated. However, private investors have developed several new space launch vehicles in conjunction with NASA, which will be used to detonate multiple nuclear warheads on the surface of the asteroid. Since Russia is the only other nation with the launch vehicle capability and guidance system technology to put a nuclear warhead on the asteroid, they have agreed to join the United States in this humanitarian effort. The explosion from the fleet of nuclear warhead-laden rockets is expected to alter the course of Genesis a fraction of a degree, causing it to miss the Earth by an estimated 40,000 miles."

Mumbling to himself, Jonathan objected, "You can't do that! Malachi said God is in control of Genesis, and the asteroid can't be stopped, and the trajectory can't be altered. You're just wasting precious time. You should begin evacuating Glenway, now."

"Jonathan, please stop talking to the television. You can't help them now. It's completely out of your control."

"Well, James, that's certainly good news."

"Yes, but NASA has reviewed the paths of other cosmic bodies they track and have identified numerous other asteroids that appear to have deviated from their normal trajectories as well. However, because of their distance from Earth, it may be years before these bodies are close enough to even be considered a threat to our planet. We're scheduled to give an official report to Congress in an emergency meeting October 17th, and we will provide additional updates to the public as soon as we obtain more information."

"Dr. Morrison, before you go, wasn't there a Professor Whitfield in the news a couple of months ago, who testified before the House Committee on Homeland Security and predicted this exact scenario would take place? I recall he even gave the committee the exact coordinates of the impact you just gave our viewers. How could Dr. Whitfield have possibly known about the change in the path of the asteroid and the impact coordinates before NASA?"

"Yes, that was Dr. Jonathan Whitfield. Although Dr. Whitfield is a recognized expert in the field of archeology, he is not an astronomer and has no expertise in astrophysics. I believe he said he had a

dream or vision about an asteroid and honestly believed it was true. Of course, he had absolutely no factual evidence to back up his prediction."

"Are you saying the target coordinates of the asteroid Dr. Whitfield predicted several months ago that you just demonstrated to be incredibly accurate is just an astonishing coincidence?"

"Yes... I would say so unless... well, unless he is a psychic! I'm sorry, Dr. Whitfield. I apologize for that comment. Everyone has a profound respect for you and your work as an archeologist, but let's face it; you're not an astronomer."

"See, Grace, they all think I'm a kook!"

"Dr. Morrison, I recall Dr. Whitfield said that a man in his dream called Malachi told him the asteroid would impact Earth regardless of any attempt to alter its course. The announcement of the asteroid targeting Earth ahead of NASA detecting it was to validate his message from God. Considering this very real threat from Genesis that authenticates his story, do you believe him now?"

"No. I absolutely do not believe his story. His prediction and the change in the course of this asteroid is purely coincidental. However, we're sure we have a plan that will save the city of Glenway and nearby areas from any harm. I assure you there is no danger and absolutely no reason for anyone to panic."

"Dr. Morrison, I believe Dr. Whitfield also reported there would be additional asteroids targeting Earth if America refused to turn to God. He said this was the beginning of God's judgment called the Tribulation in some religious circles. Based on your recent discovery of other asteroids millions of miles in deep space with trajectories targeting Earth, have you considered the consequences of ignoring Dr. Whitfield's warning? What if this asteroid is actually a harbinger from God, and Dr. Whitfield is a modern-day prophet?"

"I can't address that question, and I have no further comment. I don't want to get into a discussion about religion. I'm a scientist, and I must deal only with facts. Right now, I'm only concerned with doing what I can to save mankind from Genesis. In fact, this plan to deflect Genesis will be a practice mission for similar asteroids approaching Earth in the future."

"Just one more question before you go, Dr. Morrison. Are you related to Dr. Whitfield?"

"Uh...yes, as a matter of fact, he is my brother-in-law, but that doesn't and will not change anything I said. By the way, let me remind you once again he is an archeologist, not an astronomer or prophet."

"Well, thank you, Dr. Morrison. Please keep us updated with the latest information from NASA. Now we will return to our regularly scheduled programming."

Every other day, there was a news report updating the progress on the plan to deflect Genesis safely away from Earth. The image of the massive space rock speeding toward Earth was glaring and growing larger with each passing day. There were also sporadic reports of cities in Europe and South America that had suddenly lost all communications capability. However, the events were explained away as unusual solar activity that interfered with the Earth's magnetic field and was expected to be only temporary.

Shaking his head, Jonathan knew exactly what was happening. "Grace, I think the Electromagnetic Pulse Generator (EPG) is being tested on a few cities around the world before targeting the United States with the technology. The effects of the magnetic storms caused by solar activity are providing Iran's military with excellent stealth cover. Everything I witnessed in the vision is coming to pass faster than I could have imagined."

Late at night on October 23, while Jonathan and Grace were watching one of their favorite television programs, the regularly scheduled programming was interrupted by a special news bulletin.

James Donaldson, CBN News television anchor, announced, *"NASA and the military have finalized plans to launch multiple nuclear warheads into space to intercept the asteroid Genesis and alter its course so that it will pass safely away from Earth.*

"The launch date is scheduled for November 29. At the time of launch, Genesis will be approximately 500,000 miles from Earth or about twice the distance to the moon and traveling roughly 25,000 miles per hour. There will be a total of six rockets launched from two locations, three from Vandenberg Air Force Base in the United States

and three from the Baikonur Cosmodrome in Kazakhstan, Russia. At the time of impact, Genesis will be approximately 250,000 miles from Earth.

"It will take ten hours for Genesis to reach Earth even if the nuclear explosion fails to deflect the asteroid out of Earth's path. Thus, authorities will still have ample time to conduct an orderly evacuation from the target zone if necessary. Of course, NASA is confident that the plan will be 100% successful."

"I will cover the launch of Project Genesis in its entirety with CBN Nightly News live from Times Square on November 29. With flashing neon lights, giant digital billboards, brilliant Broadway marques, and costumed characters and musicians, Times Square provides an iconic backdrop each December 31 for the world to experience the spectacular celebration of the birth of the new year. What more appropriate place to broadcast this once in a lifetime performance of mankind's challenge to thwart the deadly attack of the monster intruder Genesis from deep space. I hope you will join us for what I believe will be a historical event."

Following the special news bulletin, Jonathan and Grace sat down to eat dinner but were interrupted by Jonathan's cell phone ringing. Seeing the caller ID marked "unknown," Jonathan mumbled, "It must be a sales call." After hesitating for a moment, he decided to answer the phone.

"Hello, is this Dr. Jonathan Whitfield?" said the authoritative voice on the phone.

"Yes, it is. Who is this?"

"I'm James Donaldson, a journalist for CBN Nightly News."

"No kidding, but why are you calling me? I just watched your news bulletin, and I must tell you; I'm fearful of what will happen if they don't begin to evacuate Glenway immediately. But what can I do for you?"

Out of curiosity, Grace slowly rose from the table and came to Jonathan's side, quietly placing her ear next to Jonathan's ear and his cell phone.

"I'm calling to invite you and your wife to accompany me during the broadcast from Times Square when I cover the launch of the Genesis Project on November 29. Since you first brought the prediction that this rock from space would target earth to the attention of our nation, I thought it only appropriate to have you on the air with me as the drama unfolds."

"I don't know," responded Jonathan, "I did all I could to warn America of the danger, and I don't know if I can take part in your broadcast and watch it take place."

Listening attentively, Grace looked at Jonathan with a twinkle in her eye and shook her head vigorously. When Jonathan pressed the mute button on the phone, Grace whispered, "You have to do this! Think of the platform you will have to speak the truth to the nation one more time."

"I guess you're right, Grace! You're always right!"

Releasing the mute button, Jonathan responded, "Mr. Donaldson, are you there? Ok, well, Grace and I will be happy to accept your invitation."

"Great. I will send all the details to you in a few days and have someone pick you up for the trip to Times Square on the day of the launch."

November 28, the night before the launch of Project Genesis

With the imminent launch of Genesis weighing heavily on his mind, Jonathan was shaken out of his thoughts by a knock at the door. Cautiously cracking the shutters on the window near the front door, Jonathan took a hasty half-step back in shock at what he saw.

CHAPTER 42

ADOPTED

Opening the door, Jonathan immediately recognized the man on the porch.

"Good evening, Dr. Whitfield, my name is Jack."

With anger in his voice fueled by years of grief and hatred, Jonathan shouted, "I know exactly who you are. You're the man who murdered my wife and son. How could I ever forget that face? What are you doing here anyway, and why aren't you in prison where you belong?"

After a long silence, the man broke down and began sobbing. "I'm so sorry, Dr. Whitfield, for the loss of your wife and son, I really am, and I would do anything in the world to bring them back if I could. The Parole Board released me from prison last week for good behavior, and they said I'm a free man now, although I'm far from free. I'll always be shackled to the chains of the horrible memories and the strangling guilt of what I did that destroyed an innocent family, your family."

"I guess you come here looking for forgiveness!"

"No, and I know I don't deserve forgiveness."

"Then what do you want, and how did you find me?"

"You've been in the news so much lately, you were easy to find."

For a few painfully long, awkward minutes, Jonathan stood motionless and stared at the man. Overhearing the conversation, Grace slipped quietly to Jonathan's side. While he was contemplating what he would do or say next, Grace opened the door wide, reached out to the man and motioned for him to come in. "Please, come inside."

As the door closed, everyone stood quietly for a few minutes. Jonathan glared at Jack and finally spoke up as he choked out the words.

"Jack, at the trial, I vowed I would kill you if I ever saw you again."

"I understand, and I don't blame you."

Moving closer to his side, Grace pleaded, "Jonathan, please don't...!"

"It's all right, Grace. I don't want to hurt you, Jack. In fact, I want to forgive you."

Shocked and overwhelmed with emotion, Jack blurted out, "How can you possibly forgive me for what I did?"

"I can't, Jack, but by the grace of God, I can forgive you, and I do. You see, Jack, I didn't deserve forgiveness for the sin in my life either, but God forgave me, and I can forgive you."

Jack was speechless at Jonathan's offer of forgiveness, and his unexpected manly hug brought tears to the eyes of both men. Grace joined them in a group hug and shed tears of joy.

"This is proof that you're truly a changed man, a born-again Christian, Jonathan," Grace whispered. "God gave you the power to forgive Jack, something you would not and could not possibly do yourself."

"I can't tell you what your forgiveness means to me, Dr. Whitfield, and I know I don't deserve it. The only thing I have ever had in this world that was worth having was the girl I met in Franklin High School and later married. She was a wonderful Christian lady and was very involved in a local church. She begged me for years to attend church with her, but I would only go on special days, and then just to please her. I wanted nothing to do with the church or God.

She loved me anyway and stayed with me despite my drinking habit and the way I mistreated her. After years of encouraging me to get help, I finally did."

Fighting back the tears, Jack continued. "She suffered a long, painful battle with cancer and died a few days before the…well, before the accident. I blamed God for her death and started drinking again. After the funeral, I decided to go for a drive toward the ocean and stopped at several bars along the way. As I continued to drink heavily into the evening, I was on my way home when… well, you know the rest of the story. I have nothing to live for now, Dr. Whitfield, and only the promise of eternity in hell when I die. I desperately want what you have, but I don't know what to do. After what I did, I know it's a lot to ask from you, but will you tell me how I can have eternal life in heaven?"

Reminded of his past life with Deborah and her passion for Jesus and the church, Jonathan stood shocked at Jack's request. In a way, he was a lot like Jack. Grace sat down across the room and began to pray silently for both men as they continued to talk. Unable to hold back the tears, Jonathan shared the simple gospel of Jesus Christ with Jack the best he could. They prayed together, and Jack was wonderfully transformed by the awesome power and amazing grace of God. Several cups of French coffee and a slice of Grace's freshly baked carrot cake topped off a celebration of the occasion. After an hour or so, Jack thanked Jonathan and said he should be going.

As they were getting up from the sofa, Jack stopped and looked at Jonathan without saying a word for several seconds.

"Is something bothering you, Jack?"

"Yes, Jonathan, there is one more thing I have to tell you before I go."

"Sure, Jack? What's on your mind?"

"I understand your dad, Raymond Warren Whitfield, died in WWII a few months after you were born, and you don't know much about him."

"Yes, but how did you know that?"

"That's not important, but before Ray and your mother Ann were married, he was married to my mother in Philadelphia for about three years."

"What?" With a lump in his throat, Jonathan swallowed hard and sat back down. With his arms stretched out, he gestured for Jack to do the same.

"Yes, we moved to California after I was born, but two years later, my mother divorced Ray, and we moved back to Philadelphia, where I grew up."

"I learned later that Ray was drafted into the army and stationed in Houston, Texas. So, you see, Ray was also my father, but I didn't know him either. My full name is Jack Warren Whitfield. I was named after our Dad, and I'm your brother...well, I'm your half-brother."

"Wait a minute, I remember the judge introducing you at the trial as Jack Williams."

"Yes, I was six years old when my mother died suddenly. Since she had no living relatives, I was adopted after spending a year in an orphanage in New Jersey. My new family changed my name to Williams, Jack Warren Williams. I even brought copies of my birth certificate and the adoption papers to show you."

Jonathan and Grace were speechless as they studied the documents.

"The man who took the lives of my wife and son is my brother? This sounds impossible. How did you learn we were related?"

"When I grew up, I was visiting with some of Ray's relatives who told me they met your mother when she brought you to visit them in California. You were just four years old. My aunt Loretta said she met you when you and your wife Deborah visited them in California about fifteen years ago. They gave me this picture of you and your wife with my aunt, and when I saw you on the news, I recognized you instantly. Of course, I was shocked when I learned that the man whose family I killed is my half-brother."

Apologetically, Jonathan said, "Jack, at the trial, I was willing to kill you on the spot. Tonight, with the help of the Holy Spirit, you gained a place in heaven for all eternity, and I gained a brother."

Jonathan and Grace wished Jack the best in life and promised to stay in touch. As Jack walked toward his car, he looked back and shouted to Jonathan. "I will see you both in heaven someday. Thank you for everything!"

Hugging Jonathan, Grace whispered, "You know that man will be in heaven because of you."

Later that night, as Grace was busy packing, she said to Jonathan, "The CBN News representative will be here at 8:00 in the morning, Jonathan, to pick us up and take us to meet James Donaldson in New York City. Will you please finish packing?"

"I will, I will. I just don't have a good feeling about the entire Genesis Project or about us being in Times Square with CBN News when the launch is being broadcast."

"Jonathan, you have done all you can do. You can't take any personal responsibility now for whatever happens."

Early the next morning, a CBN News representative arrived in a stretch limo, picked up Jonathan and Grace, and took them to a hotel in Times Square where James Donaldson was to meet them later that evening.

CHAPTER 43

LAUNCH

"*Good evening. I'm James Donaldson, reporting for CBN's Nightly News live from Times Square at the corner of Broadway and West 47th Street in front of the Times Square Ticket Booth. I am thrilled to have Dr. Jonathan Whitfield and his lovely wife, Grace, with me during the broadcast tonight. You may remember Dr. Whitfield testified in a congressional hearing several months ago that the rogue asteroid Genesis was going to strike Earth. Dr. Whitfield, do you have any comments for our viewers about the impending impact of Genesis?*"

"Yes, I do! If our nation's leaders would have heeded the warning, none of this would be happening."

"*Surely, you're not still claiming this astronomical event is being caused by God?*"

Feeling frustrated, Jonathan replied, "What is it going to take, Mr. Donaldson, to bring America back to God?"

"*Well, whether Dr. Whitfield is truly clairvoyant, has an inside line with God, or Genesis is simply an astronomical phenomenon as NASA affirms, we will be here throughout the night to bring you complete coverage of what promises to be one of the most historic nights in history. Temperatures have plunged below freezing and light snow is falling, but the weather has not been a deterrent for the thousands of spectators who came to witness this ominous event. All eyes are fixated on the huge digital countdown clock recently installed on one of the enormous electronic video screens that scales the height of the One Times Square Building, just down the street to my right. Giant brilliant red numbers displaying the time are in stark contrast with the coal-black background of the clock.*

"The bustling advertising mecca of enormous digital billboards around me sporting flashing neon lights typically dazzle crowds with announcements for everything from M&M's to the latest Broadway plays. But tonight, the colorful displays are projecting a chilling image of the monster asteroid Genesis barreling toward Earth from deep space at more than 25,000 miles per hour. Less than a minute ago, the countdown clock flashed ten minutes until 'time zero,' the beginning of the Genesis Mission scheduled for 10:00 P.M. Eastern time.

"We are now streaming concurrent live video coverage of the launch sites at Vandenberg Air Force Base in California and Baikonur Military Air Base in Russia. Standing like soldiers at attention on their launch pads, the fleet of rockets seem to be waiting impatiently for the signal to begin their journey into deep space. You can hear a pin drop here in Times Square as the crowd holds their breath.

"The wispy trails of vapor you see coming from the fuel tanks indicate the rockets are fueled and ready for launch. In less than a minute, multiple rockets armed with nuclear warheads will be simultaneously launched into outer space from opposite sides of the world for a life-saving humanitarian mission.

"Let's listen to NASA's Mission Control at the Vandenberg Air Force Base in California."

The voice of Mission Control methodically counting down the last few seconds reverberated throughout the still, frigid air of Times Square. No one moved or spoke.

"T minus 10, 9, 8, 7, 6, 5, the engine start sequence has been initiated, 4, 3, 2, we have ignition on all rocket engines and all launch vehicles are go for launch."

With excitement in his voice, Donaldson articulates the drama on the screens as the seconds tick off.

"With all rocket engines roaring to life, the colossal video screens overhead light up the moonless night sky. Shrouded in smoke and flames from the powerful engines, each rocket shakes like a caged animal struggling to free itself from the stranglehold of the massive launchpad. It's an awesome sight to behold! Everyone strains to see the rockets that are now obscured by a veil of smoke."

The voice of Mission Control pierces the silence of the frigid night air.

"T-Zero. The required thrust for lift-off has been obtained on all launch vehicles, and the hold-down arms on all launch towers have been released.

"T+2 seconds. We have confirmed a successful lift-off of all launch vehicles as they just cleared the launch towers."

With a lump in his throat, Donaldson reports, *"With that word of success from NASA, there is an audible congregational sigh of relief here in Times Square. Crowds are standing to their feet, applauding the success of NASA. Laughter has erupted, and many in the crowd are shedding tears of joy as they watch the rockets rise majestically and unhurriedly toward their bizarre appointment in space."*

The next update from Mission Control silences the crowd.

"It's a textbook launch of an unprecedented mission with all systems go. After each launch vehicle successfully completes the roll program necessary to achieve the target trajectory and jettisons the booster stage, all rockets will proceed to the designated rendezvous point in Earth orbit."

The announcement of success from Mission Control results in another standing ovation from the crowd bursting with euphoric praise for a successful phase of the mission.

"All roll programs have been achieved, the boosters have been jettisoned, and all second stage engines have been ignited and obtained full thrust. The fleet of launch vehicles carrying their payload of destruction has begun the ten-hour journey from Earth orbit into deep space and is scheduled to impact Genesis in 9 hours, 54 minutes, 30 seconds. Now we wait!"

As the spectators take a well-deserved breather after the emotional launch, James Donaldson returned to the microphone.

"Dr. Whitfield, it looks like Project Genesis is off to an amazing start. Tell me, do you still believe this mission will fail, and Genesis will impact earth as you testified earlier?"

"Yes, James, I believe regardless of how successful the mission has been so far, Genesis will strike the earth precisely as I testified."

"Well, our viewers heard your prediction, Dr. Whitfield, and we will be here as long as it takes to see Project Genesis to completion, but I have to tell you, it looks to me like these missiles are right on target and NASA is very optimistic. Of course, we all hope you're wrong.

"While we wait for the next update from NASA on the progress of the mission, we will return to our regularly scheduled programming. Coverage of the Genesis mission here in Times Square will resume in approximately nine hours and thirty minutes, but we will return immediately if there are any new developments."

James Donaldson and the Whitfields returned to their hotel rooms nearby.

For almost five agonizing hours, the spectators in Times Square snuggled anxiously under coats and blankets to escape the icy air and light snow. Those who couldn't sleep sipped fresh hot coffee provided by street vendors and speculated with friends and strangers alike on the possible outcomes of the mission. Others were out walking around visiting coffee shops and restaurants to pass the time and stay warm.

Hours later, the anxious crowd applauded loudly as the Whitfields returned with James Donaldson to Times Square to resume broadcasting.

"Good morning again. This is James Donaldson, reporting live for CBN Nightly News in Times Square, where it's a little past three o'clock in the morning, Eastern time. We just received word that NASA flight directors have successfully achieved a planned mid-course correction in the trajectory of the rockets which are approximately halfway to Genesis. As you can see on the screen above my head, the images of the rockets hurtling into space toward

their target are being broadcast live around the world from the world's newest and most powerful telescope in space. Approximately thirty minutes before the rockets impact with Genesis, NASA will provide another update.

"We're going now to the CBN Morning News desk in Washington D.C. for ... wait...wait just a minute!"

Suddenly the words "BREAKING NEWS!" flash across the screens.

With his head tilted down looking away from the camera and his hand clutched tightly to his right ear, Donaldson strained to hear the voice in his earpiece.

"What did you say? Are you sure?"

Then, with a grimaced expression, he faced the camera but hesitated before speaking. With hearts pounding like bass drums anticipating the news, the chatter of the crowd is silenced.

Jonathan and Grace saw fear in Donaldson's eyes.

CHAPTER 44

IMPACT

Reeling from the latest NASA news bulletin with his voice cracking, Donaldson updated the viewers.

"NASA just announced that something completely unexpected occurred immediately following the successful mid-course correction of the rockets' track to Genesis!

"We have asked Dr. James Morrison from NASA's Jet Propulsion Laboratory's Deep Space Network in Goldstone, California to brief us on the latest bizarre development in the Genesis mission.

"Good morning, Dr. Morrison. Please bring our audience up to date on what has happened and explain exactly what it means to the success of the Genesis mission."

"Thank you, James. Just minutes after the textbook mid-course corrections in the trajectories of the rockets were completed, scientists at JPL detected a slight wobble in the path of Genesis. Without any apparent stimulus, the asteroid began to exhibit an unusual, erratic, tumbling motion totally uncharacteristic of this cosmic body. Unfortunately, due to the constant movement of the target area, NASA scientists have determined they may be unable to detonate the nuclear warheads at the precise location necessary to ensure a successful mission."

"Please explain to our viewers in layman's terms what this

means, Dr. Morrison."

"Of course. To guarantee that the trajectory of the deadly space rock is altered sufficiently to safely bypass Earth by approximately 40,000 miles, the detonation of the warheads must take place within the narrow target area highlighted in yellow on the surface of the asteroid as indicated on the screen. Due to the wobble of the asteroid, it may not be possible for any of the warheads to hit the precise target area. However, NASA is still hopeful that the violent nuclear explosions will alter the path of the asteroid sufficiently to cause Genesis to ricochet off the Earth's upper atmosphere and hurtle harmlessly into deep space."

"Dr. Morrison, in light of the latest information received from NASA, can you give us a probability that Genesis may come closer than predicted, but not actually strike the Earth?"

"No, even though we're optimistic, the odds are definitely not in our favor. I believe it will take something beyond our scientific knowledge and ability to ensure Genesis does not impact our planet."

"Excuse me, what do you mean something beyond our scientific knowledge and ability? Who or what are you talking about?"

"Please understand, Mr. Donaldson. I'm not a religious man, but I'm just saying I believe the initial alteration in the rogue asteroid's path was caused by some cosmic power beyond our ability to comprehend. It's also unnatural and suspiciously coincidental that Genesis began to tumble uncontrollably immediately after we signaled the rockets' guidance systems to deliver the nuclear warheads to the bulls-eye of the target area."

"So, what are you saying?"

"I'm just saying it's as though some supernatural force beyond our world is observing every move we make and preventing us from changing the course of that asteroid."

"By supernatural force, do you mean God?"

"I don't know if God or perhaps some highly intelligent alien life form from deep space is responsible."

"Excuse me, but I believe Dr. Whitfield, who is with me tonight in Times Square, said this would happen if you tried to change the

course of Genesis."

Nodding his head yes and making hand jesters to get his hands on the microphone, Jonathan whispered, "I would like to say something."

"Not now, Jonathan, perhaps after the commercial break!"

"Well... yes," Donaldson replied, "but since the asteroid now appears to be on an unavoidable collision course with Earth, we must quickly address and prepare for the consequences. The warheads are scheduled to detonate on the surface of Genesis exactly four hours and thirty minutes from now. If the trajectory of Genesis is not successfully altered, we are estimating impact at ground zero approximately ten hours later. Even though we're still hopeful Genesis will miss our planet, NASA is recommending the evacuation of Glenway begin immediately."

"Can you explain to our viewers what they should expect as Genesis approaches Earth?"

"Yes, let me direct your viewers' attention to the computer-generated simulation prepared by NASA for this turn of events, although, truthfully, they never expected to use it. This video describes what you should expect to see and experience as Genesis enters the Earth's upper atmosphere from the west over Asia and hurtles east toward impact on the California coast approximately eighteen minutes later.

"As Genesis, now defined as a meteor, streaks across the heavens high above the Pacific Ocean at more than 100,000 feet and 25,000 miles per hour, it will pass safely over the Hawaiian Islands at an altitude of more than 75,000 feet. The first sign of the approaching asteroid, as it plows through the increasingly dense atmosphere, will be a blinding white ball of light. The surface of Genesis will ultimately experience temperatures approaching 3,000 degrees Fahrenheit.

"Plummeting through an altitude of 40,000 feet, Genesis will scribe a billowing white condensation trail in the heavens. Melted particles spalling from the white-hot surface, combined with burning gases, will form the tail of Genesis and stretch miles into the atmosphere.

"Racing high above the Pacific Ocean, Genesis will rapidly descend through an altitude of 10,000 feet as it barrels toward the Earth. At 1,000 feet, with the California coastline in its crosshairs, the track of Genesis will be preceded by an enormous tidal wave, thirty to forty feet high. Slicing through an altitude of 300 feet, a half-mile wide corridor of the Pacific Ocean in the asteroid's path will be instantaneously vaporized, sending clouds of superheated steam exploding into the atmosphere. Streaking across the pristine coastline of California at treetop level and supersonic speeds, Genesis will be preceded by a violent shock wave generating hurricane-force winds with searing temperatures. Everything in the path of the meteor will be destroyed by the scorching heat, raging winds, and the tidal surge. An earsplitting sonic boom will follow the shock wave and produce widespread damage to homes and other structures for miles in every direction.

"The impact of the meteor will activate powerful earthquakes and deadly atmospheric electrical storms over an extensive area of California—possibly even triggering displacement of the subterranean plates in the San Andreas Fault. The lethal rock's journey through space will terminate in a mammoth devastating explosion at ground level with the energy of 500 kilotons of TNT or a force of more than thirty times more powerful than the atomic bomb dropped by the United States on Hiroshima, Japan, in 1945. Genesis is expected to plow a crater more than a half-mile long and up to sixty feet deep. Anything and everything within a mile of the blast will be instantly vaporized, with power outages and interruptions in all forms of communication.

"The entire L.A. Basin should be avoided, and anyone remaining within ten miles of the city limits of Glenway should take cover below ground in basements or underground shelters due to flying glass and debris. Open countryside, high-rise buildings, as well as areas along the coastline, should be avoided at all costs."

Jonathan whispered to Donaldson, "You do realize there is no time now for people to escape Glenway. Thousands of people, maybe more, will die because they would not listen to the warning."

Overhearing the comment, Grace responded, "Well, Jonathan, a few months ago, I'm not sure you would have listened to the warning either."

"Thank you for that, Grace."

Ignoring Jonathan, Donaldson continued, *"Thank you, Dr. Morrison, for that critical update, and please keep us informed of further developments. We are now going to our CBN World News correspondent in Tel Aviv, Israel, where we have more breaking news. The President of the New World Union is speaking at a news conference already in progress."*

The president of the New World Union is speaking. *"Because of the imminent threat of nuclear war against Israel, I'm proposing a peace treaty which can be renegotiated after seven years. I plan to meet with the Prime Minister of Israel in a few weeks and sign the document in Independence Hall in Tel Aviv. The momentous occasion will take place in the same building where Israel was given their independence as a nation in 1948. Right now, I want to pray for those in the path of Genesis hurtling toward the Los Angeles area of the United States."*

The camera turns to the CBN World News correspondent covering the news conference.

"The news conference has just concluded, and the President of the New World Union has left the stage. We will now return to New York City, where CBN Nightly News anchor James Donaldson is reporting live in Times Square on the Genesis mission."

"Good morning again, this is James Donaldson reporting live for CBN Nightly News in Times Square. It's now less than an hour before the nuclear warheads are scheduled to detonate on the surface of Genesis. Crowds that wandered away from Times Square have returned and are jockeying for the best view of the enormous video screens."

With the crowd becoming impatient, the voice of Mission Control causes an eerie hush to come over Times Square.

"Time to impact is one minute and counting."

In a whisper, Donaldson reports, *"Everyone is on their feet and nervously counting down in sync with the voice of Mission Control."*

"Ten seconds, nine seconds, eight seconds, seven seconds, six...

five...four...three...two...one...impact!"

Dr. Whitfield stood as hopeful and helpless as the crowds in Times Square, but he had an uncomfortable, burning sensation in his gut about the outcome.

Donaldson attempted to describe the picture displayed on the massive video screens.

"There was a colossal explosion, and the mammoth video screens just flashed completely white. Wait..., now the screens are black. Something else is happening...there I see something...a very blurred image with a lot of dust. Look, the picture is coming back into focus...and there it is! There is Genesis big as life! It looks completely intact, but we will have to wait for NASA to determine if there was any change in the path of Genesis. Perhaps it's just the picture...but...yes, Genesis appears to have stopped tumbling."

After a few agonizing minutes that seemed like an eternity, the NASA spokesperson appeared on the screen. People were holding their breath, hoping and praying for good news but prepared for the worst. Hearts were pounding for those who had family and friends in and near Glenway while relieved they were in New York City, out of harm's way.

"This is Dr. James Morrison reporting again for NASA. It's with great sadness that our worst fears are realized. NASA scientists have just concluded that the attempt to redirect Genesis safely away from Earth has failed. Genesis is still on the identical path as before the detonation of the warheads."

Bowing his head, Jonathan whispered, "Why wouldn't they listen? This didn't have to happen!"

Gasping in unison, the crowd seemed to suck the air out of Times Square! Many were sobbing openly for their friends in the strike zone, believing they may not escape the death sentence from space. Everyone was convinced NASA would not—could not—fail, and they were certainly not prepared for this devastating news.

Dr. Morrison continued. *"Genesis mysteriously stopped tumbling immediately after the warheads detonated and is predicted to impact Glenway, now designated ground zero on the California coast, in approximately ten hours. There is absolutely nothing we can do now to stop, slow down, or alter the path of Genesis. The Federal Government is working with local authorities in Glenway and nearby towns and cities to immediately begin the evacuation of everyone in harm's way. The military has dispatched C-140 aircraft to all nearby airports to airlift as many people as possible out of the area."*

"Dr. Morrison," Donaldson asked, "What about the other asteroids that are on a collision course with Earth?"

"James, after the unsuccessful attempt to alter the course of Genesis, NASA has concluded a new laser technology under development may be our only hope short of what some religious people call 'divine intervention.' NASA estimates there will be global destruction and a massive death toll if the gargantuan foreign projectiles continue their paths and strike heavily populated cities. Our sophisticated intellect, strategic weapons, and advanced technology seem to be no match for whomever or whatever is behind this deadly assault on our planet. Perhaps there is some truth to the message Dr. Whitfield gave us several months ago. He said, 'This asteroid could not be stopped' and warned there was more to come if America didn't return the nation to God! I believe he called it the Tribulation. We may be witnessing the beginning of the end of our world as we know it."

"James, I would like to respond to Dr. Morrison's comments."

"I'm sorry, Dr. Whitfield! We are short on time and it is just not possible."

"We will continue to bring you regular updates in the next few hours on the progress of Genesis as it races toward the California coast. Our first update will be in approximately nine hours, forty minutes, when the asteroid is expected to enter the Earth's upper atmosphere.

"Well, thank you, Dr. Morrison, although we're devastated to hear that report. Now we're switching to our Los Angeles correspondent and affiliate WLC News for the latest information on the evacuation of the Glenway, California area that is already underway."

"We're bringing you live coverage above Glenway from our WLC News affiliate in their chopper. With less than ten hours until impact,

there are reports of chaos on the entire West Coast. People living in Glenway, as well as residents of nearby towns and cities as far away as Los Angeles and San Francisco, are terror-stricken. As you can see, residents are facing heavily congested highways in their escape from Glenway and surrounding areas. Throngs of frightened people are even jamming the LAX airport and private airport terminals hoping to get a flight out of the danger zone in time. People have been seen driving onto the runways of airports hoping to grab a seat on the military C-140 aircraft while waiting to take off."

"Grace, this is making me sick!"

"Jonathan, you can't take responsibility for what is happening. You delivered the message, and each person has to make their choice!"

"This is James Donaldson again for CBN World News in Times Square where live videos of the terrified residents and vacationers fleeing the approaching holocaust share the massive video screens with images of the killer asteroid. The crowds here are comatose watching the horror in California unfold from the safety of their vantage point in the Times Square sanctuary. We will return to Dr. James Morrison, NASA spokesperson, as soon as Genesis enters the Earth's atmosphere."

Several hours later, the massive video screens came alive again with Dr. Morrison giving the latest update on Project Genesis.

"This is Dr. James Morrison with NASA's Jet Propulsion Laboratory's Deep Space Network in Goldstone, California, to provide a live update on Genesis.

"Six minutes ago, Genesis entered the exosphere or upper layer of the Earth's atmosphere over Asia. Racing toward earth on the predicted trajectory, the deadly intruder is expected to impact ground zero in approximately twelve minutes. As Genesis rips through the dense layers of the atmosphere, thousands of rock particles or meteorites have been detected spalling from the surface. These particles are expected to produce a spectacular meteor shower in the heavens during the predawn hours before they burn out. Some of the larger fragments are predicted to strike the Earth's surface throughout the west coast of California and beyond but are anticipated to have minimal impact on people and... wait a

minute...! What?... How can you be sure?"

Clutching his earpiece, Dr. Morrison covered his microphone, whispered to the Project Command engineer, and returned to the broadcast.

Even before Dr. Morrison spoke, Jonathan could see fear in Dr. Morrison's eyes.

Now, what has happened? Jonathan thought to himself.

CHAPTER 45

NIGHTMARE IN TIMES SQUARE

"We have obtained radar confirmation that Genesis just passed over the Hawaiian Islands and is now predicted to impact the West coast of the United States in a little less than six minutes.

"However, JPL just confirmed a large fragment, weighing approximately 1,000 tons, has spalled from Genesis. NASA is predicting this fragment will skip through the heavens like a flat stone across the water at more than thirty times the speed of sound and impact on the East Coast of the United States in less than twelve minutes. With an energy level of approximately 45 kilotons of TNT, the fragment is expected to explode as it strikes the earth with a force three times more powerful than the atomic bomb dropped on Hiroshima."

"This is not possible," Jonathan said loudly to himself. "Malachi didn't say anything about collateral damage; this was supposed to be a warning, a dress rehearsal for the Tribulation."

Overhearing Jonathan's comment, James could not resist asking the question. *"Well, Dr. Whitfield, if you were given all the information about this disaster by the fictitious Malachi who you claim obtained his message from God, why didn't he tell you about this fragment targeting the East Coast?"*

Jonathan was speechless.

Hearing Dr. Morrison's announcement, desperate cries erupted from the throng of people in Times Square. "We're on the East Coast! Where is it going to hit?"

As if Dr. Morrison could hear the question, he continued. *"NASA is predicting the fragment will impact New York City somewhere in a five-square mile area of Manhattan. The Manhattan area should be evacuated immediately in an orderly, safe fashion. If you're unable or choose not to leave the city, take cover in an underground shelter as soon as possible and avoid all windows and other openings."*

"That guy must be crazy," shouted Jonathan, "They can't evacuate the city in twelve hours, much less twelve minutes. The impact zone was supposed to be limited to Glenway, California. If that fragment hits the Times Square area, a million people may die."

"Jonathan, you have to trust God and have faith in what He is doing," said Grace.

Screams from the stands of the Times Square Ticket booth amphitheater pierced the frigid night air. "He's got a gun!"

A young man vaulted from the stands to the street below and broke into a run, yelling, "Yes, and I'll use it. Get out of my way!"

As the gunman vanished among the sea of fleeing bystanders, a father in the stands hugged his terrified wife and children and cried, "Let him go. It's too late for all of us, anyway!"

"Dr. Whitfield, you and Grace stay close to me. I'm calling for a helicopter to get us out of this maddening crowd. I will continue the broadcast from the helicopter."

Gunshots, followed by muffled screams for help, were heard in the distance.

Donaldson, Jonathan, Grace, and the TV tech were running toward an area roped off by the police for the CBN News helicopter to land when Grace shrieked and stopped abruptly. A young woman had fallen in front of her.

"I think she's hurt badly," cried Grace. While she bent down to examine the girl's lifeless body, the frenzied mob running for their lives thoughtlessly trampled them both. Struggling to shield the helpless girl against the onslaught of panicking spectators with her own bruised body, Grace screamed, "Jonathan, please help her!"

Donaldson barked at the TV tech, "Help me protect the girl from the crowd and get some shots of her and our good Samaritans at work."

On his knees, Jonathan gently turned over the unresponsive girl laying in a pool of blood only to find a bullet wound in her chest. After checking for a pulse, he looked at Grace and shook his head, "She's gone! It looks like a stray bullet from a shooter in that crazy mob took its toll on her."

"Everyone has gone mad," yelled Grace, standing to her feet and trembling with fear. With every nerve on edge, she shouted at the crowd as if they could hear her or even cared what she was saying, "You're all acting like a pack of wild animals! What's wrong with you?"

Buffeted by the throng of people freaking out, Donaldson labored to continue broadcasting while Jonathan tried to calm Grace and move her away from the crowd.

"As you can see Times Square, an enchanted wonderland of fun and entertainment that dazzles visitors from all over the world, has become a horrifying toxic war zone tonight, bringing the city to its knees. This is James Donaldson for CBN News, bringing you live coverage of the night from hell. We're reporting from the corner of Broadway and West 47th Street near the Times Square Ticket booth amphitheater, where thousands of spectators are rushing through the streets like stampeding cattle trampling anyone in their path. News that the fragment of Genesis will strike somewhere right here in Manhattan in a matter of minutes has created a nightmare in Times Square."

Suddenly, a man breaks from the crowd and attacks Donaldson, knocking him to the ground while shouting, "This is all your fault!, You should have given us more warning!"

Jonathan helped to fend off the attacker and returned to Grace.

Leaping down the twenty-seven rows of the ruby red glass steps of the amphitheater, another crazed spectator heaved a young woman and her baby out of his way over the handrail. On her knees wiping blood from a gash on her head, the woman cried, "I can't move.

Somebody, please help me find my baby!"

"Grace, stay with James. I'm going to try to help that woman and her child."

Spotting the young woman just a few yards away, Jonathan fought his way through the crowd to reach her.

Donaldson continued. *"I can't believe my eyes..., everyone is freaking out! Just moments ago, the crowd that packed Times Square was calm and passive. Now bodies are tumbling head-over-heels down the amphitheater steps as panic-stricken bystanders clamber over each other to reach the street level like a pack of hungry wolves in pursuit of wild game."*

A terrified newlywed separated from her husband by the mass of people cried, "I never dreamed it would end like this."

After reaching the bleeding woman crying for help, Jonathan spotted her traumatized child standing helplessly by the statue of Father Duffy near the north end of Times Square. Fighting his way through the crowd like a salmon swimming upstream, he reunited the two and helped them off the street to safety in the nearby Starbucks café.

The roar of an approaching helicopter is heard over the clamor of the crowd. Illuminated by the brilliant lights of the animated billboards above 7th Avenue, the bright yellow CBN Air One News helicopter descended over the McDonald's Restaurant and attempted to land in the roped-off area in the plaza to pick up Donaldson and his passengers.

"Stay away from the windows, and you and your child will be safe in here," Jonathan said to the injured woman. "I have to get to my wife."

Approaching the landing area, Donaldson reported, *"I'll continue broadcasting live from Air One above Times Square."*

Suddenly a frightened young man shouted to a terrified group of followers, "Get that chopper. It's our only way out of here!"

"Stop, or I'll shoot!" An NYPD officer guarding the landing area shouted to the crazed mob rushing toward the chopper, but he was trampled before he could draw his weapon.

Just as the helicopter touched down, it was inundated by the throng of desperate people. Donaldson and his tech agreed the scene was too dangerous to go any closer.

Standing on a stationary bench, Grace strained to see over the crowd and cried, "Jonathan, where are you?"

Pulling Grace down off the bench, James shouted, "Come with me, Mrs. Whitfield. We have to leave this area."

Fighting his way through the crowd, Jonathan caught up with Grace and Donaldson, who were running from the landing area.

"Jonathan, I was worried something happened to you. How is the girl?" Grace asked.

"She and her child are safe now, and I think they will be fine."

Donaldson continued to broadcast while looking back over his shoulder and hurrying from the landing area. *"The rebels have opened the cockpit door and are forcing their way inside. It looks like the pilot is attempting to take off, but dozens of people are dangling from the open door and landing skids like clothes on a line. They won't let go! What a horrifying scene. The main rotors of the chopper are whirring close to the crowd like four giant razors threatening death to anyone in their path.*

"Oh my God, the extra weight is causing the helicopter to rotate uncontrollably, slinging screaming bodies onto the street like rag dolls."

"I'm begging you to let go! You're going to kill us all!" the pilot screamed over the PA system.

Donaldson thought to himself, *"It's true; if only they would have listened. Dr. Whitfield warned the White House and members of Congress of this harbinger of death and destruction months ago, but they all ignored the warning. I guess I'm as guilty as the rest of them."*

Donaldson continues to broadcast. *"Oh my gosh, the helicopter is thrashing in the air like a wounded bird, tilting violently from one side and then to the other side. The pilot is fighting desperately to keep the machine airborne, but with the extra weight of so many people hanging on, it's a losing battle. Now the chopper is tipping dangerously close to the ground. I'm afraid it's going to...I can't look!*

"Oh, my God, the chopper just rolled over into the crowd and exploded in a fireball right in front of us. Spinning dizzily like a flaming top, the wreckage is spewing burning jet fuel and shrapnel everywhere."

At that moment, Grace screamed and fell to the ground, grabbing her right leg where a piece of shrapnel struck her like a bullet.

With Grace in writhing pain, Jonathan wrapped his tie around her leg to stop the bleeding and tried to encourage her, "Good news, it looks like a flesh wound. The shrapnel is not embedded in your leg, but we have to get you to a hospital."

"The smoke is suffocating, and I didn't see the pilot get out. This is horrible, people everywhere are screaming for help, but there is no one to help!

"The streets of Manhattan look like something out of the War of the Worlds movie, littered with trash, broken glass and the bodies of those poor souls who died under the press of the fleeing crowd and the helicopter crash. It's too late now...time is running out, and there is no way to leave the area. By my watch, there are only two minutes until the Genesis fragment impacts somewhere in Manhattan. In fact, we should see the flaming face of the fragment appear in the western sky at any moment. We'll continue to bring you coverage of the impact of this rock from hell as long as possible.

"An ear-piercing sonic boom just shattered store windows everywhere, creating a snowstorm of pulverized flying glass, signaling the unwanted visitor from space is less than a minute away.

"Thousands of people still trapped in the city are scrambling to take shelter in stores, hotels, and apartment buildings.

"My camera tech, Jack Weathers, and I are taking shelter in a nearby building."

"No, James!" Grabbing Grace's arm, Jonathan shouted, "We don't have time, and the buildings have too many windows. Follow me across the street to the 49th Street subway station!"

Limping badly, Grace shouted, "You have to help me, Jonathan;

you know I can't walk."

Picking up Grace, Jonathan shouted to the others, "We have to hurry, but we'll be safe in the subway station below street level."

With Grace in his arms, Jonathan started across the street, but a speeding car careered out of control, climbing the curb and bouncing off the concrete safety barriers. The rogue vehicle narrowly missed them but struck and killed two innocent young people.

With her throat dry as cotton, Grace choked out, "When will this nightmare end?"

The group cautiously hurried across the street and started down the stairs of the subway entrance.

Suddenly, a veil of darkness rolled across Times Square and covered the group like a shroud of death as the large video screens, blazing with images of the impact of Genesis minutes before, became dark.

Jonathan volunteered, "The searing heat of the approaching asteroid fragment must have damaged the transmission lines providing electrical power to Times Square, causing a massive power failure."

Donaldson and his tech stopped in the stairway for a last look at the western sky, straining to catch a glimpse of Genesis with their camera. Groping through the darkness, Grace and Jonathan continued down the steps, clumsily climbed over the turnstiles, and finally reached the subway platform. The emergency lighting created eerie shadows of the rioting crowd. The shadows danced on the walls as the crowd fought and struggled to pull open the doors on a commuter train which was now stranded without electrical power.

Standing against the back wall of the platform safely out of the way of the maddening crowd, Grace muttered out loud, "Can you believe those people are risking their lives to board a train that is going nowhere?"

With a furrowed forehead and wrinkled nose, Grace swung her head slowly from side to side in the darkness, straining to see and sniffing out loud like a bloodhound on the trail of a fox.

"Jonathan, what is that horrible smell?

"I'm afraid that's the smell of burning flesh. It looks like several people were pushed off the platform on to the electrified rails by the frantic crowd. Sadly enough, a few minutes after the people died, the rails were no longer electrified due to the power outage."

From the subway stairwell, Donaldson pointed to the sky while continuing to broadcast. *"Look, there it is, the face of the demonic fragment! Quick, get the camera over there! It looks like all of hell has been unleashed on us. We will continue to broadcast live as long as the mobile satellite truck is intact. I'm told the operator abandoned the vehicle, but the signal transmitter is on automatic. Come on, Jack, let's get down to the train platform where it's safer."*

Winded, Donaldson bolted down the stairs and scrambled over the subway turnstiles, tripping and falling in the darkness.

Looking back, Donaldson reported, *"Glass from shattered store windows is being propelled into the stairwell like bullets by the hurricane-force winds.*

"Wait! Where is Jack? I thought he was right behind me!"

Getting up and looking back across the turnstiles, James saw him standing midway up the stairwell. With his face wrapped in his jacket to avoid the violent windstorm of shattered glass, he was continuing to broadcast live video of the approaching space fragment.

Screaming at the top of his lungs, Donaldson called for his close friend and longtime colleague to seek safety. "Jack, forget about the pictures and get down here before…!"

CHAPTER 46

THE AFTERMATH

Several weeks after being treated for burns, multiple cuts from flying glass, and a broken leg, James Donaldson appeared on the CBN 5:00 o'clock Evening News from the CBN newsroom in Washintgton, D.C. Fighting to hold back the tears, the celebrated journalist gave a very moving, emotional account of the horrible aftermath of Genesis during a special nationally televised CBN News documentary.

After Grace was treated for the shrapnel in her leg from the helicopter crash, Jonathan and Grace returned home and watched the newscast from the comfort of their home.

"First, let me say how grateful I am to be here tonight. My life was spared from the nightmare in Times Square by Dr. Jonathan Whitfield, who first brought the warning of this menace from space. Dr. Whitfield led us down into the 49th Street subway station, where we were safe from the asteroid strike. Unfortunately, among others, I was pushed off the subway platform onto the rails below by the press of an inflamed crowd trying to commandeer a subway car. Thankfully, I suffered only broken bones since the rails were not electrified due to the power outage. In my entire life, I've never been more thankful for a power outage!

"Ignoring my appeal to seek safety, Jack Weathers, my camera tech, remained in the stairwell to continue shooting video of Genesis

and became a statistic of the space rock from hell. A nearby street sign ripped from its foundation was propelled like a spear down into the stairwell by the hurricane-force winds and killed him instantly. The death of my colleague, who lived to bring the best television pictures possible to our viewers, is a great loss to me personally as well as to CBN News. He will be missed greatly as well as the CBN News helicopter pilot who died in the crash of his chopper!

"Although NASA could not have possibly predicted the large fragment would spall from Genesis, it was a miracle the 1,000-ton rock from space exploded in the Upper New York City Bay just south of Liberty Island and the Statue of Liberty, falling short of the crowded Manhattan Times Square area. The blast caused by the impact of the meteor in the bay produced billowing clouds of steam and a blinding light show over water that was visible for miles. Windows were shattered throughout New York City and New Jersey by the sonic boom that preceded the fragment. Waterfront warehouses and other structures near the water within a three-mile radius from ground zero were destroyed by scorching hurricane-force winds and the tidal surge generated when the space rock plummeted into the bay.

"Tunnels and subways throughout New York City were flooded, and there were several feet of water in Manhattan as far inland as Madison Square Garden. If the fragment had impacted the Manhattan area just a few miles farther north of ground zero, there might have been hundreds of thousands of people killed in Times Square alone. It's unfortunate that even though the city was spared a direct hit by the fragment, many lives were lost due to the chaos incited by mob violence in the streets and the crash of our CBN News helicopter. That Saturday night was truly a nightmare in Times Square and will never be forgotten.

"Sadly, NASA accurately predicted Glenway, California to be ground zero, where the main body of Genesis struck. However, without enough time to conduct a complete, orderly evacuation of the area near ground zero, hundreds of people died instantly, and thousands more sustained severe injuries. The entire city of Glenway was literally vaporized, and everything within a two-mile radius of the one-half-mile, thirty-foot-deep crater plowed by Genesis was incinerated by the explosion of the deadly projectile from outer space.

"As you can see in this photograph of the aftermath, the only structure still standing at ground zero where the city of Glenway was located is a fifty-foot high cross in front of the charred remains of the First Baptist Church. I recall, in his message to Congress, Dr. Whitfield said to look for a sign at ground zero after the impact of Genesis. Perhaps this single remaining structure is the sign he was referring to, but what does it mean?"

Watching the newscast from the comfort of their home, Jonathan smiled at Grace as he addressed the television. "I can tell you the cross means only the Church will escape the coming apocalypse. Those who have accepted Jesus Christ as Savior make up the true church, and they will not have to endure one second of the Tribulation that may now be imminent."

"Jonathan, please stop talking to the television."

The report continued. *"There were billions of dollars in direct and collateral property damage to homes and other structures for miles up and down the California coast. The impact of Genesis triggered a 7.2 magnitude earthquake along the San Andreas Fault that was felt as far away as Oklahoma. The earthquake sent hundreds of luxurious homes perched on the cliffs of the California coastline into the Pacific Ocean as far north as San Francisco. We may never know the complete extent of injuries or even the number of deaths on the ground as well as on all the planes, trains, and ships with desperate people trying to escape the impact zone.*

"Only those who evacuated the area early as a precaution after hearing Dr. Whitfield's initial warning survived without injuries. Many of those who escaped confessed they were just being cautious while others believed Dr. Whitfield's message and his warning with all their hearts. These new believers have now joined the swelling ranks of Americans who embrace Dr. Whitfield's message to return America to God. I understand Dr. Whitfield is even receiving emails from new believers all over the world convinced that God's judgment is imminent if there is not revival in America."

Jonathan turned to Grace. "We should hear from Donaldson soon. Remember, I agreed last week to be interviewed by phone on his 5:00 o'clock newscast today regarding the aftermath of Genesis, and it's after 5:30 P.M. Like you said, it will be another opportunity to share God's message."

Donaldson's report continued. *"With that report on the aftermath of the impact of Genesis, let me review the reaction by the White House and the effect of Genesis on world markets.*

"The President of the United States expressed his genuine sorrow at the loss of lives due to the tragedy of Genesis. Vowing another disaster like this one will never happen on his watch, the president resolved to fully investigate the cause of this catastrophe and expedite funding for new technology to prevent similar asteroids from striking Earth in the future. He reminded the nation that 'America will not be taken down by mindless rogue space rocks lobbed at the Earth by some fictitious cosmic power.' He also promised, 'I'll not allow any spiritual fanatic to paralyze our great nation with the unwarranted fear of an apocalypse regardless of their religious beliefs.' Well, from what I've experienced during the last few days, I'm not sure what the president or anyone else can do about this prophecy of destruction.

"To fulfill his promise to the American people, the president has already called for a Congressional Commission to be set up immediately with NASA scientists and the military to determine how something, or someone, could change the trajectory of an asteroid. Scientists are also designing a new powerful laser which can be launched into Earth orbit within two years to destroy or redirect the trajectory of future oncoming asteroids like Genesis."

"Do you see, Grace?" Jonathan said. "They think they're smart enough to prevent the inevitable chaos. At least this tragedy resulted in many people all over the world believing in God and accepting Jesus Christ."

"Wall Street jitters are causing investors to flee the financial markets and invest their savings in long-term supplies of food, water, fuel for automobiles, and guns and ammunition," Donaldson reported. *"Stock prices for these commodities have burst through the roof, ignoring declining markets in general. People believe the threat of more asteroids targeting Earth may signal apocalyptic war. Many people are constructing underground shelters reminiscent of bomb shelters advertised in the Popular Mechanics magazine in the 1950s and 1960s."*

Donaldson signaled for the producer to bring up a video of rallies supporting Dr. Whitfield's message for Americans to return to God.

CHAPTER 47

ARE YOU THERE?

"As you can see in this recent video, organized groups of evangelical Christians are holding huge public rallies in major cities across the nation to share the message Dr. Whitfield brought to the White House and members of Congress. You will recognize a few bipartisan congressional members of the House and Senate in the crowds speaking on behalf of Dr. Whitfield. Of course, these rallies are being met with large groups of angry protestors from every religious background that claim Dr. Whitfield and his message is offensive and has absolutely no solid basis. Although the demonstrations are, for the most part, peaceful, local police are standing nearby to suppress any violence that may develop.

"This evening, we'll have the privilege of talking to the man who not only brought the first warning of Genesis to our attention and accompanied my team and me during the broadcast of Project Genesis from Times Square but jump-started the powerful evangelical movement that is sweeping across the nation like a forest fire. Dr. Jonathan Whitfield has agreed to an exclusive interview with CBN News and will be on the phone with us from his home in New Jersey in just a few minutes. You don't want to miss this interview!"

Clutching his earpiece, Donaldson listened intently to the voice in his receiver. *"I'm told we have Dr. Whitfield on the phone now."*

"Good evening, Dr. Whitfield, it's a pleasure to have you on the

show."

"Thank you for having me, James."

"By the way, we asked our viewers to tweet any questions they have for you during the interview."

"Great, I'll be happy to answer any questions."

"Dr. Whitfield, it's been several weeks since the deadly impact of Genesis. Do you realize that the entire nation is paralyzed with fear because of your doomsday message and the coincidental impact of Genesis?"

"Wait a minute, what do you mean the coincidental…?"

"Excuse me, Dr. Whitfield, but I'm sure you have heard that after a thorough analysis of the Genesis phenomenon, NASA has concluded that the change in trajectory was due to powerful magnetic fields caused by intense solar storms on the surface of the sun."

"Now, wait a minute…"

"Let me finish, Dr. Whitfield. The same solar activity is also believed to be responsible for the recent temporary loss of communications in many cities around the world. With all due respect, Dr. Whitfield, NASA scientists are the only ones who completely understand the physics of the vast universe, and the results of their analysis are very compelling."

"But how can you say…"

"On another subject, people have been flooding our phone lines with calls asking what they can do to survive the future impact of meteorites like Genesis in the unlikely event other asteroids targeting Earth cannot be stopped. Will you please explain to our viewers what you and your followers are doing to survive future attacks from space?"

"Mr. Donaldson, thank you for finally allowing me to speak to your viewers. I had hoped Americans would believe that the supernatural change in the trajectory and impact of Genesis I announced several months prior to NASA identifying the threat was a clear, undeniable message from God. Now that a peace treaty between the President of the New World Union and Israel is being negotiated, I don't believe we have much time."

"What do you mean, 'We don't have much time?' I don't follow you, Dr. Whitfield. Will you please explain yourself?"

"If you recall, I affirmed in my address to Congress that prophecy in the Bible promises the signing of a seven-year peace treaty with Israel will trigger the beginning of the deadly, supernatural apocalypse called the Tribulation, the ultimate judgment of God."

"Okay, but let's talk about something more relevant."

A picture of the horrendous blackened impact crater of Genesis in California flashes up on the screen.

"What about this cross next to the charred remains of a church on the edge of the crater made by Genesis? Is that the sign you said we should look for after the impact of the meteorite, and, if so, what does it mean?"

"Yes, and thank you for pointing that out. The cross is the sign that if America rejects the message from God, the only ones who will escape suffering and dying during the coming Tribulation are members of the church."

"Jack B from California just tweeted, 'I believe everything you're saying, Dr. Whitfield, but can you tell us which church will survive the apocalypse and can I join that church online? Can you give me a link to their website?'

"What do you say, Dr. Whitfield? I would like to know the answer to that question myself. What harm could it do to join a church if it provides a safety net from suffering, death, and destruction during the Tribulation? If you will give me the link to the website, I'll put it up for our viewers."

"That's a great question, Jack, but the church I'm talking about is not made up of people who proclaim affiliation with a religious denomination like Catholic, Baptist, or Methodist, or even those who attend religious services in a church building or watch them online. The true church I'm talking about is made up of people who have accepted Jesus Christ in their hearts by grace through faith in God and faithfully embrace His words for righteous living. As I explained earlier, the true church and all children will be supernaturally removed from this Earth by what is called the Rapture before the Tribulation begins. Since those who accepted Jesus Christ will not be on this planet, there is no need for them to make any other preparation for the impending apocalypse."

"Admittedly, regardless of how or where you obtained your information about Genesis, you were right on target, if you will excuse the expression. Now please explain to our viewers the basis for your outlandish prediction that all the children and believers you refer to as the church will somehow be removed from Earth during this Rapture. You're an archeologist, not a theologian. By the way, do you even have any theological training?"

"Well, no, I don't. but..."

"Do you have any idea how many quacks have predicted the end of the world in the last fifty years? By the way, if you haven't noticed, after all the wacky predictions, the world is still intact, and we're all still here. Besides, who or what has the capability to remove all the so-called 'believers' from planet Earth and where will all those people be taken? Are you proposing a modern-day 'Noah's Ark' rocket to take those people to the moon or some other planet?"

"No, Mr. Donaldson. All the believers who have accepted Jesus Christ in their hearts will be supernaturally and instantly taken to heaven by God to live with Him for all eternity. I admit I have been as blind to the truth as you and thousands more are most of my adult life. Now I'm sharing the simple gospel message of Jesus Christ with as many people as possible in the time we have left. Returning our nation to the fundamentals of God on which it was established is the only way to delay the Tribulation and the ultimate judgment of God. Frankly, Mr. Donaldson, I just don't know how much longer God will allow our nation and the world to continue rejecting Him and abusing the Bible and his messengers.

"Mr. Donaldson, there are many Americans who understand the message from God I delivered and recognize that the impact of Genesis authenticated that message. In the weeks following the destruction in Glenway and New York City, revival has broken out throughout America and many parts of the world. Many churches are packed on Sundays now, and some have large crowds on other days as well. I also understand some members of Congress are having prayer on the steps of the Capitol Building in Washington, D.C. reminiscent of the days after 9/11. My prayer is that this is the beginning of a spiritual revolution that will save America before it's too late."

"Well, you must be elated that your religious campaign has been so successful, although you seem to be very narrow-minded as to who may escape this great Tribulation as you call it."

"Even though I'm thrilled at the response of so many people accepting Jesus Christ in these last days, I am very disappointed that the numbers are still small in comparison to our total population. We are praying that the revival will spread throughout America to the leaders of Congress and even the White House in the time we have left. I would even like to take a few minutes and briefly share the gospel message with you and your viewers and answer any questions they may have."

"Well, thank you for the offer Dr. Whitfield, but I don't know if I can believe in a God who claims to mysteriously remove some people from Earth and leave the rest of the population to suffer and die. However, I will put a link to your website on the screen so that viewers may contact you for more information."

"You will be interested in this news, Dr. Whitfield. I've just received word from our Washington correspondent Sam Nicholson that a small group of Christian Congressional representatives who embrace your message brought a bill to the floor of the House today in the face of strong opposition. Their bill calls for an impressive sized 'Ebenezer Monument' to be erected on the National Mall between the White House and the Washington Monument, as you suggested. As a symbol of national religious solidarity, the monolith would demonstrate the nation's commitment to begin the arduous process of returning our nation to God, as requested in your message. In fact, the bill is being debated on the House floor as we speak, and I may have a report on the progress of the vote later in the newscast."

Clutching his earpiece, Donaldson listens intently. *"Wait a minute! Please stay on the line, Dr. Whitfield. Sam Nicholson in the Capitol is telling me there is breaking news from the floor of the House of Representatives. Hello, Sam. What's all the commotion about?"*

"James, we just received word from the floor of the House of Representatives that the erection of the Ebenezer Monument on the

National Mall has been determined to violate the Constitutional rights of certain religious groups and human rights organizations. Representatives of these groups have lobbied members of Congress objecting to any monument with a Christian connotation being constructed on federal land. It looks like it may take some time behind closed doors to garner enough backing for a compromise bill."

"Thank you for that report, Sam. Well, there you heard it live with our viewers, Dr. Whitfield. I know you're probably disappointed, but do you have any comments on this congressional action?"

"Yes, I certainly do! How will we ever return America to God when our congressional leaders refuse to make the commitment to do so? I believe God is heartbroken, as I am, by the refusal of our leaders in Washington to even begin the process of leading the nation back to God when we're clearly in the crosshairs of impending destruction."

"Excuse me again, Dr. Whitfield. I'm sorry for the interruption, but there is late-breaking news from our CBN World News correspondent in Israel. Please stay on the line, and I'll get right back to you."

After the conclusion of the news update from the correspondent in Israel, Donaldson returned to the air to continue his interview with Dr. Whitfield.

"Dr. Whitfield, the newly elected President of the New World Union, is in Israel and has just announced that he and the Prime Minister of Israel are ready to sign a peace treaty for an initial term of seven years. Negotiation of this treaty has been deadlocked for months with absolutely no sign of an agreement on terms and conditions. Suddenly, without notice, both Heads of State came to an understanding on all points of the document late tonight and agreed to sign the treaty in an unprecedented early morning news conference at one A.M. Israel time or six P.M. eastern time. Since we have a television crew in Tel Aviv covering the negotiation, we'll be able to bring our viewers live coverage of this momentous event when it takes place.

"Proposed to protect Israel from their enemies for at least seven years, this treaty will be signed in Independence Hall on the historic

Rothschild Boulevard in Tel Aviv, Israel. This is the same building where the Declaration of Independence for Israel was signed in 1948. Dr. Whitfield, this treaty will undoubtedly help to further your cause for peace throughout the world, so I'm sure you're very excited."

"Did you say the treaty will be signed between the New World Union and Israel this morning?"

"That's correct. The peace treaty with Israel is expected to be signed at one A.M. Tel Aviv time, which is just a few minutes from now." Clutching his earpiece, Donaldson listens closely. *"I'm told we're receiving live video now from Independence Hall in Tel Aviv, where the final treaty has been prepared for signatures, and the news conference is in progress."*

"Mr. Donaldson, don't you realize…?"

"Excuse me, Dr. Whitfield, but we're broadcasting live from Tel Aviv."

The press conference from Tel Aviv concluded with the Press Secretary of the New World Union speaking.

"Having just signed a seven-year peace treaty, the President of the New World Union and the Prime Minister of Israel have each expressed their whole-hearted approval of the terms of the treaty and look forward to a new era of extraordinary peace in Israel."

Following the speeches and the signing of the document, each of the heads of state smiled and shook hands for a photo-op to mark the momentous occasion.

After the newscast from Tel Aviv, Donaldson returned to the phone with Dr. Jonathan Whitfield.

"Please stay on the line, Dr. Whitfield, for a few more minutes. We're going to our Washington D.C. Correspondent, Sam Nicholson, who is live in the Capitol building talking to Senator Jason Waldrop, Chairman of the Senate Armed Forces Committee. Let's get Senator Waldrop's reaction to the historic Israeli peace treaty.

"Well, I thought we were going to hear from Senator Waldrop, but I'm told he is on his way to the basement of the Capitol building, and Sam Nicholson is following him.

"What's going on, Sam? Now what… I think we just lost the audio and video…no, we still have video, but all I see are the stairs of the Capitol building. It looks like the camera is on the steps. Wait a minute! I think Sam is calling me on my cell phone."

"Sam, is that you? What is going on there?"

Out of breath clambering down the stairs, Sam choked out, "James, the congressional chambers shook violently a few moments ago, and at the same time, the air was filled with an ear-splitting sound that some are saying was an enemy missile or supersonic aircraft. The military has been alerted, and everyone is scrambling for cover in the bunker downstairs. Did you hear anything where you are?"

"No, I can't hear anything from the outside in the CBN soundproof newsroom where I am broadcasting."

"James, the consensus here in Washington is that America is being attacked."

"Attacked? Attacked by whom?"

"I don't know, James. It all happened so fast, but I need to get to safety in the underground shelter. I'll get back to you when I know something. You need to find shelter."

"Dr. Whitfield, thank you for holding. I'm very sorry, but I have no idea what's going on in Washington. Since we may be under attack, we will have to get back with you later to finish this interview. I really apologize for all the inconvenience I've caused you. By the way, I've changed my mind about talking to you about your God and the gospel message. After everything that's happened, I would like to know more when you have time!

"Is that all right with you, Dr. Whitfield? Do you have time to talk with me privately about God and the gospel? I don't know anyone else to talk to. Do you hear me, Dr. Whitfield? Are you there? Did you hear a loud noise or see any signs of an attack?

"Hello, hello, Dr. Whitfield. Well, now I believe we lost the connection with Dr. Whitfield. I can't blame him. He was probably frustrated with all the interruptions and just hung up. We're returning now to our CBN News desk in Washington D.C. to obtain an update on the latest breaking news of the alleged enemy attack

on Washington, D.C."

After the cut-away, Donaldson thought, *I remember Dr. Whitfield said there would be a loud noise in the heavens just prior to the Rapture and that it would happen when a peace treaty was signed between Israel and the New World Union. I wonder now if the noise heard in Washington after the treaty was signed in Tel Aviv signaled the Rapture and the beginning of the Tribulation. Maybe the asteroid strike was indeed a warning of coming judgment and Dr. Whitfield was telling the truth all along. That means there is no attack on America from an enemy, at least not right now, and this is the...*

CHAPTER 48

IT'S ONLY FICTION BUT...

Well, now, you know Dr. Jonathan Whitfield's story. Of course, the people, places, and some events in this story have been fictionalized, but the narrative is based on historical facts, actual current events, and prophecies recorded in the Bible in the books of **I and II Samuel, Daniel, II Chronicles, Jeremiah, and Revelation**.

The message Dr. Whitfield delivered to America is based on the indisputable grace of God and the Biblical prophecies of the future Rapture, the Tribulation, and the second coming of Jesus Christ that are coming to pass today at the speed of life. Make no mistake about it! America is at a spiritual tipping point, and the sands of time are rushing like a waterfall through the fingers of those who can make a difference, but there is still hope for the future of America.

America is accelerating on an unprecedented collision course with destiny at the intersection of unquestionable Biblical prophecy and undisputable world events. The lives of people everywhere hang in the balance, depending on whether they accept the simple gospel message of Jesus Christ.

Like many people, Dr. Whitfield is a good man as far as society defines 'good' and is respected and well-liked in academic and professional circles throughout the world. Being a moral and generous person, it was difficult for him to understand why he would spend eternity separated from God without Jesus. The key to Jonathan's heart was not through a message from a preacher on Sunday morning, but through his obsession with archeology and his unquenchable quest to learn the secrets of the ancient past.

So, you may ask, "If America is on the precipice of destruction, what can I do to save our nation?"

First, recognize that in 2016, God orchestrated a historical political revolution in America that resulted in the election of a man for President of the United States who had never held a political office. Without allegiance to seasoned politicians, lobbyists, or special interest groups, this man has been instrumental in advancing the economic and financial health of America as well as being the catalyst to attempt to restore Godly principles to the nation. With a groundswell of support against insurmountable odds, this peaceful uprising in America was in many ways like the Brexit revolution in Great Britain. No one believed it could happen, but it did! However, no man, not even the President of the United States, can reverse the deteriorating spiritual condition of the nation by himself.

Americans must begin the arduous process of changing the direction of this spiritually corrupt vessel of democracy that is speeding toward annihilation in the dark waters of complacency and blind tolerance. Before it's too late, a definite course must be established to return America to the Godly nation that was established more than two hundred years ago by the founding fathers. It has taken decades for America to reach this stage of disappointing spiritual debauchery, and it will take many years to make substantive changes, but the process must begin now. With the recent unprecedented change in the White House, God has given the nation one last opportunity to stop the spiritual freefall, but he will not continue to wink at the mockery Americans are making of God's word, His messengers, and His church.

America has become a melting pot of cultures and religious factions with a government that encourages the acceptance of all religious beliefs, except Christianity, and welcomes integrating them into society, public schools, the legislative system, and even the judicial courts. While embracing the religious demands of all other cultures that mandate altering the American way of life, everything that stands for the traditional values of God and Christianity is being methodically extracted from America's landscape.

Americans must go to their knees and repent and restore God to His rightful place in this great nation by:

- Giving the one true God, the Bible, the Ten Commandments, and the cross the recognition and respect they deserve;

- Restoring Christian values in the schools and in the books that are taught in the schools;

- Allowing every baby formed in the wombs of mothers the right given by God and promised in the Constitution to be born and to do their best to live and succeed in life;

- Respecting and embracing marriage strictly defined by the union of one man and one woman as God ordained;

- Recognizing and valuing the family unit as the backbone of the nation's societal well-being and ultimate economic and financial success;

- Restoring the freedom to pray to God in the schools, athletic events, and any other occasions by all those who wish to do so;

- Enacting legislation by and for the people based on the Godly principles that this nation was founded on with absolute transparency and honesty;

- Arresting the downward spiral in moral values promoted by Hollywood and embraced by society;

- Maintaining freedom of religion without sacrificing the sanctity of core beliefs in the one true God;

- Refusing to tolerate the infestation of principles of false gods in the courts, the legislature, the education system, and even the penal system that threatens to alter the American culture;

- Restoring the Sabbath to be the day set aside to give everyone the freedom to worship God as it was intended by our Creator, without penalizing those in the labor force;

- Restoring America's relationship and support as a strong ally for Israel.

As America begins the time-consuming journey of restoring their relationship to God, the following must also be embraced:

- Reestablish America as a beacon for peace and democracy to the world with a military presence second to none and a nation that demands respect and doesn't offer an apology to anyone for their God-given greatness;

- Back the men and women of the military to the hilt, making them proud to serve their country. Care for and respect the military and their families when they return from active duty;

- Teach children at home to respect God and all figures of authority, beginning with their parents;

- Operate America on a sound financial basis;

- Secure and protect the borders to give American citizens the security they need and deserve.

The list may seem a bit daunting, and one may even believe there is little that can be done as individuals to save the nation and stop the spiritual freefall that is accelerating at an alarming rate. Those in political power who oppose the Godly principles on which this nation was founded can be voted out, and the men and women who are willing to embrace and support those principles can be voted in. However, the efforts at the polls do not guarantee there will be change, and even if change comes, it will arrive with a price and take valuable time to implement. The powerful political machines in local, state and federal government bureaucracies will always strive to run on the tracks of selfish personal gain that seasoned politicians, special interest groups, and lobbyists have laid for them decades before.

On the other hand, you can definitely do something about your own destiny. You may be like Dr. Whitfield, who was in grave danger of spending eternity separated from God. There may be something in your past that prevents you from accepting God as the awesome creator and Savior that He is, something for which you blamed God as well as yourself or others. Remember, everyone will spend eternity somewhere. That's right! The Bible promises you will live forever somewhere after you breathe your last breath on this planet. I pray you will set your own Ebenezer Stone down today as a symbolic marker of the transformation of your life. Ask Jesus Christ to become the Lord of your life and totally transform your life today by praying this very simple prayer:

Thank you, God, for sending your son Jesus Christ to save me and forgive me of all my sins, past, present, and future. I am sorry for my sins and for failing to recognize Jesus as the Son of God. I accept Jesus Christ into my heart at this very moment, and I promise to serve you and honor you in everything I do for the rest of my life. Thank you for saving me.

God does not promise anyone another day or even another minute as far as that goes. Be sure you're ready for eternity, since the Tribulation could begin at any moment, or your life could just suddenly end at the next tick of the clock due to an accident or physical trauma.

It may be that you're a Christian, one of God's creations that He wonderfully transformed at some point in your life. However, you've wandered far from God, caught up in the relentless but empty pursuit of happiness that the world promises.

Or, you've settled your place in eternity with God, but you find it difficult or impossible to forgive someone for something that has happened to you or your loved ones. Your sad, heartbreaking spirit cries out, 'Why did this happen to me? What did I do to deserve this? Where was God when I needed Him?'

The fact of the matter is God never promised that life would be without heartaches, and it's unrealistic to think any of us will sail through life without having sadness and disappointments. God only promised that He would be there to comfort us when we needed him, and He is there all the time. So, look up to God. Thank Him for the blessings in your life, and then forgive that person who wronged or hurt you. Ask God to forgive you right now, and He will! Promise to serve God the rest of the days that He gives you on this Earth. I promise, you will be a happier person.

Like Jonathan, maybe you just can't find the time in your busy schedule to enjoy life and the world God has created for you. Perhaps you need to spend more time with your family and those you love. Spend less time with those who only look to gain from what you can do for them but who have little or no interest in you as a person.

Well, now you know what you need to do, and today is the first day of the rest of your life.

www.ingramcontent.com/pod-product-compliance
Lightning Source LLC
Chambersburg PA
CBHW021133110726
47900CB00002B/329